Praise for Johnny Diaz and *Boston Boys Club*!

"Breezy . . . fun . . ."
—*Edge (Miami)*

"A charming cocktail."
—*Out*

"Make way for the boys of summer! Johnny Diaz has written a sexy beach-read romp that you won't be able to put down."
William J. Mann, author of *Men Who Love Men*

"Sexy, funny, you savor every page . . . a great summer read . . . all you have to do is sit back and open it and enjoy."
—*Eureka Pride*

"*Boston Boys Club* entertains, amuses and is the perfect compliment to a long, lazy day at the beach and cold tropical drink of your choice. But don't be fooled, there is a serious side to this book, which make it all the better a slice of LGBT life. There are issues and illnesses, losses and things falling apart. But in the end, things come together and these boys will win your heart. This book is a keeper and Johnny Diaz had better start working on a sequel."
—*La Bloga*

"*Boston Boys Club* is racy, funny and smart. With his unforgettable trio of narrators, Johnny Diaz ushers the reader through the sex-filled, weirdly skewed world of contemporary gay Boston. You're going to love this book."
—Scott Heim, author of *Mysterious Skin*

"In case you haven't heard the buzz, *Boston Boys Club* is the book to read on the beach this summer . . . fast paced and lighthearted."
—*Bay Windows*

"A fun summer read . . . one hopes that the author will grace readers again with another story of New England's favorite city."
—*AfterElton.com*

"A bubbly beach read . . . the author clearly knows Boston inside and out, and readers from New England will appreciate the attention paid to the surroundings and the many local insider jokes."
—*Bay Area Reporter*

Please turn the page for more outstanding reviews for
Boston Boys Club!

"A love letter to Boston."
—*The Gay & Lesbian Review*

"A winner . . . sexy, rich and charming, this one is a true page-turner."
—*Out Smart*

"Sure to make an appearance on many a beach towel this summer."
—*Here! Magazine*

"A winning book, especially for a summer read."
—*Boston Spirit*

"Johnny Diaz brings to palpable life the ins, outs, ups, and downs of gay city life and its most dangerous pastime: dating. In chronicling the love lives—or lack thereof—of three good friends who meet weekly at a popular watering hole, Mr. Diaz gives us situations, hopes, fears, and, especially, characters, that all readers will identify with, and may even recognize as themselves. At turns comic, touching, and tragic, *Boston Boys Club* is sure to serve as a testament of American gay life in the new millenium, and the timeless search for Mister Right—or Mister Right Now. An addictive read."
—J.G. Hayes, author of *This Thing Called Courage*

Miami Manhunt

Johnny Diaz

KENSINGTON BOOKS
http://www.kensingtonbooks.com

Acknowledgments

I'm such a goof. I forgot to write my acknowledgments the first time around with *Boston Boys Club* so this one will be a little long. So sit back.

A big thank you to my editor, John Scognamiglio, for his patience, kindness, and literary insights. Without John, *Boston Boys Club* and *Miami Manhunt* would not be in your hands.

I'd like to thank Juan and Milagros Diaz for supporting their only gay Cuban son even though they can't read in English. Their support is boundless and not limited to Spanish. A thank you to my sister, Cary, who supports me in her own quiet way.

I'd like to give a shout out to my Boston Boys Club: Antonio DiPierro and my Cuban *"loca"* Rosco Cortinas for making Beantown feel like home. To my Miami Boys Club: Tom Welhaf and Carlos Castillo; Eric Vasallo and Eric Boylan who make leaving Miami so hard whenever I visit. To the Perez and Cuervos, my big Cuban family in Miami. A special gracias to Maria Sanchez, my loving godmother in Duxbury, Massachusetts. She has been one of my biggest readers since I began writing her letters from Miami when I was a lonely 12-year-old boy.

I want to thank my first creative writing teacher, Ricki Weyhe from Miami Beach High who always pushed me to show more than tell. A big thank you to my first real news editor, Patty Shillington, who saw something in a skinny, curly-haired 16-year-old kid and hired him as an intern at *The Miami Herald* in high school.

A heartfelt thank you to my old friend Rene Rodriguez, my newspaper mentor and dear friend for the past 10 years, even though we always disagree on movies.

I'd like to dedicate this book to the late Maria Krok, of Miami

Beach, who wasn't just a caring neighbor but who adopted me as one of her grandchildren. She not only invited me into her home every Thanksgiving and *Noche Buena* for 10 years, but she also invited me into her heart. By her example of helping others, this world is a better place, and I know her favorite granddaughter Cynthia Casanova would agree with me on that.

A huge thank you to *la doctora* Isabel Gomez-Bassols and her family, the Vasallos, for making me an honorary Vasallo all these years.

A thank you to dear FIU college friend and former *Globe* intern, summer of 1995, Anne "Martinez" Vasquez for always believing in my talent and looking out for me, especially when I was homesick during our first weeks in Cambridge. Ditto to Joanne Skerrett, another former *Globe* intern and fellow author.

A special thank you to my dearest friend Ryan Andrews for his unconditional support and love and for all those late-night, long-distance chats these last seven years when I needed to bounce dialogue and some ideas off him.

And last but not least, an infinite thank you: to my blue-eyed "Muggle."

Author's Note

Many of the Miami and Boston businesses, locations, and events that appear in this book are real. The narrators and their supporting characters are not. The businesses and locations were used to make the settings as realistic as possible for the fictional characters who are products of the author's imagination.

1

Ray

Three stars.

That's what I'm giving *Miami Vice II: Back to the Beach*. It's not a bad movie with its muscular camerawork and steely blues and grays à la 2004's *Collateral*. Like the first installment, it didn't paint Miami in pastels or reek of '80s' vice. This movie is just unnecessary. Did we really need to see Colin Farrell and Jamie Foxx running side-by-side through the streets of Miami chasing drug lords again? No, we didn't. Did we need Michael Mann casting Miami as a bullet-riddled metropolis through gritty shootouts and inky skylines one more time? Nope! But *Miami Vice* opened at number one in the summer of 2006, grossing more than $50 million in its first weekend, and it held up modestly after that. It had good box office "mojo" (Sonny's aptly named go-fast boat in the movie). And in Hollywood, if your movie makes a hefty profit (cha-ching!), you're guaranteed a sequel. But that doesn't mean it's a good idea. Think: *Basic Instinct II* and a taut-faced Sharon Stone showing off what God (and, apparently, her plastic surgeon and Botox technician) gave her while she recites some truly terrible dialogue. That's why I slaughtered the film in my review, commenting tritely, "Follow your basic instinct and stay away!"

Before I dissect any more movies, perhaps I should introduce myself. My name is Ray Martinez, and movies are my life. Sometimes, my life feels like a movie. I can see the trailer playing in my head now. *Coming to a theater you,* The Miami Movie Critic *starring Ray Martinez in his debut performance.* The camera zooms in on me sitting in a mostly empty theater screening another movie just like I did this afternoon. So yes, I write 700-word critiques on the latest films for South Florida's biggest newspaper, *The Miami News.* I attend at least three screenings a week at the new Carnival Center for the Performing Arts in downtown Miami or at the South Beach AMC theater on Lincoln Road, where I just caught *Miami Vice II.*

As the credits roll, I emerge from the darkness of the chilly theater into the buttery afternoon light of South Beach, my home. I light a cigarette, my fifth of the day. (I can't seem to quit the evil weed.) Bronzed rollerbladers breeze by as I stroll back to my car. I'm heading to the *News* building across the calm glassy waters of Biscayne Bay that part Miami and Miami Beach. I want to get my review done today so I can relax with the guys tonight at Score (not just a place but a goal), but I'll get to that in a minute.

Everyone thinks I have the best job in the world. Sometimes, I feel that way. Other times, I never want to see another movie again because it doesn't leave me much time for off-screen romances. I have a passionate love affair with my craft, and I know most other movie critics have a love-hate relationship with their jobs. To understand what we go through you have to be a member of our club, but I'll do my best to explain. My job, like a cigarette, is also my illicit lover; it seduces me and, at times, abuses me. My work also serves to distract me from dating other men, the same way my clingy Cuban family does, but I'll introduce the Martinez clan in just a bit.

On a sun-dappled Miami day like today, when I screen a movie that is marginally entertaining on multiple levels, I have a lot to work with in my review, and that makes my job rewarding. I dash back to my cubicle on the fourth floor of the *News* building—a five-story, mustard-colored fortress anchored off the bay—and return to my computer screen, analyzing the plot, the lighting, the acting, and the pace of the film. Not that I can't get side-tracked. Between sentences, I may catch myself gazing out the window at the colossal cruise ships docked at the Port of Miami, imagining how those metal vessels stay afloat. I notice how the sun glistens against the aqua bay water like a liquid carpet of shimmering crystals. It's highly distracting, but that's Miami, a tropical wonderland. If it were a movie, it would be called *Pastel Paradiso* because it overdoses on art deco. And I mean that in a good way. Like a tie-dye tapestry, the pale blues of the sky mix with the peach and candy-pink building tops of South Beach. Miami is a living, washed-out canvas of watercolors, and I wouldn't want to work or live anywhere else. We could use more trees for shady respites, but that's something a Metro reporter can talk to you about. I write reviews, not news.

So yes, this gig has its perks beyond my postcard office view. I watch movies for free and then write what I think. It doesn't get any better than that. Well, it does. I also get to travel to Toronto, New York, and L.A. for movie junkets to interview stars and directors about their latest projects. In 2007, I interviewed Brad Pitt in New York City for *Ocean's 13*, which for the record was the film equivalent of empty calories, but you didn't feel like you were duped by Danny Ocean. Pitt's rugged masculine sexuality mixed with his angelic beauty threw me off balance. I kept losing my focus, even dropping my digital recorder twice. When I replayed the 15-minute interview, (that's as much time as you can expect from a big star), I noticed how much I stumbled over my words. How embarrassing or, as we say in Spanish, *"Qué pena!"*

So that's one perk, the up-close (if not personal) chats with beautiful Hollywood actors that I wouldn't have a shot with in this lifetime. And did I mention the fabulous views from work?

My fellow reporters and writers have critic-envy, and I can see why, but I earned my place at the *News* after years of freelancing and writing obits. Also, my little mug shot accompanies each of my reviews in the paper and online, which makes me feel important, like an authority. In Miami, it's all about the scene and being seen, and having my Kodak moment out there helps in the status department and, occasionally, with dates. Only columnists get their picture in the paper, and I'm the only critic outside the sports and Metro departments who has his photo run with each commentary.

Racso, my straight, macho twin brother, makes fun of that photo all the time. He gets off on being my big brother (by four minutes, people!) and my biggest critic, especially of my pack-a-day smoking habit. He refers to me as "Miami movie boy" to his colleagues at Coral Gables High, where he teaches English and writing. He also makes fun of my blog, which is called "*Rated R, for Ray.*" (Hey, my editors came up with that.) Racso also thinks it's really gay with its Art Deco, pink-colored fonts and movie reel images, but then he takes it back when he wants to tag along for the screening of a big blockbuster. (I got him in for free to watch *The Da Vinci Code,* and he bragged about it to his students and faculty members the next day.) I love my brother and he loves me, and despite our competitiveness and constant brotherly bashing, I know he'll always have my back even if he doesn't agree with all my reviews in the paper and on my blog. Speaking of my blog, I use that to respond to readers' emails, of which I get plenty. That brings me to my next point.

That's part of the downside to what I do. Everyone has an opinion about my opinion, and folks in Miami don't hold back what they really want to say, tossing me rotten tomatoes via email in both English and *en español.* My mailbox swarms with some of the nastiest letters out there, but that's understandable. People are passionate about the movies, whether they like them or not. Going to a movie and being whisked away into another world is a personal experience, and I know I wield a lot influence in that arena. When people see a movie after reading my review and disagree with my perspective, they blame me for their bad time. They chew me out with such comments as "You stupid idiot. *Pirates of the Caribbean* was great. What movie were you watching that night?" or "You should be rated R, for ridiculous. You thought *United 93* was good? It made me want to leave the theater screaming. You owe me $8 asshole!" Hey, it's hard out there for a movie critic, as the song goes from *Hustle and Flow* (which I gave four stars, by the way).

Speaking of *Hustle and Flow*, I almost got hit by a car just now as I was crossing Lincoln Road at Alton Road. I have to learn to control my tendency to start forming reviews in my head the moment I leave a screening. (I even do it during the occasional date.) As I wait for the light to change, I take a deep drag from my cigarette while cherry-red convertibles and sports cars with spinning rims zoom by me in a blur of mechanical purrs. Traffic grows worse by the day as more people move to our town, a mere ten minute drive to the *News*. Sometimes, I bike to work along the Venetian Causeway, which connects a series of residential islands with inspired Italian names like San Marco and Dilido. After spending hours in a movie theater a few times a week and being stuck behind a desk writing reviews, I savor the moments of sunshine and the Atlantic-whipped tropical vapor. It's refreshing on a day like this even as I watch Miami morphing by the minute into a mini-New York of the South. In the distance, I see a condo development rising, another addition to the growing forest of sexy glass towers against the bay. Sometimes, it seems like there are more cranes than bodies in Miami. The city is a carnival of construction crews.

At the stoplight, a lunky Miami-Dade transit bus screeches to a stop, and I spot my old college friend Ted Williams. Well, it's not really Ted but his photo splashed on the side of the bus. It's a Channel 7 ad with Ted showing off his ultra-white grille, holding two thumbs up pointing to the station's catchphrase, "Just One Station." Some background notes on Ted. He's one of my Miami buddies and a famous face in South Florida. Aside from this bus ad and the billboards off Interstate 95, Ted really does have a big head. He's the region's star news reporter, with the morning perkiness of Kelly Ripa and the edgy professionalism of Anderson Cooper. If you've ever visited Miami, you may have seen Ted. He's the guy in the yellow raincoat holding on to the swaying coconut tree for dear life as he covers the latest hurricane. He also cohosts *Deco Time*, our snarky local version of *Entertainment Tonight*. Sometimes, he has me on the show to talk about the movies opening that weekend.

And thanks to his hosting duties on *Deco Time*, Ted gets to highlight the new nightlife offerings, gets me and our mutual friend Brian into the clubs for free. Not that Brian needs the free-bies, but I'll soon explain.

As the bus limps lazily along Alton Road like an old man with a cane and crosses Seventeenth Street, I wave goodbye to Ted's big head. I finally cross the street and unlock the doors of my sea-blue Nissan 300 SX. Mother Nature must be in a bad mood because she has turned up the temperature a few boiling notches. It feels like ninety-something even though the beach breeze blows against my skin. My long-sleeved Gap T-shirt is quickly becoming sticky with sweat.

While watching *Miami Vice II* was worthwhile, I still have to see the bad movies, another con of my job. At least you, the moviegoer, can get up and walk out of a theater if you don't like a movie. I can't. I have to sit through two, sometimes three hours of a bad film, and that's torture in itself for a lover of cinema who first caught film fever after seeing the first *Godfather*. But I digress. Oh, and another thing, it's hard for me to go on a date to the movies because the theater is the last place I want to be after a week's worth of screenings. Can you blame me?

That's why I can't help but look forward to meeting up with my two *locas*: Ted and Brian. We rendezvous every Friday night at Score on Lincoln Road to shoot the shit about our hectic lives. While we gab, we eyeball the younger hotties who are sprouting in South Beach like palm trees—and those new glassy condo towers. When you're twenty-nine, you have more of an appreciation for sitting outside with your *chicos*, drinking a cocktail, and watching the man-flow of guys pour in and out of the bar.

While Ted and I have common journalism ties (we met at the

University of Miami's Communications School as undergrads ten years ago,) that's where our similarities end. He's half Irish, though you wouldn't know it by looking at him. He has natural dark, tanned skin and matching brown eyes, like his Portuguese forefathers from Cape Cod, and thick short-cropped black hair. The only white thing about him is his Colgate smile, a job requirement for TV. He's also extremely cheesy with his sound bites, which he does on and off the air in his TV news voice. But he has a heart of gold, and I can always count on him to listen as I vent about my latest frustration with the paper, my brother Racso, or my unsuccessful attempts to quit smoking. (I've tried three times to no avail. Damn the nicotine!)

Speaking of Racso, I look just like the dude (we're identical twins after all!). People also say we look like two different versions of actor Paul Rudd (most famous for playing Alicia Silverstone's geeky love interest in *Clueless*.) But our distinct styles make Racso and me stand apart like Miami-Dade and Broward counties, similar from a distance but definitely not the same up close. While Racso and I both have light-blue eyes that reflect the South Florida sky and thick black straight hair, I spike mine up with Aveda products and keep it short while Racso wears his down and parted in the middle, like a mop. Racso has a more sculpted body, thanks to his home gym, and I'm telephone-pole lean from biking to work and around South Beach. In case you're wondering, Racso's name is Oscar spelled backwards, after our father. I was named after our grandfather Raymond, but everyone calls me Ray. Racso also calls me Gay Ray, ever since I officially came out to him in college.

It wasn't easy coming out to my straight brother who always enjoyed talking about how much he liked women. I thought I did a good job of cloaking my invisible life from him until one spring night. We were out drinking in the Grove, celebrating the end of our first year in college when he asked me point blank, "Bro, are you gay? It's okay if you are."

I spat out my Corona, spraying the bar counter and our fries.

"*Qué cosa?*" I stuttered. I dated some girls in high school, but I knew deep in my heart that I liked men. Actually, I lusted for men. I just wasn't ready to tell Papi, Mami and most of all, Racso who always finds a reason to make fun of me. The last thing I wanted to hear was him ragging on me for being *un pato*.

"Ray, it's cool. I kinda sensed it. You never really talk about girls, and you're into your movies and your writing. And let's face it, your new friend Ted at UM isn't the most masculine dude. He's kinda girly, and you guys are always hanging out and giggling like two schoolgirls on the phone."

And so that night, I came out to Racso. He listened as I told him about my secret crushes at Gables High. Rick on the track team. Dan on the football team. Jake at the school newspaper. Racso was surprised to hear that I had liked so many guys he knew from school. I remember sitting there at the bar, my nervousness replacing the warm buzz from my Coronas as I spilled my guts. But it was a relief too. Hiding took so much energy and effort. I always made sure my eyes didn't linger too long on a cute guy if I was out with my brother and our parents. It felt good to share all of this with Racso even though he began probing me as if I were a Reese's-loving alien from *E.T.*

"So you're a homo-sex-ual," he said, elongating the word and teasing me. "Have you gotten it up the butt? Are you a gay virgin?" Racso teased. And from then on, I decided that my twin didn't need to know everything about me. My sex life remained private. I could share those details with Ted. It's not that I don't love Racso, but he didn't understand why I was attracted to guys while he was drawn to women. (And he was a future educator at the time. Go figure!) I grew tired of explaining it to him. A few months later, he helped me tell Mami and Papi, who didn't seem so shocked. They said they suspected I was different and they loved me regardless. But Papi had to add, "If this is what you are, we accept you. But we will not have a son dressing up as a woman and performing at La Copacabana on Calle Ocho." Mami, in her Cuban dramatic fashion, stormed over to me, hugged me, and said, "*Mi hijo, mi hijo!*" and then gave me a long lecture about safe sex, as if I hadn't known. It was awkward for those first few months, but then they realized I was still Ray, or as Racso began calling me, Gay Ray, which Mami and Papi never liked him doing.

My bro and I are both fair-skinned, and we both have the same amount of freckles dotting our nose and shoulders. Our propensity for sunspots harkens back to our pre-Cuban roots, back to Madrid, Spain, where our grandparents were born with milky white skin. We always stood out against our olive-skinned, tanned Cuban cousins and friends growing up in Coral Gables.

Fifteen minutes, two large armpit sweat stains and another cigarette later, I pull into the main parking lot of the *News's* main offices. That's Miami for you. A two-block walk in this soupy heat sends your pores into overdrive even if you're walking under the awnings of local boutiques. I'm about to enter the massive lobby, home to two rising and descending escalators, when I feel my cell phone buzzing in my pocket. I whip it out. It's a text message from Brian. I bet it's about tonight.

Hey, we're meeting at eleven tonight, right? Daniel's leaving on a business trip, and that means I can find myself a hot Latin papi.

Brian is ready for another Miami manhunt tonight, which only happens when Daniel is in New York on business, where his printing company is based. To Brian, hot dark-skinned Latin guys are human catnip. He can't wait to roll around with a Latino when his other lover is away.

I punch in a text message as I ride the escalator to the fourth floor.

Yeah, we're still on for tonight. I just have to finish this review and answer some emails at work. I think you're gonna like *MVII* when it opens next week.

Brian text messages back.

Cool. I can't wait. See you later, man. I already emailed Ted. He'll meet us after his *Deco Time* taping tonight.

How do I explain Brian? Where do I begin? He's the craziest and hottest of our trio and the youngest at twenty-eight. He was born in North Carolina and dreamed of becoming a full-time singer, à la Josh Groban. Brian still dabbles with his music and occasionally produces demos when he can focus. (He has ADD.) He has light, sandy hair combed up with a matching goatee and dark blue eyes that remind me of the blue found only in rolling storm clouds over the Everglades. He's 6'1" (about three inches taller than Ted and me), with an average build, yet he manages to nab all the Latin cuties. (It's those piercing mysterious cobalt blue eyes, I tell you.) He has a wealthy Israeli entrepreneur partner that he's been with for seven years. Brian doesn't work because Daniel prefers that he oversee the renovations at their waterfront McMansion off the Venetian Causeway or at their condo in Chelsea. Brian also doesn't work because he can't stay focused on one thing at a time (the ADD, remember?). That may explain his boy craziness.

Daniel and Brian have this understanding that Ted and I have never understood. Daniel and Brian have an open relationship. They don't have sex with each other (they lost that connection a long time ago), but they can have sex with other guys as long as they stick to one simple rule: no seconds with the same guy. And it works, they say.

With Daniel flying back and forth between Miami and New York, Brian gets to play on the side at their beach house. I guess I'm more conservative, like Papi and Mami and Racso with his college sweetheart Cindy. Our thinking is that if you're going to want to be with someone else, then don't be committed to your partner. Set him free and be single. Brian and Daniel seem happy, but Ted and I can't help but think that one day, Brian is going to fall for one of his tricks, when he truly feels a passionate connection. When that happens, will Brian be able to leave his life-partner and all the good things their life together has to offer, like that slamming Land Rover and his Rolex watch? It's almost like a gay version of *Unfaithful*.

It's 6 p.m., and I have just filed my *Miami Vice* review. I decided to go with three and a half stars instead of my original three. The movie grew on me on my drive back to the office as I mulled over Michael Mann's hypnotic use of his high-definition lens. He's a cinematic virtuoso who uses rock-and-roll action shots to dazzle the viewer in this dark reupholstered version of Miami.

"Hey Patty, have a good weekend," I tell my Arts editor as I pass her grand office. It's down the hall from my tiny cubicle, which is covered in mini-mountains of DVDs under posters of the *Godfather* and Winona Ryder flicks. I grab my messenger bag and swing it over my neck as I head down the hallway, passing the mostly empty cubicles that sit under rows of ultra-bright fluorescent lights. I'm not surprised that most of the Arts writers are gone for the day, leaving the newsroom a ghost town on a Friday afternoon. The only people left here are the over-caffeinated and overstressed copy editors and designers who are getting to work on tomorrow and Sunday's pages as well as our Web site.

"You too, Ray. I've only read the top, but nice *Vice* review. If I have any questions, we can deal with it Monday. Take it easy," Patty says, returning to her computer screen. I finally get to leave this place for the weekend. I walk out of the building through the front entrance and hop back into my Nissan. I'm about to turn onto the Venetian Causeway with Miami's small forest of skyscrapers filling my rearview mirror when I hear my cell phone playing the theme song to *2001: A Space Odyssey*. I check the caller ID, and I see that it's Racso, probably wanting to bug me about something.

"Hey, little brother! How was *Miami Vice* today?" he asks in his butch guy's guy voice, which I don't have. Mine is a little more sarcastic and whiney.

"Well, you'll just have to read the review next week." I approach the white Spanish-style tollbooth at the causeway and fly right through, thanks to my SunPass.

"Oh please! If I focus hard enough, I can probably sense what you thought. Let's see. Hmmm. You kinda liked it. You thought it was entertaining, but you didn't see the reason why it needed to be made, right?"

Damn it! My brother is good, really good at reading me, even from across town. I hate how he knows what I'm thinking. It's like he has this twin telepathy thing that gives him a secret access to my thoughts and emotions, but it only works one way. He can sense me, but I can't sense what's going on with him. Why was he born with that ability and not me? Because of that twin ESP, he always knew when I was lying when we were growing up. It's just another thing that makes Racso more special to our parents.

"Close but no cigar," I tell him, passing Brian's majestic house with the grand black gates on San Marco Island. I see that he's home. His silver Land Rover sits in the driveway.

"Yeah right, Ray! You know I'm right. You just hate admitting it when I am. Listen Miami Movie boy, I need to know if you're gonna be able to pick me up from the dealership tomorrow. My car is acting up again. Cindy is tutoring some students in the afternoon, and I think Papi and Mami are going to Abuela's house in Kendall."

"Yeah, I can pick you up. Call me when you get to Miami Toyota," I tell him, passing all the island estates. "I still think you should get a new car. That Toyota Corolla is nine years old, *chico*."

"Well, when I make the money that you make at the paper, then I can afford something nicer, but for now I'm on a teacher's salary and I might as well be paid in magic beans. This Corolla will have to do. Thanks for giving me the ride tomorrow. Talk to you later," Racso says

"No problem," I say before flipping my cell phone closed, crossing the last island on the causeway, and hanging a right on West Avenue.

It's 6:20 p.m., and I'm only a few blocks from my condo. I'll have plenty of time to walk Gigli, my rascally black mutt of a dog named after a really bad J.Lo movie (admit it, you read my review and decided not to see it). I'll have just enough time to drop by Puerto Sagua restaurant on Collins Avenue for a *media noche* sandwich and mamey shake and then take a disco nap before tonight. Once I walk inside my one-bedroom apartment and toss my keys on my kitchen bar counter, I start to think that maybe I should have given *Miami Vice* three stars because it really wasn't all that good—but I know tonight with the guys will be.

2

Ted

"And now we leave you with the newest video by Paris Hilton shot in our very own backyard. See if you recognize the bar in the club scene and spot, ahem, a certain dashing Channel 7 reporter. For *Deco Time*, I'm Ted Williams."

"Oh Ted, you're so modest. Not!" my co-host cuts in and turns my way. She squints and sticks her tongue out while shuffling a fake script in front of her. We ad-lib this so much that our producers never know what's going to fly out of our mouths anymore.

"And I'm Trina Tucker. See you next time on *Deco Time*."

The producer cues the Paris Hilton video, and her computer-enhanced vocals starts to play. My producer gestures that we're about to go off the air in 5 . . . 4 . . . 3 . . . 2 . . . 1.

I flash a smile as wide as I can, keep my gaze locked on camera one, and wink at Trina, who sits to my left. She turns to me and then to camera two for her farewell closeup. We playfully hit each other with the unnecessary script as the picture fades into the Hilton video with the show's credits rolling over it.

"And you're done!" Sheila, my producer, says into my earpiece, which I gladly start unhooking, but I'm not going to let Trina off the hook that easily.

"You bitch!" I tell Trina as she takes off her earpiece and tucks her Beyoncé *un-be-weavable* straight hair behind her ears. She also detaches her mini-microphone, which is amazingly nestled out of sight between her bodacious boobs. I'm surprised we don't need to call Miami–Dade Fire Rescue to excavate the darn thing like the Big Dig in Boston. If her boobs were any bigger thanks to Dr. 33139, we'd have a wardrobe malfunction. I secretly think Trina wishes that would happen so her face—and tatas—would be flashed all over the news, and on the real *Entertainment Tonight* and *YouTube*. It doesn't take much to make the news these days, as I prove every week with my stories on *Deco Time*.

"I was just playing, Teddy. You get all fussy over nothing. It's *Deco Time*, remember? We're supposed to be playful, tongue-in-cheek, and everything in between, you know." She grabs and squeezes her tits to emphasize her point. She gets up from her side of our hot pink news desk with its big white sign behind us that blinks "DECO TIME," like the infamous Hollywood sign. Flanking the sign are two fake yet lush palm trees. *Very* Miami.

"Watch out! I'm going get to get you back on next Friday's show. You can count on it, Trina Fucker . . . *Oops*, did I just say that? I meant, Tucker."

"Oh, whatever Teddy. Don't let your pink feathers get all ruffled over this. You're not a pink flamingo at Metro Zoo. You're still the star of the station," she says, flailing her arms like a diva as she walks back to her desk. As she struts, her heels echo through the studio.

She's right. She was just playing. I just don't like looking like an ass on TV, but that's hard when you host a wanna-be *ET* show called *Deco Time*. If Trina pulls another one of her cheap shots on air, this show is going to be called *Deck her Time*.

I follow Trina's lead and head back to my own cubicle, maneuvering around the cameras, sound equipment, and lights of the news studio. The only thing I care about right now is that it's Friday. Thank God! What a week it was. Let me give you a recap. I spent Monday covering the double suicide of a mother and daughter in Hollywood Beach. The women hung themselves in their house. *Bizarre!* My Tuesday went to covering an eight-car pile-up on I-95 on the Dade-Broward line all because some driver lost control of her Lexus SUV while applying some lipstick. (I'm surprised it wasn't Trina who caused that wreck layering her L'Oreal foundation.) Wednesday was all about the President rolling into town for a surprise appearance at the University of Miami. *Love her!* That story is a keeper for my "Best of Ted Williams" news reel. Thursday, what did I do yesterday? Oh yeah, it was my turn to do a follow-up on the Miami real estate robber. He's the guy who pretends to look at homes in Coral Gables and Pinecrest with pretty agents and then snatches their purses. *Scary.* It's making the property values dip for the neighbors of the listed properties. So with all this gloom and doom reporting, I don't mind spending my Fridays taping *Deco Time* or my occasional *Wednesday's Child* segments, where we highlight a local youngster who wants to be adopted. I enjoy hanging out with the kids we feature because they're regulars at the South Beach Boys and Girls Club. It's for a good cause. Those segments and *Deco Time* provide outlets to gently ease into the weekend, except when Trina pulls one of her cattylicious lines on me.

With all the make-up they put on her, you'd think there was a drag queen sitting next to me on the set. People know me more for my *Deco Time* segments than my breaking news reports, so I don't mind the actual duty. I just sit back and comment on all the video we have about our local and out-of-town celebs frolicking on Ocean Drive and Collins Ave. and at Oprah's Fisher Island digs. Every now and then, I grab our camera guy Carlos, and we hit the clubs to dish about the hottest bar in South Beach or downtown, and I take Ray and Brian along for the ride. In the past few years, downtown Miami, a place you'd avoid at night at all costs, has become a clubbing destination. It really has stolen South Beach's club thunder because there's plenty of parking and you don't have to deal with the causeway caravan clogging the streets. Besides, South Beach has become more international heterosexual than it was young and homosexual in the '90s when Ray and I were at UM.

The round newsroom clock reads 9 p.m., and I'm sitting at my cubicle (no, most TV reporters don't have their own offices unless you're BaBa WaWa). I loosen up my baby pink tie and check my emails before I take off. There's one from Ray from 6 p.m.

I'm getting ready to leave work. I saw *Miami Vice II* today. Will tell you all about it later but you won't be missing too much if you skip it. Anyhoo, see you at Score, TV whore!

Ray has such a way with words. He's always been more of the writer. I've been more of the give-me-the-facts ma'am reporter. I read some more emails from viewers, mostly realtors complaining about my story last night. They say they've had cancellations for house tours because of my reporting. To be nice, I write them back with kindness.

Hi, thank you for your email and for watching Channel 7. I appreciate your feedback. Send us your news tips.

Sometimes, these people just want a response.

I log off and shut down my computer before walking out of the studio's main doors off the 79th Street Causeway in Miami Beach and toward the parking lot. I have a reserved space that reads "TWILLIAMS" for my cherry-red BMW. Once inside, I glance at the digital clock and notice I have just enough time to get to my home in mid-Miami Beach, and get ready for tonight.

In case you were wondering, I do share the same name as the famous Boston Red Sox slugger. It was my dad's idea. Being a Williams, he always thought it would be great to have a son named Ted after his favorite ball player. Little did my Irish dad know that I would grow up hating sports, so the name is kind of ironic. The only ball I could hit was the glittering one in the club on '80s nights in Beantown. I also take after my mother's Portuguese family with the dark tanned skin, which confused people back home when I was growing up because of my last name. It could have been worse. I could have had her maiden name, San Paolo. Then I would have been Ted São Paolo. Sounds like a tasty dish, huh?

Fifteen minutes later, I pull up into my brick-paved driveway, and walk up my winding cement walkway to my small cottage off Pine Tree Drive. I love living here, along the Intracoastal Waterway and within walking distance of the beach. Because of my boost in salary after I received a competing offer from Channel Four, I am able to afford this little real estate gem. It's a one-story white bungalow from 1936 with two bedrooms, an office, and a small backyard. Several red, yellow, and pink hibiscus trees ribbon the exterior of the property. This is my little beach oasis from the daily news grind.

I tinker with the keys, and hear some scratching and whimpering on the other side of the door. That's Max, my sandy chihuahua, just like the doggie from those old Taco Bell commercials. "*Yo quiero* Ted Williams," I always joke to guests. When I do that, I hold up Max and mimic the Taco Bell dog's Spanish-accented voice.

"Calm down, Max. I know you've got to go." The moment I open the front door, Max starts scratching at my gray slacks, trying to climb up me. He's so sweet. He's excited to see me because he's been cooped up inside the house all day.

"Now, now. Let me put your leash on, and we'll go, OK?" Max follows me to my Mexican-tiled kitchen, where I toss him some treats, grab the leash, and hook it around his neck.

We walk outside and down Pine Tree Drive, passing the majestic gated estates with flowing fountains that dwarf my little house. The sidewalk is wet from the automatic sprinklers that water the manicured green grass and trees. Max sniffs around and finds his spot under a palm tree next to the Weinsteins' home.

"There ya go! Good boy!" Max starts peeing like Oprah in that scene in her movie *Beloved* where she gets so excited upon seeing Danny Glover's character that she pisses like a racehorse. As we walk back to the house, I feel the beach breezes soothe my skin and spirit like the winds off Cape Cod, my hometown. I can't help but wonder at what a good life I have and how blessed I am. I have the job of my dreams, a dog that adores me, friends who love me, a nice big Irish-Portuguese family back in Massachusetts, and a beautiful home in one of the most beautiful cities in the world. But I can't help but feel like I want more. Even though I'm a famous reporter in South Florida, where I get the best stories, I come home to Max and no one else.

During weeks like this, I fantasize about how nice it would be to come home to Max and a boyfriend. Someone who would have dinner ready and a romantic night with flickering vanilla-scented candles softly lighting the rooms. Someone who wants to share his life with me as much as I want to share my life with him and Max and perhaps another dog or even a kid. Maybe I could adopt one of those *Wednesday's Child* kids with a partner one day.

As beautiful as this city is to live in, Miami is just as ugly when it comes to the dating scene. It is like a beautiful unique shell, the kind you find in the Caribbean with swirls of radiant tropical colors. It seduces you with its sexy veneer and perpetual Technicolor hues. But on the inside, the city is hollow and lacking substance. South Florida is the southern capital of saline implants (for men, too) and Botox injections (guys, too). Most of the guys only care about what car you drive, what gym you work out at, and how much you make. At least back in Boston, I'd get into these heavy conversations about world politics, religion, and gay marriage. In Miami, books are used as towel weights.

If I sound bitter (do I really?), it's because I haven't had a boyfriend since I moved to South Florida from Boston four years ago. Cupid has had terrible aim when it comes to me, and I'm hard to miss, with my face plastered on every billboard and bus. Cupid did find me love back in Boston where I worked the weekend shift at the other Channel 7. Louie was my partner for the three years I was a general assignment street reporter. He was basketball-player tall and built, with aqua eyes and brown velvety fuzzy hair from his crew cut. He had one of the most endearing smiles, a good heart, and an infectious Boston accent. He was head director at the local Boys and Girls Clubs organization, and I often helped him with events by accompanying him to after-school basketball games or field trips with the kids during the summers. We'd go to Provincetown during the summer weekends and visit my family in nearby Sandwich on the Cape. Everything seemed to point that we were going to be together forever. He even put up with all my social and speaking engagements as one of the few Portuguese-American journalists in New England. My heart melted when he began taking Portuguese classes at the Boston Center for Adult Education to better communicate with my relatives on my mother's side. We were planning a trip to visit Portugal when everything fell apart.

One afternoon, I came home early from work. I wasn't feeling well due to a stomach bug. It was four and I walked into our bedroom and found him in our Beacon Hill bed with one of his college-age coaches from the center. I literally caught them with their pants down. No matter how much Louie begged and tried to explain that it was a mistake and would never happen again, I couldn't get past the situation. It replayed in my mind relentlessly like a *This-Just-In* news alert at the station. I wasn't just hurt. I was disgusted he would do that to me, to us, to our future! A fire churned in my gut from all the pain, and sadness hijacked my heavy heart. Work kept me grounded, but when I was alone, the tears would well up in full force.

We broke up. And just as I was planning to find a new place to live, our sister station in Miami offered me a job. It was perfect timing, and I thought coming back to Miami, where I studied at UM, would be a nice way to start again. I already had Ray here as a friend, and we roped Brian into our little group this past year when he and Daniel bought their estate on the Beach. So far, the move has been everything I had hoped for except in the dating department. That has been a big flop. Guys here seem more interested in saying, "I went out with the Channel 7 reporter," or "I hooked up with Ted Williams." I know this because I've overhead my former dates and tricks gab in the bars and bathrooms at Score. To them, I'm *that* Ted Williams and not just Ted.

"So, it's just you and me, Max, right?" He jumps up and scratches my knee playfully. We continue walking, passing other couples pushing their strollers and small children on Pine Tree Drive. I really hoped that was going to be Louie and me one day, but one mistake dissolved that dream into nothing. *Asshole!*

Max and I venture back into the house, where I feed him some more of his favorite treats. I check my mail (credit card offers galore!), and find my mortgage and BMW lease statements have arrived.

I slip out of my clothes and into my egg-shaped gleaming white tub. I take a nice long hot bath with rose-scented bubbles in my Jacuzzi. This is my getaway from the big 7. I come here, let the water fizzle up to 90 degrees, and feel the tickling bubbles rush up and down my back. As the steam rises, the heat clears my face and sinuses. I scrub the layers of make-up off my face, slip underwater, and feel the water envelop me into a liquid cocoon, lulling me into a dreamy state. I feel warm and safe down here. No news to chase. No guys to date. Just a silent peacefulness. I stay in the tub for half an hour before I start to get ready for tonight.

It's 10:55 p.m., and I'm strutting down Lincoln Road toward Score like a whore on the go. Parking was a bitch tonight—even worse than Trina Tucker—so I had to park in the municipal garage two blocks away.

I bet I'll be the first one here since I'm always on time. Ray tends to be on Cuban time, and Brian, well, he stops by whenever it suits him. I pass the baristas whipping up coffee and mocha lattes at the corner Starbucks, and I catch a glimpse of straight couples dancing in the Cuban cigar lounge. I meander through the traffic of stylish trimmed, tanned, toned, plucked (and tucked) people hitting the strip with the same confidence and attitude as if they were starring in their own music videos. Hey, at least I have a good excuse for my purposeful stride. I'm on TV five days a week reporting the news, and I'm a member of the smart set, the small but growing intellectual circle here. I find I am forced to read *The Boston Daily* and *The New York Times* online to tame my appetite for layered stories with substance. Locally, I must make do with *The Miami News*, no offense Ray.

I finally arrive at Score, and notice the guys lounging in the café table chairs outside, watching all the man-traffic coasting in and out of the bar. I grab an empty table and slouch back in my chair and relax. I'm the first one to arrive.

The word "Score" is emblazoned in big bold black letters on a sign above the entrance, the banner radiating what the word means, get it on, win, hook it up. *Score!* The thumping bass and electronica float from the South Beach clubs and over Lincoln Road, reminding me of many other Friday nights in South Beach.

I order a vodka with grapefruit juice from the baby gay waiter, who looks like he should be on Nickelodeon with his spiky blonde hair and boyish bod. I stare at my watch a few times as the minutes and the men go by. Score soothes me. Being here on a Friday sands the sharp edges off my day.

"Oh my gosh! Like aren't you *the* Ted Williams, star reporter for Channel 7?" I hear some queenie-lisping guy gushing from behind my seat. Must be a viewer, a fan. I'm used to this. I turn around ready to sign an autograph or shake a hand when I see a certain Cubano with blue eyes and a burning cigarette in hand. It's Ray, pulling my leg, as usual.

"And aren't you Miami's most fabulous and chronically tardy movie critic?" I fire back, getting up to give my bud a big hug and trying to avoid any falling ashes from his ciggie.

"Good to see you, Ted, even though I see you on the buses in front of me on the road and on the news and in Flamingo Park trolling for tricks at 3 a.m."

"Oh no, you didn't! Besides if you saw me there, it's because *you* were there. I was just looking for you, fucker," I tease Ray back. We have this ongoing inside joke about Flamingo Park, where desperate horny guys go after not scoring at Score, Twist or even online. Flamingo Park is the last resort, and the guys are there until sunrise moseying around, rustling through the bushes and trees. I've never been there. Ray swears he hasn't either, but we can't help but joke about it like those "Your Mama's so fat" jokes.

"Well, my deep throat sources told me you just came from there, and that's why you're late, as usual!"

"Only because I was looking for you Ted," he says, blowing a plume of smoke my way. We burst out laughing (I cough a little from the smoke). Our heads bob, me from my giggles and Ray from his dry heaving.

"Well, grassy-ass!" I say, my way of pronouncing the Spanish word *gracias*.

We sit down and the man-boy bartender reappears to take Ray's order. Ever since we met at UM, Ray has had a thing for Coronas. He said his dad Oscar would drink them with his uncles during baseball games when he was a teen and he ended up catching the buzz when he got older. I remember watching the Canes football games with Ray, and he always had a Corona in his hand. I go for more of the classy drink that gives you a warm buzz from the vodka and yet a sweet but tarty taste from the grapefruit.

"So what's new with you? I saw your story last night about the real estate robber. That's messed up. I don't get how you do the TV thing. You have to rush and run around town for a one-minute, or even a two-minute, time frame to tell a story. I'm all about sitting down, taking my time, and massaging my words for my reviews," Ray says.

"But see, I can't imagine watching three movies a week and then writing about them. I like being out on the scene, getting the story, chasing tips," I say, sipping my drink. The bartender comes back and brings Ray his Corona. He stuffs a lime down the bottle's neck.

"Any cute guys tonight?" Ray asks, taking a swig from his beer.

"Just the usual. I feel like I've met everyone here."

"*Oye*, Ted, that's because you *have* met everyone. You're always out. You're overexposed like Britney Spears. You've clocked more club hours than Paris Hilton. If you were on Friendster or MySpace, you'd have the whole city on your friends list."

"Well, I am on TV *after all*. My face is out there. My name is out there. I have to be out there to keep up my profile. Look, you're the one with the mug shot in your paper every Friday, so I wouldn't talk."

"Yeah, but I don't do the party scene and take Channel 7 with me like you do. Maybe you should take a break from all the partying and being-seen scene."

I know what he means. It's hard to stand out when you're everywhere, but I can't help it. It's part of my persona, my job. I feel like I'm doing community service by attending various functions and events, like I'm promoting Channel 7 and myself in the process. There's always cuter and younger faces out there waiting for me to screw up so they can steal my job. I know I'm good at what I do, but I also know I'm not a looker by South Beach standards. I'm not all-American boy handsome like Brian, or even boyishly Cuban cute like Ray and his twin. I stand out here and yet, I don't. Makeup cleans me up well for television. But one thing I've got under my belt is my Magnum P.I. (Portuguese-Irish) dick. It's the size of a hand-held Channel 7 microphone, at least that's why my tricks have told me. I'm happy that I take after the Portuguese in that respect.

"I just think that if I get myself out there, I'll find that guy, you know?" I tell Ray, scanning the surrounding tables for other cute guys.

"I know what you mean but I bet there's a whole layer of guys out there who go to book clubs, or the Gallery Walks in Coral Gables. It's those guys we have to find," Ray says, holding up his beer for a toast.

"Amen," I click my glass to his.

"Gay men!" Ray says looking around. "Speaking of men, where's Brian?"

It's almost midnight, and Score is packed. The Venezuelan bouncer with the fake blonde hair is turning people away at the door. The DJ inside starts mixing Christina Aguilera's *Ain't No Other Man*. It's a good thing we have our table outside. We only go inside when we have to dash in for a bathroom break. Friday nights are about the three of us catching up, not so much about manhunting, though Brian would probably disagree.

I think I see him over there by the Starbucks, talking to some muscular Latin guy. No wonder he's late. He's chatting it up with a hot Puerto Rican. A few minutes later, we see Brian coming our way with a big grin on his face. I notice that Brian is dressed in his usual attire: white Polo T-shirt accented by a thick silver necklace, blue jeans, and sneakers. No matter how many times we've told Brian that he has the money to dress better, he doesn't listen. He prefers to be ultra-casual.

"Hey, *chicos*. Sorry I'm late. I, um, got sidetracked," Brian says, looking up as if he just ate the canary and the cat that was eyeing it, too. He gives us each a bear hug that leaves us momentarily breathless. Ray and I are like midgets next to him.

"Good seeing you, Brian," Ray says, with a return hug and a loud masculine pat on the back.

"Yeah, I saw what distracted you, a six-foot-tall, dark, curly-haired Puerto Rican with a deep-fried tan and biceps the size of the grapefruits, probably the ones that made my drink. Does that sound right?"

"Yeah, just about, Ted. Wasn't he hot?" Brian's eyes dance mischievously as he talks about the guy who sort of looks like Adam Rodriguez from *CSI: Miami* but with a slightly bigger Latino fro. Brian plays with the golden brown whiskers of his goatee. "I'm gonna meet up with him inside later after we all hang out. *Qué rico!* His name is Eros. He's a Puerto Rican with a Greek name. How hot is that?" Brian says, taking his seat next to Ray.

"You know, you better be careful with that one," Ray pipes up. "Eros in Greek mythology was the god of love, lust, and sex. His Roman equivalent is Cupid," Ray says, lighting another cigarette. "Even worse, his name is sore spelled backwards." Ray is always giving us some pop or historical trivia. He does this with movies, literature, history or anything else that comes to his mind. He's a human Wikipedia. Call him *Ray-ipedia*.

Brian grins. He obviously seems smitten, or just lustful, from the few minutes he was talking to this guy.

Even from my seat across the café table, Brian's eyes seem luminous, a slice of the Atlantic on a stormy day. The guy has the looks, the money, a rich partner, and the life. But yet, it never seems to be enough for him. He wants more.

Don't get me wrong. I really like Brian. He's a good guy and means well, but does he have to have it all? Let Ray and me have the single guys to ourselves. Brian already has a man, a very wealthy one. Do I sound a little bitter? Maybe I am. I guess because deep down inside, I've always had a tiny crush on Brian, but that could never be. He has a man at home and another always waiting on his Miami horizon.

The manboy bartender returns and fetches a drink for Brian. He likes vodka and cranberry.

"So what's going on, guys? How's your other half, Ray?" Brian asks, sipping his reddish drink.

Ray tells him that his brother is good, as always, and that he'll see him tomorrow. He tells us about *Miami Vice II* and what to expect, but doesn't ruin the movie. I recount my crazy week and my little encounter with Trina Tucker.

"You called her Trina Fucker?" Brian asks, his blue eyes widening.

"*Oye*, that's hysterical," Ray jumps in. "Too bad that wasn't on camera. It could have made the people news in the *News*."

Catching up with these guys is the right way to end the week and begin the weekend. We chat for another hour or so, ordering more drinks and talking about what's coming up in our lives.

Brian says he's doing his best to complete the renovations on his new house on the Venetian Causeway while having Daniel call him about every little thing every hour. Daniel expects things to be done yesterday, every day. It may explain why he's a multimillionaire. Too bad we haven't met yet. Brian says he doesn't like to socialize.

"Daniel hates it when the contractors fall behind schedule. That's why I have to stick around here for the next few weeks to watch things. I don't mind. That's more time to play with my new friend," Brian says, prowling the outside of the club for Eros.

Ray has two movies to review next week, *Ocean's 14*, and a new movie by Pedro Almodovar. He also has to help his father and Racso with some house repairs. If he's not at work or with his dog Gigli, Ray is with his super-needy Cuban family.

By 1 a.m., just as things start getting good outside of Score, Ray decides to call it a night.

"*Oye*, I'm exhausted guys. I had a long day, and I have to help my brother tomorrow. So in the infamous words of the *Ah-nold*, *Hasta la vista*, baby." He takes one last swig of his third Corona, and he high-fives each of us as he disappears down Lincoln Road.

Brian decides to use Ray's exit as his exit. It figures. He's always seemed more comfortable with Ray than with me. It was through Ray that I met Brian. It's always been me and Ray since college, but Brian makes a nice third to our group. I know what it feels like to be the new kid on the block in a new city, not knowing anyone so I felt I should give Brian a chance and welcome him to Miami when he joined our little clique a year or so ago. Besides, it's fun listening to Brian's stories about his latest hookups and the renovations to his homes. He's quite a wild character.

"Hey, Ted, I think I'm gonna go look for Mr. Puerto Rico. I told him I would meet up with him after hanging with you guys a bit. Is that cool?"

"Yeah, go have fun, Brian. At least one of us should get laid tonight," I tell him, getting up and giving him a hug. When we hug, I catch traces of his Tommy Hilfiger cologne. It never fades from his skin, and I feel a slight warm tingle breathing it in.

"Talk to you soon, Ted. Go and have fun inside, will ya?" Brian walks off and then disappears into the black darkness of the club.

With the guys gone, I decide to sit back and order one more drink. I watch all these younger guys with their lives ahead of them, some are with couples, others have met tonight. I twirl my straw in my empty drink as I await its replacement. I can't help but think it's just another Friday night in South Beach. Some men walk by and say "Yo! Mr. *Deco Time!*" Some older women stop by and ask me to autograph a napkin for their children.

At 2 a.m., I decide to call it a night, too, since I don't notice anyone I like or anyone new. I leave the man-boy waiter a ten dollar tip. As I head back to the parking garage, I get a text message from Brian.

Eros has such a big cock! Whew. *Qué rico!* I felt it in the bathroom. I'm gonna have so much fun tonight. Hope you get home okay. Talk to you soon.

That's great, Brian. Be safe. Be careful,

I reply. I drive back home to Max. Like I said, another Friday night in South Beach.

3

Brian

"Yeah, yeah! *Yeah* . . . just like that, chico. That feels so good, Eros."

"*Te gusta?*" He tugs at my hair, which makes my back curl up into an arc.

"*Si, papo. Me gusta*, a lot!" I whisper back in my Spanglish. I'm still learning Spanish to meet Miami's Latin *papichulos*. I love the culture, the food, the music. Such warm and passionate people. Maybe that's why I'm drawn to them.

Eros is lying on top of me, our bodies flowing up and down, our skin producing suction noises that I haven't heard in a while. I stare straight into those deep mocha eyes of his, like patches of night. His tight curly fro tickles my face whenever he nuzzles his nose into my neck. Every time he leans in, I notice his bicep tighten into a smooth ball, with a rope of a vein in the middle.

I taste every bit of him. I kiss his biceps, lick his smooth, dark, tanned chest, which is as hard as the jetties off Government Cut. I feel his muscular legs and arms pinning me into submission. I give in easily. I'm his, and I feel that he's mine. I can just sense it. Eros radiates such a powerful spiritual and physical energy that I haven't felt in years.

"You close, *papito*?" he says, thrusting his fat Puerto Rican dick faster in between my legs. I feel the warmth and wetness of his rubber-wearing cock jetting in and out of my ass.

I turn my face away. Looking at him makes my insides want to explode. I can't take this much longer. He suddenly grabs my face and makes me look at him. He puts his finger on my mouth, traces my lips, and tickles my goatee. Our eyes lock, and I disappear into those trance-inducing eyes. I take a deep breath.

"Yeah, Eros. I'm . . . I'm . . . oh wow! . . . *really* close."

"Yeah, you like that?" He pushes deeper into me, like a Puerto Rican drilling machine.

"Oh . . . oh . . . God . . . BRIAN!" He pushes more than before which sends wild waves of insatiable tingles all over my body. I can't take this anymore.

"Oh . . . Eros . . . ahh . . . oh God!"

I instantly come with him, shooting my load all over his tight abs. I see the cum trickle back down onto my stomach like clear dripping paint. He lets out a big sigh and collapses on top of me. I feel the wetness of his hair against my face again and the moistness of his skin from the sexual workout. His grassy cologne smells even sweeter than when I first caught its trace on Lincoln Road, outside the Starbucks.

"Whew, *chico*. That was intense," Eros says, catching his breath and speaking in his Spanish-laced English. His voice reminds me of a far-away island in the Caribbean, the crashing of waves against a shore and sunsets smeared with orange and purple ink.

"Yeah, tell me about it. I can't remember the last time I came like that." I feel a peaceful exhaustion that makes my eyes flutter and want to stay closed. Eros moves to my right side and holds me close to him. I swing my arm around him and tickle his left shoulder softly with my fingers. I smooch the top of his arm, which carries a tattoo of a sunburst. It's hot, not just because he's gorgeous but because his body feels so warm right now after our romp in the bed.

He passes out as we lay in my king-size bed, the one in my

bedroom, not the one I share with Daniel. That would be the master bedroom, and only Daniel and I sleep in there. No tricks are allowed. That's one of our rules.

My bedroom is somewhat smaller than the master bedroom. Sometimes I sleep in here when Daniel and I erupt into one of our vicious arguments. When you have two Scorpios together, things are going to get loud every now and then. We're like two alpha males always trying to be in control, two roosters trying to be the big cock. It's always been like that, ever since we met seven years ago, when I was twenty-one and Daniel was thirty.

The image comes to me as I lie here and look out the grand windows of my bedroom and see the cruise ships sit still in their berths glowing with their nighttime lights at the Port of Miami. With the windows open, I smell the saline scent of ocean wafting into the bedroom and cooling me off. Seagulls chirp above and a tug boat chugs by and sounds its horn. Those sounds transport me back to Chelsea Piers, where I met Daniel.

I remember walking along the waterfront to pick up some dinner, which in those days was a slice of pizza and a Coke. I had just finished my shift at Food Bar and had a hankering for a pizza and a view of the water. It was a bright sunny April day, and I wanted to be outside around people as soon as my shift was over. As I walked up to the window at the pizza place, I noticed a handsome George Clooney type in a three-piece suit staring my way from across the skate park. I thought he was one of the hottest Latin men I had ever seen, with his olive skin and dark features. I smiled. He nodded. A minute later, he crossed to my side of the pier and introduced himself.

"Hello! My name is Daniel, and I have to say you're one of the most beautiful men I've ever seen. What's your name?" he said, gripping my hand in the strong handshake of a straight man. I noticed the masculine strands of black hairs on his arm.

"I'm . . . Brian," I paused. His salt-and-pepper hair and the penetrating gaze from his big brown eyes almost made me stutter.

I was like a gushing schoolgirl. It was my first year in New York City after leaving Charlotte, North Carolina, and I still wasn't used to meeting guys from all sorts of backgrounds.

"Can I buy you another slice of pizza? Maybe you can join me for a bite. I'm hungry myself," he said.

Daniel didn't just buy a slice. He bought a whole pizza heavy with chicken, green peppers, and tomatoes. We sat by the edge of the pier, where it faces the high-rises on the cliffs across the Hudson River on the Jersey side. We ate and talked for hours.

I learned that he was born in Israel, where he served as a captain in the Israeli army. He dreamed of being a successful businessman in the States to help support his two brothers and three sisters in Tel Aviv. He came here five years ago when an old family friend asked him if he wanted to help run his printing press. Within two years, Daniel rose from supervisor to manager and saved up enough money to buy half the company. When his friend decided to move back to Israel, he sold Daniel the entire business. Immediately, Daniel began expanding, taking on more clients, such as post-card companies and small newsletters for local colleges and other businesses. He eventually bought two other printing companies in Brooklyn and Queens and now owns four all together. On the side, he buys and sells real estate.

"You've done so well for yourself, Daniel. I'm sure your family is very proud of you," I said, shoving the last piece of pizza into my mouth. I couldn't believe I ate more than half of the pie, but I was hungry and he paid.

"My goal was to be a multimillionaire by the time I turned thirty. I'm almost there," he said in his Israeli accent, which completely threw me off at first. I figured he would have greeted me with an *Hola* or *Como estas* or a *Que tal?*

I told him how my mom raised me as a single parent in Charlotte and how I always felt like I was the parent. Milly—I call her by first name—was always having trouble paying the bills and keeping debtors away, so I remember growing up eating cereal for dinner and watching a lot of TV while she worked odd jobs, from selling newspaper ads for *The Charlotte News* to Avon beauty products.

As soon as I turned sixteen, I got a job at the Gap folding clothes, and I worked part-time at a karaoke bar where I would get up and sing at least once a night to a standing ovation. I was never much of an academic type. I always had a hard time focusing. Teachers told my mom I had ADD, and they were right, something I've learned to accept and deal with. My dream was to be a singer, so I went to the local community college in Charlotte and studied music. But learning all the different music styles and studying operatic music (I was a baritenor) wasn't my thing. I just wanted to go out on a stage and sing, and sing I did, every Sunday at church and with the school choir. At twenty, I decided my dreams couldn't be contained in Charlotte, and I set my sights on New York City, where I've been searching for my big break. I haven't found it yet, but I know it's out there. I can sense it.

"Let me hear you sing, anything," David said, sipping his Diet Coke. The way he looked at me made me feel so special that afternoon, like I was the only boy in Chelsea, or even in New York for that matter. His eyes were completely on me and no one else, not even the sweaty, hot muscle boys running and skating up and down the pier in their too-small shorts and too-tight tank tops.

"Okay, but remember, my voice isn't warmed up."

I sang him a verse of Foreigner's *I Wanna Know What Love Is*—one of my favorite classic rock ballads—and I wasn't pitchy at all. He just held my stare as I sang and, apparently, I sang on key because a small crowd gathered and began tossing coins and dollar bills into our empty pizza box. That money went to my dinner fund for the next night.

"That was great, Brian. You have the voice of an angel and the blue eyes of one, too," David said, leaning in closer to me as he spoke.

So that was our first date, and from then on, we were inseparable. Three months later, I moved into his Chelsea two-bedroom, and my life continued to improve. We took trips to Israel to meet his family and weekend getaways to a condo in Newport, Rhode Island that Daniel ended up buying on impulse. My creativity and eye for design helped Daniel decorate our homes, and my spirituality helped soothe and center him when he was stressed out from work. Daniel's business savvy and direct in-your-face approach to life taught me how to deal with people and how to get what I wanted. We were a good match. We understood each other. Our personalities balanced one another's. We were two Scorpios in harmony. But over the years, something began to fade and, like a disappearing sunset, I can't pinpoint the exact moment it happened. The sex grew infrequent. Daniel was working more and seemed less interested in being with me. I had more to do with overseeing the renovations and home projects in our upscale two-bedroom condo in Chelsea, our little condo in Newport, and then a new parcel of land on the Venetian Causeway, where we were building our waterfront villa.

I yearned for sexual intimacy and Daniel wasn't interested in having that with me. As I got older I started shedding my boyish look and began to look more like a man. I grew a goatee and gained a little weight around my waist. (It was all those grand dinners at restaurants in Chelsea and in Newport.) I could sense that Daniel wanted a younger-looking boy toy to play with. I didn't seem to turn him on anymore, like when we first met. I was old at twenty-five. Although I was attracted to Daniel, I eventually lost my sexual desire for him, too. (He wasn't the hot Latino *papi* I first imagined he would be.) We fell into a pattern more befitting roommates, best friends, and business partners. We just weren't sexual partners anymore.

And that brings to me to this gorgeous Latin man sleeping at my side. Eros's simple touch arouses a deeply hidden sexual desire in me that drives me wild. If only I felt this way toward Daniel again, but I don't and neither does he. Three years ago, after months and months of a sexless relationship, Daniel and I agreed to extend the boundaries of our relationship to allow us to have sex with other men. Our rule: we can hook up with other guys but never more than once because that could poison our life-partnership. It was hard for me at first, knowing that Daniel was going out there and doing all the things we used to do, but with other boyish guys. But then I realized I could hook up with those Latin guys that have always turned me on, ever since watching Eric Estrada on *CHiPs* or Lorenzo Lamas on *Falcon Crest*. I can't imagine my life without Daniel. I do love him, and I know he loves me. He even likes my flaky mom, who can be a handful during the holidays, trying to delegate what we're going to eat and where we're going to sit. The sexual part of our relationship is dead, and I don't think anything, not even sweet nostalgia, will revive it.

People don't understand my situation with Daniel, especially Ted and Ray. They are great guys, and I'm glad I've become friends with them in my adopted city. I have a hard time making friends because once they see my Rolex, my Land Rover, and one of our houses, they see the wealth and the opportunities that the money can bring them. I've recognized the look over the years from users, so-called friends who have a business agenda. Ted and Ray aren't like that. They seem grounded and interested in me only as a friend, not as a liaison to Daniel and his investors. Neither has ever made a move on me either and for that, I knew they could be good friends of mine in Miami when I visit. I don't have many close friends. Most of my friends are Daniel's business associates, and I don't relate to them.

In case you're wondering, I met Ray first, online for a possible hookup one night on manhunt.net. From his posted photo, I thought he was cute, and when he said he was Cuban, my eyebrows shot up with excitement. But when we met in person, the sexual vibe wasn't there. (That's the thing about online connections. You can't make an accurate assessment until you come face to face and read the person's energy.) I immediately sensed he could be a potential new friend in Miami, and we left it at that and started hanging out. But never at the movies. I can't sit through a two-hour movie. I like listening to him talk about his twin brother and his wacky but loving Cuban family. I wish my upbringing was more like that, instead of me parenting my mom. I had to be the man of the house at a young age because my dad wasn't around. He wasn't part of the Anderson household, but I've dealt with that. My father, if you can call him that, decided that going out and boozing was more important than helping my mom raise me. He abandoned us before I was born. At twenty-three, he wasn't ready to be a father. I yearned to have that father figure when I was younger. I watched fathers pick up my classmates after school. I envied my friends when their dads sat in the audience and watched us in school plays. I eventually accepted the hard truth: I didn't have a father. I survived without one. As time went on, I didn't need him in my life. It doesn't make a difference to me whether he's dead or alive. Milly did her best, and Daniel has been my family and my rock. When my father resurfaced three years ago and wanted to be part of my life, I said no. But at Daniel's urging, I agreed to meet him for lunch, and that has become our yearly get-together. I do it out of obligation. It turns out my father has liver problems from his years of alcohol abuse, and he wanted to make amends before it was too late. I wish he had that epiphany when I was a boy, when I needed support in dealing with another drinking parent. The reason I meet with him once a year is that I want to know in the future that I made an effort in getting to know my father. I want to prove to myself that I am a better person that he ever was or ever will be and that I am nothing like him.

"Hey . . . you okay Brian?" I hear Eros waking up.

"Yeah, I'll be right there *guapo*. Just looking out at the stars over Miami. I'm over here on the balcony."

I look at the bed, with its flowing white sheets. Eros lays there like a tanned Puerto Rican statue coming to life. He sits up and winks at me.

"Come over here *papito*. I want to hold you," he says, gesturing his hand toward me. The bay breeze blows the bedroom curtains softly like the sails from a boat that has just found a new wind. The clouds swallow the sentinel moon over Miami. The bay's water laps against our twenty-foot boat and our two jet skis, rocking them rock back and forth, a lot like my thoughts right now.

What is it about this guy? I feel like I've met him before but yet, it all feels so new at the same time. Ever since I first glanced at him at Starbucks tonight, I have felt this incredible pull toward him, like the gravitational force the moon has on Miami's tides. I feel so warm and so safe with him. I feel alive. I told him earlier about my situation with Daniel, and he didn't seem to care. Now I have to tell him what I tell all my tricks. We were a one-time deal. But for some reason, I don't think I'm going to be able to do that. There's so much about Eros I want to know more about. I want to know what it was like for him growing up in San Juan. What is his favorite food? What's his favorite place? What are his dreams, his goals in life? I don't know much about him. He works as a waiter at a Cuban restaurant on South Beach, and lives in an apartment near Flamingo Park. He seems like a simple guy and a hard worker, but there's so much more to be explored. I can feel it.

"Brian, come back here. I want to see those beautiful blue eyes of yours," he says. And with that, I tiptoe on the cold white marble tile, slip back into bed and into Eros's strong arms.

As we kiss and cuddle again, I hear my cell phone vibrate on the tile. I have a feeling it's Daniel.

4

Ray

Beep beep!

I honk the horn twice. Where is Racso? I'm sitting outside the Toyota dealership on Le Jeune Road waiting for my chronically-late brother. That's one of the few things people say we have in common besides our looks, our penchant for tardiness. But at least I was on time this Saturday afternoon.

I finally see him emerge from the gleaming windows of the dealership, home to all those snazzy Scions and the new Camry. I keep telling Racso he could use a new car. His Corolla, with 110,000 miles, is on its last legs, which is why he's back here for another repair. He approaches my Nissan 300 SX and sticks out his tongue at me. I do the same.

"*Oye*, it's about time." He opens the door and hops in.

"What are you talking about, little brother? It's 11:05. I told you 11:00 yesterday," Racso says, buckling his seatbelt.

"It's 11:12," I fire back.

"Well, my watch says five past eleven," he says with a snicker.

"So what's wrong with your car this time, Racso?" We pull away from the dealership and head back to Papi and Mami's house off Miracle Mile in the less upscale part of Coral Gables, better known as "The City Beautiful."

"It's the catalytic converter. It's shot. It'll cost me about five hundred dollars," he says, fiddling with the stereo and stopping on the country station. Faith Hill belts out her old hit *This Kiss*. He's doing this to irk me. He knows I hate his country bumpkin music. Who has heard of a Cuban liking country music *en Miami*?

"Your car is barely worth five hundred dollars! In a few months, something else will go and I'll have to pick you up all over again on my day off," I say, as we drive down Le Jeune, passing the Blockbuster and the old Sears at the Miracle Mile intersection. I hang a left and switch the radio back to the new Madonna mega-mix CD. It has a new version of her hit *Hung Up*. I can't wait to see her in concert again this fall with Ted and Brian, if he's in town.

"Ray, we've been through this before. I'm a schoolteacher. I make almost half of what you make. I can't afford a new car. I'm still living with Papi and Mami. I'm saving up to buy a house one day. No good comes from renting like you. All that money I save by living at home can go to buy me and Cindy a new little starter home maybe in Kendall or somewhere when we get married."

"But all the money you're pouring into your car can be a down payment on a *new* car! If you can pull off a new car, why not?" I tell him, grooving to Madonna with my right hand. When I'm not switching gears, I let my right hand do the dancing.

"Well, one day you'll see that I'm right. I'm thinking about my future, Ray. Maintaining this Corolla and living at home will pay off for Cindy and me, you'll see. If you met the right person, ah, I mean the right guy, you'd know what I'm talking about. You learn to sacrifice more. I'm not just thinking about me but about her too," he says, changing the station back to the country channel, which has Keith Urban crooning *It's A Love Thing*. Racso is really irking me right now, and I can't help but show it by grinding my gears and gunning the car while making a right on Ponce de León Drive. It's my Cuban passive-aggressiveness. Good thing we're only a few blocks away from the house.

As I pull onto Ponce, passing rows of convertibles and sports cars parked in those slanted metered spaces in front of little bou-tiques and restaurants, Racso's words replay in my head. *If you met the right guy.* Yeah, tell me about it. I've never really had a serious boyfriend. Just dates and hookups—no one serious enough to bring home to pass the Martinez inspection, which includes Papi, Mami, and Racso. And, of course, Gigli. If she doesn't like the guy, which has happened before, I move on. I'm not going to bring just anyone home.

It's hard finding someone who lives up to my standards. Professional (lawyer, teacher, fellow writer, intellect.) Lives alone (not with the ex-boyfriend, ex-wife, or his mom and dad). Out to his family (No bisexual or in-the-closet stuff). Good-looking (he has to be somewhat cute). Speaks English and Spanish. (This is Miami after all). HIV negative (I'm a little of a hypochondriac. Sorry). More or less my age (Give or take five years or so). Good taste in films (Scorsese, Manning, Spielberg, Almodovar). Then there's the other Martinez standard. I hate to admit this, but I want the same thing Racso has with Cindy. As much as my brother heckles me, he has a great girlfriend and loving relationship. He and Cindy met at FIU where they were both education majors. She's half Cuban and half Irish, with dark brown straight hair that falls to her chin, light brown eyes, and a very outgoing personality. No matter who she meets, she wins them over with her charm. She's funny, too, and has cracked me up countless times with her witty comments. She and Racso started dating in their senior year of college, graduated together and went on to get their master's in education at FIU. Mami and Papi immediately loved her, recognizing that she was a pretty Cuban girl who happens to look a lot like Neve Campbell, the *Scream* queen. She also converses with them in Spanish. The fact that she wanted to be an elementary school teacher just sealed the deal. Anyone who does that for a living must have patience and a heart of gold. Anyone who can put up with my sometimes obnoxious jock of a brother deserves a gold medal. When I see Racso and Cindy together, they just gel. There's devotion in their eyes and a certain magic between them, similar to the way Papi and Mami interact with each other. They each know what to say to make the other laugh, as if they have their own secret language. I haven't met my guy version of Cindy yet. Hopefully, when I do, Papi and Mami will take to him the same way they have embraced Cindy, who they consider the daughter they never had. She's even invited to join us on family vacations, and her parents and my parents have bonded. But I know how uncomfortable my gayness makes Papi at times, so we just don't talk about it. At least Cindy is cool with it, and I appreciate that. She always asks me if I've met a new guy and inquires about my nightlife experiences with Brian and Ted. Racso is really lucky to have her in his life.

I pull into the grassy driveway of our childhood home on Menores Ave., and I see Papi mixing his exterminating chemicals by the garage. We're the third house in from Ponce de León. Our house is small and homey, but to Papi, it's as special and majestic as the waterfront estates in Cocoplum. You see, Papi, aka Oscar Martinez, killed a lot of roaches to pay for that house. When he came here from Cuba in 1968 with Mami—Ana—he found a job as an exterminator through an old friend from Havana. He worked for Javier for a few years before earning his own exterminating license. With that, he opened his owned business, R and R Pest Control, named after me and Racso. The name is emblazoned on his little white Toyota pickup truck.

He hoped one day my brother and I would take over the business, but we had bigger dreams. I wanted to be a writer. Racso wanted to teach. In the end, Papi was happy that his two sons had ambitions beyond carrying a can of pesticide. He worked hard and sacrificed so much so we could grow up and have good lives in the United States. Papi and Mami personify what "good Cubans" are all about. They're sincere, humble, honest, and kind-hearted souls open enough to share with you their life stories at the drop of a hat, especially tales from Cuba. But as much as they love me, I know they don't share one particular story with many people, that their movie critic son is gay and hangs out at gay bars on South

Beach. They tend to tell people about my reviews, my car, and even little Gigli.

There's a Latino awkwardness in sharing that aspect of my life in casual conversation, though I wish it wasn't so. Everyone *en la familia* knows that this twin likes guys, but they somehow dance around the issue of dating when we have family gatherings or birthday parties. That conversation always involves Racso, and he doesn't have to say much because Cindy will be at his side, socializing with our big Cuban family as if she had always been a part of it. When my parents talk about Racso and Cindy, Mami and Papi glow bright enough to light up the American Airlines Arena. It's just how things are, and I've grown accustomed to this double standard because I love my parents. I just hope one day they will extend the same courtesy to my boyfriend as they do to Cindy.

"*Hola*, how are *mis hijos* doing?" Papi greets from the garage door. He's wearing his khaki work pants and white wife-beater shirt. He's still wearing his R and R cap.

"Hey, Papi. Your cheap son needed a ride from the Toyota dealership," I tell him, patting him on his sweaty back. The Miami sun is beating down on the city pretty hard today, and Papi wears a sheen of sweat. His crow's feet crinkle into the sweetest smile whenever he looks up at us, as if he had just glanced at us for the first time at the Mercy Hospital baby ward.

"My car will be ready by 5 p.m., Papi. Do you think you can take me back there?" Racso asks.

"*No hay problema*, Racsito," he calls him by his nickname. Mine is Raysito. Pick any Cuban kid, young or adult, and their nickname will be their name plus "ito—or, like me, plus sito."

"Go inside, *tu mama* has made one of her super *dulce* flans," Papi says, returning to his chemical concoction.

"I love seeing *mis hijos* together and helping each other. No matter what happens in jou lives, jou are always brothers and best friends. Jou will always have each other," Papi tells us.

Racso rolls his eyes and walks ahead of me as I pat Papi on the shoulder. Whenever Racso and I would argue or get into a fist-fight, which happened every minute when we were younger (with Racso often being on top of me), Papi would forcefully separate us and repeat that saying. We've heard it a thousand times.

Racso and I walk inside. The aroma of boiling evaporated milk, eggs and caramel wafts through the air, the sweet smell of my childhood. We follow our noses down the main hallway, where Papi and Mami have created a mini photo gallery of us as kids. There's Papi and Mami each holding one of us at five years old in front of Parrot Jungle with bright red and orange birds posing on our shoulders. There we are at eight years old with matching white suits for our communion. We were both missing our front teeth. There we are at ten years old with matching buzz cuts, blue tank tops, and shorts, smiling with the captain of the cruise ship from our end-of-the-school-year trip to Mexico. There we are at sixteen, standing proudly in our used Honda Accord hatchback that Papi surprised us with on our birthday. And there we are at eighteen, standing in white graduation gowns and with diplomas in our hands and our arms around each other.

The photos also remind me of the old Miami, when Gloria and Emilio Estefan performed at local *quinceañeras* rather than cloaking themselves behind their publicists in their rich and fabulous lives on Star Island. When Miracle Mile was home to a grand Woolworth's store before it was replaced by another Barnes & Noble and Starbuck's cafe. When the hotels on Ocean Drive were rentals for aging retirees, waiting for their next destination, and not jammed with too-cool hip-hoppers trying to *keep it real*. When families descended on Calle Ocho to watch new movies at the Tower Theater for two dollars instead of dishing out five dollars just for popcorn at the flashy Lincoln Road Cinema. I remember when Miami Beach was simply referred to as *la playa*, not SoBe.

I can't help but smile at the framed family album on the wall and all the memories it brings back. The photos are gentle reminders of our happy childhood and all the places we went as a family. These days, most of my trips are to movie junkets or down to Key West for a quick getaway or here, to the house, to help Mami and Papi with their errands.

A little bell rings furiously. It's Mami summoning us to the kitchen.

"Are jou here, Raysito y Racsito? I made jou some flan and two *media noche* sandwiches for lunch," she says, emerging from the kitchen and greeting us in the dining room, where there are more photos of the family.

I don't know why Mami is so happy to see Racso. He still lives here.

"Raysito, how is *mi nene*, my baby," she says, hugging me and giving me a kiss on the neck, as she did when we were younger, in front of our friends at Ponce de León Middle School.

"Jou never come over anymore. I have to call jou and see how jou are doing. I see more of jou movie reviews than I see jou," she says, taking my hand and leading me to the breakfast room where our sandwiches and slices of flan await us.

"Yeah, Ray is never here. Because he lives sooo far, *tu sabes*? South Beach is what, ten miles away?" Racso interjects, while hunched down browsing through the refrigerator for a Sprite.

"Mami, I get busy with work. Besides, I was here last Saturday, helping Papi change the air conditioning vents."

We sit and chow down on our food, the whole time Mami watching us, probably imagining us as little kids eating her dinners. While we eat, I hear Mami's Spanish soap operas playing on the small kitchen radio that never seems too far away from her reach. She listens to the morning run of dirty jokes from Cuban DJs, the latest local news, and, of course, her novellas.

Racso finishes his sandwich and flan and thanks Mami. Then he then heads off to our home office to grade some papers.

"Hey, little brother, thanks again for the ride today. I appreciate it," he says messing up my hair.

"Leave my hair alone. I'm gonna have to gel it again."

"Oh, no! God forbid the famous movie critic is seen without

every spiked hair in place," Racso winks. "Keep Mami company for a little while. She feels like she never sees you or knows what's going on with you, little brother," he says, leaving the kitchen.

So it's me and Mami and that darn little kitchen radio. I can feel it coming any minute now. A Ricky Martin or Shakira song will start playing, and Mami will start feeling the beat and whip me onto the kitchen dance floor, like she would when I was little. When no one's home, she breaks out in dance with an invisible partner. Mami is wacky like that. While she whips meringue or a rich flan, she spins herself on the beige-tiled kitchen floor. If she's stirring some rice and beans, she twirls herself to the music of Celia Cruz.

I hear Ricky Martin's newest song come on and to avoid the dance routine, I ask her for a favor. I do this every once in a while, and it's that time again. I need Mami's help to use Nair on my back.

"Mami, can you do that thing you do for me on my back? It's time," I ask her.

She winks, knowing exactly what I'm talking about. I don't believe in waxing, and I can't reach that far down my back to shave. But Nair takes care of that small patch of hair I get on my back.

"*Si, como no*," she says, grabbing her yellow dishwashing gloves for operation Nair. "Anything for my baby!"

We head into my old bathroom where she keeps the bottle of Nair handy for these mother and son moments.

I take off my shirt and sit backwards on the yellow toilet seat, facing the sky-blue wallpaper with streaks of yellow. Mami squeezes the bottle and smears the Nair in the middle of my back. For some reason, Racso has a smooth back and doesn't have to deal with this, but his chest is much hairier than mine. Funny how genetics works. We're identical twins, so identical that people can't tell us apart. But if you spend five minutes with us, our differences emerge. Racso is spontaneous and physical. He likes to punch me in the arm, allegedly playfully. He has a deep Cuban masculine voice like Papi. I'm more organized and stick to a routine. I'm not very physical except with the keyboard to write up my reviews or with the stick-shift on my Nissan. When Racso punches me, it hurts. When I try to wrestle him, he flips me on my back and nails me down. For Halloween, Racso enjoyed dressing up as Superman or Batman. I preferred to be Green Lantern, slipping into green and black tights and a mask, or Aqua Man because of the bright orange suit. And I got to wear a blonde wig.

Oh, and Racso is cheap, and I like to splurge. You should see the balance on my *Miami News* expense card. (One time, I went a little crazy at Bed, Bath and Beyond with picture frames and towels, but that's between you and me.)

The Nair is cold on my back, and immediately, I feel the tingling sensations. The hair-eating glob is chewing away at my roots.

"Jou know, Raysito, I was listening to *el radio* the other morning and the *locutor* was talking about *la SIDA* and how there has been more infections *aqui en* Miami. I hope jou are using protection when jou go out *con tu amigos*. It's getting *muy bad aqui con todos los gays y touristas,*" she says.

I don't even want to turn around and face her when she starts talking like this. Just because I'm gay doesn't mean I am going to get AIDS. I'm super careful. Besides, I rarely hook up. I bet she doesn't give Racso the same talk.

"Mami, *por favor!* I don't need you to tell me what I can do and can't do. I work for a newspaper. I read the news. I know what's going on. I'm educated." The Nair is burning as much as I am right now. I hate when she does this to me when we're alone.

"I know jou are smart. I am just telling you what I heard *en el radio*. I tell jou Because I love jou, *mi amor,*" she says, grabbing a towel and dousing it with hot water to wipe the Nair and little black hairs off my back.

I know she means well, but it's so awkward when she says these things. I begin to wonder whether she's thinking about me having sex with some guy. It's too weird. I wish people would stop equating AIDS with gay men. It's everyone's disease, not just gay men's.

"It never hurts to take extra precautions, *tu sabes*. All it takes is one mistake, Raysito. One mistake!" She wipes my back up and down with the warm towel and washes it in the sink.

"Now see, you have no more *pelitos*. Jou hairs are gone. *Tu espalda* is all clean now." She pats me on the back, and I turn around and see her staring at me with her big blue eyes, the same ones that Racso and I have. Papi has light brown eyes, which I think are more unique and look more Cuban, like my cousins Betty and Idelys.

I take a quick look in the mirror, and my back is as smooth as a baby's behind. I smile. If this were a movie, it would be called *She's Got Her Son's Back*.

"*Gracias*, Mami, for your help," I tell her, kissing her on the cheek.

"*No hay problema*," she says before heading back to the kitchen and back to her radio. Come to think of it, I hate that little kitchen radio.

"Just be safe when jou go out. Remember what I told jou."

"I know, Mami!" I tell her. "I know."

After I brush off the remaining little hairs, I put on my Urban Outfitter's T-shirt, the one with the *Fight Club* logo on the front. I'm reading the paper in the dining room when I feel my cell phone buzz in my pocket. It's Ted.

"*Oye*, Ted . . . what's up!" I say, taking the phone outside in the yard, where Papi has his small crop of banana trees and remove the large shady mango tree. He's always secretly dreamed of having a farm one day, like his dad did back in his native Matanzas, Cuba.

"Hey, Ray. What are you doing tomorrow afternoon?" I can sense he's up to something.

"I was gonna go to the beach, take Gigli for a walk along the seawall. Maybe hit Lincoln Road. Why? Wasssup?"

"Remember how you said how I'm overexposed and I go out too much?

"Yeeeah . . . and your point, Ted?

"Well . . . you're gonna loooove this. There's a new gay book club starting up at Books & Books near your parents' house in the Gables. Wanna check it out?" he says.

A gay book club? Hmm. I do love to read. I just read the latest Dean Koontz suspense thriller. And I'm looking for something else to read. It could be fun and something different.

"That sounds cool, Ted. Wanna pick me up? I'm on the way. We can drive with the top down to the meeting. What about Brian?"

"Deal, but I don't think Brian would be interested. He doesn't read that much. Besides, I think he has his hands full with Eros, the Puerto Rican love god."

We both laugh.

"I'll swing by your place about noon. The meeting is at one."

"See you then, *chico*!" I say, closing my flip phone.

5

Ted

"Do you think there will be some cute guys?" I turn to Ray who is sitting shotgun in my BMW grooving to the Scissor Sisters. We're cruising along the MacArthur Causeway with the Port of Miami to our left and Star Island to our right. It's another sun-drenched South Florida day, and I'm glad I put on my Clinique moisturizer and sunscreen although I don't think I can get any darker than I am. It's my Portuguese DNA. My Portuguese cousins and I look like we could be Greg Louganis's relatives even though he's Samoan. My cousins from my dad's side of the family look like your typical Boston Irish descendants with the fair skin and blue or green eyes. And some of them shared the same racist attitudes, looking down on people not quite as light as them and making people feel like outsiders. I remember one time at my Uncle John's birthday party in Quincy, my cousins Trish and Marty, part of the Williams, Cunninghams, and Cavanaugh brood, kept calling me and my sister Lourdes sand-niggers and spics. We were ten years old, and it stings just as bad now as it did then. It was one of the last times my mother ever let us visit, and the incident put a further strain between my dad and his family because you know the kids picked the words up from my uncle and aunt. So I always felt more at home with my mom's side of the family, and among Latinos especially, with the last name Martinez. My mom's side of the family and even Ray's *familia* are a lot like me, very affectionate/lovey-dovey/let's-throw-a-party. My dad's family is stiff, silent, and let's-go-to-prayer-meeting people. Among Cubans or just Latinos in general, I feel accepted and loved. I feel I'm among my own, especially here in Miami where I'm part of the brown rainbow of Hispanics and Latinos. In Boston I usually stood out in the bars and school and surprised people by speaking English perfectly sans accent and being (surprise!) on TV.

"I don't know Ted. This is a book club, *not* Score. We're hear to read and engage in lengthy discussions about specific literary works. I want to find a new book to read and perhaps, meet some other intellectual men to interact with beyond the 'Where do you work out?' bronzed muscle gods we meet out and about. I dunno about you though," Ray says, lifting his sunglasses and his thin black eyebrows to make his point. When he's done speaking, he lets his shades fall back into place. I now can see myself talk again in the reflection of his Ray-Bans.

"Well, you never know. There might be a hunk in the crowd that never goes out. I doubt these guys go out much if they're meeting on a beautiful Sunday afternoon . . . in a bookstore!"

"*Bueno*, we'll see." Ray says, wearing his *Lethal Weapon* black T-shirt, another freebie from his job, his Old Navy shorts, and Converse sneakers. He looks like a big kid who would be seen hanging outside a mall and smoking a cigarette. I went for my usual preppy look: a beige Polo shirt, dark blue khaki shorts, and boat shoes. "If anything, Gilbert's Bakery is around the corner. We can get some *cafecito y pastelitos*. Yum. They make the best ones. You can smell their succulent aroma while driving down Le Jeune. My parents would take me and Racso there on Sundays after lunch at La Carreta when we were little."

Fifteen minutes later after passing rows of bridal shops and hair salons on Miracle Mile, I pull up to a meter outside the small bookstore. I see a small crowd gathering inside. I pop my top back up on the BMW, and Ray and I walk into the store and take off our sunglasses in slow motion like David Caruso on *CSI: Miami*.

And so it begins.

"Hey! Aren't you Ted Williams from Channel 7?" an older woman in her sixties with bright red dyed hair that matches her nails greets me. I smile and shake her hand, thanking her for watching the station. Ray rolls his eyes. This rarely happens to him, but I guess he's used to it happening to me. It's those bus ads and billboards, I tell you.

We pass a cashier standing in front of a wall of books and magazine racks. We make our way deeper into the store. In the back, a small group of chairs form a circle and we see about ten men sitting there. This must be it. Ray and I sit down side by side, and we make ourselves comfortable as some classical music softly plays in the background. This is quite cozy. I've been to Books & Books on Lincoln Road, but guys use the books there for towel weights for the beach. It's also a stopping ground when guys get to Score too early. They come in to mosey around the store and pretend to eye some good book or magazine when they're really eyeballing each other. I know this because I've done this myself. But I do pick up the *Wall Street Journal* there sometimes and *Newsweek*. I'm more of a newsmagazine guy.

The Gables Books & Books is much larger, with a courtyard in the middle. It's really quiet in here. It reminds me of the kind of place that makes you want to sit on the floor, hide in a corner, and read a good book, like I did back at the Sandwich Public Library on the Cape when I was younger.

"They have some coffee. Want some?" Ray offers, getting up from his seat.

"Sure, low-fat milk. I'm trying to watch my figure, Ray." He rolls his eyes again at me. With his glares, Ray should be called Captain Obvious or Sarcastic Martinez.

I'm sitting here in a half-moon group of chairs, and the ten other guys are waiting for the book club organizer to arrive. Some of the guys start introducing themselves. I hear a Todd, Omar, Tom, Bill, Jose and Mark among the exchange of greetings. Not the handsomest bunch with their beer bellies, big noses, receding hairlines and unkempt hair. Most of the guys here appear to be in their thirties and forties. This could easily be a meeting for the Unlucky In Looks club, but I shouldn't talk.

"Hi, I'm Ted Williams. Nice to meet you all. This is my first time at a book club meeting."

"Hi, Ted!" the group greets me back, as if I were in an AA meeting or something, not that I've ever been to one.

Ray returns back with two small coffees from the little café inside the bookstore and hands me my drink.

"This is Ray everyone!" I say.

"Hi, Ray!" the group responds. Ray nods, smiles, and sips his coffee as if embarrassed by all the attention. The guys all smile at him.

I see a tall handsome man, in his forties I suspect, approach the group from the backroom of the store. He sits in one of the chairs with some books in his hands. I'm smitten. This man has salt and pepper cropped hair, icy-blue eyes, thick charcoal eyebrows, and a chiseled jaw. He's got some crow's-feet around his eyes, but it works for him. I notice his biceps framed by the snug navy blue Polo blue shirt and beige khaki shorts. (We match!) He's about to speak. I elbow Ray in his side so he can check out the guy.

Ray widens his crystal blue eyes to give me another one of those will-you-stop-it looks. This reminds me of our time at UM where I wrote him silly notes during our Law and Ethics or Feature Writing classes.

"Hello everybody! I'm so glad you all could make it to our inaugural Books & Books Gay Book Club gathering. We've wanted to do this for a long time. My name is Richard, and I'm a manager here at the store. Let's all introduce ourselves."

We already did that but we do so again because it's what Richard asks, and if he asked me to, I'd give him my car. He's that hot! He reminds me of some of the older Irish guys in Boston with their blue-collar street hunky appeal.

We all introduce ourselves, and as I say my name, Richard's eyes lock on me for one . . . two . . . three seconds. He's interested. I knew it! I may have an exclusive here, people.

Richard continues with the formalities.

"Since this is our first meeting, I wanted to bring some new and old gay literary books that we could decide to read. The idea is to pick two books out of the batch and then we'll meet up in a month and dissect them. Forgive me if you have read any of these. I tried to choose a wide range of gay novels," he says handing out a list of ten books for us to choose from.

He holds up each book and talks a little about them. There's the Anderson Cooper memoir *Dispatches from the Edge*. I notice some guys make some smirks and tsssks. One guy makes a gagging vomiting sound in the corner. Luckily, I'm blessed to work for a station that embraces and encourages me being open in public, but then again, I'm not an anchor. Just a reporter and a co-host of *Deco Time*. I wonder how they would feel if I was the main anchor?

Richard holds up a fairly new book called *Boys of Boston* by Tommy Perez, a former *News* writer now at the *Boston Daily*. I knew him peripherally, and I've heard through the gay media grapevine that he's a good guy, but I've never officially met him. He worked in Fort Lauderdale. My stories are mostly in Miami.

"This one's a debut novel, about dating in Boston and told through the viewpoints of three different guys. Like a *Same Sex in the City*. A fun read that explores various issues among today's gay men," Richard says enthusiastically.

That sounds like a good book. I'm sure Ray and I could relate. Me because it's in Boston, and Ray, because he's Cuban-American, like the author who worked at his paper. Richard continues to rattle off the other books. There's *Where The Boys Are* by William J. Mann, an author in Ptown not far from where I grew up on the Cape.

"This is about three guys finding their place in each other's lives amid the drug circuit party crowd," Richard explains. I can't believe I've never heard of these books. I don't have time to read but if I want to keep seeing Richard, I'm going to have to squeeze in some reading rainbow time.

Richard goes on to name the other books, *Mysterious Skin* by Scott Heim. Ray looks at me and whispers to me that he saw the movie and gave it three stars but wouldn't mind reading the book to compare the differences.

Richard mentions two other books that don't seem to stir any interest.

"I vote for *Boys of Boston*," announces a stocky guy with a shaved head and brown doe-eyes. He reminds of Charlie Brown, the cartoon character, all grown up. Omar, the Dominican guy with the crew cut and the reading glasses who gagged on the Anderson Cooper book, chimes in, too.

"Yeah, those seem like two different books. Let's give them a try," he says.

Richard seems encouraged by the interest among the guys. He leans and holds up the nominated novels.

Just as he does this, I hear *Sadeness* by Enigma playing in the background. You know the song. It came out in 1991 with the French woman breathing and speaking French to an addictive flute hook. I remember everyone buying the CD to have sex or at least a massage to it because it's very sensual. I zone out Richard for a second and pick up the song in my head. I see Ray just noticed the song as well. We look at each other with a smirk on our faces and we read each other's minds. We start to sing some of the French lyrics outloud.

We forget about the book club and start giggling, and some of the other guys give us nasty looks. That's probably the most French we'll ever know.

"Um, excuse me fellas. This isn't a karaoke bar. It's a book club. Can we get back to the book list?" Richard says, gesturing with his hand for us to join him back to reality.

"Sorry, Richard. Ray and I used to always make fun of that song in college," I say.

"We couldn't resist," Ray says.

"So what's it going to be?" Richard asks.

Ray and I are elbowing each other to speak up and to stop laughing from our Enigma or un-enigmatic performance. We're like the male versions of Laverne and Shirley.

"I think those two books would be a great start for this book club, right Ray?" I turn to Ray who catches my drift as I point to the Perez book and *Mysterious Skin*.

"Yeah . . . yeah . . . we should have lively discussions on both novels," he says. "I would be curious to see how much the movie was adapted from the book."

So Richard decides we'll read those two books and announces our meeting. He passes a paper around for us to jot down our names, numbers and emails. I fill mine out, keeping one eye on the sheet and the other on Richard. There's something about this guy. I've never seen him out. He seems to be passionate about books and writing. There's an unassuming twinkle in his blue eyes. He must work out or at least run, because his calves are well-defined, so tight that I could just bite into them. He seems a little older, but maybe that is what I need, a mature guy, not these club twinks or fame fuckers.

"If you go to the cashier, you'll be able to buy some of these books new or used. Thank you all for coming, and I look forward to meeting with you again," Richard says, getting up and shaking each of our hands. "Feel free to hang out here and get to know each other."

As the other guys pull away in different directions, I use this chance for some one-on-one time with Richard. He smiles as he sees me head his way.

"Thank you for coming out Ted," he says, standing in the middle of the circle of chairs as the other guys head to the cashier to buy the two books. Ray waits for me in the romance section, and he points up at the sign and starts laughing.

"Thank you, Richard. I can't wait to read these two books. I'm a big reader, you know."

Ray hears me and pretends to gag his finger into his mouth without Richard noticing.

I turn around and glare at him to stop it and then regain my composure to flirt with this Magnum, P.I. silvery clone.

"I see you all the time on Channel 7 doing your news stories and *Deco Time.* Maybe you can do a story on the book club one day and show people that South Floridians do enjoy a good book now and then and we're not all about the beach and the bars," Richard says, leaning closer to me.

"That sounds like a good story idea. Maybe down the road once the club finds its rhythm," I say to him, paralyzed by his eyes and his friendly presence. I can see Richard and me having dinner one night on South Beach, taking a long walk along the seawall on Ocean Drive, maybe even having a picnic at Vizcaya's lush gardens. As I drift deeper into the daydream imagining him hugging Max in my house, I hear his voice summoning me from the dream.

"Ted . . . Ted . . . are you with me?" he says, and oh yes, I'd love to be with him I think to myself.

"Yeah, still here."

"Well, it was nice meeting you. I have to go help some customers and make some phone calls on some orders in the back. Thank you for coming, and we'll see you next month," Richard says as Enya softly begings her *Orinoco Flow* on the store's speakers. I haven't heard this song in ages. I shake his hand firmly again.

"Yeah, same here. See you soon."

He walks off and thanks Ray and the other guys for coming as well.

Ray walks toward me with a mischievous look on his face.

"So I guess you scored at Books & Books," Ray says, carrying his two books around in his arms as if he was in high school. Ray really does have this boyish thing about him. Because of his black hair, blue eyes, and slight build, he reminds me of a real-life, adult version of Pinocchio but one who smokes Marlboro Lights.

"Well, not exactly. He didn't ask me out or anything. The way I see it, I can win him over with my deep understanding of gay fiction. It will be like reading books for our lit courses at UM all over again."

"Don't you mean gay dick-tion, Ted?" Ray teases, making a phallic gesture with his tongue and the side of his cheek.

"Yeah that too Cuban boy! Did you like any of the guys from the book club?" I ask, standing behind Ray at the cashier.

"No one is really my type. I can't imagine bringing any of these guys back to my parents' house." Now I'm rolling my eyes at Ray.

"Just because you can't picture it doesn't it mean it can't happen. Look, I found Richard to be interesting. Maybe you can find one of the other guys interesting too," I say, as Ray pays the elderly woman working the register.

"What are you, the gay Yoda?"

"No, just a friend who wants you to give someone a chance for once," I say.

"We'll see Ted. We'll see," Ray answers. When he doesn't know how to respond to something, he says "It depends," or "We'll see." They're his diplomatic answers for any situation, and you know what? It works.

"I'm looking forward to reading the Tommy Perez book. I've never read Hispanic gay fiction before. His picture is cute too. Now see, Ted, this is my kinda guy. Young, Cuban, a writer. Too bad I never had a chance to meet him when he was at the *News*. People think everyone knows each other at the paper, but it's like one big city with bureaus all over the county and Broward. So sometimes, we meet other writers and editors by accident."

"Well Ray, maybe your fellow cubanito writer may come down and do a book reading or something here since he's from here," I say, paying for my two books.

"We'll see. We'll see," Ray says. And with that, we leave Books & Books and head back outside in the unforgiving Sunday heat to my BMW. We both put our sunglasses back on.

"Gilbert's Bakery?" Ray asks, as soon as he hops back into the passenger seat.

"Definitely," I say, as I pull away from Andalusia Avenue and head to Gilbert's. The whole drive there, I notice Ray skimming the Perez book as if it were a lost treasure he just discovered. I really do think he's going to like it as will I. But I have something else sweet on my mind besides the Cuban pastries, and his name is Richard.

6

Brian

"No . . . no . . . *NO!* Alex! Your men are doing this all wrong. I wanted the coconut palms on each side of the main gate on the outside, not on the inside of the property. Daniel and I want our guests to pull up to a small forest of lush palms which opens up to our brick-paved driveway. Grr!"

"I must have misunderstood Mr. Anderson. I'll get my men to replant the trees," Alex says, all apologetic in the morning light.

You know, overseeing renovations on our homes really is a full-time job. Daniel sometimes forgets how much of my time requires me to supervise our small army of workers here and in Newport, and as you can see, things can go wrong pretty fast. He thinks I'm just here goofing around, spending our money, and meeting hot young Latinos to fuck around with. I only do that part of the time. I may not have a regular full-time job, but this is close enough to one. With Daniel barking on one end of the phone from Manhattan and me having to look after these workers, I can get stressed, very fast. Sometimes, our relationship feels like a working one.

I'm standing in the foyer with my hands on my waist and staring through the large glass windows that face the driveway. I watch the workers, mostly Mexican and Guatemalan, and their Caterpillar cranes scurry back into action. As I study their tanned muscular arms, my mind drifts back to Eros. *Qué guapo*. I can smell his scent on me, and I'm immediately turned on. He left a few hours ago before the workers arrived. I gave him fifty dollars for a cab back to his South Beach apartment. We couldn't keep our lips off each other when we said goodbye. He gave me his number, and I put it away in my top drawer. Daniel returns this Friday for a weekend away from New York. I don't know if I'm going to be able to see Eros again. My tricks are one-hit wonders. No encores as Daniel and I have agreed, but I can't get Eros out of my head. Being together with him felt so deeply right, and I can't explain why. My intuition tells me there is something special about him. My heart tells me we connect on an intimate level, even though I met him less than twenty-four hours ago. I don't believe in coincidences. Things happen for a reason, and I know the universe sent him my way for a reason. I read a lot of spirituality books, and I'm a big follower of Char Margolis, the spiritual reader who's been on *Regis and Kelly* and on *The Insider* communicating with dead celebrities. She's the real Ghost Whisperer. I've even had readings with her on the phone.

Just six months ago, she told me that I'd meet a man with a Greek name who would be my destiny, someone who would awaken feelings and passions that I thought were dormant. She also said in our two-hundred-dollar phone session that my life was going to take a big change. She said there was some emotional turbulence on the way which could alter my home life and finances. I dismissed it after a few days when nothing happened. And when I least expected it, I met this beautiful creature named Eros whose name alone suggests he was made for sex and lust. There's so much more I want to know, no, I *need* to know about him. The intensity of his gaze told me there was so much passion and love that I wanted to explore. Perhaps he came my way to make me realize that my relationship with Daniel is rich in some ways, such as comfort, safety and trust yet lacking in many others; sensuality, passion and love. I do love Daniel, but I don't feel that overwhelming magnetic pull with him, physically and emotionally. But, Eros, oh my! When we talked and touched, it felt like two brush fires in the Everglades coming together, burning hard and bright. I feel him so powerfully in my heart, and I don't know why. We're like two energies complementing each other, pulling and drawing one another in.

I put my hand on my neck, and I feel the platinum necklace Daniel gave me for our anniversary years ago. I've never taken it off. I can't see Eros again and damage my imperfect relationship with Daniel despite these newborn desires. Our pact! Besides, who has a perfect relationship? Daniel is my life-partner, and I've been very happy with him.

I gently fidget with the necklace as I walk up my marble cream-colored staircase and head back to my bedroom to take a shower. I grab a T-shirt and shorts, and I notice a brown wallet. Hmm. Eros must have left it behind. I'll call him later and see how he wants to get it back. Maybe this is the universe's way of sending him back my way for another meeting. I hold the wallet, and I feel Eros's presence here with me in this mostly white bedroom. I like the color white. It represents purity and cleanliness. Our walls are white, our sheets are white, our marble tiled floor is white. Our furniture is mostly beige and brown tones from Restoration Hardware to complement the white hues. White is a protective color that wards off bad energy and spirits, from what I learned in my readings. The sage incense I lit earlier has finally reached the upstairs rooms and has been spreading its protective smoke everywhere. The sage also wards off bad energy, which there's a lot of when you have wealth.

With the incense soothing my spirit and cleansing the house, I walk into the gleaming bathroom, again all white, and turn on the hot water. The shower window offers a view to the houses across the bay on Star and Hibiscus islands. I think I see Rosie O'Donnell's house from here. I strip off my clothes from the night before and descend into the wall of vapor. I let the water cleanse me of all the thoughts I have for Eros. I'm hoping the cascading shower will wash away my desires for this Puerto Rican stranger who entered my life and won't seem to vacate my thoughts. I want to see him again. I need to see him again.

Twenty minutes later and feeling all refreshed, I'm sitting in my white bathrobe on a leather loveseat chair in our den with the wallet in my hand. I hold it tightly and smell it. He's going to need his wallet. I have to call him. It's unavoidable. I finally dial his number on my cell, and he answers on the second ring. I get pebbly goosebumps all over my skin at the sound of his tropical voice.

"*Hola*!" Ero says on the other end.

"Eros, hey! This is Brian from last night. *Como estas?*" I say, holding back my enthusiasm and bending my knees up to my chin.

"Ah Brian. *Muy bien, y tu, chico lindo?* I can't talk too long. I'm on my way to work at the restaurant," he says.

"I just wanted to say I had great time last night and that you left your wallet here *en mi casa*," I say in my broken Spanish.

"Oh, wow. *Gracias* Brian. I've been looking for it. Luckily, you had paid the taxi. Can I come by and pick it up tomorrow? I don't get out of work until one a.m."

I picture Eros showing up on my doorstep wearing his sexy smirk and a tight white tank top that shows off his smooth tanned chest and arms. He tends to talk with one side of his mouth higher than the other which drives me crazy. His dark skin makes his white teeth more pronounced and sparkly and just more beautiful.

"Yeah, tomorrow is fine. I'm here overseeing some renovations. Come by whenever."

"Okay Brian, *nos vemos a las dos*," he says, settling on two p.m.

"Adios, Eros!"

"Adios, blue eyes!"

I think I need another shower. My inner butterflies want to fly away, but they're trapped inside my stomach. I lean back on the sofa, close my eyes, and run my hands under my robe and across my chest, imagining Eros's tender touch. Something about Eros flipped a switch inside me and unleashed a torrent of bottled heat. That switch wants to stay on as much as I try to fight it to turn it back off.

I'm lost in my thoughts when the house phone rings on the desk. I look at the caller ID. It's Daniel. My dream state quickly extinguishes.

"Hey, Brian! What's going on at the house? How are the workers today?" Daniel asks.

"They're working. They screwed up with the coconut palms, but I got on top of it. By the time you get here, we'll have a small forest of these beautiful trees for our little beach villa." I get up from the sofa and walk back out to the foyer to make sure Alex and the workers are doing the job right this time.

"Well, make sure they don't charge us for the hours they're using to fix their mistake, or I'll get on the phone with them and tell them where they can put those trees, and trust me, it won't be on our property," Daniel yells. He tends to yell a lot. I think it's an Israeli thing because his family is also very loud. "Everything else okay? How was last night with your Miami reporter friends?"

"We had a blast at Score. Ted and Ray are doing well but feel overworked. They're media guys. They're always working. You should meet them sometime. They're good people. I met this Puerto Rican boy. We messed around. Big, beautiful cock. Don't worry. We used my bedroom, not ours, and I was safe as always. He left this morning. Nothing else going on," I say, stoking the whiskers of my goatee. My eyes glance out the den's windows, and I stare at the white sailboats rocking in Biscayne Bay and seagulls soaring above. The water must be choppy today.

"Brian, you're holding back. What was this guy like? Did you like him?" Daniel asks. It feels more like a mini-Inquisition. Daniel knows me so well. I can tell that he can tell that I kinda like this guy. It's our Scorpio connection and years of being together. He can read me from New York City.

"He's a nice guy, a waiter in South Beach. Curly dark hair,

black eyes, thick eyebrows. Nothing much. He left his wallet. He's coming back tomorrow to pick it up."

"Well make sure that's all he picks up! I'm sensing you like this guy. Be careful. He's a Puerto Rican waiter and money hungry. He probably has dollar signs in his eyes after seeing our house," Daniel warns me. He's had hookups with young blonde boys who become too interested in what we do and how much we make and want to somehow have a part of it. Hence, our one-trick rule.

"Honey, I *know*. I'm not stupid. Jesus! He's just coming to get his wallet. That's all!"

"Well, get back to work. Make sure these workers don't screw up again today. Good help is hard to find in Miami. Everyone wants to milk us when they see the Land Rover and Mercedes or learn of our addresses."

Daniel and I say our goodbyes, and I make my way back downstairs to the black grand baby piano in the living room. We had the piano imported from New York so I could play it whenever I wanted to down here. I'm spending more time here anyway, and Daniel rarely gets to leave New York like he used to. My fingers start tapping the keys as if another force guides them. They flow effortlessly over the ivory as if being steered from something greater. I hum a new slow sensual song, something Alicia Keyes would come up with. I'm not sure where it's coming from, but I have an idea. Eros.

7

Ray

One star.

That's what I would give the Fort Lauderdale International Film Festival (FLIFF, if you will) if it were a movie. It's utterly pointless. Organizers erroneously think that showing one hundred movies in twelve days at the Riverwalk Theater in downtown Fort Lauderdale makes them a contender in the film festival circles. Thing is, the Miami Film Festival is the local event that culls the most media and high-brow prestige, not to mention better films. Not this joke of a film festival (I call it FLUFF), which gets the leftovers, the rejects from the MFF, and the occasional sound previews to upcoming movies. But since *The Miami News* endeavors to cover all of South Florida, it is my duty (I'm forced to do this, to maintain my nicotine addiction and snazzy sports car) to write at least *something* about the festival. If not, the organizers will harass my editors to death.

I told Patty, my insightful editor, that I'd do a small preview with some online capsule reviews of the better indie offerings for our obsessive cinephiles and to appease the festival coordinators. Besides, I still have to review the mainstream fare this week, which includes a *Jackass* clone. This is my secret guilty pleasure because Johnny Knoxville is one fine looking guy (especially lean and shirtless), even though he acts like a crackerjack with his crew. I forgive him for *Dukes of Hazzard*. He did it purely to get closer to Jessica Simpson. The other new release I'm reviewing is *Mission Impossible IV: A New Mission*, starring Brad Pitt. Thanks to Paramount's decision to let Tom Cruise go in 2006, Ethan Hunt took an early retirement from fieldwork after a stray bullet stopped him in his track. Of the three movies opening Friday (count them, three!) at the Fort Lauderdale festival, only one of them, *Ma Vie Est Bleu*, is worth seeing because it not only features Paris as its glittering, stunning backdrop, but it's a tender coming-of-age story about a boy named Rene who thinks he's a girl. So I have a lot of work to do this week. Friday, where art thou?

I'm in my Nissan 300 SX, driving back to Miami from the screenings for the Fort Lauderdale Film Festival. I can bang out this preview and the review capsules pretty quickly for the blog and then move on to my real work for the printed newspaper. With the direction my industry is headed, I'm eventually going to be writing primarily for the paper's Web site. The blog is the beginning of that transition, and I can't help but feel that my craft is participating in its own destruction by giving its content away for free online. Mind you, anyone can read anything online these days, but we're the single best newspaper Web site to provide unique content and news about Miami. I do my best to enhance my stories and reviews with a South Florida flavor so I don't end up without a job. Movie critics nowadays are becoming an endangered species because as newspapers attempt to reinvent themselves to survive, the corporate brain trusts continue to eliminate our jobs and reassign us to other beats.

The mental giants who sit behind glassy offices at the newspapers believe they can save money by picking up wire copy or movie reviews from the bigger papers and importing them into the Features section. Top managers are finding that the public's appetite for our feedback is fleeting, and that angers me because I am passionate about my craft. As long as I maintain my colorful presence in the paper and online, I think I'll be okay and remain relevant, but you never know.

These job-survival thoughts come as I begin my drive out of

Fort Lauderdale. Who lives in Fort Lauderdale? It's so blah, South Florida's vanilla compared to Miami's colorful burst of tropical sorbet. It's a wanna-be Miami with its high-rises along the New River and cafés and restaurants on Las Olas Boulevard. While the city has become more gay in recent years, I just can't imagine myself living or working here. No offense, Mimi Bauers (my nemesis at *The Broward Daily*, who was born in Fort LaTiDa). I only come up here if I absolutely must, for work or to fly out of the airport. JetBlue offers better flights to Toronto and Los Angeles than too-congested Miami International. Even film companies know to stay away from Fort Lauderdale for local shoots. The last movie filmed here, if memory serves correct, was *There's Something About Mary* with Cameron Diaz. They shot several scenes at Plantation City Hall and the golf course in Pembroke Park. The rest of the movie was filmed in Miami and Providence.

As I floor my Nissan on 95, I feel a sense of relief approaching the green traffic sign that says "Aventura" up ahead. I'm about twenty minutes away from downtown Miami. The Broward zone is growing smaller in my rearview mirror.

I whip and weave through the traffic like a Cuban speed racer in the Mach 5 when my cell rings. It's Brian. "Hey, Ray! How are you, amigo?"

"Hi. Doing well, just leaving Fort Lauderdale. Getting close to the office. What's up with you? How did things go the other night with Mr. Puerto Rico? Did you get to see his big flag?" I say, turning down U2's *Achtung Baby*, one of my favorite CDs of all time.

I hear Brian take a deep breath as if recounting a delicious dream that he didn't want to wake up from. I'm going to need a cigarette just to hear this story.

"Oh . . . things went really well. He's coming over today to pick up his wallet. I think we're gonna hang out here at the pool or something, maybe get a bite to eat."

I can tell Brian has a crush on this guy by the soft voice he uses to talk about him. But I find that Brian's crush makes absolutely no sense since he already has a partner. Gay rich white boys, I tell you.

"Actually, Ray, I can't wait to see him. There's just something about him. I know I'm breaking my rule about the one-time hookup thing, but I'm just following my gut and letting the universe guide me. I need to see him again."

I have a feeling Brian just invited some huge drama into his life, worthy of a frantic Julianne Moore movie, and I didn't need Char Margolis or a psychic to tell me that.

"Well, it's your dick that's guiding you. Look, do what you have to do but be aware that you are committed to someone else and that you are very much tied to him in a lot of ways, especially financially. You have to weigh whether seeing this guy again is really worth compromising all the things you and Daniel have worked for. I mean, just consider your house here. It's something out of *Scarface* without the thugs and mounds of cocaine."

I exit off the I-195 ramp to Biscayne Boulevard, passing the Taco Bell and McDonald's on the left and that weird curvy glassy high-rise that sits on a spit of land between the Julia Tuttle Causeway's east and west lanes. I hang a left at the Wendy's to grab a medium chocolate Frosty in the drive-thru. Besides Johnny Knoxville, Frostys are my other guilty pleasure. I'm a few minutes away from the newsroom so this one quick stop won't delay me much.

"Yeah, I know. I can't help but feel this is happening for a reason, Ray. I mean, have you ever met someone that really got under your skin, that you just wanted to explore in so many ways that you can't explain it?"

Actually, no. That guy has been an elusive figure in my life, like a fugitive on the run from a nice and cute movie critic. I've done the hookup thing and the casual dating thing, but no one seems to stick full time, so I don't really know where Brian is coming from, to be honest. I know it's because of my rules. I won't date a guy who is married, bisexual, or has a boyfriend. I won't date a friend's ex-boyfriend or former trick. I won't date someone who just broke up with his boyfriend. Tourists are also on my no-date list. They're only here for their fun-in-the-sun vacation. So who does that leave? Not a lot of guys. And then there are those guys who are trying to look airbrushed in real life. Miami is a city of image and illusion. I would love to have a nice cutie who is grounded by family to call my boyfriend. I don't need a super Amazonian model, the type that's found on every café corner here. On second thought, I wouldn't mind hooking up with those model guys.

It's probably so much easier for straight guys like my brother Racso. They go out and bang. They have a slew of women to pick from, who actually want to settle down and build something. Not like these South Beach man hos who include Ted and Brian, by the way.

"Well, be careful. You're in a complicated situation as it is, and it's only going to get more complicated if you allow this guy into your life any more than he already is," I say, picking up the $1.35 Frosty from the friendly drive-thru cashier. I take off the lid, which is smeared with cold chocolate, and lick it clean before plunking my Wendy's spoon into the thick frozen shake.

"Yeah, I know, but wasn't he hot. Wow!" Brian says, as if to justify the emotional spider web he is weaving.

We talk a few more minutes about my reviews, then he tells me about Daniel coming into town this weekend. The whole time, I shovel spoonfuls of the Frosty into my mouth. Mmm. *Yum.*

While I have known Brian for about a year, Ted and I have never met Daniel. Yeah, we've been to their McMansion but only when Daniel wasn't there. From what I gather, it seems that when Daniel is with Brian, he demands all his attention. So we only see Brian when he's not busy with Daniel. It reminds me of *Sleeping With The Enemy,* one of Julia Roberts' earlier movies after her break-out role in *Pretty Woman.* Not that I think Daniel is ruthless or trying to kill Brian. It's that he keeps Brian on such a tight leash with his wealth and doesn't allow him to work. Like the movie, they live in a glass house on the water. In some ways, Daniel also reminds me of Charlie Townsend of *Charlie's Angels,* the show and the Drew Barrymore production. We hear him and know what his money can do, but we've never been face to face with him.

"So you wanna meet up Friday night at Score for some drinks?" I ask, but suspect the answer will be no.

"I can't this Friday. Daniel is coming for the weekend, and I need to spend time with him."

See what I mean.

"Okay, well have fun with your new guy Eros. I just pulled into the *News* lot. We'll talk soon."

"Sounds good. Have a good day, amigo!" Brian says.

"*Igualmente,*" I say.

I hope for Brian's sake that he understands the emotional mud he's about to slosh into. This can get messy, like Miami after a hurricane.

All done with the Frosty and having managed not to get any on me or my car, I hop out of my Nissan and click my remote to activate the alarm. Ever since the new performing arts center opened across the street, I've noticed that the panhandlers on Biscayne Boulevard are more aggressive, relentlessly asking patrons and passersby for money. I always keep my convertible top up when I drive around here. They follow the dough.

I emerge from the *News* garage and approach the lobby. My phone rings again. It's Racso. Why does everyone call me during the day? Everyone seems to think I have all this time on my hands because I spend my afternoons watching movies. It's work. The reviews don't write themselves.

"Hey little brother, what's going on?" he asks.

"*Oye,* Racso, I'm about to walk into work. I have some reviews to write. What's up with you? Shouldn't you be in school right now?" I say, lingering on a bench outside the building as the breeze off the Port of Miami blows through my spiky hair.

"Yeah, I know you're busy. I can sense that from school," he says, referring to our one-way twin sick sense of his.

"So, *qué tu quieres?* I have to post something on the blog for the Fort Lauderdale film festival and start on my movie review," I tell him, moving to the shaded outdoor patio where all the smoking staffers are relegated to perform the nicotine dance. I smell the puffs of smoke and surrender. I light up a cigarette, inhale deeply, and watch the wind send the smoke I slowly release toward down-town.

"Well, I have a surprise for you. What are you doing this Friday night?"

Hmm. What is Racso up to? I smell a Cuban conspiracy—or maybe it's the smoke I'm inhaling. I know he's plotting something. I bet he wants to borrow my car.

"I'm probably meeting up with Ted and Brian later at night but that's at eleven or so. *Por que?*"

"I wanted to invite you to dinner with me and Cindy Friday night. You haven't seen her in a while, and I thought it would be nice for all of us to chow down somewhere. We can hit Versailles, like we used to with Mami and Papi. I know how much you like the breaded chicken steaks there and the chocolate flan. Dinner is on us!"

Racso is willing to pay? Now I'm convinced something is up. He prefers to spend Friday nights with Cindy, after a long week of work. They have dinner and go to the movies, based on one of my reviews, of course. Perhaps Racso is just being nice. It can't hurt. I'll just go with it.

"Sure. I can do dinner. I'll have my work done by six."

"Great, little brother. Cindy may invite one of her friends from school so it won't be a threesome, but I'm not sure who the fourth will be."

"Yeah, I'm cool with that and I'm especially cool with you pay-ing for dinner. I'll remember that when I order the side of scrump-tious plantains and a bed of rice with a topping of black beans. Maybe I'll get two desserts. The *tres leches* are tongue-tickling. Yum."

"Whoa, whoa! Don't go overboard. I'm still on a teacher's salary, remember Ray?"

"Yeah, how can I forget? Your car says it all."

"Funny Gay Ray. *Bueno hermanito*, let's meet at Versailles at eight p.m."

"Sounds good, Racso."

"See you then, little brother."

I hang up the phone and stroll into the newsroom. I think about how nice it was of my brother to invite me out to dinner with him and Cindy. Maybe he wants to pay me back for picking him up from the dealership on my day off the other day. But I can't help but think something is going on. Inquiring minds want to know. Maybe Mami knows. She's like Radio Bemba. She knows everything that goes on in our house and then announces it to all her friends and our family. Her station would be 106.5 MAMI!

Five minutes later, I settle into my corner cubicle, but I can't stop thinking about dinner Friday night. I call Mami on my work phone to find out what she knows.

"*Hola*, Raysito! *Cómo estas?* Shouldn't you be *en el trabajo?* Is something wrong? Jou never call this early, *mijo.*"

"Hi, Mami. Everything is fine. Listen, I just spoke to Racso. He and Cindy invited me to dinner Friday. What I want to know is . . . what are they up to? You must know. You're like the *National Enquirer* of Coral Gables."

I hear Mami laughing on the other end, but I don't know if her laughter means she knows something or she thought my joke was funny.

"Ay Raysito . . . jou hermano loves you. I think it is bery sweet of him to invite you to eat with Cindy. Just go and have fun. Stop overanalyzing this. This is not a movie to review, *tu sabes?*"

Maybe Mami is right. I tend to overanalyze everything. My critical mind works overtime.

"Thanks, Mami. How is Papi?"

"He's exterminating the Days Inn on Collins Avenue. That's one of his bigger *clientes*. Call him later and get back to work, okay?"

"Thanks, Mami. *Hasta luego.*"

I hang up and start writing my reviews, but my mind wanders to Friday night at Versailles. Maybe Racso really is just being nice. Besides, Cindy will be there. What could he do?

8

Ted

"We're coming to you live from the Carnival Center for the Performing Arts in downtown Miami where vandals spray painted the front windows of this fairly new center. The vandalism has left city and art officials singing a sour note."

Carlos, our camera guy, cues the video showing the big graffiti letters scrawled across the front of this glimmering glass arts house. (Think: Miami's version of Lincoln Center.) My voice-over kicks in with interviews from a Miami police spokesman, the president of the center, and some shocked art aficionados.

While my video package plays, I grab my compact and dab some more foundation on my face. The waves of heat, probably eighty-five degrees if you factor in humidity, are making a Portuguese puddle out of me. I have to use my Lord and Taylor handkerchief to wipe down the beads of sweat. I would hate to look too shiny on camera or for that cute muscular guy in the sleeveless shirt and baggy shorts who just walked by. *Hello! Can I get a sound bite or just a bite?*

A few blocks away east, I see reporters streaming in and out of the *News* building's lobby. I bet Ray can see me from there, and I bet they'll have a big story about this online today and tomorrow in the paper. Miami's first state-of-the-art performing arts center defiled by vandals. It may not sound like it, but this is a big local story because Miami waited five years for this jewel of a glass house to be built so that we can say that we are culturally high brow and more than the bars, the beach, and Gloria Estefan. Urban visionaries have been saying that downtown Miami will eventually pop, making the area the most desirable place to buy and live. Despite the local clubs that have opened on this side of the bay, I just don't see this area happening. This arts center is already in the red, and it's brand spanking new. Those glassy towers cutting a new view on the downtown horizon? People aren't buying them. It was a great sales gimmick.

"Ted, we're coming back to you for the tag in 5 . . . 4 . . . 3 . . . 2 . . ." my producer Sheila pipes in over my earpiece. I watch the rest of my package unfold on the little monitor to the right of our cameraman. I'm on again. I love this part, my sign-off.

"Police are still investigating the crime. Right now, they say there aren't any leads. In the meantime, workers have begun washing off the graffiti that has temporarily scarred Miami's newest arts institution. For Channel 7 News, I'm Ted Williams. Back to you in the studio, Craig."

And I'm off the air for the six o'clock show.

"Good job Ted," Sheila says. "Channel Four didn't have the arts center director, and Channel Ten didn't have the art fans. We beat them today."

"Thanks, Sheila. I hustled my ass all day rounding up all these people," I say, as another film of sweat forms on my forehead. I pull the earpiece out, loosen my tie, and hop back into the air-conditioned blue and white station van parked on the sidewalk off Biscayne Boulevard. Because of all the news vans, angry rush-hour traffic snarls up and down the street. Drivers are slowing down to see why we're all here, like an accident on I-95. We're causing a traffic jam but, hey, we're just reporting the news, performing our community service. *So stop honking, people!*

I have one more live-shot for the ten o'clock news, and then I have to tape another version of my story for *Good Morning South Florida*, our early morning newscast. And then, I'm outta here for a few hours. I also have to tape a small nightlife segment tonight at Club Space for *Deco Time*'s weekend edition. The club is hosting a fashion show benefit tonight for the *Wednesday's Child* adoption and foster kid program, so I know my extra late night reporting will be for a good cause. Miami is many things, but it's never boring. There is always something to report on or something to do, and I feel it is my duty to inform Miamians about one or the other through my on-air reports.

Thinking about the adoption fundraiser reminds me how much I would like to be a father one day. I can see myself taking my son or daughter to school in Miami Shores or to the TV station on *Bring Your Child To Work Day*. I see myself showing the kid how to walk Max or take him running at nearby Fisher Park near our home. But I would hate to do it as a single gay dad with my hectic reporting schedule. I think every child should have a mother and father figure, and I'd rather share that responsibility with someone I love one day the same way Mom and Dad did with me and my sister Lourdes. Maybe one day it'll happen. Lourdes would make a great aunt with her patience and enthusiasm for books, and Ray would make an awesome Cuban uncle, as long as he doesn't smoke around the kid. Who knows, maybe by then, Ray would have quit smoking once and for all and may have a kid of his own.

I'm sitting here inside the van trying to get started on my morning version on the arts center story. I'll have some downtime between stories. I brought my copy of *Boys of Boston* with me to pass the time in between shots as I wait in the van before I go on air again for the ten o'clock show.

It's not a bad book but not great literature either. It's easy reading, and I'm enjoying seeing Boston through this Miami guy's eyes. The book makes me miss home. My parents are still there in Sandwich, which is about sixty miles south of Boston on the Cape. Lourdes lives in Dorchester, the urban gentrified neighborhood of Boston, where she works as a copy editor for *The Boston Daily*'s Arts section, my all-time favorite paper other than the *New York Times*. (Don't tell that to Ray. I always tell him how much I love the *News* which shrinks a tad in staff and substance every year. It's losing readers faster than a bulimic drops calories. I also think Ray packs one too many adjectives like "visceral," "white-hot" and "high-octane" in his movie reviews, but that's another story.)

I miss the seabreeze off the Cape, the way the buttery sand dunes meet the ocean in Provincetown. I miss the chilly steel blue water at Herring Cove beach which is beautiful to look at but not to swim in. (It feels like you're diving into a big bottle of rubbing alcohol compared to Miami's warm bathwater ocean) I miss driving my old BMW on the reliable Bourne and Sagamore bridges which look like art sculptures in the sky, majestically defying gravity and hanging over the blue waters of the Atlantic. I even miss the *whoosh whoosh* sounds of the spinning blades of the Coast Guard choppers that fly in and out of the Coast Guard Air Station Cape Cod.

I also miss my family. My parents and Lourdes have come down to Miami, but it's easier for me to go up there since there's only one of me. I think the reason why I've settled in so well in Miami is because, in some way, it reminds me of the Cape. I am surrounded by water and that certain beach breeze that magically makes you feel better at the end of a long day. I can always go to the beach whenever I want. There's something soothing about living near the water. I feel calm here, and Max enjoys the walks along the boardwalk.

I'm thinking of home because I plan to be in Boston next month for the annual National Lesbian and Gay Journalists Association Conference, which will be held at the Boston Park Plaza Hotel on the South End/Back Bay border. Organizers asked me to be on the *Being A Gay TV Reporter* panel along with four other journalists. I'm actually excited about this opportunity. I'll be able to network with other print and broadcast reporters, and I'll be able to visit my parents and Lourdes and my friends in Beantown. I talked Ray into going too because it might be a good chance for him to meet recruiters from other newspapers such as the *New York Times* and for him to get away from his super-clingy

Cuban family. Besides, we can cruise the convention and hit the bars together. Ray has already agreed to let Max stay with his parents and Racso while they watch little Gigli. Like us, our dogs are pals and always have fun together.

I begin to record my voice-over for the arts center story to make it seem like more morning-friendly for the early bird viewers. Hopefully (*yawn!*), I won't be too tired tomorrow from working tonight at Club Space.

"Hello *Deco Timers*. We're here at Club Space for a very special cause: Fashion For Foster Kids. Let's take a look," I say, leading the camera backstage where a frenzy of models are slipping on the latest clothes by Armani and Versace. I see many familiar faces, mostly past contestants from *America's Next Top Model* and other reality TV shows such as *The Amazing Race.* They'll do anything for a free flight and exposure. I gesture to Carlos to take a sweeping shot of the crowd with close-ups of some of the celebrities in the house.

"Make sure you get Gloria and Emilio sitting over there in the front row. Oh, I think I see Paris Hilton with her on-and-off again gal pal Nicole Richie." I hear they're in town doing a Miami version of *The Simple Life* or what they're calling *La Vida Facile* because the show's producers are moving the girls into homes of people who only speak Spanish. That should be fun to watch later next season.

After Carlos gets shots of these people on tape from a distance, I lead him back into the dressing room where I interview some of the models. I ask second season ANTM winner Yoanna House, about who's she wearing. She turns around in her make-up chair. She's all smiles with her pasty white skin.

"Well . . . I'm wearing a new Versace gown. You like? It's part of an upcoming collection," she says, giving good face the same way she won the show in 2003.

"Fabulous honey! Now why did you want to take part in this event?"

"Because I've had several friends who were in foster care growing up, and I know what a difference these programs can make for them," she says directly into the camera. She has really come a long way since landing a steady gig on the *Style Network* called *The Look for Less.* She's a pro now.

We give each other air kisses, and I let her get back to shellacking her face.

Carlos and I make our way deeper backstage to the men's dressing room where I see some models and industry folks noshing on sushi and sipping wine. In the corner, I recognize a long-legged cutie who I remember from another reality show back home.

"Kyle! Welcome to Miami. Nice to see you doing some runway work here again," I tell him, as he zips up his flowing khakis.

"Oh, why thank you Ted Williams of the one and only *Deco Time.* It's my *pleasure* to be here for such a good cause," he says, towering over me in his open black blazer. His hair is still as bouncy, blondish and curly as it was in his *Real World: Boston* days and when he modeled in Miami.

"So, who are you wearing?" I ask Kyle who now suddenly hijacks my microphone and deadpans to the camera.

"Only the best baby. Versace. It's always about Versace with me. This reminds me of another fashion show I did years ago in Paris, or was that Milan? Or maybe it was here in good old Mee-ami. Anyway, as I was saying . . ." he begins to babble. I see an open shot to quickly grab my mike back and wrap up his interview, if only he'd shut up.

"Well, thanks Kyle. Good to see you back on the runway. You can still work it." As Kyle is about to say something, I turn my back to him and continue my interviews.

I hear him say in the background, "But there's more to see back here. I haven't even told you about my latest project. I . . ." His voice drifts away while and Carlos and I tape another segment by the backstage curtains and away from the Kyle. He probably wanted to tell me about his new talk show on LOGO TV called *Kyle's Korner* which sounds, how do I put this, corny.

"The show is about to begin. We'll have more of these fash-
ionistas when *Deco Time* returns after this break." I motion to
Carlos to cut.

As the show begins, Yoanna struts her stuff in her gown as she
walks a transparent runway over a reflecting pool. She's trailed by
other former ANTM contestants including Yaya and Camille,
who do their signature walks. Then the men come out, led by
Kyle who was followed by Reichen Lehmkuhl, the hunk who
won *The Amazing Race* a few years ago with his ex-partner Chip.
How did I miss Reichen backstage? Maybe he arrived late. Maybe
I need to do a follow-up interview with him and ask him about a
sequel to his memoir *Here's What We'll Say*. (I know what I'd say.
He's a mighty fine hunk.) He commands the runway with Kyle
along with some other men who I don't recognize. Just before the
last model twirls and sashays to the music of Missy Elliott and
Ciara, small armies of little kids come out wearing some fashion-
able jeans, tops, and shorts. This is so cute. I point to Carlos for
him to shoot the kids. When the Gloria Estefan remix of *Conga*
and *Coming Out of The Dark* stops playing, the kids bow as if
they're at the end of a school play. Everyone stands up in applause,
including me. The kids are like little Dunkin' Donut munchkins.

I get in position near the lip of the stage so that the camera
shot will catch the Estefans to my right, as well as Paris and Nicole
"I am hungry" Richie applauding. I do my tag for the night.

"On another night out on the town for a good cause, I'm Ted
Williams for *Deco Time*." Now I can go home, feed Max, and get
some rest because tomorrow night I'm gonna need it for a night
out with Ray and Brian at Score.

9

Brian

"Ah man. This is so nice," I tell Eros, who is laying next to me in the lounge chair by the pool. Okay, I couldn't resist. As soon as he came over this afternoon to pick up his wallet, I couldn't pry my hands off him. We started hugging, kissing, licking, sucking, massaging, nibbling, fucking, and just about any other good-sounding action verb. We already came twice when we jumped in the pool and I splashed and climbed him in the deep end. I straddled Eros in the shallow end and let the water jets blow concentrated bubbles up and down my back and legs. Now we're cooling off in the lounge chairs like we've known each other for a long time and we're on vacation.

The sun glistens against Eros's dark skin and highlights all the watery droplets that dot his body like mini-rhinestones. His underwear looks bleached white against his smooth dark skin. I had a feeling I wasn't going to able to keep my hands off this Puerto Rican god. He's my forbidden fruit, the one I can't seem to get enough of.

"Hey baby . . . you okay over there?" Eros says, leaning over on his side and tracing my goatee with his fingers. When he does that, my dick immediately throbs.

"Yeah, Eros. I'm fine. I was just thinking about you and how right you feel by my side, here in my house." I turn on my side and lean on my elbow to face him as well. I'm level with his beautiful brown eyes.

I ask him about his upbringing, his family, his life. I want to know everything. When he talks, I can see a fiery passion behind his eyes, a zest of life and yet an appreciation for all that he has, which I can tell isn't much. He's a waiter and doesn't have a car, yet he seems so fulfilled and content with everything, as if he's at peace with himself. I'm drawn to that.

"I grew up in San Juan, running in the fields below the mountains with my sisters while *mi mama* cooked us rice and beans and chicken. We would drink the sweetest juice from the coconut palms that lined our backyard," he says, looking away at the bright blue sky with a dreamy expression. He then locks his gaze on me again.

"*Mi mama* would love you, Brian. She's very down to earth and a simple good woman. She'd melt the moment she saw those blue eyes of yours and your handsome face."

I peck him on the cheek after he says that.

"When me and my sisters, Gladys and Maria, got older and started to work, Mami made it a point that we all meet at the house every Sunday for lunch, no matter what. And we always did that, each of us in charge of a different food. I brought the desserts from the bodega. Maria would bake fresh bread. Gladys would make us shakes to cool us off, and Mami would handle the big meals, usually the chicken or pork. I miss doing that with them," he says, a sad glint in his eyes.

"Why did you come to Miami if you're family is in Puerto Rico? Your eyes light up when you talk about your home," I ask, drifting away with the images of Eros in his youth running in the lush tropical valleys and with his family in San Juan.

"The economic situation in Puerto Rico is unstable. The government had to shut down a while ago for a week because it couldn't afford to pay everyone. It's the biggest employer. I lost my job at the library as an assistant in San Juan. My boss is now doing two jobs on her salary. Even schoolteachers are out of work.

Tourism isn't as strong as it was. People are suffering there, even though we're a commonwealth of the United States, we're really on our own. We're like second class citizens because we're American but we can't vote in national elections from the island. One of my cousins told me that I could make some good money working at Puerto Sagua where he works as a waiter. I decided to check it out for a little while until I save enough money to go to college and get a professional job. I send *mi mama* some money every month. Financially, I have a better life here than in Puerto Rico, and the weather is pretty much the same. I can walk where I need to go in South Beach."

My heart melts as he talks in his accented English. He's a family man, helping support his relatives back on the island. I hold his hand as he continues. I notice he doesn't mention his father.

"You don't realize how lucky you are, Brian, to have this beautiful house, your cars, your wealth. My whole family could live here, and there still would be extra room for two more large Puerto Rican families." He laughs.

"I know how lucky I am. Remember, I used to be a waiter in New York when I met Daniel. Sometimes it takes someone to help you out when you need it the most." I grin at him. "What about your father? Is he in the picture Eros?" I gently ask.

"*Ese pendejo* left us when I was fourteen. He met a younger woman, and he moved out and ditched my mother and sisters. He's a selfish *comemierda*. I guess he didn't want to be around us anymore. He was a truck driver, so he would be gone for days at a time. We got used to him being gone, so it wasn't too bad. I just had to be there for *mi mama*. I would catch her crying in kitchen in the afternoons when she thought she was alone. But she's a strong woman. She survived."

"And you haven't seen your dad since?"

Eros looks away and lays back on the lounge chair. "What kind of father would do that, abandon his family? We didn't have much, but we had each other, *tu sabes*. He doesn't exist in my mind. I would never do that if I had a child."

I caress the side of his cheek with the back of my hand, and I see the beautiful contrast of colors between our skin.

"Maybe in time you can have a relationship again. I'm sure he probably regrets it. I mean, how can he leave such a wonderful son like you? My father and I didn't talk for years until recently. Now we meet up once a year for lunch. You deserved a better father, so did I, but we can't pick our flesh and blood."

I deserved a father who would be there. I wanted a father to take me to a concert or the annual carnival in Charlotte. I wanted a father to take me to Sears to buy me new clothes and a backpack for the school year. I wanted a father who would visit me in college and hear me sing during my solo performances. I wanted a father, like those TV dads or the ones in Hallmark commercials who attend their son's high school graduation or throw big surprise birthday parties at arcades or amusement parks. I wanted a father who loved me, Brian Anderson, and all of me. It sounds so simple: Love me and yet, he couldn't do it. When I see my father for our yearly lunches, there is no love. We are two strangers sharing empty conversations about the happenings in our lives. I don't think anyone would think we were related except for our blue eyes and brown straight hair. He spikes it up as I do, which I find weird. When I sit in front of him, I see a man I hope I will never be like but who undeniably has a biological connection to me. A long time ago, I wished he had an emotional connection to me. But since he didn't love me, I don't love him.

I get up and sit on the edge of his chair and hold and kiss Eros's right hand. What is it about Eros that gets under my skin? His body? His accent? The warmth and compassion that pours out when he talks about his family and his love for Puerto Rico? He's like one of those rare guys you meet who have a certain something that you can't put your finger on, yet you sense they are good guys. There's a whole other set of transactions between us that extends beyond words and physical electricity.

I plant a wet kiss on the lips and then grab us some us some cool Sprites when the house phone rings. I put on my white robe and skip into the house along the chilly tiled floor to answer the phone in the kitchen. My nipples harden from the cool central air.

"Brian, it's Daniel. Did the workers fix the problem from the front yard?" he says in his typical greeting.

"Yeah, they're all pretty much done up front. I was just in the pool and hanging out."

"Did *that* Puerto Rican waiter pick up his wallet?" Daniel asks in a suspicious tone.

"Yeah . . . he's still here. It was so hot that we decided to take a swim. He's leaving shortly Daniel," I say casually.

I can sense Daniel is going to have one of his Israeli freak-outs. He starts yelling. "Brian! I want him out of there, *now*! I've decided I'm flying in a day early in the chopper and will work from home for the day. I'll be there tomorrow, and I don't want to hear that this guy was there again, you got it?"

Daniel is pulling his Alpha Male rank on me, and he knows that the more he tries to control me, the more I resist, but he can't control his temper sometimes. I don't know why he's getting all worked up but then again, he always yells and stresses out about everything, hence all our vacation homes and his high blood pressure at forty years old. I sense he's coming a day early to keep me in check, and I slightly resent that.

"Daniel, okay. I heard you loud and clear. I'll tell him to leave. I just wanted to go swimming with someone and you're not here and my friends Ray and Brian work all day. Watching these renovations and our workers can be boring and lonely sometimes. I get restless. At least you have lots of people around you at the office to talk with."

"Well get back to work, and make sure our workers don't mess up again. I'll let you know tomorrow what time I'm flying in."

"Sure . . . see you tomorrow, Daniel," I say.

"Oh and one more thing, Brian."

Great, he probably wants to me to do five more things before he gets here. My list of projects never ends. Sometimes I feel like one of his employees.

"I love you," he says. "You know that, right?"

And then he knows what to say or do to rope me back in.

"I love you too, Daniel, just calm down okay? It'll be you and me this weekend. No distractions."

I place the phone back in its cradle. I look out the window, and I study this beautiful creature lying on the lounge chair so peacefully. I think to myself, how do I kick this guy out of my life when I want him so much to be a part of it? I feel a chill that sends ripples of goose bumps all over my arms. I'm not sure if it's from the air conditioning or from the cold truth I'm about to tell Eros.

I walk slowly over our iridescent tiled floor in the living room with two cool bottles of Sprite and step outside into the bright light of the day. The later afternoon sun immediately warms my face like the soft flames of a fireplace. Eros smiles at me and reaches out to hold me.

"*Qué te pasa muchacho?*" he asks. He unpeels the top of my robe and massages my shoulders. My dick quickly responds again by saluting north toward the house. I have to resist and tell him I can't see him anymore. I hate this.

"Eros, listen. I'm really fond of you and I want to get to know you some more, but I do have a partner and he's coming tomorrow for the weekend. I'm not going to be able to see you, even though I really want to." I feel like a seventh grader professing his innocent deep crush on a classmate, but it's more than that. I feel something strong hatching in my heart for this guy.

Eros turns me around and holds my hand.

"I'm a free spirit. I go with the flow, and I sense you do too. I think that's why we connect on so many different levels. You were upfront with me about your partner from the beginning, and I will always respect you for that. I knew this wasn't going to go anywhere, but I trusted my instinct and enjoyed my time with you. I make the most of the moment, the now, Brian."

"I feel the same exact way. It's just, ugh, frustrating Eros. Here I am with everything a gay man could want, a handsome partner, riches, a life of leisure, my health, but I feel there's a hole in my soul and in my relationship. I want passion, love, lust, feeling, and now you've spoiled me by giving me a taste of some of those things again."

With his index finger, he outlines my goatee which turns me on so much, and he rubs my eyebrows gently with his thumb. I look down at the whiteness of the cement flooring that surrounds the pool.

"Brian, don't be sad. I feel that our paths will cross again. Just be with your partner. You must love him on some level to have been with him for so many years. I should be going. I have to be at work in two hours."

Eros leans in, kisses me so deeply that I taste the lemony Sprite he just drank. I think I could drink all of him if he'd let me. I get that tingly feeling inside me, like I'm falling off a ten story building, and I don't want to be caught. It's a feeling so foreign yet familiar wrapped in one. I want to keep feeling this, but I know I can't.

He hugs me tightly and then starts collecting his clothes. I pick up our towels and throw on a T-shirt and jeans. I offer to drive him back to his apartment. The whole fifteen-minute ride to his apartment, we hold hands tightly and we don't say much. When we arrive, he gives me another one of those passionate kisses, and he gets out of the Land Rover and waves goodbye through the tinted passenger window. As I pull away, he grows smaller in the distance. I can't help but look back at the man that temporarily reawakened dormant feelings and desires I haven't felt in so long.

What the fuck am I going to do now?

It's about the same time the next day when I hear a chopper buzzing the house. I get up from the leather couch where I was watching *Dr. Phil* while the brown-muscled guys outside continue landscaping the front yard. The chopper has to be Daniel or Channel 7 working on a story nearby. I toss the remote on the sofa and walk out in the pool area where I place my hand over my forehead and scan for the helicopter. Over Watson Island, I see the navy blue Bell 222 Delfin chopper that Daniel loves more than life, even me. He bought the former Coast Guard twin-turbine engine helicopter from a hospital in New Jersey. He had the chopper re-decorated on the inside to make it more comfortable for passengers, and he removed the uncomfortable fold-out Guard seats. Daniel even has a small replica of the chopper on his desk at work. I see the chopper disappear out of sight, which means Daniel has landed. The *whoosh whoosh whoosh* sounds of the blades fade. He's home.

I hop in the Land Rover and drive west on the Venetian Causeway past the *News* and Omni Hotel to pick him up on Watson Island. Within fifteen minutes, I'm there.

Sometimes I forget how handsome my partner is. He has his helmet in his hands, and he's wearing his Polo shirt and jeans. His tanned olive skin, salt and pepper Caesar cut and black sunglasses make him look like George Clooney's twin brother. Just seeing him puts a smile on my face this afternoon. I wave to him, and he waves back as he walks toward the Rover.

"Hey, Bri!" He calls me by my nickname. He gets into the passenger seat, gives me a kiss on the cheek, and rubs the back of my head with his hand.

"Hi, Daniel. Good to see you. How was your flight? Any bad turbulence?" I pull onto the MacArthur Causeway and head east toward the beach. Daniel tells me that he had turbulence over New York but then clear skies down to Charleston, South Carolina, where he refueled. The coast was clear until Georgia where there were 40 knot winds. He then had smooth air once he passed the Georgia-Florida border. I prefer to fly JetBlue, but Daniel finds some manly pleasure being his own boss and his own pilot even though the chopper flights to and from New York take him eight hours. But that's one thing I've always admired about Daniel. He writes his own script in life. Together, we've been rewriting our own, with rules that wouldn't necessarily apply to other couples, such as being apart for days or weeks at a time and taking on other part-time lovers.

We arrive at the house in less then fifteen minutes, and immediately Daniel inspects the work the contractors have done in the front yard. He seems pleased with it because he doesn't utter a word, not even a complaint. That's a good thing. The last thing I want to hear is Daniel complaining about something again.

Inside, he tosses his keys, wallet, and Rolex on the kitchen counter, drinks some Perrier, and sighs.

"It's good to be back, Bri. I've been so stressed out at work with the changes in the printing presses and some lazy employees we have. I want to take it easy this weekend. Just you and me!" he says, coming over and giving me a big hug. I smell traces of his Angel cologne which carries a particular sweet powdery scent.

I hug him back tightly.

"It's good to have you home, Daniel." We hold each other for a few minutes, and I feel so safe in his arms, like when we first met at Chelsea Piers.

Daniel messes up my hair and goes upstairs to take a hot shower. He's exhausted from the long trip, but I know he likes to be self-sufficient.

"Bri, I'm gonna take a nap after my shower. Let's plan on going out to dinner somewhere later on. I've worked up an appetite. By the way, go into my bag and open the back pocket. There's something there for you."

"Sure, Daniel," I say from the bottom of the marbled stairs as he walks up and strips off shirt. "I'll make reservations at China Grill, your favorite place." As I hear the showerhead begin to spray Daniel's hot shower, I go into his bag and pull out a CD from the back pocket. I turn it over, and I see a new photo of myself and on the cover it says, "Brian Anderson." I look at the index on the back and I recognize the songs. Apparently, Daniel had a DJ remix some of the songs I've written over the years. The CD looks slick and professional, a perfect demo to hand out to some labels. I hold it in my hands, and I smile, looking at the photo of me with the blonde highlights I got so I'd look more like a boy band pop star.

Daniel must have done this to surprise me. In his own way, he is the biggest sweetheart I've ever met, and he's my biggest fan. He loves to surprise me, and he does it in an understated yet thoughtful way. That's one of the things I love about him. I'll never forget what he did on my twenty-fifth birthday two years ago. I walked into our Chelsea apartment and found thirteen vases of lilacs and roses set all around the living room making it look like a florist's shop. Each vase had an envelope and a letter for every word in Happy Birthday Brian. When I opened each envelope, I heard a Happy Birthday melody play, as if coming from the vase. When I reached the last vase, for the letter "N," I heard someone sing "Happy Birthday Brian, from your honey, Daniel." I started crying right then and there. No one had done something so thoughtful and creative like this for my birthday. When Daniel arrived an hour later from from the office, I hugged him tightly and kissed him repeatedly on his beautiful, thick lips He looked at me with his big brown eyes, his love for me pouring out. There is a strong and pure love between us. It just might not be your typical Nicholas Sparks novel type of love but it's there. When Daniel surprises me like this, he really does make me feel like the world is lucky to have me in it. He just has this gentle caring way about him that is often cloaked by his in-your-face bossy style.

I look out the front glass windows of our door and my mind drifts briefly back to Eros. I wonder what he's doing right now, but I know I should just focus on Daniel. He needs me to relax this weekend. And although he can be loud and complain sometimes and appear bossy, I know deep down that he's my soul mate, my life partner. I take the CD and pop it into our stereo. I lay back on our sofa, with my hands tucked under my head listening to the remixed songs. I smile and mentally thank Daniel as my voice fills the room.

10

Ray

I'm going to kill my brother! I decide this future homicide after walking into Versailles Restaurant in Little Havana to have my free dinner with Racso and Cindy. This brightly lit Cuban palace has accented wall-to-wall mirrors, green borders, and dazzling fake chandeliers and the smells of café Cubano mixed with the succulent aroma of fresh garlic butter bread. In the corner, I spot my twin brother, Cindy and another guy or (is that a kid?) at their table in the corner. I realize that's no kid but a little man, but worst of all, a blind date. I've been ambushed! By the end of the night, there will be only one Martinez twin left if I have my way. *Lo voy a matar!*

The guy sitting with them is about twenty-seven or so, with receding dark brown straight hair, light brown eyes crowded by thick eyebrows and olive skin. He looks short, about five-feet-five from what I can tell. He wears a forest-green Polo shirt which defines his thin, diminutive build. How did I not see this coming? Did I mention how I hate blind dates? I arrange interviews with major movie companies and their stars. I don't need help in the romance department. But what I hate more is that my brother thinks he's actually helping my lackluster love life by setting me up with a Teletubby.

I glare at Racso and I imagine I have Superman's heat vision when my brother greets me with a warm hug. I don't reciprocate. Cindy approaches me next, and I find it hard to be mad at her because she's so sweet. She hugs me and kisses me on the cheek, and I respond as cheerily as I can. I catch a trace of her floral yet sweet Estée Lauder perfume when she begins to pull away.

"Hi, Ray! So glad you could make it tonight. You look so handsome! I want you to meet our friend Arnie." She gestures to the little guy who stands up to shake my hand. I was right about his height. He has little hands, too.

"So good to meet you, Ray. Racso and Cindy have told me a lot about you," he says, firmly shaking my hand.

"Nice to meet you too. I wish I can say the same thing since my brother hasn't told me *anything* about you. This was a surprise."

I sit down all annoyed and take a seat across from the midget. I have Racso to my right and Cindy to my left. I kick Racso under the table, and he stomps my shoe in return. Everyone settles in and places their napkin on their lap. During this brief opportunity, Racso turns to me and silently mouths, "Behave. Be nice. This was Cindy's idea. Okay? Don't mess this up." I look up, and I see Arnie and Cindy smiling back my way.

"You guys really are identical twins. Wow. Except for the haircuts and the builds, it would be hard to tell you two apart," Arnie says, his eyes like a tennis ball bouncing back and forth between me and Racso.

"Yeah but I'm the better looking one," Racso teases. That joke is so old. "I always tell people my brother is *hot!*" Racso says.

"And gay!" I tease back. "People confuse Racso as the gay movie critic sometimes which I find very funny. Actually, it's hilarious. He hates it when that happens."

"Yeah, I do, and it's not funny little bro," Racso says, his eyebrows furrowing in annoyance. "Because I'm not into dudes. That's you and because everyone knows the Miami movie critic from your outings in South Beach with your Channel 7 sidekick, they assume I'm you. No offense. It's not easy to explain that no, I'm not the movie critic and no, I'm not gay. At the beginning of every school year, I have a hard time convincing my students that I don't moonlight at the *News*. I have to explain to them and their curious parents that I don't get to see movies for free and that I don't have connections to Lindsay Lohan and Tobey Maguire. They think I know Spiderman and the new Superman. Whenever a new block-buster comes out, it's all about the movies and what I can get out of you for the school. It's very distracting, dude," Racso says.

"Admit it, you secretly wish you had my job, Racso," I say.

"Not your job little bro, but your paycheck. In fact, you should be paying this with your almost six figure salary. And Papi and Mami could use some of your financial help. Business isn't as good for Papi as it used to be," he lashes out.

I've always suspected that Racso has been jealous of my pay and job and that's why I'm the target of his barbs. Now I'm sure of it. Hey, he could have been something else other than a lowly-paid teacher. No one forced him pursue education. But what he said about Papi disturbs me and stays with me. Papi is so proud, cut from the same cloth as many older Cuban exiles that came here in the 1960s. If Papi needed money, he wouldn't let me know. That's just how he is. I'm going to have to ask Mami about the financial issues later. I can write them a check here and there. I had no idea.

"Remember, this is your treat! This was your idea." I fire back to Racso, gulping some water and squinting at him. No one talks. Arnie looks confused and drinks some water as well until someone speaks up.

Cindy, being the sweet and good person she is, then tries to fill the awkward silence like a good hostess.

"So Ray . . . how has your week been? Any good movies that we should see this weekend?" She smiles and tucks her straight black hair behind her ears, looking like Neve Campbell's twin. Cindy could easily fill in for her in *Scream IV* if she wanted to.

"If you want the high-energy popcorn fare, then go see *Mission Impossible 4*, with Brad Pitt. I'm sure it'll do well. It isn't perfect, but it delivers a jolt and is surprisingly entertaining for the fourth installment of this franchise. People are curious to see how Mr. Angelina Jolie will pull off the Ethan Hunt role. But I'd hold off and avoid the crowds and catch the Pedro Almodovar movie marathon at the Miracle Mile theater this weekend. They're showing his greatest movies, including *Volver* with Penelope Cruz and *Bad Education*."

As mad as I want to be at Cindy, I just can't be. I know she wants to help me and her friend out. She's always trying to help people, from her students to the kids she tutors on the weekends. She even takes Mami shopping sometimes on the weekends at Merrick Place. Now Racso is a different story. I'll get my revenge on him later.

"That's a good idea Ray. Arnie loves the movies. He's a fellow teacher at my school. He reads your reviews. He's a fan," Cindy says, winking at him and smiling back at me.

Mr. Little Man finally jumps back into the conversation while Racso scans the menu. I don't know why he even bothers. He always gets the *ropa vieja* which to me looks more like dirty laundry than shredded beef.

"I was impressed with your roundup of the Fort Lauderdale International Film Festival. I've been reading your reviews for quite some time. Do you ever get sick of seeing movies since you see so many?" Arnie asks, in a whiney tone. His voice cracks in mid sentence. He seems like a nice guy, and I sense he's a little nervous. I guess I should behave and make the most of the dinner. It's on my brother, but right now, I feel like literally putting the dinner on him.

I tell Arnie that sometimes, the last thing I want to see is a movie theater but when I get to review a good movie or an acclaimed work by Scorsese or Clint Eastwood, then my job is both fun and challenging. Arnie tells me about his favorite movies, which all happen to star Sandra Bullock. I want to throw up. Ugh.

"Did you see her in the *The Lake House*, with Keanu Reeves? I loved her in *Infamous*, the Truman Capote movie. Everyone thinks she's this goofy funny *Miss Congeniality* character, but when she's serious about a role, she shines," he says.

I muster a smile and nod as he talks. He's trying, but I don't feel like talking about work so I switch topics.

"*Oye*, so you work with Cindy? Are you a teacher or a counselor?" As I speak, the slight, cute guy waiter with short dark cropped hair and boyish smile brings us the steaming garlic bread and glasses of ice water. Now, I wouldn't mind having him as a blind date. He's more my type.

"I teach eighth grade U.S. history. I love sharing insights about our country's complicated yet intriguing history. Right now, we're discussing World War II. The challenge is getting the kids to see what a critical time this was in world politics, and I try to do that by asking them to trace their family's roots. By doing this, I can explain and help them understand how their family's native countries were affected by this. In order to make history relevant, you have to make the students to connect with it in some way," he says, ripping a piece of bread in half.

"I'd love for the kids to see Berlin and what's left of the Berlin Wall and where Hitler killed himself. I was there last summer, and it really helps you understand how different the world was back then. When you see history up close, you have a better understanding of it," Arnie continues. His eyes flicker with excitement over the topic.

Racso sits to my right nodding and raising his eyebrows as if to say "This is an interesting guy, no?" Cindy sips some water and nods in agreement, her hoop earrings shaking.

"The kids love Arnie, or should I say, Mr. Beggy. He gets them excited about learning. Arnie was teacher of the year last year at Coral Gables Middle," she gushes, as if she were Arnie's publicist. Whenever she finishes a sentence, she flashes her big smile and giggles. It's infectious. When she laughs, I notice Racso looking at her in an admiring way, that shows he's proud of his girlfriend. And after she says something, her eyes search for his. *Ahh*, love!

"That's great. I remember how some of my teachers made a big difference with me in high school. That's one of the reasons why I went into film critique and why Racso became a teacher himself," I say, taking a bite out of the scrumptious bread.

"That's right little brother. All it takes is one good teacher to make a difference in a young person's life. I think that's why all three of us have gone into this profession. Definitely not for the great pay. We educate children, and yet we get paid crap," Racso says.

The waiter comes back and takes our orders. I get the *arroz con pollo* with a side of black beans and a Diet Coke. Cindy and Arnie both order the chicken steak sandwich. Racso orders *la ropa vieja* as I expected and a pitcher of sangria for the table.

"Oh, and can I have a side of shrimp?" I ask the waiter. Cindy and Racso look at me with bug eyes. Oops, my bad.

"Ah, never mind. I think it'll save some room for a little dessert," I tell the waiter who looks annoyed now that he has to scribble off the shrimp side.

This Arnie dude seems like a nice guy, but I have to admit, I'm not attracted to him. I can tell he likes me because of the lingering stares I catch whenever I look up. He's sitting across from me so I can't help but avoid meeting his eyes. I don't know if it's the receding hair or his height, but I'm just not feeling it. Cindy must have recognized something special in this guy to have us meet. I bet it's because he's pretty smart and likable. But heterosexuals seem to think that just because you're gay, you would automatically click with any other gay. Not true. They assume since you're a minority you can connect on various different levels. Wrong again. Being a gay man, one who lives in snooty South Beach, I know instantly if I'm going to get along with a guy or be attracted to him on a more intimate level. Perhaps Cindy senses I've been getting lonely and she tossed this little man my way, but it's not how it works. Yes, gay men can be shallow when we should be supporting each other. We know what we like and blind dates are more of a curse than a blessing. They hardly ever work out. They're usually trolls, no pun intended.

As I pour my Diet Coke into a glass filled with ice and I watch the brown liquid fizz to the top, I just want to dive in and get out of here. I look around and I hear all the other chatter. Versailles is abuzz with activity as usual. That might be because of the funeral home nearby and the cemetery down the street. I see tables of over-dressed baroque Cuban ladies shoving the garlic bread into their mouths. I hear them gabbing about the person whose funeral they just attended and the obscene amount of make-up that was painted on the corpse. The women seem like statues, their years of living etched by the deep tanned lines in their faces. They smeared their faces with heavy make-up as if this was their night on the town but also to recapture some of their youth probably spent at social parties in Havana in their majestic homes. Mami and Aunt Betty could easily fit into this crowd since they always talk about who is sick or is dying and fill conversations with their sweet nostalgia for the good old days in Cuba. In the background, I hear an organic beat-filled song by Celia Cruz, which calls to mind colorful rumba dancers shaking to the infectious conga rhythms. They would all fit in seamlessly in this neighborhood. Tint the scene with sepia-tones, and this could be Cuba North.

Versailles is known for its quick service and generous portions, and our food arrives a few minutes later. We all dig in and keep on talking with Cindy playing moderator. I can't help but feel bad for not trying as hard to make conversation with Arnie so I toss him some questions for the sake of chatting and to make this dinner fly by.

"So what do you do when you're not teaching? Do you go out much besides the movies or Hitler's former hangouts?" When he laughs at my joke, I hear a wheezing sound which makes me grin because I make the same sound when I laugh. I thought I was the only one who did that.

Arnie swallows his big bite of his sandwich, wipes the napkin at the corner of his mouth and smiles. He has a big piece of chicken jammed between his teeth. I don't say anything so I won't embarrass him. How do you casually tell someone they have food in their mouth without making them feel self-conscious?

"I love bike riding and walking my dog Harry. Yeah, I named him after one of my favorite singers, Harry Connick, Jr., but this Harry is a sweet English bulldog. He'll lick you to death. I usually go biking in Key Biscayne or the Everglades. There's nothing quite like it. You're riding on a narrow concrete ribbon with alligators lazily sitting in the swampy marshes," Arnie says, taking a sip of his sangria.

"That's so adventurous, right Racso?" Cindy pipes in. "Maybe one day, we can all go bike riding in the Everglades. It would be so much fun, and I could take pictures for our students. Everyone thinks Miami is all about the beach and the bars. There's so much more to do here that is educational. I always try and get my students to understand that when they talk about MySpace and their other favorite Web sites."

"Yes, Cinderella, that sounds like a good idea." Racso calls Cindy by his nickname for her. I glare at him again. If my blue eyes had any heat-producing abilities, Racso would have evaporated by now.

Like the faux chandeliers above us, Arnie lights up at the idea.

"Yeah, anytime. I'd love to show you my favorite spots on the trail. One time, I came face to face with a deer, just like Bambi. It's like a savannah out there. Really relaxing and away from the city."

Now I see why Cindy and Racso wanted me to meet this guy. He can hold a conversation. He's obviously educated. He has a dog named Harry, and he loves to cycle. So we have some things in common. But as I sit here, I can't imagine myself bringing this guy home to Papi and Mami. I'm not even the tiniest bit turned on by him. This may sound shallow, but I need that burning passion, that lustful attraction, if I am going to date someone. I would like someone who's not of Lilliputian height. I want that same charged electricity that Brian felt when he saw Eros the other night.

Arnie is missing that physical spark that I'm looking for. I've found it in other guys, but then they lacked the smarts and reading ability. I find pieces of my ideal man in different guys but never in one package.

"If you guys will excuse me, I'm going to use the little boy's room," Arnie casually announces, and I try to hold on my laughter at the unintended pun. He stands up and pushes his green-leather chair back in before searching for the restroom.

When he's clear of our table, Cindy gives me the Cuban Inquisition.

"So, *te gusta*? He's a really nice guy Ray, the kind of guy who would make a good boyfriend or even a new friend." Cindy tilts her head to the side which makes her straight dark brown strands of hair move in the same direction.

"So little brother, you like?" Racso leans in, with his sangria half gone and staining his lips.

They seem so excited for me, and I hate to burst their Miami episode of *Blind Date*, but I am brutally honest. This blind date gets one star.

"*Oye*, guys, listen. I really appreciate what you're trying to do for me. Arnie seems like a sweet guy. He does. But I'm just not feeling it. Sorry."

"Oh, Ray, give him a chance, at least a dinner alone with him or something. Don't look at his size, but consider the size of his heart. Maybe you and Gigli can spend the afternoon with him and Harry," Cindy encourages.

"Yeah little bro, give the guy a shot. Just one date or afternoon. You never know."

These two are not going to let up. It would be nice for Gigli to have another play friend for the afternoon. She's always cooped up in the apartment when I'm at work and attending screenings. Every now and then, Ted brings Max the Chihuahua to play with her at Flamingo Park.

"Psst. Arnie is on his way," Cindy blurts out and swats my arm with her hand. "Change the subject."

Arnie comes back and sits down, and Cindy starts babbling about real estate.

"Yeah, and so the market is softening so maybe Racso and I can find a cute little starter home in Miami or the Roads," she says, opening her eyes wide at me so that I'll follow along with the conversation. "Being together and living in our old childhood bedrooms is getting old, fast."

"Oh yeah . . . Give it a few months or another year, and you'll have all the foreclosures piling up from the hot market from two to three years ago. It would be great to see you guys living together. It seems like you've been dating forever," I say, scraping the last of my yellow rice with bits of chicken with my fork.

Racso winks my way when Arnie readies to say something.

"So Ray, would you like to go out sometime, just you and me." He wiggles his thick eyebrows and bares his teeth like a bulldog. I notice his tooth doesn't wear the stranded piece of chicken anymore.

Cindy looks my way. Racso focuses on my face. Arnie pleads with me with his light brown eyes. I can't help but look north at his receding hairline. I hope that wasn't obvious. Shit, the pressure.

"Well . . ." I take two gulps of Diet Coke to buy me three extra seconds. "Maybe we can set up a play date for our dogs. How about that?"

I hate it when people put me on the spot like that. Usually, if someone likes you and you don't like them, you take their phone number and don't call them. But in this case, I have Cindy and my soon-to-be-violently-killed twin brother involved.

Cindy and Racso breathe a sigh of relief. Arnie smiles like he just won the Lotto or discovered some historic find in Berlin.

"Great, I'll get your number tonight and call you over the weekend," Arnie says, smiling as he looks down at his plate. He does seem like a good guy, even a little shy. One afternoon date won't hurt, and I know it would make Cindy happy.

After Cindy and Racso pay the bill, we all walk out to the parking lot near the café window where all the Cuban old men gather to talk Fidel this and Raul Castro that. I see one of our Metro reporters, Dan Maynor, interviewing some of the customers about the latest development in Cuba. We all grab cafecitos and call it a night. Arnie asks for my number, and I scribble it on the back of my *News* business card.

"Ray, thank you so much for coming out with us" Cindy says, giving me a smooch that leaves a red smudge on my cheek.

"Anytime *chica*." I hug her back.

"Little bro, talk to you later," Racso says, playfully punching me in my arm, which hurts. This is going to leave a mark. No sleeveless shirts for me this weekend.

Arnie extends his hand and says, "It was really nice meeting you Ray. I'll call you soon." His hand lingers for an extra second or two as he retracts it.

I realize I totally tower over this dude.

The three of them walk toward their cars. I parked in front so I'm already here. The only thing I want do now is hightail it out of here and meet up with Ted at Score. It's Friday night, and I could use a drink or two and maybe, a guy my height.

I pull out of the parking lot and shoot down Calle Ocho toward 95. Passing the rows of bodegas, boutiques, and used car dealerships, I can't help but feel some resentment toward my brother for doing this to me. At a red light, my cell vibrates. It's Racso.

"Hey little brother! I wanted to see how you're doing?"

"*Oye*, I know what you were trying to do, but I don't need your help finding a guy, okay? It's not like I'm fugly or anything. I look like you!" I snap at him. "Don't ever do this to me again you asshole!"

"So you're pissed, huh?" Captain Obvious asks.

"Duh! You think?" I say.

"Hey, calm down. I just thought Arnie was a good guy for you to meet. It's not like he's Frankenstein or anything. You always talk about how you'd like to have something similar to what I have with Cindy. Well, I was trying to help you meet a nice guy, and besides, Cindy's a great judge of character."

"Yeah I know, but I don't have a problem meeting guys. I'm fine on my own. Don't ever get involved in my personal life like that again, got that?" I scold him. I get on the ramp that swirls around to take me to 95 with the downtown skyscrapers beckoning like industrial lighthouses to my right.

"I just want you to be as happy as I am, little brother. I thought I was helping. I'm sorry about tonight. I thought it was something nice, and this really came from Cindy. She was so excited planning this. Papi and Mami worry that you're gonna end up all alone the day they die. We're all worried about you, little brother."

My annoyance, as fiery as it is right now, begins to fade as I listen to Racso and hear the sincerity in his voice. I can imagine Mami telling Racso that she doesn't want to see me living alone as gay old man with another dog while Racso and Cindy and our cousins enjoy their grandchildren. I know Racso loves me and wants the best for me, but being gay and meeting the right guy is never easy. Some guys never end up falling in love or being in relationships. It just seems so much easier for guys like my brother and my straight co-workers at the *News* because of the abundance of places and opportunities for them to meet and find a potential love connection. In Miami, it's pretty much Score, Twist, the on-line chat rooms, and yes, Flamingo Park, not that I would ever go there or anything.

"*Oye*, I'll let you off the hook this time, but promise me you'll never set me up on another blind date. If not, I'll come to your school and tell your students about the time you shit in your pants when we drove down to Key West with Papi and Mami and we were stuck in traffic."

"You wouldn't! We were fifteen at the time, Ray! That could happen to anyone."

"Yeah, but it happened to *you*, and I'll never forget the look on your face. It was all those Betty Crocker chocolate chip cookies you ate the night before. It gave you massive diarrhea."

I start laughing thinking of the incident and how Mami tried to hold in her laughter when we pulled over at the next McDonald's. Racso starts to laugh at the situation too.

"Okay, you've got a deal, little brother. No more blind dates or trays of chocolate chip cookies for me."

"Deal!"

I laugh the whole drive to South Beach and Score thinking about that moment, but the laughter doesn't shake off the lingering resentment I sometimes feel toward my brother. Why does he have to have it all?

11

Ted

As usual, I'm the first to arrive at Score even though I took my time tonight after taping *Deco Time* and walking Max up and down Pine Tree Drive a few times. He seemed to appreciate the extra laps because he passed out in his doggie condo as soon as we got back to the house. Max was maxed out.

"Grapefruit juice with vodka please," I tell the boyish blonde waiter. He scribbles down the order because it's so hard to remember, you know. He disappears into the crowd of twilight visitors that linger outside the main entrance door. It is ten minutes past eleven, and I'm sitting at our usual table, holding down the pink fort until Ray arrives. Brian is with Daniel—or perhaps Eros or who knows what other Latin boy toy—this weekend so he'll probably be a no-show. Besides, Ray and I always have a good time with or without Brian, but it's nice when he's around. His youthful good energy adds to the festivities, and I love hearing about the latest episode of *The Fabulous Life of the Rich and Brian*.

I'm leaning back in the wicker chair looking at the guys walking up and down Lincoln Road as if it were *America's Next Top Model: Miami*. I see some muscle queens wearing shirts two sizes two small as if they bought them in 1999 on sale at Old Navy or at the Abercrombie and Fitch outlet at Sawgrass Mills in Broward. I see the Hispanic twinks, the baby gays, with their super gelled hair that looks perpetually spritzed with water. They've got that young Antonio Banderas thing down to every wet strand. Even at night, the men here look like they are covered in Crisco because of the oily sheen from their daily face and arm moisturizers. I see a mix of lipstick and butch lesbians cavorting three tables over. Their laughter punctuates the air as they swap stories about a recent *Ellen* and *L-Word* episode. Some of the ladies puff on cloves which sends a pipe-scented cloud my way. Cough! I try to wave the smoke away. You smell more cologne than perfume here because of the guys gathering here tonight. Basically, it's your typical Friday night at Score.

Fergie of the Black Eyes Peas purrs from the speakers inside the club and my feet tap along to the thumping beat just like the 1988 song *Supersonic* she sampled.

"*I'm Fergalicious . . .*"

If I could, I'd change the song to "*I'm Tedalicious.*" It has more snap like that. Hey, I'm just glad the bar isn't playing the Miami urban version of the song, you know, *Chongalicious*. In case you're scratching your head, a chonga is a ghetto Hispanic chick, most often found in greater parts of Hialeah and the Miami suburbs of Kendall. The two girls who sing that version of the song fit the bill using Sharpie markers to outline their blood-red lipstick and glue sticks to keep their hair shiny and smeared tightly on the sides of their heads. The song was remade here in Miami by two drama high school students who were featured on *Deco Time* last year. Their follow up song: *I'm In Love With A Chonga*.

South Beach's cool tropical breath hisses softly like two hands rubbing together, through the palm trees on Lincoln Road. The manboy bartender returns with my icy drink. I take three long sips, letting the fruity yet tart liquid swish inside my mouth before chilling down into my throat.

Where is Ray? I'm surprised he makes deadline at the paper. He's late for *everything*. Dinner at Versailles can't take *that* long. The older waitresses with the wigs usually shoo you out the door to make way for the lobster-red tourists.

"*Oye* boy, you gotta light, bro?" some gang banger asks from behind me. I turn around, and it's Ray, standing in a rapper's pose as if to say "Word to your mutha." He always catches me off guard. My eyes were locked on some Latin cuties in tank tops passing by.

"Very nice, Ray. I'm sure your editors would be impressed with your grasp of Cuban eubonics and gangstah speak. How are you? How was dinner with Racso and Cindy? I want the exclusive. News at 10!"

Ray sits down, rolls his eyes and takes a deep breath. He's got a story to tell. This should be good.

"They set me up with Mini Me!" he deadpans. "It was a blind date with *Little Man*."

I breathe in an astonished gasp imagining the Wayans brother from the movie with the same name. My mouth open forms the letter "O."

"No! They wouldn't! You're shitting me! I could see your twin doing that as a joke but Cindy? She's not the prankster type." I toss back another swig from my drink.

"They invited me to dinner so I could meet one of Cindy's gay teacher friends from her school. They thought I would hit it off with him because he's—get this—gay! And on top of that, his name is . . . Arnie!" Ray raises his thin black eyebrows and holds an unlit cigarette in his hand to emphasize his point. He uses the candle on the table to light up. I cover my mouth in disbelief at the news.

"No way! Do they know your type? Well come to think of it, what is your type Ray? You can never seem to make up your mind as to what you want or who you like. And how short was he? I hope he's taller than Max."

"Yeah Ted, he's just a *few* inches taller than your Taco Bell chihuahua. Actually, he seemed liked a nice guy. Not the best looking guy but sort of cute in his own dorky way. He's a history teacher, he has a dog, and he reads my reviews. He's educated, and he obviously has great taste in movie critics."

Ray winks at me and orders a Corona from the manboy when he comes around again.

The blind date couldn't have been that bad if Ray is saying some decent things about Arnie. So far, the only negative I've heard is his height. I try to picture myself dating a substantially shorter man. I guess it depends on the whole package. If he has a cute enough face, lofty goals and a great personality, I may be able to overlook the height disparity. Would I be able to take him to a Channel 7 party? Maybe, if his personality outsizes his stature. It must be hard for Arnie, being in South Florida, the land of Amazonian men, women, and trannies. Oh, who am I kidding? I wouldn't date someone who was a lot shorter than me. I would be uncomfortable with how it looked. This reminds me of that *Golden Girls* episode when Rose brings home a little bearded doctor friend, and Dorothy and Blanche grow extremely uncomfortable around him because everything they say is a synonym for the word short.

"Does this mean you're going out on a date with him or did you NEXT him like the guys on that MTV show?"

"He put me on the spot with my brother and Cindy right there. I told him I'd be up for hanging out some afternoon to let our dogs play." Ray takes a deep drag from his cigarette and exhales a cloud of second-hand smoke which rolls my way. I hate when Ray does that. He thinks it's cool. It's extremely unhealthy. His lungs must be as black as the Miami River. The smoke is also bad for your skin.

"Wait, Gigli is having a date with his dog, behind Max's back? This could be an episode of *Paws of Our Lives*. Are you taking them to your favorite late night hang out, Flamingo Park?" I tease him.

"Don't go there, Ted, but then again, you do go there! Your name is etched on the trees in the baseball field from your late night undercover reporting there. There's a big Channel 7 logo under your name there."

"Well, if my name is there, it's below yours, Ray Martinez with four stars."

We start laughing, and we high five each other. I'm happy for Ray. He's got a date. Well, more like Gigli has a date. Maybe Ray will see Arnie in a different light if they're alone, but it seems like he's doing this more for his dog and his brother and Cindy than for himself which is typical of Ray. He's been guilted into this. Cuban guilt is something Ray and most Miami Cubans know well. It's a powerful manipulative weapon among families here, and Ray is often a victim of it, with his mother and his brother calling him to do favors for them, as if he's the on-call gay son with no life.

"Can I casually drop by the park when you're having your date? I can bring Max and make it look like a total coincidence. I want to see what this guy looks like."

"*Oye* . . . no! You'll be so obvious and I don't want the guy to think that I arranged for you to drop in on us and rescue me," Ray says. He jams a lime in the Corona the boy bartender just brought him.

"Oh please . . . pretty please. I promise, I won't be conspicuous. I can make it look like a total accident. I want to see who this great little guy is that Cindy and Racso went through so much trouble to introduce you to. Besides, I might meet a cutie there myself. I'll even bring my copy of *Boys of Boston* to read there to look even more *au natural.*"

"You're gonna do what you're gonna do, Ted. I can't talk you of something once you make up your mind. Just don't embarrass me, Arnie, and of course, Gigli."

"Trust me. You won't even know I'm there. It's not like I am going to show up with a Channel 7 camera and put this on *Deco Time* or *Help Me Howard.*"

Ray tells me that he'll make the play date for Sunday afternoon at the park, which will be swarming with guys. He can't do it tomorrow because he's going to help his dad fix the garage door and then take his mother to Costco for their monthly food shopping trips. (It's the Cuban good-son syndrome he has.)

As we catch up from our week and check out the guys walking by, I notice a certain North Carolinian in his usual white T-shirt and blue jeans walking our way. It's Brian. I guess Daniel let him out of the house tonight.

"Hey guys. Did you save me a seat?" he says. He hugs Ray and then pats me roughly on my back. He probably wrinkled my Armani light green T-shirt which goes great with my baggy Diesel jeans. I'm casually dressed tonight. No TV suit like my other typical Friday nights because I got out of the *Deco Time* taping earlier than usual. Now I feel like the little man next to Brian.

"Where's your man, or should I say, men?" I ask Brian, who scoots into his chair and waves to the bartender to come our way.

"Daniel had a long flight yesterday so he went to bed early, and I wasn't sleepy and wanted to go out."

"And Eros? How's he doing?" Ray asks as if he already knows the answer to his own question. Ray is already on his second cigarette.

Brian smirks and looks down. His hands tap the side of the chair like a drum as if he's nervous about what he is about to discuss.

"I had to say goodbye to him. Daniel didn't have a good feeling about him and he was getting upset that I kept hanging out with him." Brian leans back in his chair and puts his feet up on the empty fourth chair which I'm sure he wishes Eros was sitting in.

"But it sounded like you really had a connection with this Puerto Rican guy, like you liked him," I say, finishing up my drink. I feel a warm, light-headed buzz coursing inside me. The vodka is doing its job. Giddiness bubbles up from within me. "But then again, you already have a husband. You're in one complicated situation. You don't need another."

"Yeah Brian. It's hard enough to be with one man, but juggling two can't be all that easy or fun despite the benefits," Ray interjects. "I can see where Daniel is coming from. It's completely disrespectful to your unique relationship to continue with Eros."

Brian takes a deep breath and his eyes drift away to somewhere else before settling back on both of us.

"Look, I know you guys don't understand. Sometimes, I don't understand my relationship with Daniel. We love each other. We're together and we're committed, but we can play on the side. Daniel sensed I was getting attached to Eros, and he's right. I had to cut it off. I can't stop thinking about him, but I told him we couldn't keep hanging out. The pull is too strong between us. Whew!" he says, fanning his face with a white cocktail napkin.

"But wouldn't you rather be with someone with whom you have this incredible physical and spiritual connection?" I turn to Brian. "Isn't that what we all want? I had that with Louie in Boston until the stupid faggot cheated on me. I know I'll find that guy again one day. Are you listening to me Anderson Cooper or Chris Cuomo from *Good Morning America*?"

"*Oye*, I think that's the ideal we all want," Ray says. "Perhaps Eros came into your life to remind what you don't have. I'm not saying to break up with Daniel. I'm just saying that maybe, just maybe your situation isn't fulfilling what you really want and requires closer examination. It never hurts to take a personal inventory of what you have and don't have."

The manboy arrives with Brian's vodka with cranberry, and Brian slurps a quarter of it immediately.

"Tell me something I don't know, Ray. I know you guys mean well, but I have to sort this out on my own. Will I always be with Daniel? I don't know. Things are good for now. We're going shopping this weekend for new furniture for the Venetian house, and we're planning to spend the day in Vero Beach looking at some properties. Who knows, he might meet a cute younger blonde boy that he connects with the same way I connect with Eros and leave me for him. Nothing is guaranteed, but I do know that Daniel loves me and I love him in our own special way."

I wish I had Brian's dilemma, caught between two men especially one that is a multi-millionaire and owns a grand apartment in Chelsea and a helicopter. I don't understand why he can't just break up with Daniel. It's half of a relationship. This is what it breaks down to: they are really good friends, business associates and roommates. Sex is absent in their life together. So why be together? As much as I like Brian as a new friend, I think he and Daniel are being plain greedy, holding on to each other when they should let each other go and find that true love, that passion that evaporated from their relationship so many years ago.

"I'm really tempted to call Eros, to have lunch or something. Maybe we can be friends. I still don't know that many people here in Miami besides you guys and the construction workers at our house." Brian eyes the crowd outside of Score. I bet he's looking for Eros. "My intuition tells me we're going to see each other very soon. I feel strongly about this, and I can't help that feeling."

Ray leans closer to the table, crushing his cigarette into the ashtray.

"Brian, what will you do if you bump into this guy again? Do you really think you can walk away from him knowing how much great sex you guys had and the highly charged sexual connection that exists between you?"

Brian twirls the straw in his vodka and cranberry, creating a reddish tornado inside. It probably reflects the storm of emotions he's been feeling lately. He takes a few seconds to respond.

"We'll find out when it happens," he says.

"Well, here's your chance. Eros just walked into Score," I blurt out, raising my right eyebrow and nodding up toward the entrance.

Brian looks like he's itching to leap out of his chair like one of those Mexican jumping beans to chase Eros inside the club, but he manages to stay put. We move onto other topics. I start talking about the celebrities I saw last night at the fashion fundraiser, and Ray talks about the recent movies he reviewed. He also recounts his blind date experience to Brian, causing him to laugh.

An hour later, after we've all gabbed the upcoming gay journalism conference in Boston, Brian, who seems bored by our shop talk, finally ditches us for his Puerto Rican man. He denies it and says he's going into Score "to walk around." Ray and I know better. We're journalists after all. It's not that easy to snow us.

A few minutes after Brian leaves, Ray realizes he's run out of cigarettes. He decides to take off to buy a new pack and call it a night. He says that his two Coronas and the *arroz con pollo* and the black beans rumbling in his stomach aren't agreeing very well. I personally think it's the cigarettes along with the drinking and the *arroz con pollo* that gave him the stomachache.

"Yeah, I'm gonna take off, Ted. I think I'm having a Maalox moment." Ray rubs his stomach, the pain evident in his cringing face. He readies to leave, and I don't want to be around when his insides explode.

"Try some Pepto while you're at it. Sounds like you could use whatever stomach ammunition you can get your hands on."

Ray slowly walks away toward Meridian Avenue and his car. Now it's just me sitting here, on my third grapefruit and vodka. I'm slurping the last bit of the drink when I hear a sweet German-accented voice.

"Hallo! Do you know vere I can find a bank machine?" I look to my left and I see the face of a Nazi, but a cute nice one. He has green eyes, sandy blondish straight hair combed to the side like a book page. He has a big honker, but it's overshadowed by his other qualities. He's wearing a short-sleeve, buttoned down light blue shirt and a cute skinny black tie and khaki slacks. He's a German Gap ad in the flesh. I take back the Nazi comment. He can feed me currywurst anytime.

"Hi, there's one inside Score, but they'll overcharge you in bank fees. You're better off using the one over there, across from the Starbucks." I point to the ATM next to the art gallery.

"*Danke schoen*," he smiles bashfully, nods, and walks away.

I don't know Ray's type, and neither do Racso and Cindy, but this German boy is the kind of guy I like. He reminds me of one of the kids from *The Sound of Music* but all grown up, in his mid-twenties. I sit back in my chair, sloppily slurp the rest of my drink, and watch Mr. Germany boy's tight bum defined ever so beautifully by his form-fitting khakis which scream H & M. I can't tell if he's gay. Most Europeans with their manicured nails, moisturized faces, gelled up spiky or combed down hair, ultra lean bodies, and fashion savvy look gay but aren't necessarily. I make a toast to myself at my empty table, "To hottie Germans. May they all look like that guy." The lesbians at the other table toss me some strange looks after catching me talking to myself.

"Don't worry ladies, I wasn't talking to you," I tell them. They shoot me some nasty looks. Oh well, beef curtain eaters.

I'm feeling very buzzed, all warm inside. The chairs in front of me look like they're shifting from right to left. I feel like I'm swaying when I'm sitting still. I face it. I'm a little drunk. I can't drive like this. So I decide to walk it off. I get up. *Whoa*. I have a hard time balancing. *Focus*, Ted, *focus*!

I leave a ten dollar tip for the manboy bartender, and I start walking on Lincoln Road past all the art galleries, shops, fellow club goers, and late night diners eating alfresco. I hang a left on Lenox Avenue and keep on walking, past the shoulder-to-shoulder Deco apartment buildings that are probably packed with gay men fucking right now, doing some blow or G, or watching my re-aired telecast from tonight. I stumble across Fourteenth Street under the whitish glow of the light posts. I follow their trail and a few minutes later, I'm passing a row of cars parked diagonally. I see men sitting in each of the cars eyeballing my every move. I follow the sidewalk, and it leads me into the park. I almost trip a few times on some tree roots. It's almost pitch black here except for the glow of the light posts that surround the property, providing some light and casting shadows on the playground and baseball field. A chorus of crickets chirps as I stroll by the basketball courts. Some bushes suddenly rustle and startle me. The grass is soft and moist, and my Merrell sneakers sink into them like goo.

I'm getting ready to leave the park when a man about thirty and built like an international male model stops me in my tracks. I stand face to face with his tight hard chest. He looks like one of those blue-collar, macho types from Boston with the dark hair, big blue eyes, and fair skin. I look up and see this ruggedly handsome guy in a tight T-shirt and sweat pants. I'm not scared. I'm turned on.

"Yo man, wanna get sucked?" he says in the most masculine voice I've ever heard. It reminds me a boxer or a tough prison guard barking orders. My cock gets instantly hard.

All I could mutter is, "Hi! How's it going?"

Next thing I know, he grabs my hand.

"Come this way." I don't resist as he leads me to a corner of the park where it's really dark and desolate, where some bushes and trees meet near the playground. I can barely see anything in front of me including this hot stranger. I try to keep up, but my legs feel heavy, as if I'm dragging some cement blocks with each step in the soggy grass.

When we stop, he starts unbuckling my belt and unzips my pants. My dick flings out through my Calvin Klein boxers.

"Yeah man, that's what I like, some nice dark big cock," he says. I don't even think about what's happening. I just go along with it.

He squats down and starts sucking on my dick, stroking it up and down with his tongue. He makes some slurping sounds, and I reflex forward at few times because the sensation feels so deliciously tingling that my knees want to buckle and surrender. I haven't been this turned in so long. His tongue swirls all around my cock and up and down my shaft. I feel the soft wet insides of his cheeks and the occasional tooth.

"Man, you've got a great cock," he says, before returning to his sucking post. "Are you Brazilian or Dominican? You're like a tripod."

"Well, why thank you!" I say, in my slurred speech. I wish I had a third leg to keep me standing on the two I'm on.

I'm just doing my best to keep from falling forward on him. The trees, bushes, and the lights in the distance are all a blurry haze. I look up and see specks of silver in the night's constellation.

"I'm Portuguese-Irish from the Cape," I slur. "Ever been?"

He ignores the question. I look down and see the sculpted V-shape of his back through his shirt. I see the crack of his smooth ass because his sweat pants are pulled down. I then realize he's sucking my shaft up and down hard and jerking himself off at the same time. That causes me to rock back and forth a bit like a man machine. The motion and the sight of his dick makes me want to come right there. I steady my right hand on his shoulder blade to keep my balance. No commercial interruptions tonight. I lean my head back and stare at the starry sky and dig my fingers deep into his muscular back muscles. I close my eyes.

"Man, I'm about to come . . . I'm so clo . . . *wow!*"

He ignores me and sucks with more vigor, like a machine on an assembly line. I look down again, and I see his head bobbing up and down like a yo-yo.

"I can't hold it . . . I'm . . . I'm . . . Oh . . . God!" I explode, feeling bursts of my warm cum blast into the back of his throat. I hear him moan and hmm. He licks my cock dry.

"Yeah, I love that dark dick cum," he says, still licking.

He breathes heavily and rapidly. I hear him rasping in our little sex corner, then I hear a guttural moan.

Squirts of his cum torpedo in front of me and in between my legs, leaving the stench of fresh cum in the air.

"That was hot man," he says.

He stands back up and catches his breath. He then tops off his dick of any excess fluid and pulls up his sweat pants. He wipes his mouth. I can only see half his face in the darkness.

"Thanks man," he says. "Gotta go." He jogs off and disappears into the darkness. I stand there alone looking around me for any spying eyes. I try to stay balanced and the smell the sterile cum still fills the air around me. I pull my jeans up and ruffle my T-shirt back into them. I keep looking around, and I see other distant figures roaming the park like lost zombies. How did I get here again? Where the hell am I? *What the fuck?*

I squint my eyes and search for my way out of here. Then it hits me. All the jokes Ray and I have said about this place are on me. I got blown in Flamingo Park. I feel deeply ashamed but even more embarrassed. I'm a respected and well-known, professional journalist. How could I stoop so low in my drunken stupor? What if this guy had been a cop? My career would be over. I'd be the top of the news instead of reporting it. Mom and Dad would be so disappointed. Ray would be embarrassed to be seen with me here in South Beach. Even more troubling, what if this guy has an STD? I've always been clean and safe. The vodka made me do this. It was the vodka's fault.

My heart races. The adrenaline from the oral sex and the gravity of what I've done conspire to sober me up somewhat. I quickly walk out of the park with my head down and my hands tucked in my pockets. I take the least busy streets back to Lincoln Road and to my BMW, hoping and praying that no one saw me here. What happened tonight in Flamingo Park will stay there. There are some things you can't really share with other people especially your friends, even best friends like Ray. I would hate for him to know that one of our jokes has just come true, in more ways than one. I'm the joke.

12

Brian

"Whoa, what a wave!" I shout to Eros from my jet ski. "Did you see that?"

He's laughing his heart out as I spray him with my watery exhaust.

"Stop that, Brian! You're too much, *chico*!" I just jumped a wave and flew in the air like an aquatic cowboy, leaving the whipped water of jet ski behind.

We're shredding the waters just off Government Cut with the azure Atlantic all to ourselves. I slow down, cut the engine, and bob up to Eros's jet ski. This is his first time on a water bike, and I'm glad I'm introducing him to something new. He looks so sexy wearing the red life vest, water droplets falling from his curly hair. His toned dark arms tense and flex as he keeps a locked grip on the jet ski's handle bars.

"Having fun *guapo*? This is one of my favorite things to do when I come down to Miami. There's nothing like jumping on a jet ski and zipping by the cruise ships and the little Biscayne Bay islands."

"Yeah, this is fun *chico*." I pull up to him, and we kiss, our jet skis bobbing side by side. "Thanks for taking me out like this."

In the distance, we see the bright-white sandy South Beach shore dwarfed by the row of pastel Deco hotels and buildings on

Ocean Drive. A Royal Caribbean cruise ship gently eases out of Government Cut on its way to the Caribbean. Eros and I wave to the passengers like an episode from the *Love Boat*.

We passionately kiss again as the jet skis rock back and forth from the waves stirred by the cruise ship. I rub the back of his head and tickle his ears.

I know what you're thinking. Why am I with Eros? Where's Daniel? I could just imagine Ray and Ted with looks of disappointment, shaking their heads in disapproval. They just don't understand.

I swore I wasn't going to see Eros, but when Ted told me last week that he saw him walk into Score, I felt a jealous pang in the pit of my stomach. The thought of him in Score looking for another guy to hook up with began gnawing inside me. I have no right to feel this way. I do have Daniel, and Eros is single and free. He can do whatever he wants with whoever, but just the thought really irritated me. After hanging out with the guys, I looked for Eros and I found him at the bar, sitting by himself stirring a red straw in his Cosmopolitan. When I approached him, he looked up at me with those dark brown eyes, and a huge smile slowly spread across his face. I had the same reaction. I sat with him, and we talked. He'd been tired from working hard at the restaurant where he's on his feet for ten hour days. He talked about talking to his family earlier that night. I told him about Daniel, our planned drive to Vero Beach, furniture shopping, and the new song I've been working on. I also told him how I felt.

"I missed you so much. I've been thinking about you non-stop."

"Me too *chico*. I've never wanted to be with someone who had a boyfriend. This is new to me," he said.

We couldn't go back to my place that night since Daniel was there. When I asked Eros if we could go to his place, he said he had a straight roommate who didn't know about him. Hmm. That was news to me. I always thought the reason he never wanted to go back to his place was because he was embarrassed by his apartment. When I dropped him off the second time we hung out, the building looked like one of the few subsidized apartment complexes left in South Beach. It looked slightly ghetto and run down as if the landlord abandoned the property and only stopped by to collect the rents.

"So you're gay, but your roommate doesn't know?" I asked him that night at Score.

"*Chico*, I never said I was gay. I'm bisexual. I go both ways," he said, taking a long sip from his drink.

"But you know you're gay, right? You obviously like men more, Eros."

"I had some girlfriends in Puerto Rico before I moved here. But I like having sex with men. My roommate doesn't know about that part of my life. I don't feel comfortable telling him," Eros said, slightly defensive.

So much for my intuition. I could have sworn he was gay. He takes it like a power bottom.

"So what do we do tonight then? I want to play."

"Let's park somewhere," he suggested, winking at me. The idea gave me an instant boner. We left Score, hopped into my Land Rover, and I drove around looking for a place. Eros seemed to know exactly where to go. I'd rather have sex in a bed than in a car like high school students, but we didn't have much of a choice.

"Near the park over there. It's pretty dark," the so-called bi guy pointed out.

I pulled into the corner of Flamingo Park off Eleventh Street near some houses that face the park's running track. One of the bulbs of the light posts was burned out, so we were in a darker space than the other parked cars. The Land Rover had tinted windows so I didn't worry about anyone seeing us. As soon as I turned the engine off, Eros immediately unzipped my jeans and went down on me. His warm wet mouth covered my entire dick. Within minutes, I instantly exploded in his mouth and the tingling sensation lingered for a few minutes afterward. He wiped my penis dry with his tongue. Then I returned the favor. His guttural moans filled the

Land Rover when he reached his intense orgasm. We sat in the
Land Rover and held each other as the moon shone through my
sun roof. I stroked the back of his head with my fingers. When I
saw the digital clock read 3 a.m., I knew I had to get going back to
the house before Daniel woke up.

When I offered to drive Eros home, he said matter-of-factly, "I
can walk. It's not that far." We kissed each other a few times, not
wanting to let go. I told him I would call him when Daniel left on
Monday.

"Call me whenever you want, *chico*," he said, as he got out of
the Land Rover. He winked at me and disappeared into the park.
As I watched him leave, all I thought about was how much I
wanted him to stay the night with me. Maybe another time. As I
began to drive away, I noticed men walking up and down the
perimeter of the park ogling every car that cruised by. One guy
looked familiar, really familiar. I slowed down as I passed him and
did a double take. It couldn't be. Ted? I stopped the car, but he kept
walking by as if in his own world. He looked like he was talking to
himself because I could see his lips mouthing silent words. What
was Mr. Respected Reporter doing here at this time? He would
never be caught in a place like this. His shirt was wrinkled, and his
belt sloppily unbuckled. I thought about offering him a ride but I
didn't want to explain what I was doing in the park myself. I have
a feeling he had the same reasons for being here too. I also had to
get back home. I knew Ted would be fine. He was probably walking back to his BMW and headed home.

A big splash in my face brings me back to this sunny afternoon
with Eros. After jumping some more waves, we head back through
Government Cut, along the docks of the neighboring homes on
the Venetian Islands until we arrive back at my dock. We towel off
and take a nice hot shower in my bathroom. I bend Eros over and
fuck him right there as the steamy vapor fogged up the shower's
glass doors. I don't know if I'm sweating from the vapor or from
the mechanical feel-real-good sex. When I finally come, I feel my

knees wanting to buckle from the sensation. I lean against the tiled wall and go down on Eros a bit until he comes. There's something about the sex with Eros. It feels so carnal, so pure, as if our bodies can't help themselves but seek each other out. Just Eros's touch arouses me like a sweet addiction. I know I shouldn't but I can't help it. He's becoming my sex crack, and I don't know if I'm going to be able to stop. It feels too good with him. We eventually dry ourselves off and head to the Van Dyke to get something to eat.

Twenty minutes later at the restaurant, we sit at one of the outside tables as people strut up and down Lincoln Road in the bright daylight. I try to hold Eros's hand, but almost by reflex, he pulls it back, which boggles my mind.

"What's wrong? I just want to hold your hand?" I ask him, as I browse the menu. All that water action, on the jet skis and in the shower, makes me want to chow down on a burger.

"Nothing. I just don't like being affectionate in public," he says defensively. Ah, ok. This comes from the guy who sucked my cock like a popsicle the other night in a park.

"I'm not like you Brian, so open and free. I have my cousin here on the beach, and not a lot of people know that I like to play with guys. My family doesn't know."

Could I have misread this guy? I always assumed—more like felt—he was gay and proud. Now I'm getting another side of him. I tilt my head to the side and stare at him with curiosity. But that only lasts for a few seconds because I find him absolutely stunning to look at it. Then again, something seems different now from my view. My intuition tells me I am not getting the entire story from him. But I still want to fuck him again as soon as we're done with our late lunch.

The waiter returns for our order. Eros asks for the salmon with a side of crab cakes and a glass of red wine. I order a cheeseburger, fries and a shake. Eros also asks for an appetizer of avocado egg rolls. The boy doesn't waste any time ordering and he orders a lot.

We talk about his goals.

"I really want to quit my job at the restaurant. I feel I can do so much more with my life. It was fun at first but after a few months, being a waiter wears you down," he says, drinking some of the iced-filled water the waiter brought.

"What do you want to do then?" I ask.

"I don't know, take care of you and that beautiful face of yours," he says. Eros has a way with words. It's that Latin charm which I fall for all the time. A guy can talk about the weather in a Spanish accent, and I'd be turned on and nodding as if it was the most interesting conversation I've ever heard.

"Maybe I can get a job at the library like I had in Puerto Rico. You see all sorts of interesting people there and I get to play on the computers."

"And what do you like to do on the computers?" I ask, sensing the answer I already know.

"I like to read news Web sites about Puerto Rico. The *News* only really cares about Cuba this and Cuba that which doesn't interest me. Being online makes time go by pretty fast. It's also a good way of meeting people."

The waiter returns with our appetizer which interrupts my train of thought. I feel a stinging jealousy come over imagining him chatting with men online and sending them photos of his eight-inch Puerto Rican cock. He must go online and hook up with guys, probably on Manhunt or AOL chat, especially if he's not out to his roommate.

"What does your roommate do?" I ask as I taste the avocado egg roll.

"He runs a women's boutique on Ocean Drive. He's offered me a job doing some bookkeeping and managing the clerical stuff. But I think we might get sick of seeing each other too much," he says, already on his second egg roll. This boy is either really hungry or a little uncouth. My mom would probably think he's low class because of the way he looks. Mom is old school American, from North Carolina. She'll think Eros is black or something along those racial lines because of his dark complexion.

"And you think your roommate is straight, even though he runs a boutique for women? Sounds pretty gay to me Eros."

He laughs back and keeps eating. The waiter returns with our food. For the rest of the meal, we devour our entrees. Eros reaches over and eats some of my fries, which annoys me. It's not like he doesn't have enough food on his plate. I don't like plate invaders.

Half an hour later, the waiter clears our table and leaves the bill. I grab it and look over the sixty-five-dollar bill. I notice Eros stays quiet. He doesn't offer to pay or even try to take out his wallet. One thing I do appreciate about Ted and Ray is that they always make the effort to pay or insist about paying if I paid our round of drinks the week before. It's classy. Maybe I'm reading too much into this bill with Eros. He'll probably pay next time. I'm more than happy to pay. I like to treat people. It's one of the privileges of having wealth.

"I got this," I announce.

"Thanks, *chico*," he says, leaning back in his chair and winking back at me. "I'll pay next time."

The next few days, Eros and I hang out at the house and we seem almost inseparable. We have several sex-a-thons in my bedroom, in the pool, in the kitchen, the staircase, the backyard, on the boat and in the yard. I can't help it, and my dick is raw from all the shagging. My body yearns to be with his and as soon as we have a round, we fall asleep and recharge for the next. My abs are tightening from fucking Eros with a ferocious intensity. A sheen of sweat covers my body after each episode. And he loves it. When we don't have sex, Eros plays with my X-Box in my home office or heads back to work at the restaurant. One night, he spent the day cooking and prepared us a nice dinner of pork chops, yellow rice, and an apple pie, which I appreciated. Maybe I was reading into the late lunch at the Van Dyke too much. I'm just used to people offering to pay even when I insist on paying.

I haven't talked to Daniel as much this week because he's had a lot on his plate at work. We've exchanged some emails and a quick phone call here and there, and I didn't mention what I've or who

I've been doing while he's been in New York. Sometimes I think Daniel knows me better than I do my own self. I wouldn't be surprised if he senses I've been hanging out with Eros. I don't know how to explain this pull I feel for Eros, yet I don't want to let go of Daniel either.

13

Ray

"*Oye*, Gigli! Stop biting Harry." Gigli ignores my commands, and she looks away when I tell her not to do something. She seems annoyed as if she doesn't want to be here. I know the feeling. She takes after her papa. She's not used to Arnie's bulldog or Arnie for that matter. We're here at the corner of Flamingo Park, near the baseball field, hanging out with Arnie. I don't know if you can call this a date. Maybe one for our dogs, but Arnie's not my type, and I'm guessing Harry's not Gigli's type either.

"I think Harry has a little crush on Gigli," Arnie says, wearing khaki shorts and a blue Polo T-shirt. He's definitely a guppie (gay yuppie). His über-hairy legs look like Captain Caveman's but with nice calves, probably from cycling in Key Biscayne. Whenever Arnie speaks to me, he finishes his sentence with a big grin. There's no food in his teeth this time. Harry is persistent about trying to hump Gigli, and well, Gigli's not that kind of pooch-lady. Like me, she's picky and selective. And if you come on too strong, she bites back. I will too. Not that Arnie is coming on too strong, but it's obvious he likes me and I'm just not feeling it.

"I think they would make a perfect boyfriend and girlfriend, don't you?" Arnie asks, rubbing Harry's big white face. His drool flies everywhere. Harry is such a fat bulldog. He waddles when he walks. Gigli easily outruns him, and whenever Harry gets close enough to try and hump her, she gallops away. If she could talk, Gigli would tell Harry, "You're not getting a piece of this pretty ass, dawg!"

Other dogs are here too, sniffing the small patches of grass surfacing through the cracks of the sidewalks on this sun-soaked February Sunday. Other dogs sit under the shady trees or near their owners watching the spectacle of *When Harry Met Gigli*. I know it isn't going to kill me to hang out with Arnie, but I'm feeling pretty bored. We've talked about my job, how I go into it, Sandra Bullock movies. We had an interesting exchange about Penelope Cruz rising from the unrewarding B-list movies to her Almodovar comeback in Volver.

"I bet she'll never make another *Sahara* again," Arnie says.

"Yeah, she knows better now. She's unappreciated by American audiences because she's never translated well on screen here. Yet in Spain and Europe, she's today's Sophia Loren. Her accent is off-putting here, but when she speaks Spanish, she seems more comfortable in her roles." I light up a cigarette and blow the smoke away from Arnie. The aroma mixes with the smell of the dry grass and earthy mulch near the giant oak tree near our bench.

Then the conversation tumbles again. Arnie starts repeating why he loves to teach so much and rehashes his trip to Germany and how much Racso and I look alike. We can't seem to keep a steady conversational flow. It's like Arnie is trying too hard and maybe I'm not trying enough. It's our dogs that seem to pick up the conversation whenever it dips.

"Has anyone told you how cute you are Ray? The moment I saw you, I couldn't keep my eyes off of you. You don't see many Cuban guys here with blue eyes," he says, looking down with a grin, twiddling his thumbs as Gigli outruns Harry near the other benches. The other dogs, which include a gray pug, a black and white Boston terrier, and a white poodle, bark at them when they whoosh by. Tail wagging with gusto, Gigli seems to be enjoying torturing Harry with her catch-me-if-you can strategy.

"I can't believe you don't have a boyfriend. You seem you like you have your act together," Arnie continues, leaning in closer into my personal space. I back up a little on the bench to maintain my personal bubble. "Most of the guys here are more concerned about their looks than their jobs. You've got both things going for you."

"Thanks Arnie. That's sweet of you. I think I'm okay looking, nothing like the Hollywood actors that star in the movies I review. It's a pain in the ass dating in Miami. I just haven't met the kind of guy who sends ripples of goose bumps all over my skin or makes my heart melt, someone who inspires me and gets me excited about seeing him again. You know, sort of the way Racso and Cindy do." As I say this, Arnie's grin vanishes. He looks serious as if he just realized that I'm not into him. I should have watched my words more carefully. I just made it painfully obvious I don't like him that way. If this were a movie right now, it would be called *The Crush*, like that movie with pre-pubescent Alicia Silverstone. Come to think of it, Cary Elwes played a writer in that film. Hopefully, Arnie is not Alicia-crazy like in that movie.

"Oh. I just thought there might have been a chance for us to get to know each other better or something. You just seem like such a nice guy Ray, talented too, and smart. I don't meet guys like you that often. Most guys here don't take me seriously because of my height," he says, looking down.

Ay dios! I feel really shitty right now, but I can't date Arnie because I feel bad for him. I can't imagine what it must be like for Arnie to date in such a vapid place as Miami. You're judged like a book cover here. If you don't grab someone's attention in a good way, you might as well not go out. It sounds callous, but it's true. I can imagine what the queens here in Miami must think when they see Arnie at a bar climbing up on a stool for a drink. I bet if Arnie lived in another city, maybe in the Northeast, which isn't as looks-obsessed as Miami, he would have better luck meeting guys.

"I'm sorry Arnie, but I don't see things escalating here beyond a friendship. I have to tell it like it is. I usually know right away." I look at Arnie. A sadness leaks from his eyes. Ouch!

"Then why did you agree to hang out this afternoon if you weren't interested?"

Oh great, he wants a review of the whole situation. If someone's not interested, they're not interested. There's no way around that. Why even bother to ask? Who wants to know why they were rejected, what they lacked? I wouldn't want to know. I'd move on. But it's usually me who's not interested, so I haven't really been on the other side of the situation.

"Because you seem like a nice guy and because Cindy thinks very highly of you. I love Cindy to death, and I trust Cindy's judgment, even though she's dating my cocky brother. She's allowed one flaw, you know."

"Ah, ok."

In this moment of thick awkwardness, my hero saves the day.

"Is that you Ray? I thought I saw Gigli running around or more like running away from an overweight bulldog. Someone needs to put *that* dog on a Purina TRIMSPA." It's Ted with a big fat smirk on his face, approaching us with little Max in tow, trotting like he knows he's the hottest dog in the park, like his owner.

I try and act surprised.

"Oh hey, Ted! What brings you out here? This is Arnie, a friend of Cindy's from work." Ted sizes him up. I want to bust out laughing, but I can't. I don't want to be rude to Arnie. I may not be into him, but I'm not an asshole either.

"Nice to meet you Arnie. Any friend of Cindy's is a friend of mine." They shake hands.

"You're the Channel 7 reporter, right? I see you on the eleven o'clock show. Good reporting. Dramatic sometimes, but it grabs my attention while I'm grading papers."

Ted feigns offense.

"Well, in this age of media distractions, from the Internet to iPods, you need to literally grab the viewer and pull them in. So I raise my voice sometimes to get people's attention, and it seems to be working. So what brings you guys out here on this splendid afternoon. The Channel 7 forecast calls for clear skies through Tuesday."

"We're here with our dogs. What about you?"

"Oh me too. I decided to bring Max out to play and then walk Lincoln Road and see who's out and about."

As we talk, Max tries to run off to play with the other dogs, but Ted hasn't unleashed him yet. He barks repeatedly toward Gigli's way to get her attention.

Arnie tries to pet Max and the chihuahua tries to bite him.

"Whoa, mean dog. '*Yo no quiero* strangers?'" Arnie asks, making fun of Max's twin in those old Taco Bell commercials.

"His bark is worse than his bite. Deep down inside, Max is a big pussy cat, like Ray. I think Max is jealous that Gigli has a new friend over there. Is that your dog?"

"Yeah, the fat bulldog, as you said, the one that's about to collapse. They're not very physically active. They have trouble breathing too, but they're the sweetest, gentlest giants around."

"He's well, so wide," Ted says, using his hands to show how wide. "But a cute face. I'm going to let Max play with them."

The moment Ted unhooks Max, he rockets toward Gigli. They start jumping all over each other like two long lost friends. Poor Harry. He's given up. He lays on the grass, his tongue dangling like a small red carpet unfolding and his legs splattered in opposite directions on the ground. From my perch at the bench, I can hear him breathing heavily.

Arnie walks over to Harry and brings him some water from his Evian bottle, leaving me and Ted alone for a few minutes.

"Oh my gosh, you were right. He's a Teletubby! Now I know why you're not into him," Ted says, taking the seat next to me on the bench.

"Shh! Don't say that too loud, Ted. Yeah, he's a little guy. Nice and all but not for me and not because of the height disparity, okay?"

"Actually, come to think of it, he kind of looks like his dog, short and stocky and somewhat dorky."

Ted always cheers me up. He's literally saved the day by being here. Now things won't be so awkward because Ted knows how to fill the air with some witty or catty comment, the same way he does on *Deco Time*. He always makes me laugh.

"So how much longer do you have on this doomed date? I say by the looks of Harry, not much longer. The dog is completely wiped out." Ted leans back on the park bench and puts his arm around my neck as if to playfully choke me.

"Probably a little while longer. I've been bored here with Arnie. I'd rather do something else."

"Well, our book club meeting is later today, at six. Do you still want to go? I finally finished *Boys of Boston*, and I'm a little more than halfway into *Mysterious Skin*," Ted says, wiggling his eyebrows excitedly. He just wants to see Richard, the handsome coordinator of the book club, again.

"Yeah, I'm up for that. I almost forgot that it was tonight. I finished reading both books. *Boys of Boston* was a fun read. It got me excited for our trip to Boston. Thanks for reminding me. We can meet there, once I drop off Gigli at my parents house. Papi and Mami miss babying her. She's the closest thing they have to a grandchild these days. My mom also is ironing my suit for the trip, so I have to go there anyway."

"Deal! Let's get there a little early, like five forty-five so we can scope out the place," Ted says, getting up and wiping the back of his cargo shorts, in case they got any dirt on them from the bench.

"While we're at the bookstore, I want to pick up a map of Boston," I tell Ted as a chorus of barks echoes in the background. "Our gay journalism convention trip to Boston is next week, and I want to be prepared as much as I can to see all the historical hot spots."

"Ray, you won't need to buy any map. I'll be your human MapQuest. I know Boston like the back of my hand. We're going to have a blast. I already have some outfits picked out for the panels and workshops. We're going to hit Club Café, the place Tommy Perez writes about in his book."

"Maybe we'll meet some hotties there, since it's print and broadcast gay journalists. Maybe Anderson Cooper will be there?"

"I doubt it, Ray."

I start laughing as Ted gets up, and Arnie walks our way carrying Harry.

"I think he's done for the day. I'm going to get him home. He doesn't look too good," Arnie says, concern painted all over his face.

"Yeah, he looks exhausted. Poor Harry. I guess he had a hard time keeping up with princess Gigli and Max." Ted pets Harry's head. Meanwhile, Max and Gigli sprint around our section of the park, like two mini-greyhounds or gayhounds.

"Well, Ray, it was nice hanging out with you this afternoon and meeting Gigli. Nice meeting you, Ted." Arnie says, shaking my hand and then Ted's.

"Same here, Arnie," Ted responds.

"Yeah, I had fun Arnie. Say hi to Cindy for me in school tomorrow," I say, taking a deep drag from my second cigarette of the afternoon.

"Give me a call some time, if you want," Arnie says meekly. "Take it easy guys."

"You too!" I say.

"Au revoir!" Ted announces with his little French from the University of Miami. He only took it because he was sick of hearing me speak Spanglish in college.

Arnie walks away, cradling Harry. Ted and I call Gigli and Max back, and they race toward us. We all walk through the park and back to our cars to get ready for the book club meeting tonight.

14

Ted

"Welcome back everyone. I hope you enjoyed the two books that we're going to discuss today," says Richard, who looks to die for, as we all settle into our circle of chairs. Ray's wearing one of his infamous movie T-shirts. I'm glad he changed from the clothes he was wearing at the dog park, but he still could have worn something a little nicer than the *Apocalypto* shirt with the angry Mayan chief on the front and his Nike shorts. It's hot outside, so I don't blame him. I smell the last cigarette he smoked in my BMW on him. Thank God I had the top down because I would hate for my convertible to smell all ashy. I took a lot of notes for the *Boys of Boston* discussion. Yellow Post-its pop out of my book for me to refer to during the chat. I'm ready to analyze and impress Richard. Maybe I can get a date out of this meeting. I don't want to wait another whole month to see him again. He doesn't seem to go out, because I never see him. What does he do at home all day? I wonder what his deal is.

"So who wants to begin?" Richard asks the group, which is made up of the same guys—the baldie with the glasses, the serious Dominican guy, three other fugly guys wearing similar bowling-type shirts, Ray, me and (sigh!) Richard.

"Well, I thought the book was an easy read. Very conversational. Being a Bay State boy, I thought Tommy Perez captured the voice and the rhythm of Boston, which is not easy to do for an outsider. I really enjoyed the romance between him and the cute South Shore blue-eyed boy. It was very Nicholas Sparks. I'm a big romantic at heart," I say. All eyes are transfixed on me. I see Ray looking down, smirking, and trying to hold in his giggles. He's not doing a good job of it. I jab him quickly with my elbow, and he coughs.

"That's an interesting observation, Ted. So you found that the book was authentic to Boston, even though the author is a Cuban from Miami? Yes, I too enjoyed the blossoming romance between the Cuban character and his all-American boyfriend. It was very real," Richard says, rubbing his tanned, hairy kneecap with his right hand as he holds the book with his left. He's looking right at me. I know he wants me. I can feel it.

"I wasn't that much into the romantic aspect of the book," Ray pipes in, now that his giggles have waned. "What intrigued me the most was the relationship the Cuban guy had with his family in Miami and how accepting they are of him being gay. You don't hear a lot of that. There's still very much a taboo don't-ask-and-I-won't-tell-you-how-gay-I-am policy in Hispanic families. Tommy breaks that by showing the character's parents traveling to Boston to spend Thanksgiving with his boyfriend's Irish-Italian family on the Cape."

Everyone in the group seems enlightened by what Ray says because they're all nodding or rubbing their chins as if they're deep in thought. I try and steer the discussion back to the romance and moi.

"But wasn't it sweet how the Cuban guy and his boyfriend decided to make gifts for the holidays instead of spending money on each other? Then they decide to use the money they were going to spend and buy toys for needy Boston children. That just tickled my Portuguese heart. I'd love to do that with my next boyfriend, giving to charity during the holidays. It brings people together. I can totally see this being a movie, right Ray?"

"Well, not a movie *per se*. Maybe a TV show on LOGO or

something. It's written in short scenes with punchy and breezy dialogue," Ray says.

We continue talking about the book's plot, and the surprise double-twist near the end in Provincetown. Then we move on to *Mysterious Skin*. But since a lot of the guys didn't finish it, we decide to hold that over for the next meeting.

As the gathering comes to a close, we all get up, stretch, and shake hands. I walk across Books & Books to Richard's side and flirt with him.

"So Richard . . . would you want to hang out sometime, you know, just me and you, us, alone, for dinner, drink, or dessert? We can talk more about the book or other stuff. I know this great little place in South Miami . . ." I tell him, leaning closely toward him. I can smell his minty breath from the gum he popped inside his mouth. I also smell a whiff of some musky cologne or aftershave. Ray grabs some coffee from the café as I talk to Richard.

Just as I tell Richard about this cute eatery in South Miami, he cuts me off.

"Sorry Ted, I think the book discussions should remain in the book club so that members don't get the wrong idea," he says, folding his arms which defines his round tight biceps sprinkled with freckles. As my eyes scroll down from his biceps to his forearms and finally to his hands, I notice there's a ring, a *wedding* ring? Huh?

"I don't go out much anyway. Bill, my partner of ten years, and I are usually home taking care of our two children, Matt and Mikey. They're a handful. Want to see photos? They're eight years old now," he says enthusiastically. He opens his wallet and unveils his perfect all-American gay family.

"Oh," is the only response I can muster. "I didn't know you had a partner. I'm so sorry for flirting with you. I sometimes get carried away. I didn't mean any disrespect to you, your partner and your boys." I feel like such a dufus. This is worse than the time I referred to Aretha Franklin as Urethra on a story and everyone in the studio started laughing out loud. How did I not notice the ring before? Ray comes back with his steaming black coffee. He picks up on the situation and saves me.

"*Oye*, Ted, I think we should get going. I need a ride back to my parents' house to pick up Gigli," he says, putting his hand on my upper back.

"Richard, we'll see you at the next discussion next month," Ray says. "Good seeing you."

"Yeah, same here. Keep reading *Mysterious Skin*. It's a sexy yet layered book about adolescence in Kansas and how coming to terms with your past helps your present even if it might involve UFOs and aliens," he says.

I just wave to Richard and give him my fake *Deco Time* smile. My shoes stomp against the bookstore's tile as Ray pulls me outside.

"Nice going Big Head Ted! You totally threw yourself at the dude like a cheap slut on Biscayne Boulevard. Next time, ask a guy if he's single before you make your move," Ray says, lighting up another cigarette, rolling his eyes, and taking a deep drag.

"Well, he gave off the single vibe. Who knew? At least I tried. I had so many hopes with his guy. He's totally my type, all Boston-blue collar like."

"*Oye*, we're going to see the real thing Thursday in Boston at the gay journalism convention, so forget about Richard. It was an honest mistake. You'll be over this, in what, five minutes," Ray chides me. We start laughing as we walk back to my BMW and get on our way to Ray's parents' house.

"Yeah, you're right. Richard wasn't *all* that. Oh who am I kidding . . . yes he was. But we're bound to meet some cuties in Beantown."

As I turn the ignition, Ray and I look at each other and shout, "Boston, here we come!" and we high-five each other.

15

Ray

After I watched Ted shamelessly throw himself at the book club organizer only to learn that the guy has been in a committed relationship for ten years and has absolutely zero interest in Ted, I drive back to my parent's house to pick up Gigli and my suit for the upcoming journalism conference.

Whenever I stroll up the bricked walkway to the front door, I feel like a teenager coming home from school or a night out all over again. I hear Mami in the kitchen talking to Gigli as if she were a baby girl.

"Now Gigli, show me how jou sit. Bery good. Now go and give Oscar the ball to play with jou," she says.

"Bery good Gigli! Bery good *preciosa!*" I hear her say, and I see Gigli running across the living room to Papi's bedroom with a ball in her mouth.

Mami spots me as I make my way into the kitchen. She comes over and hugs me.

"*Cómo estas* Raysito? How was jour afternoon?" she asks, as she makes me a turkey sandwich. I don't even have to ask for it. She knows I want one.

"Ah, it was okay. Racso and Cindy introduced me to this teacher that she works with at the school. We went to the park with our dogs this afternoon."

"Did jou like him? If he's a friend of Cindy's, he must be *buena gente* Ray." Mami carefully smears mayo on both sides of the bread covering every inch. She tightly rolls up the slices of turkey and tucks them in between the bread.

"Yeah, he's nice Mami, but I don't like him like that. He's not for me." I always feel awkward talking to Mami about these things, but she seems to be willing to drag it out of me. I suspect she enjoys hearing about my dates with men to substitute for the talks she has with Racso about dating Cindy.

"Jou have to go with what feels right, Raysito. When jou meet the right muchacho, jou will know like I knew when I met tu papa. Jou heart will tell jou and jou won't have any doubt." She cuts the sandwich in half and adds some potato chips to the side of the pink plate. We walk over to the table in the pantry, and she pours some Sprite in a tall glass for me. We sit down. I love being back at home. It reminds me of when I was little and Mami would make us lunch on the weekends after Racso and I went bike riding along the lush verdant green golf course at the Biltmore Hotel.

"*Gracias* Mami. I believe that too. I just hung out with Arnie as a favor to Cindy."

"Like I said, when jou least expect it, bam!" she says, clapping her hands in a thunderous sonic boom to emphasize her point. "Jou will meet the right guy. I was talking to Emi the other day, and she read my cards, and jou know what came up, Raysito? Jou came up and the cards said that jou would meet someone bery especial soon *y super lindo. Un escritor* too."

Mami and her best friend Emi are into tarot card readings, and Emi has always been dead-on in her predictions—like when she told Mami that I would be a movie critic at the *News* or when she said that Racso would meet a beautiful young woman in college named Cindy. This is one of their hobbies when they're not listening to the dirty jokes on Spanish radio and giggling like two schoolgirls. It's just as funny watching them in the act, proving that no matter how old you are, you can be hilariously free-spirited.

"At first, I thought the cards were talking about Racso but

Emi showed me how it was about you and another muchacho. I was so happy when I saw that. I want jou to be happy and with someone who cares about you," Mami says, filing her red-polished nails and looking up at me whenever she talks. "The cards said he was going to make jou feel something jou've never felt before but let's not talk about it too *mush* because that could be bad luck. Emi also said jou and the muchacho would face some difficulties, but let me stop talking. The more jou talk about things, the less they will happen. Remember, keep this to jourself Raysito, okay?"

"*Oye*, you can't leave me hanging like that. What does he look like? What happens?" I ask her, as I chow down my sandwich and munch the salty chips.

Just as she's about to answer or dodge my question (Mami is good at doing that), Papi comes in. Gigli is trotting right behind him and jumping on his leg. Mami and I change the subject. Papi hates it when Mami does her tarot readings with Emi or her secret religious things like walking around the house with a bunch of blessed flower stems and branches or smoking a thick cigar to rid the house of any evil. My mother would never admit this, but I know she's a Santera, a follower of the Afro-Cuban religion. Most older Cubans are. They just don't talk about it, like they don't talk about their son being the only (known) gay in the family. Santeras just practice the religion on the down low. Papi doesn't buy into any of that. He also doesn't like hearing about me being with guys. It's that whole Latino code of silence. Papi loves me and accepts me, but he doesn't want to know the details. He has even told me so.

"Jou are homosexual, but I don't want to see you dressed like a woman or talking about *pingas* or whatever it is you people do. No one needs to know that jou are *un maricón*. Keep it to yourself when you come into this house," he told me once. In fact, he's never met anyone I've dated because I wanted to avoid the potential awkwardness of the whole situation.

"Raysito, how's my handsome *hijo*?" Papi says, patting me on the back and kissing the top of my hair. Gigli runs up to me and puts her paws on my knee. I pet her playfully as her tongue wags.

"Doing good Papi. Just here with Mami talking about work and stuff."

Mami gets up to make Papi some food as he sits down across from me and plays with Gigli. We talk about my movie reviews and Papi's latest roach encounters from exterminating the hotels on the beach.

"The cucarachas were falling from the ceiling and flying out of the cabinets. It was raining cucarachas in that apartment. When I drove here, there were some on my shirt," Papi says, all animated as he describes his latest battle with Florida's renowned insect.

As Papi continues his roach tale, I can't help but think about what Mami told me a few minutes ago. I start imagining what kind of guy I am going to fall in love with, what his name is, and what he looks like. For the rest of the night, I catch myself smiling at the thought and about my upcoming trip to Boston with Ted.

16

Ted

Ahh, Boston. The cobblestoned streets. The snow-caked Storrow Drive. The sculpted college rowers plowing the Charles River, their puffs of cold breath marking their trails. (I can follow those trails to their happy trails.) The towering Prudential and John Hancock buildings rise in the New England sky like glass fingers clawing into the sky, dwarfing all the diminutive Victorian and brick buildings in Back Bay and Fenway. It's good to be home. Forty degree weather is pleasant here, a chance to wear a nice coat or a cardigan from Lord & Taylor. In Miami, winter means sixty degrees, and it's unforgiving. It's at the top of the newscasts, on the front page of the *News*, and the number one topic at every Cuban café counter. Miamians freak out and buy bundles of logs to fire up their dusty fireplaces. Even the palm trees seem like they're shivering miserably.

I arrived last night with Ray, and we checked into the Colonnade Hotel on Huntington Avenue where tony Back Bay and the uber-gay South End intersect. Ray visited Boston years ago when I was a reporter for the local Channel 7. But he always got lost in The Hub, so I agreed to drive the rental car last night. Ray's biggest complaint about Boston: "*Oye*, the streets go by names. They're not numerical like Miami. So if you don't know where one street is, you're not going to know how to find the other. What were these, cow paths?"

And then there was his other complaint: "*Oye*, what's up with these rotaries? They are like the car version of revolving doors. Why don't they have traffic lights?"

Because we arrived late last night, there wasn't enough time to go out and hit the scene. We did have dinner at one of my favorite places, Bertucci's. It's an Italian chain restaurant in New England, and they serve the best bread rolls ever. After dinner, I returned to my room and collapsed. I knew I had a full schedule for the next two days. I'm supposed to man the Channel 7 booth for the job fair for two hours and rotate with other staffers from our sister station in Boston. I also was booked as a panelist for a discussion called "Off Camera: The Challenges of LGBT TV Anchors and Reporters."

It's 11 a.m., and I'm on my way to the session. I walk through the lobby of the Colonnade Hotel to the convention hall where the conference is being staged. About six hundred gay journalists, editors and photographers are expected here. Ray said he would meet up with me later because he wants to drop by the job fair and drop off his resume and clips at *The New York Times* and *Entertainment Weekly* booths. I don't think for one second he would ever leave Miami and his super-clingy Cuban family behind, but I encouraged him to at least get his name out there beyond South Florida. Who knows, he may get an offer that he can't say no to.

I make my way deeper into the hotel to the registration booth. I pick up my convention badge and bag, which is full of promotional goodies like pens from NBC, notepads, cardholders, paperweights and magnets from the different news organizations. My favorite: the small reporter pads from CNN.

It's been a few years since I've attended this gay journalism conference. Since it was being held in Beantown this year, I couldn't resist. This would be a good chance to meet new people, engage in heavy dialogue, and share in our newsroom and gay experiences. I could also take a quick road trip to Sandwich and see my family Saturday morning.

"Hey Ted, welcome to the convention. So good to see you," says Thomas Roberts, the hunkiest reporter on TV. He's one of the few guys on TV who looks better in person than on his newscasts. As he hugs me and pats me on the back, I feel the boulder-hardness of his through his shirt.

"Long time no see, Thomas!" My, he looks dapper-casual in his tight-fitting black Polo shirt and khaki pants that perfectly define his bum. I'm in a white dress shirt, pink tie, and black slacks. Donald Trump has nothing on me.

"We're both on the same panel. This should be fun. I hate doing these things, but I know they're for a good cause, to inspire younger gay reporters. I stuck my head in a minute ago and the meeting room is packed!" Thomas says, towering over me with his six-foot-two frame. As we chat, other gay men swoon and do double-takes when they spot this gorgeous creature in front of me. It's one of the rare times I feel invisible. "They're bringing more chairs inside. Let's go in and get settled," the former CNN hunk says.

We stroll into the meeting room and take our perch on the panel, along with three other anchor and reporters. There's the adorable Itay Hod from LOGO. He has always reminded me of the cute guy on CBS's *NCIS*. He's such a ham, but aren't we all because we are on TV. The pages of a newspaper aren't big enough to contain our colorful personalities and bigger egos. There's Randy Price, from Boston's Channel 7. He's my old mentor and he always grand-marshals the annual Boston Pride Parade. We get started and the journalists or wanna-be journalists in the audience start tossing their questions at us. I get the first one. I guess I still have some fans in Boston.

"Mr. Williams, is it hard being gay off-camera? Has the fact that you're gay hindered your job opportunities?" a green-eyed young man with a blonde buzz cut and matching goatee asks me from the third row.

I take a sip of water and gladly answer him. I really want to do something else to him, like plop a big kiss on those soft red lips, but there will be plenty of time for that later at Club Café.

Here I go.

"I'm fortunate to work for a company where being gay is a non-issue. South Florida is diverse in so many ways. I've hosted the annual AIDS Walk in Miami, and like Randy, I've been the grand marshal of the Pride Parade. Every now and then, I do receive some nasty emails from some homophobes, but I've developed a thick skin and have learned to move on. If you're in this business, you have to learn that not every one will agree with you or like you."

Thomas Roberts jumps in as I take another sip of water. He speaks in his calm and compassionate voice, something that endeared him to his viewers on CNN. Too bad it wasn't enough to keep him on air. He's now on *The Insider*, reporting on how the latest pop tartlet is ruining her life.

"Our personal lives shouldn't be an issue on air. We're journalists. We're objective. We focus on the story at hand," he says, all eyes fixed on his every word and vein-defining bicep.

He continues to talk about the time he came out to one of his co-workers at CNN a few years ago.

"Are you involved with anyone?" he recalls her asking him.

Then he told her his partner's name, and he got this reaction.

"Oh . . . oh . . . OH!" she had told him.

Everyone in the audience erupts in laughter. Thomas blushes a little, and he continues. I love this guy, but he's hogging up the discussion. Whenever I want to jump in, he keeps talking. Media *hog*!

"I've been in a relationship for the past eight years. I had been all buttoned up before about being out at work," he says, leaning closer into his microphone. The men in the audience all gaze at him with saucer eyes.

"It's about timing yourself with your honesty . . . and owning it," he says of coming out at work.

Everyone applauds including Randy Price, Itay, and me.

"At LOGO, well, we're all out so it doesn't affect us that much. But I think I would probably have a hard time being taken seriously if I wanted to jump to CBS News or another major news network," Itay says. I agree with him. Every correspondent at LOGO is obviously gay. In a way, they've pigeonholed themselves as gay reporters.

A chubby man in his early thirties with thick curly hair asks Itay a follow up question.

"Would you want to jump to another network or are you happy at LOGO? It's a great channel, and you give us the kind of news that we're interested in hearing," the man asks.

Itay smiles like a Cheshire cat. He snatches the spotlight off Thomas Roberts for a little bit.

"I'm happy being a LOGO journalist. We covered the Gay Games. Can you really see NBC or, ahem, CNN, for that matter doing that story. Um, I don't think so!" he says. "We go where the major news outlets don't dare to."

After an hour of more questions such as the lack of lesbian broadcast journalists, we wrap up the discussion. I sign some autographs from guys who come over to pass the time as they wait in line to meet Thomas Roberts and uber-cute Itay. Not that I blame them.

It's about noon, and I excuse myself from the other panelists with air kisses. I then head over to meet up with Ray in the job fair next door.

"Take it easy, Ted. I'll catch ya later," Thomas says, firmly shaking my hand and giving me a hug. I smell the Dolce & Gabana cologne on him, which makes me horny.

Randy hugs me as well.

"I'll see you my friend at Club Café tonight, like old times," says Randy, still handsome at fifty-eight with his snow-white, short cropped hair, twinkling blue eyes, and gray mustache. He's the oldest and yet most popular anchor in the Boston market, and he still delivers the top ratings at 11 p.m. He gives me hope that I may have a long professional shelf life in this industry. But more than that, he's been with the same man for thirty-one years. He's my professional and personal hero.

I stroll out of the conference room (I only signed one autograph) and walk into the hall next door where dozens of booths represent the various news organizations. Tie-wearing men and women in business suits and skirts armed with their resumes browse the various tables. There's NBC, *The Boston Daily*, ESPN, and *The Miami News* to name a few. I spot Ray standing at the *News*'s booth chatting with an editor there.

"Yeah, this is great. This is my first time here. Who knew there were so many gay journalists?" Ray tells Steve, the paper's Metro editor.

"Yeah, everyone comes out of the closet for this convention. It's like a journalists' circuit party," Steve responds with a laugh. Ray is sharing in the joke when he turns around and sees me.

"Hey, so how was your panel?" he asks, wearing a long-sleeved chambray blue dress shirt, a black sports jacket, blue jeans and sneakers. That's Ray for you. He never dresses up. He gets away with almost dressing up.

"It went well. Thomas Roberts got most of the questions, but it was a great session. I heard we were the most packed of the sessions so far."

"Yeah, I heard people raving about it for a few minutes as they walked by. So what's next on the agenda Mr. Beantown?" Ray asks, showing me his bag of convention collectibles. He holds up a small fuzzy moose with *NYT* on its sweater that he picked from *The New York Times* booth and a mouse pad from *People* magazine. I also see a folder from Harvard.

"Are you planning to go to Harvard or something?" I ask Ray. "Aren't you a little old to do that now?"

He pulls out the folder and smiles.

"You never know. They have the annual Nieman Foundation fellowships for journalists. They pick a group of journalists every year to focus on a particular field while taking classes at Harvard. The booth caught my eye, and the director gave me some literature on the program," Ray says, leafing through the application form.

"Oh please, Ray! I know you. You wouldn't be able to stand a Boston winter. You would leave after the first snow fall. Besides, aren't you happy at the *News*?"

He looks up and starts to put the pamphlets away into the NBC bag he picked up from their booth.

"I am, but the way print is going these days, jobs like mine are disappearing as fast as the marshlands in the Everglades. And I'm not interested in writing for a Miami Web site in the near future where my copy will be shorter and more blog-like. Not that I think I'm in trouble, but who knows what doors could open or what job security Harvard can give me. Imagine me, studying film criticism in Cambridge, where so many movies have been filmed. Call me *Legally Cuban*," he says, laughing at his own joke. "And I can tell Racso and my parents that I went to *Hah-vard*," he says, extending Harvard into words with a Cuban Boston accent if such a thing ever existed.

"Besides, you loved living in Boston. I know you miss it, Ted," he says.

He's right. I do miss living here, the seasons, the intense conversations at Starbucks or at bars. Boston is the number seven news market in the country, but living here was too difficult after my break-up with Louie. Everywhere I went, there were reminders of our relationship, our first date in the North End at La Dolce Vita, our runs along the Charles River, our brunches on Tremont Street, our hiking trips to the Blue Hills. Sometimes, memories are like their own beings, with strong presences that are difficult to ignore and escape. Boston held too many of those reminders in my daily life. Miami seemed to be the place for me after our break-up, a place to start over. It's my home now, but I still sometimes fantasize about being the anchor at WCVB-TV Channel 5, now that Natalie Jacobson retired and if the station could ever imagine having a person of color as a main solo anchor. I grew up watching Natalie and her former husband Chet Curtis anchor the evening news. The station remains number one in New England in total viewers except at 11 p.m. (that belongs to the Boston Channel 7) and continues to be the most respected for its traditional journalism. Not that I'm unhappy at Channel 7, but it caters to a different audience, one that is more interested in fast and flashy news. I want to aspire to something more than the big Seven. Besides, we can't capture the same numbers as Univision which is number one in South Florida. But for now, I'm staying put. I never had the name or face recognition in Boston that I do in Miami. I'm a brand in South Florida, and I can't ask for more that at this point in my career. I owe that all to Channel 7, the most progressive and contemporary news company.

Just as I'm about to tell Ray that we're gonna meet up at 9 p.m. for dinner at Club Café and then head to the bar in back for some drinks, an enthusiastic cute younger guy, about twenty-one or so, interrupts us.

"Excuse me. My name is Ronnie Reyes, and I'm a student reporter with the convention's newspaper. I'm writing a story about the lack of gay minorities in newsrooms and the challenges of recruiting them for print and TV newsrooms. I was hoping I could ask both of you some questions for my article," he says pleading with his eyes for us to give him some feedback for this article. It seems like there aren't many gay minorities here which is typical. By minorities, I mean journalists of color, and this gay convention tends to be a white-man's country club. Aw, this is guy is so cute with his thick black eyebrows, light brown eyes, and dark brown wavy black hair combed back. When he talks or smiles, you can see a small gap in between his two front teeth. He has good energy, as Brian would say.

Ray's eyes seem locked on Ronnie's, and I can tell he's smitten right away with the guy's boyish yet masculine demeanor which reminds me of a younger Cuban John Stamos.

"Sure, fire away!" Ray says, eyeballing him from head to toe with a silly grin on his face.

Ronnie smiles, flips the page on his reporter's pad, and begins his interview.

"Why do you think there is a lack of minority journalists in today's newsrooms? Do you find that it's harder for them or for yourselves to be out and open at work?" Ronnie asks both of us, but Ray gladly answers first.

"*Bueno*, I'm a movie critic at *The Miami News*, and while we do have some gay people there, not all of them feel very comfortable being out and open on the job and that includes those journalists who happen to be Hispanic, black, or Asian. They don't want their gayness to be the most interesting thing about them," Ray says as Ronnie looks down at his pad and jots down everything Ray says in a chicken-scratch shorthand.

"Wait, you're Ray, as in Ray Martinez, the critic? I read your reviews all the time, although I disagreed with you on the *Miami Vice II* piece. It was a muscular and kinetic movie. You barely gave it three stars. I would have at least given it three and half. The movie was about Miami. You gotta represent."

"Good memory," I jump in. "So you're from Miami too?"

Ronnie turns my way. My gosh, this guy is cute, but I can tell Ray is somehow affected by him, in a good way, and I don't want to interrupt the nice exchange they have going on between their words and their eyes. Ronnie looks at Ray with admiration.

"Yeah, I grew up in Hialeah. I'm Cuban-American. I go to FIU where I'm majoring in journalism. I'm a senior. I also work at the *News* as a part-time intern for the Beach community section. I write those stories about city hall and quirky profiles of Beach people, you know. I won a trip to come to the gay conference by interning here for the convention newspaper. This is my first time here," Ronnie says, smiling and looking down.

Ray looks like he finally recognizes who this young guy is.

"*Oye*, I know who you are now. I recognize your byline. I saw the story you wrote on the woman who plays matchmaker at the beach laundromat. Your lede was clever, something like 'She's the coin laundry cupid.' You're a good writer, Ronnie. You produce a lot for the *News*. You're well on your way," Ray says, his smile getting bigger and his blue eyes scrutinizing every aspect of Ronnie's face. I can tell that something is hatching—whether an attraction or a commonality, between them so I decide to add my two cents for his story and disappear. What are the chances of bumping into another gay Cuban from Miami in Boston?

"Back to your question Ronnie, I would agree with Ray. At Channel 7 in Miami, we have a lot of gay producers and writers but not many are out. Like Ray said, it's a personal choice to be out professionally. When you're on camera, you want to be remembered for your story, not your sexuality. I'm Portuguese-American, but because of my skin tone, I'm thought of as a person of color, but I am proud to be gay too. But that's just a part of me," I tell Ronnie, as he scribbles furiously on his reporter's pad.

"Wow, this is great Mr. Williams. You guys gave me a lot of good quotes for my story. I'm hoping I can add this to my portfolio," Ronnie says.

"Well, it was nice meeting you, Ronnie. I'm grabbing lunch with a colleague of mine, but stay here with Ray. I'm sure he can give you advice about getting hired at the paper when you graduate, and I'm sure you guys can talk about being gay and Cuban and stuff."

Ray winks at me as if sending me a mental *gracias*. Ronnie gladly shakes my hand and gives me a business card that he fashioned himself. It says "Ronnie Reyes, freelance writer" with an image of an old typewriter in the back. How cute. There's something endearing about Ronnie that goes beyond his looks. He's got spunk!

I wink back at Ray and hand Ronnie my card with the big Seven on it next to my name and the rainbow peacock in the background to represent our parent network.

"If you need anything, just email or call me. Ray, I'll see you tonight at Club Café. I'll swing by your room at 8:30, and we'll walk over to the restaurant/bar or *bah* as they say *heah*."

I walk away smiling as Ray and Ronnie head toward a small area of sofas in the corner of the job fair hall as they continue gabbing. So Ray met a nice boy here. I wonder if I'm going to meet anyone here tonight as well. Either way, it's good to be back in Beantown. Home.

17

Brian

I haven't been hanging out with the guys lately. Last time I spoke to Ray, they were heading to Boston for a gay journalists convention. I miss meeting up with them, and I feel bad about it but it's for a good reason and his name is Eros.

As Daniel has been swamped with work for the past two weeks in New York for his printing businesses, I've been busy with Eros. If he's not cooking for me or massaging my back, he makes me feel so sexually alive with the faintest touch of his hand. I haven't had time for much else besides watching the construction guys work on the driveway in front of the house. I can tell the workers are probably wondering what is going on since Eros has been spending a lot of time here. They know I'm with Daniel so they probably think Eros is my secret boyfriend, and in some ways, he has been. In our phone conversations, I've kept Daniel in the dark about Eros. I'm just not ready to tell him I've fallen for this Puerto Rican creature who understands me so well, mentally, spiritually, and physically.

I do love Daniel, but I've come to realize that I haven't been in love with him for a long time. If I had felt the same way or if Daniel was still in love with me, we'd be monogamous, right? I'm lying by the pool on this sun-soaked afternoon, looking out at the glistening Biscayne Bay, and pondering my life. I rim the top of my glass filled with vodka and cranberry, and I realize I only want to have sex with Eros. No one else. He's at work this afternoon. He spent the night, and we had another sex-athon. It's almost like an addiction for me. I just can't get enough of his smooth dark tanned skin, his white teeth, and his curly hair as it tickles my face. It's as if our bodies, our souls, were together in another life and have found each other once again. I feel in my heart that Eros came my way for a reason. Sometimes, I see a future with Eros, but other times I feel somewhat confused by his words. For one, there's the whole bisexual thing even though he lets me top him most of the time. I can feel that he's gay, but he says that I wouldn't understand his whole bisexuality because I'm not Latino like he is.

"In my family and culture, it's not cool to be gay. Gay men are considered to be *maricones, patos*, faggots. People look down on them in Puerto Rico. And I like getting it on with a girl every now and then. It feels good too," Eros said last night in bed.

"But you like cock, specifically mine. Maybe you're not ready to deal with it, but I know in my heart of hearts that you're gay. You said the other day how much you want to have a wedding one day. What straight man says that? Only a gay man or a woman would say that," I told him. I was laying down with his feet propped up against my chest. I massaged his legs while he massaged my toes at the opposite end of the bed.

"I do want a wedding one day, but I can't picture it with another guy. Sorry, Brian. As much as I've grown to care about you in such a short time, I just don't see myself settling down with a guy in that way. I do have feelings for you, which I've never had for another man. This is all new to me *chico*."

His resistance to being totally gay only fuels my resolve to get him to see the light, the rainbow light that he's a cock-sucking faggot. I'm very intuitive, and I can sense with every bone in my body that Eros is emotionally and physically drawn to men. He doesn't even look at attractive women when we go out. So that's one of the issues I've been having with Eros, his denial about being gay.

The other thing is money. I've noticed that every now and then, he expects—no he assumes—I will pay for everything. I know he's a waiter and all, but he should at least make the effort to try and pay.

The other day, we were eating at La Carreta restaurant in Little Havana, and Eros ordered the fried plantains and tostones as appetizers in addition to the breaded chicken steak and pitcher of sangria. When the bill came later for forty dollars he didn't even try to fetch his wallet to pay some of it. He sat back and thanked for me dinner and winked. Another time, we went to the Miami Seaquarium to see the dolphins and whales leap through the air. I thought it would be something fun for us to do as a couple, and we had a blast dodging the splashes of the whales and marveling the slithering stingrays as they cruised in the giant tank off Key Biscayne. But again, I had to pay the twenty-five dollar cover for each of us and the hotdogs and drinks we bought there. Whenever I feel like he's interested in me for the money, we ended up having incredible sex that night and I forget—for the time being—these little annoyances. I just wish he'd put some more effort, that's all. I feel like I do all the heavy lifting to see him. I pick him up from his apartment. (I still haven't been inside because of his so-called straight roommate.) I have to drive Eros back after we spend the day or the night together. Of course, I drive to wherever we go since Eros doesn't have a car. That's a whole other issue. When I look at Eros, I realize how independent and successful Daniel is. But when I think of Daniel, I realize how much I want to be intimate with Eros. I have this rush of emotions swaying back and forth in my head and in my heart, like the waves crashing up against my seawall here behind the house.

The phone rings in the house, and I lazily get up from my cushy lounge chair and walk over to the kitchen to answer it.

"Brian, it's Daniel. How's my baby? How's the driveway coming along today?"

"Hi, Daniel. Everything's good. Just here lounging by the pool keeping an eye on our never-ending renovations."

I lean forward against the marble white counter, and I notice that Eros left behind a note that says *"Happy Thursday* lindo*! Love, Eros!"* What a sweet note. I smile as I hold it in my hands.

"I haven't seen you in three weeks, and I miss you. I'll be down there later today. I'm having a long weekend. I'm too stressed out from overseeing my workers. Some are so lazy, and it's costing me money. I had to fire three people this week. Luckily, I have good managers to help me handle everything but still. It's aggravating me to the point this week."

"Don't worry about it Daniel. You probably did the right thing in letting them go if they weren't producing enough. Anyway, I would love to see you. I've missed you too." I fold Eros's note and put it the back pocket of my cargo shorts.

Daniel goes on to tell me that he'll land at 6 p.m. at Opa-locka Airport.

"I'll pick you up in the Land Rover. I can't wait to see you. We have a lot to catch up on," I say.

"Yes, we do. I want to hear about everything you've been up to down there. I can sense you've been quite busy."

Yes I have.

After I pick Daniel from the airport, we head back to the house. The whole ride, he's venting about work.

"And Raul took three hours off for lunch. I had it with him. I'd given him a warning before. So I fired him. He was holding up our presses with his long breaks," Daniel says.

As he releases his work rants, I hold his masculine strong left hand and rub the top of it to comfort him. I can tell work has really stressed out Daniel, and I need to do my best to give him a nice relaxing weekend. We pull into the our dirt driveway since the new one is being constructed with beautiful decorative red and brown bricks. By the time it's done, it will look like a courtyard in our villa.

"Shhh. Don't talk about work. Your veins are popping out of your neck. Just relax Daniel. When we get back to the house, sit by the pool. I'll make you your favorite drink and relax. Enjoy the Miami view."

An hour later, after Daniel has showered and simmered down, I see him lounging by the pool and absorbing some soft sun rays late this afternoon. From the large glass windows in the kitchen, I see him shirtless lying in the chair with his sunglasses on. His salt and pepper hair covers some of his chest and funnels down in a perfect line to his stomach. Daniel looks like an image from an old 1950s movie or George Clooney in *The Good German*. Sometimes I forget how dashing Daniel is, yet I don't feel stimulated. I think of how Eros was just here earlier today sitting in the same spot with a pair of sunglasses reflecting the radiant South Florida light. The breeze would lift up some of his curls and harden his tan nipples. Immediately, I feel a stirring in my shorts.

"Brian come over here. I want to talk to you about something." I grab the martini I just made for him and walk it over to the pool.

I scoot beside Daniel and hand him the drink. I sense that Daniel wants to have a serious talk with me. I caress the top of his hand again and look down. I feel so mellow today like the soft puffy white clouds above us and, yet, so conflicted inside, like a storm rolling through the distant swampy Everglades.

"I know you've been with this Puerto Rican guy. I'm not stupid. I wouldn't be where I am today if not for my instincts. And remember, I know you better than you know yourself. I know you love me, and I love you too, but you need to make a decision. I am not going to put up with you hanging out with *that* Puerto Rican waiter. I'm telling you this right now, once and for all, he's only interested in our money, *my* money."

"It's our money, Daniel. I may not bring in the business or carry an income, but I *do* work, taking care of our homes and renovations and overseeing our workers." I hate when he says *my money*. It's an insult to me. It's disrespectful.

"So yeah, I've been hanging out with Eros. I know I should

have told you, but I wanted to see if this was just an over-extended trick or something else. I'm sorry to say this, Daniel, but I do have feelings for the guy. I just connect with him on so many levels, like we used to."

I can't see Daniel's eyes because of the sunglasses, but he looks the other way as I talk. For such a tough business guy, he's a tender pussycat when it comes to matters of the heart and me for that matter.

"He's going to hurt you, Brian. If you told him that I cut you off and you had no money, he would drop you like that," he says, snapping his fingers. "He's playing you."

"You haven't even met him!"

"And I'm not going to meet him. I can smell trash a mile away. You have to make a decision. It's either me or him. You can't have it both ways, Brian. I won't put up with this."

At this point, Daniel gets up and storms into the kitchen. I can tell he's pumped up with anger now because he's flailing his hands as he talks. He comes back with another martini.

"I can't believe you would risk everything we have, everything we've built together for some a waiter guy who probably doesn't even have a car."

"It's . . . it's . . . not that simple, Daniel. Things with us aren't black and white. You were the one who decided to open up our relationship so you could hook up with that tall blonde guy Lee a few years ago. I put up with that, all two weeks of that. Then you realized he was only interested in our money, oh excuse me, *your* money!"

I get up and stand in front of Daniel. We're arguing face to face. I feel his spit land on my cheek with each word. The veins in his neck are popping up again like small pieces of rope trying to surface through the skin.

"That was different. It was the first time I had hooked up with someone in our new defined relationship. After that, we decided to have the one-trick rule, remember? And you've been breaking that for who knows how long with this piece of shit. What's his name again, Dinero?"

"It's Eros, and he's a good, hard-working guy. He works at the restaurant to send money to his family in San Juan. He's not all caught up in our materialistic life."

"Oh yeah. Has he asked you for money yet? If he hasn't, he will. He probably has the dollar signs in his eyes. I bet you pay for everything with our credit card. Tell me this, does he always come here? I bet you don't even go to his apartment or anything."

I hate it when Daniel is right. He's reading me. It's our Scorpio connection.

"He hasn't asked me for any money. And yes, I treat him because I can and want to."

Daniel paces back and forth and throws his martini glass like a baseball against one of the columns that separate the living room from the patio. Oh my God, he's really angry. He picks up the lounge chair and tosses it into the pool.

"Now you listen to me Bri. I will not put up with this. Either Dinero or whatever his name is goes or I do and so does the money and perks you've enjoyed all these years," he says, his face all red.

"Wait, that's our money. I put in my sweat equity into these homes with my decorating. You're being a total asshole, Daniel. It's our wealth. Not yours," I say, moving the pieces of the broken shards of glass with the side of my sneaker.

"Well, we'll see about that. Remember, I'll be fine without you, Brian. They're my businesses, my revenue. You're on my payroll. You can't even hold down a job for five minutes. We'll see who'll be begging to come back to me."

"Well, fuck you Daniel! And your money and your properties and everything," I say. A shard of glass slices part of my finger as I try and pick up some of the pieces. Daniel walks away.

"Well fuck you too, Brian!" He grabs the keys to the Land Rover, jumps in, and peels out of the muddy driveway.

I sit down in a pool of broken glass with a finger spilling blood and a heart bleeding with frustration. I have no idea what I'm going to do. I can't leave Daniel or Eros, and I can't keep both of them either. What the fuck do I do?

After I pick up the glass and bandage my finger, I call my mom in North Carolina. We talk several times a week, and she always seems to cheer me up with one of her funny stories about selling ads for *The Charlotte News*. But I haven't told her about my adventures with Eros yet. I've kept her in the dark, too, probably because I know what she would say.

"Millie, it's Brian," I say, taking a deep breath and holding back the tears which make my voice crack a little.

"Hey sweetie, how are you? You don't sound too good. What's wrong? Did you get into a fight with Daniel or something?"

I start telling her about Eros and how we have this great connection and about our passionate affair. I detail the fight I just had with Daniel.

"Oh, Brian. Do you realize you're playing with fire? Daniel loves you. If he's so angry, it's because he cares about you so much. He's been so good to you, even allowing you to have sex with other guys to get your rocks off. What are you doing with this waiter guy Eros? So far, it only sounds like you two have hot sex in common. With Daniel, there's spirit, love, compassion. You two are like soul mates. I love seeing how you two relate to each other when I visit for the holidays or your birthdays."

I sit on one of the stools in the kitchen and lean my head against my right fist.

"Millie, it's that I love having sex with Eros. Daniel and I have a sexless and passionless relationship. That's not fair to me or to him. We should be with someone who stimulates our hearts and our bodies. And Eros is such a great guy. He's kind and fun and super *guapo!* Whew. He just gets under my skin in a good way."

"But, Brian, can you see a future with Eros? If he's a waiter, he probably doesn't earn much. Is he out of the closet? You just met this guy. You haven't even met his family. What do you really know about him? Is he really worth wrecking everything you've built with Daniel. Do you really want to lose all that?" she says. It's one of the few times where I feel my mother is being a mother, instead of me being the parent. She's making sense and asking all the right questions that I don't have many answers to.

"He's not out. In fact, he says he's bisexual. His family is in Puerto Rico. I don't know a whole lot about his background when it comes to dating, but I know he does care about me Millie."

"Oh, Brian . . . you are about to screw up your life in such a bad way. I don't get a good feeling about this guy. Does he do nice things for you, like take you out to dinner and pay for things?"

Again, she's asking all the right questions, and I can't help but get defensive.

"Well, I pay most of the time. He's a waiter, Mom. I don't mind. He doesn't have a car so I do the driving. But he does little things that make a difference. He cooks for me sometimes or leaves me sweet notes and messages."

"Brian, I'm coming down. I want to meet this young man you're willing to risk your life with Daniel for."

"Millie, no, it's okay. It's not a good time. Daniel and I just had this bad fight, and I need some time to smooth things out with him," I say, leaning back in the stool and rubbing my goatee.

"Brian, listen to me. I'm coming down there. I suggest you stay away from Eros and spend this weekend with Daniel and give him all your attention. I'll call you with the flight arrangements. I want to see who this Eros guy is. Mothers know best."

Just what I need. My mother meddling and meeting my other lover.

18

Ray

Ronnie Reyes is so cute. Goofy but super *lindo*! Something inside me sparked like the soft crisp flame from a match the moment he came up to me and Ted at the journalism conference earlier today. There was a kindness in his eyes as he asked us about our jobs and being minorities in our workplaces. I noticed how his thick black eyebrows furrowed with deep focus whenever he scribbled down what we had to say. And when he looked up to ask another question, his eyes would widen, showing off more of his soft, soothing brown eyes. Part of me just wanted to hug him and whisper in his ear, *Ask whatever you want,* chico!

"Ray, *hello!* Are you listening?" Ted asks, as we sip some cocktails at Club Café, Ted's favorite hangout from his days at Channel 7 Boston. I'm having my usual Corona, and Ted clenches his grapefruit juice with vodka. We're sitting at the front of this bar as a stream of men flow deeper inside to the rear of the club. The monitors blare old episodes of *Queer As Folk* to the music of Madonna, Beyoncé, and the musical *Dreamgirls* soundtrack. I gave the movie four and half stars. For the record, I thought Beyoncé came off wooden and stiff in her role as Deena. She seemed uncomfortable on screen, except when she sang. Then she came to life like a wind-up, bootylicious, bouncing doll. Call her Bouncy.

Jennifer Hudson's Oscar-winning performance knocked Bouncy off people's radar, and I can understand why.

"Yeah, I'm here, Ted. My mind drifted off, that's all," I smile, taking a swig from my beer.

"I know exactly what you were thinking about. He's about 5 feet 9 inches, big smile, tender masculine quality, dark brown hair and matching eyes. He's a writer. About twenty-two. The Cuban John Stamos!"

"Noooo, Ted. I was thinking about my upcoming interview with America Ferrera. I have to prepare for it as soon as I get back home," I say, trying to hide what he accurately guessed I was thinking.

"Yeah, right. I know you, Ray Martinez. Young Ronnie has gotten under your skin even though you're going to deny it until you're blue in the face. Finally, you meet a guy who can match you in pop culture trivia and movies. Well, guess what? Mr. Young Reporter just walked in through the door, and he's looking even more adorable than this afternoon."

I glance at the entrance from our perch at the bar, and I see Ronnie, wiping the snow off his black wool coat and unwrapping the blue scarf from his neck. Snowflakes dotting his thick hair. *Qué lindo!* For the first time in my life, I can't put into words what I'm feeling, but I'll try. I feel a flock of inner butterflies floating around, gently bouncing from side to side, warming me from the inside. Ronnie reminds me of who I used to be, so ambitious with his writing. He's full of enthusiasm and hope about journalism. When we chatted earlier about the news business, I noticed he wasn't jaded like most reporters, or immature like many J-school students I've spoken to. He's refreshing, and I can honestly picture myself bringing him home to my parents and even to Racso and Cindy. I think they'd admire the jump he has on his career, with his part-time internship at the *News* and this scholarship to the gay conference. He's so ahead of the average college student. They'd also think he's a cutie patootie, too, as Rosie would say.

"Well, go up to him. Say hi or something, Ray. I think he likes you, too," Ted says, sipping his drink as other guys in suits from the convention walk among the barflies sporting long-sleeved jersey shirts and baggy blue jeans. They huddle like a gay herd waiting to order drinks.

"Oh yeah, why do you think he likes me?" I glance at Ted, curious about his answer. I'm playing reporter with a reporter. It's usually Ted who wants to know the who, what, when, where, and why. I'm more of the "This is what I enjoyed about this movie" type.

"Ray, *hello*! The guy asked you more questions than me, and he looked at you with those big brown Bambi eyes. You're like his Cuban-American idol. You guys have so much in common being gay, Cuban, and writers. It's such a great match. The critic and the young writer. I can just see the movie-of-the-week now on LOGO."

"Yeah, right. Well let's go and say hi to him before one of these Boston dudes hits on him," I say, feeling a sting of jealousy jab me.

We make our way toward the coat check where Ronnie hands his coat and scarf to the coat check guy, unaware that we're approaching him. He seems like he's in his own little world.

I gently tap Ronnie on the shoulder, and he turns around. He flashes a sweet, infectious grin. Dimples form in each side of his cheek. I want to pinch his cheeks. Ronnie has this rare quality. He looks masculine, yet when he smiles or speaks, he exudes tenderness, a unique sensitivity. That will help him go far in our craft. Who wouldn't want to open up to him in an interview? I know I would.

"Hi, Ray! Hi, Ted! What's up? Are you working undercover on a story or something?" he says, handing the coat check guy two dollars.

"Yes we are, and you're the story, young man," Ted jumps in. I can't believe he just said that, but then again, this is Ted. I elbow him, squint, and glare at him.

"Oh, we were just strolling around. Actually, Ted dragged me here. This used to be one of his hangouts when he worked at the Boston Channel 7 once upon a time," I say to change the subject.

"Can I buy you guys drinks?" Ronnie offers, now that he's free of his coat and scarf. He's wearing an olive green, nicely snug long-sleeved T-shirt with baggy blue jeans that gently hang off his slight waist. His cheeks are slightly rosy from the outdoor walk. He's a college student and all, so I don't want him wasting his money on us overpaid reporters. He's here on a scholarship, after all, to get his writing out there.

"Don't worry about that, Ronnie. This is on me," I offer.

"Great, thanks, Ray. I appreciate it. I'd love a vodka with Red Bull. It'll wake me up. I just filed my two stories for the conference newspaper. *Whew!* I'm beat," he says, as we walk toward the middle bar through a throng of guys.

I order his drink from the pony-tailed bartender, our group consists of me, Ronnie, and Ted, who is eyeballing every single guy here like he's on the hunt for a juicy story. Some of them recognize him from his reporting days and welcome him back. I give Ted a look to signal that I'd like to be alone with Ronnie for a bit. He obliges with a wink. *Gracias*, Ted!

"Well guys, I'll leave you two alone. I'm going to make the rounds here and say hi to the old townies. I just saw a hot guy with a shirt that says Italian Stallion, and I heard someone call him Rico or something. I'll call you later," Ted says, disappearing into the crowd of men. "I may just want to ride that stallion for a bit."

It's just me and Ronnie. Ray and Ronnie. That has a nice ring to it, but I'm probably getting way ahead of myself. This intense attraction I'm feeling has never happened with anyone before. I'm intrigued by Ronnie. I want to know more about this cute *muchacho*. The bartender returns with Ronnie's drink and another Corona for me.

"Thanks, Ray," Ronnie says, sipping the rim of his drink and making a cute slurping sound. His tongue gently licks the top of the glass. I am instantly turned on.

"Let's make a toast. To gay Cuban writers in Boston, the two but proud," he says, holding up his golden drink to my bottle.

"To future, cute full-time journalists," I toast back with a wink, and our glasses clink.

As we enjoy our drinks under the semi-bright lights of the bar, I ask him what it's like dating in Miami and being gay at FIU. I wonder if it's different for someone his age, seven years younger than me. I came out midway through college and I'm wondering if he has a good coming out story. It's probably easier for him and his classmates these days. They have so many positive examples on TV, from Ellen and Rosie and the guy from *Grey's Anatomy* and the character on *Brothers and Sisters*.

"Oh, it's way cool. I'm a member of the gay and lesbian student organization. The more of us who are out there and proud, the more visibility we get. You can't be happy in the closet, Ray," Ronnie says, as U2's *Vertigo* blares on the monitor. It's one of my favorite videos, though I've never understood the beginning. *Uno, dos, tres, catorce* which translates as One, two, three, fourteen? Bono needs a Spanish lesson, pronto.

"I know what you mean. My parents know about me but we don't get into the intricate details. You're only twenty-two. How do your parents deal with you being gay?" I notice Ronnie takes a big gulp of his drink. I notice his cheeks redden just as he swallows, probably from the stuffy, dry heat in the bar. His lips are so perfectly shaped and luscious, something out of a magazine. I'd like to give him a pop kiss, but I don't want to be too forward. I can tell he looks up to me and admires my writing. I don't want to taint that with a hookup.

"My parents know I'm gay, but like yours, we don't get into the 411. I've had dates, but until I meet a serious guy, I ain't bringing anyone home to the Reyes household," he says with another infectious grin.

"Right now, I'm focused on finishing at FIU and getting as much experience as I can at the *News*. I want to be the best writer I can be, like you, Ray," he says, looking up from his drink.

This guy is as sweet as a Hershey Kiss. We talk about writing some more and I notice all these Boston dudes checking Ronnie out. I shoo them away with a gaze from my blue eyes, the way a werewolf would look down at competing predators. Ronnie smiles at everyone and says hi as they pass him, commenting "You're so adorable," and "Wow, where are you from, handsome?" He stands out in the crowd, and seems a little shy now, different from the question-pelting reporter I met a few hours ago. I find this endearing. The two sides of Ronnie Reyes. I would give him five stars based on looks and another five on personality. Ronnie is a ten in my book. *Coño*, I sound like one of the cheesy gooey characters in a Nicholas Sparks novel. I have to control myself. Maybe I should slow down on the drinks.

I suggest that we sit at one of the tables by the front bar for more privacy, and Ronnie gladly agrees. As we walk, I put my hand on the small of his back, noticing the square-shaped cut of his hairline. He's so groomed. I see a little freckle on the back of his neck. I want to touch it with the tip of my finger, but I fear coming on too strongly.

We plop ourselves on the bar stools and lean close to listen to each other.

"So how do you like Boston? *Tienes frío?*" I ask.

"Oh, my gosh, it's freezing up here. You know that if we had weather like this in Miami, the city would shut down. No one would leave their house. They'd be lighting up their dusty fireplaces and calling this forty-degree weather *The Miami Blizzard, The Frozen City*. Boston is too cold for my Florida skin," Ronnie says.

"Amen! There's nothing like going to work in short sleeves," I say. "My Nissan would probably get stuck in the snow. Since I guess you don't see yourself living here, where do you see yourself in five years, Ronnie?"

"Let's see," he says, cradling this glass as if it were a crystal ball that sees the future. "Oh, I have a vision. Hold the phone! I want to be a reporter covering Miami Beach or Miami. I believe we need to be the watchdogs of city government. Without us, all those politicians would get away with murder. I want to inform people about what happens in their community. I would like to do that for a while and then move on to Features and write profiles about local celebrities and your everyday Miamians doing interesting things in the community. With our jobs, you can go from news to features, you can edit or design, the possibilities are endless—like the snow falling tonight," he says, his eyes flickering with excitement. "I won't have a lot of pull when I apply for my first job, so I'll take whatever I can get. I think I'll be happy doing whatever job I can get, as long as I get to report and write. I'm a cheap hire and a cheap date. It doesn't take much to satisfy me," he says, looking down, twirling his straw and grinning at his crystal ball scene. The right side of his lip curls up when he grins, which I find very sexy.

"What about you, Ray? Where do you see yourself in a few years?" he asks when his eyes surface again to meet mine.

"I don't know. I really enjoy what I do. I feel blessed to have a job that lets me watch movies and report on the different trends in cinema. It's always changing, so I'm never bored. As long as there are movies, there will be movie critics. I'm happy where I am now. I take things day by day," I say. "I'm not going anywhere anytime soon."

We go on to talk about the dot.comization of newspapers and our wacky Cuban families. It turns out Ronnie has a younger sister named Lisa, who's about to graduate from Hialeah High. She wants to be a schoolteacher. She knows he's gay and is cool with it, he says.

"Yeah, my brother is a teacher, too. Actually, my twin brother," I say.

"Whoa, there's another guy with your cute face in Miami? Can I get his number? Stop the presses!" Ronnie jokes.

"*Gracias, chico*. He's my identical twin, and he teaches at Coral Gables High. Sorry, though, you wouldn't be Racso's type. He's straight, with a great girlfriend. You'd like Cindy. She's really sweet and funny. And I think she'd like you, too."

"Do you guys have that twin telepathy? I saw a story on *20/20* a few years ago about how twins can communicate with their thoughts and feelings, even if they're thousands of miles away," Ronnie says, sipping his drink.

"Yeah, we have that ability, but it only works one way. Don't ask me why. I've never been able to solve that family riddle. Racso seems to have a private radio antenna that beams straight into my mind. It sucks, bro! It's like he has a private dial with my name on it."

"I wonder what he would pick up now if he were tuning into you?" Ronnie says.

"Oh, it's all good," I say, winking at this cutie. "You have nothing to worry about."

We talk about bicycling, one of my favorite things to do in South Beach and apparently Ronnie's, too. Where did this guy come from again? We have so much in common. If he tells me he has a black dog named Gigli, I'm going to freak out and think I'm being punked or something.

"Have you been to Shark Valley in the Everglades? It's so vast and beautiful and scenic," he says, his voice lifting with enthusiasm. I remember little Arnie had told me about that place during the ambush blind date, but I hadn't been excited hearing it from him. I can see myself riding that trail with Ronnie, watching him speed in front of him, point at something for me to look at in the river of grass. I bet he has nice, slightly hairy defined calves. Nine out of ten Cuban guys tend to be hairy. I know this because of a goofy *News* story on men and hairy legs that actually studied the hair follicles of South Florida's men. This is why I don't want to be a features writer. You never know what trend story or silly assignment will fall into your lap.

"I've heard about Shark Valley, but I've never been. It sounds like a lot of fun. Something to do on a weekend afternoon," I say, with a subtle hint.

"Well, I have a Jeep Liberty, not new or anything, and it has some scratches and fender benders. It sometimes acts up, but it gets me to school and around Miami for my *News* stories. It was a birthday gift from my parents during my senior year at Hialeah High. I'm sure we can fit both our bikes in the back and go biking sometime. I'd love to show you my favorite spots on the trail. You see deer, alligators, birds, even snakes." Ronnie says, his eyes widening on the word "snakes."

"Snakes? Hell no! I hate reptiles. I'll pass on the bike ride," I laugh.

"Well, I'll protect you, Mr. Badass Movie Critic. Most of the snakes are garden snakes. They're harmless. I guess that's why you didn't like *Snakes On A Plane*. I remember you gave it like two stars or something," Ronnie says, putting his hand on my hand as if to comfort me. Gosh, this guy is so incredibly sweet, sexy, smart, and yet sensitive. How does he remember my written words? I want to take him back to my room right now and explore his thin beautiful Cuban body and tickle every strand of hair poking out from his shirt. But I'm not ready to tamper with the goods yet. I like this feeling, whether it's like or lust or good chemistry. I want to keep it going, like this easy conversation.

An hour and two drinks later, I'm feeling a good buzz, or maybe it's just Ronnie's company. I've lost Ted. Oh wait, I see him down the bar trying to hit on a really handsome dark-haired Italian guy with bulging biceps, so he may be busy tonight, but the guy looks a little out of his league so who knows? I'm too focused on Ronnie, who keeps giggling at his own jokes. It's endearing. I can't help but laugh with him. He talks randomly, jumping from one conversation to the next. I can tell the liquor makes him a little more hyper than he is when he's sober.

"My mom has the worst Spanish accent. She says 'You know' like 'juno' as in the capital of Alaska, Juneau," he breaks out in laughter. I laugh, too.

"You should hear my mom, Ronnie. She pronounces 'w' as 'g.' So work sounds like gwork and Walgreen's sounds like Galgreen's. It sounds like her mouth is trying to spit something out in slow motion." We burst out laughing. When Ronnie giggles, his eyes disappear into small curvy slits and he flashes a warm smile. You can tell he's a good guy. I can feel it.

We head back to the coat check to grab our jackets, so I can smoke outside by the bar's entrance. As Ronnie reaches into a pocket, something falls out of his wallet. I bend down and pick up a piece of folded paper. It looks like some writing.

"Hey, what's this?" I ask.

"That's a poem I wrote on my flight up."

"*Oye*, can I see it? I'm curious to read your creative writing."

"Um, sure, Ray. It's no big deal. Just a little poem. I do that from time to time, write short stories, poetry. We can't really do that in journalism, so this is my little creative outlet, a way to break out of the restraints of newspaper writing. I feel I can experiment more with my words, play with them, massage them, just have fun with the process."

"I know what you mean Ronnie."

I unfold the small square of folded paper and a long poem opens up called *The Wanderer*. I read it to myself as Ronnie grabs his coat.

> *He walks alone amid the shadows and lights,*
> *Wanders aimlessly around town.*
> *No destination*
> *A half moon is in sight.*
> *He rounds a corner,*
> *Hoping to find a soul to harbor him for a night.*
>
> *He passes closed shops,*
> *Crosses wet-dewed streets.*
> *Crowds flock.*
> *People walk.*
> *Shimmering stars so high.*
> *Another night he had to lie.*
>
> *Passersby stare.*
> *Marveling his chiseled profile.*
> *A deep loneliness he tries to hide.*
> *Through his bashful smile.*

His innocent eyes.
Good looking, shy.

He continues his journey.
Not knowing where to go.
Can't figure out the present.
He just doesn't know.
Looks to the past.
Forgets the future.
He hopes the nights will always last.

He thinks of a chum.
So smart and nice.
He's cute and cool.
He envies his life.
So masculine and straight.
Nothing like me,
A gay, people hate.

Fear brews inside.
Hope is sometimes near.
Innocence fades away.
The soul remains young.
The face gets older.
Tormented, alone, afraid.
Life's getting colder.

He slinks into a club.
Eyes meet his.
An octopus of hands reaches out
They try to grab, to hold, and to touch him.

He dances away into a world he knows.
Where he forgets the future, the past,
The life he loathes.

He sways to the left.
Swirls, sweats, alive.
Beats pulsate inside.
Sounds resonate.
Life feels right.
No pain, pure fun.
No feelings to fight.

Alone he continues to wander.
The shadows are gone.
Thoughts still brood.
The night has turned to day.
It's another episode of being
Unhappy, young, and gay.

By Ronnie Reyes

I'm impressed with his simple poem that says so much. It's written in a staccato style, but it packs a potent literary punch. I'm sure a lot of younger gay guys, even older ones looking back on their youth, would feel some connection to Ronnie's poem.

"Ronnie, this is really good. Have you thought about submitting it to a publishing house or a literary publication? You've got talent, boy," I say, as we walk outside. Other guys are here smoking like human chimneys, filling the cold air with clouds of smoke. I blow my smoke away from Ronnie so he won't smell like cigarettes. He's rubbing his arms to keep himself warm and staring at me as if I'm the only guy here despite all the other cute blue-eyed, Boston boys with their pale skin and fuzzy crew cuts.

"Thanks, Ray. I can't believe you really liked that poem. It just comes out of me, like breathing. I wrote it in one sitting," he says, all bundled up again in his black coat.

"Seriously, I could relate to what you wrote. I may be going out on a limb here but it's about you, dealing with your sexuality, right?"

Ronnie looks down and back up again to answer.

"Well . . . sort of. I know I'm gay and happy with it, but that poem is about a friend of mine in our gay student group. He just told his parents he was gay, and they're not taking it too well. I feel really bad for him. One night we went out in South Beach to the bars, and I was watching him as we walked on Washington Avenue. We talked about it. On the plane up here, I kept thinking about what he told me. I was bored, and that poem came to mind."

"Maybe you should give your friend this poem. Maybe it will help him feel better about his situation, seeing it from your point of view," I offer, in between puffs of my cigarette. I fold the poem back up and hand it back to him.

"Thanks, Ray. Maybe I will. That's a good idea. I usually keep my poetry to myself, sort of like journal writing, but maybe Jake, my friend, would appreciate it."

As I continue smoking, feeling the nicotine rush into my bloodstream and mix with the slight buzz from my drinks, I notice we're both suddenly quiet. That awkward silence of what to do next. I only hear the cars zipping by on Columbus Avenue and the guys near us gabbing about who just walked in or left with whom.

Ronnie breaks the silence.

"So what are you going to do now?" Ronnie asks, standing closer to me. I want to kiss him so badly and warm my frozen lips.

"Do you want to exchange numbers? Maybe we can hang out in Miami sometime. I'd love to take you to a screening and out to dinner. Next week, I have to screen another *Die Hard* sequel. It should be called *Die Already*. I also have to screen *Freedom Writers II*, the sequel to the Hilary Swank movie about teaching in the L.A. hood. Your poem is the kind of writing that teacher would appreciate, getting her students to document what's going on their lives so that others might connect."

"Oh my gosh, that would be great. She was fantastic in that role, almost saintly, but she wins you and the students over with her naïve charm," Ronnie says, giving me his own mini review. I like this guy. I study him from various mental angles. He's got spunk, yet he seems really genuine, a nice guy. Add intelligence and ambition to the list.

He whips out his little business card from earlier and scribbles his email and cell phone number on it. He adds a big smiley face with thick eyebrows under his name. Cute.

I give him my business card with my cell phone number. He holds it in his hand and reads it over with a grin curling up from the side of lip. We stand outside as a light snow sprinkles down on us. Like white confetti, the snow quickly begins to cover his dark brown hair. Some flakes fall on his nose and mix in with the tiny freckles there.

"Well, I had a great time hanging out with you, Ray."

"Me too, Ronnie. I have an early flight tomorrow so I'm gonna go back and look for Ted one last time before I head back to the hotel."

"I should get going also. I'm pretty beat," he says.

We lean closer to one another, and I resist the temptation to grab him and pull him into me with a kiss. I don't want to break the spell I've been under tonight. Instead, I reach out and hug him tightly, catching the trace of his powdery cologne. Calvin Klein's *Escape*, I think. I pat him gently on his back.

He returns my tight hug with an even tighter embrace. We say goodnight, and Ronnie takes off into the frigid Boston night. As I stand in the doorway of the bar, I see Ronnie walk along Columbus Avenue back to his hotel or wherever he's going. He grows smaller in the distance like a figurine receding from sight, and I can't help but think that I can't wait to get back to Miami to see him again. Ronnie inspires me to want to write a poem about him. His presence warms me even on this chilly, Boston night.

After finding Ted talking to that hunky Italian guy, I leave him be and walk to the hotel a few blocks away. My phone starts to vibrate. It's Racso.

"Hey, little brother! How's it going in Beantown? Are you freezing your *cojones* off?" he says.

"Doing well. Yeah, it's a bit chilly up here, but I've been having fun, meeting a lot of different people, making contacts. *Oye*, what's up with you? How's Cindy?"

"Oh, nothing. Just had dinner with her. She says hi by the way. I called because I was sensing that you were really happy, excited about something, and I had to call and find out. Why are you feeling so good, little bro? I hope I didn't just call you in the middle of sex or something."

I'm always amazed at how Racso can read me from across Biscayne Bay—but across the country? Does this twin ESP thing have frequent flier miles or what? How is he able to do this? I can't tap into his thoughts for the life of me.

"Trust me, I wouldn't answer the phone while I was getting my groove on. Yeah, I've met a lot of people, Racso, and I'll leave it at that."

"Oh wow, this must be good then. You're not talking about it, which means you met a cute guy up there. *Cindy, Ray met a guy in Boston that he really likes,*" I hear Racso tell Cindy, who is probably sitting next to him on our couch at the house.

"Oh wow, get the details. What's he like? We want the dirt!" I hear Cindy talking in the background.

"So, what's he like, little brother?"

"*Oye*, you guys don't know what you're talking about. I met a college student, a senior at FIU, who asked me some questions about the *News* for an article he was writing. We had some drinks tonight, that's all! There's nothing more to say." Oh shit, I said too much. I know it. Me and my big Cubano mouth.

I hear Racso repeating everything I just told him to Cindy.

He comes back to me on the phone.

"And . . . what does he look like? Do tell, Ray. Do tell. Would you give him five stars?" I hear him cracking up with Cindy, who's also giggling. "If you don't tell us, I'll get Emi to do another reading on you. Yes, Mami told me everything, and it looks like it's coming true."

"*Oye*, that's it. I'm hanging up. I'm tired and I have an early flight tomorrow. Goodnight, Ronnie . . . ah . . . I mean Racso."

"Cindy, he just slipped and called me Ronnie, so that's probably the guy's name." I hear Racso talking to Cindy, who says, "Oh my gosh. Get the 411. If not, we'll grill him when he gets back. That's great, Ray," she says in the background. "We're rooting for you."

Drat. I just had a Freudian slip. Now I'm never going to hear the end of the Racso-Cindy inquisition. I bet they'll tell Mami before I even land back in Miami.

"Okay, yeah, that's enough! I'm hanging up. I don't need your obnoxious comments tonight. Nite!" I say.

"Wait . . . wait, Ray, I was just kidding. If I ask all the questions, it's because I care. I'm not trying to be a jerk. I'll pick you up tomorrow from the airport and you can tell me all about it in person. Have a good night, little brother, and put out that cigarette that you have in your hand. You really need to give those up."

"Yeah, whatever," I say. "See you tomorrow."

I hang up my cell and toss the finished cigarette on to the sidewalk like a tiny missile. I begin walking, and hang a right on Dartmouth toward my hotel, passing the subway station. Buses and cars lumber by as I look up at the Boston sky, which is blanketed with stars twinkling as if they were trying to say something to me. Are they winking? I don't know, but I can't help but wonder whether Ronnie is staring at the sky, too, maybe writing a poem about tonight. As we talked tonight, lights switched on inside me. And now, I'm like a resplendent stadium. Entering the lobby of the hotel, I carry the moment of tonight with me with the same care as if I were carrying a tray of fine china. I want to hold onto it and not let it go. I have a feeling (gosh that sounds like Brian) that my ordinary life of filing movie reviews and helping out my Cuban family will be turned up a slight notch.

19

Ted

"So what's your name Italian Stallion?" I ask this gorgeous masculine guy with green eyes that match the shallow waters off South Beach.

"Rico. Wassup?" he says. I feel a boner wringing in my khaki slacks as I look at his tight biceps defined by his blue T-shirt.

"I'm Ted, nice to meet you. I'm going to get another drink. Um, would you like one? My treat!"

"Sure, I drink Sam Adams light. Gotta watch the carbs, you know," he says, in a deep masculine voice. I can't believe this hunk is actually talking to me.

"Don't go away! I'll be back before you know it!" I pass Ronnie and Ray as they head to the front of the bar. I wink at Ray. He looks so cute with the boy. They really do make a nice couple, but right now, Rico is the story. I order our drinks from the pony-tailed bartender and make a beeline back to this Italian god.

"Here you go!" I hand him his bottle.

He toasts my drink, vodka with grapefruit.

"Thanks man! I appreciate it," he says.

We stand in the corner taking sips, and I can't take my eyes off this man. I want to rip that shirt off him and throw him onto my bed back at the hotel. I'll even settle for a few minutes in the bathroom stall. Guys like this don't come around that often, and they usually don't talk to me unless they want to be on *Deco Time*.

"So are you from here? Waiting for a friend? A guy as handsome as you shouldn't be here all alone. The guys must be all over you."

He smiles a gamma-ray smile that is brighter than my bleached white TV teeth. Where did I leave my sunglasses? I could use them right about now.

"Well, I am waiting for a friend," he says mysteriously. I wonder who he's waiting for. Well, he's alone, so he's mine for now.

"I'm from Miami. Well, I'm really from the Cape, but I now live in Miami. I'm a news reporter for Channel 7, like the one up here. I came back to Btown for a gay journalism conference. What about you? What do you do?" I ask, leaning closer.

"Real estate. The market has softened up, but I have a lot of contacts," he says, taking another chug of his drink. "It makes selling houses and condos more challenging, but I love me a challenge," he winks.

"So, this friend you're waiting for, is it someone special? If you were mine, I'd never let you out of my sight." I sip the top of my drink and stare deeply into those green eyes of his.

"Yeah, you can say something like that," Rico answers, leaning back against the wall and downing the rest of the beer. I hear his gulps from two feet away. I want to suck on his Adam's apple.

As I prepare to ask him about his gym routine (He must work out a lot to maintain such fabulous arms and small waist) I notice a tall, lean, cute guy with a velvety buzz cut and big smile approaching us. Where did Boston suddenly get these good-looking imports from?

"Well, gotta go boy. My guy is here. Have fun in Boston and *grazie* for the beer," he says, before walking away with Mr. Tall and Lean.

"Oh yeah, no problem. Anytime Rico. Nice meeting you," I say, but he's already walking away holding the hand of this boyish man. They both seem as happy as can be. Oh well. Mystery solved. I tried, again, and failed.

Even in Boston, I'm striking out as bad as the Red Sox historically have against the Yankees. Maybe I'm trying to meet guys who are too good looking for me. Maybe I'm trying too hard. I don't know what I'm doing wrong. I figured I'd be the new guy again in Boston after moving to Miami, but the guys here seem so much cuter nowadays. I can't compete with these *CW*-network type guys. I also feel overdressed, wearing my slacks, dress shirt and tie while the guys here mosey around in their Diesel jeans and Hollister shirts. I finish off my drink and head to the bar for a refill. Fuck this! Jennifer Hudson's newest dance track plays in the background, and a pack of young guys in the middle of the bar gyrate and jump up and down to the beat. They look so happy. Some are couples, blissfully in love. Ugh, I want to throw up or throw this drink at them and ruin their fun. At least Ray met someone today, and I'm happy for him. I just want to meet my own guy, my own special someone. Shades of futility envelope me. I'm a success in my job and in my friendships but a failure at love.

I decide at this moment that I need a break from men. No more dates. No more hook-ups. I am going on a dating detox, a man fast, a man cleanse, to rid myself of any residual bad karma from all these guys I've been chasing after, first the book club organizer and now Rico. No more men. I need to focus on *moi*.

Just as I begin to drown in my own pool of self-pity, I notice a handsome blondish guy ordering a drink next to me. Who's this? Forget the man fast. I can start that next week.

"Vodka mit Cola light," he says with a German accent.

"Mit what?" the bartender asks. "We don't sell mitts."

"Oh, I'm so sorry. That was German. I mean, vodka vith Diet Coca Cola," says the blonde boy. He looks my way and grins. I smile back and twirl the straw in my drink to make sure the vodka has fully mixed with the seedy grapefruit juice. This guy looks awfully familiar. I could have sworn I saw him in Miami recently, but I can't place him. Maybe I interviewed him for a story or something, for one of those man-on-the-street interviews I sometimes do for *Deco Time*.

"I remember you," he says in his German accent. "You're from Miami, no?"

"Yeah, I live in South Beach. My name is Ted and you are . . ."

"Oh, my name is Jergin. I'm a flight attendant for Lufthansa Airlines. I asked you a few veeks ago vhere I could find an ATM on Lincoln Street, and you showed me. I never forget a face especially from someone as nice as yours," he says, paying for his drink. Vodka with Diet Coke? I guess it's a German thing.

"Oh wait. Now I remember you. That was a while ago. I'm Ted. Nice to see you again. So your name is Jergin, like the soap?" He laughs.

"Yes, like the soap," he smiles back.

"What brings you to Boston?" I ask.

"Vat brings *you* to Boston?" he answers my question with a question. I like this.

"I'm here for a work conference for gay journalists. I'm also from Boston. Cape Cod to be exact, a town called Sandwich," I say, looking him up and down and up again. This is such a good surprise. I already forgot about what's his Italian face, Chico or Rico or Loco or whatever.

"Oh Sandwich! Is that near the towns of Hamburger and Fries," he says, with a grin. Okay, that was funny and cute. I will give him that. Nobody ever batted an eye about how I'm from a town that sounds like something you can eat for lunch.

"I'm here on a layover. I fly back to Berlin tomorrow. A friend told me about Club Café, and I vanted to have a drink," he says.

We stand along the bar and get to know one another. Jergin tells me he's twenty-seven and from Berlin. He says he loves traveling, and that's one of the reasons he became a flight attendant. Also, his airline pays him well, and he lives quite comfortably. I notice he pronounces all his "w's' as "v's." It's endearing, fresh, and yet different.

"Ve're not like American Airlines. Ve give you lunches and

dinners. Ve dress in nice uniforms. In Germany, being a flight attendant has some, vat is the vord, um, prestige? My English is not
so good. My apologies. I am still learning," he says, his big green
eyes, glistening under the lights of the bar.

"Your English is very good. I understand you perfectly. It's not
an easy language and neither is German."

"*Vye danke*, Ted."

We head to the other side of the bar, and I notice Ronnie and
Ray are gone. We take their old stools which are still warm from
their presence.

As we sit and talk about the airline industry and the places
we've both traveled (I've done the Miami-Boston trajectory a little
too much in recent years, and he's pretty much mentioned every
country in Europe as well as U.S. cities up and down the East
Coast) I can't imagine for the life of me why I didn't follow this
guy to the ATM in South Beach or into Score. What was I was
thinking? He seems so interesting and well-traveled. He listens
more than he talks, maybe because of his limited English which is
better than the average Cuban's in Miami, including Ray's parents.

"Is it hard maintaining a relationship as a flight attendant, Jergin?
You're single, right?" I ask as the Scissor Sisters jump around to *I
Don't Feel Like Dancing* on the video monitors above us in the
front bar. I want to make sure he's single after that fiasco back at
the book club in Coral Gables. I don't want anything to be lost in
translation.

"My ex-boyfriends have had a hard time with me traveling. But
if you love someone, you make it vork," he says, leaning back
against the wall of the bar. "I alvays found a vay to come back to
see them in Berlin, but some guys vant a boyfriend that is there all
de time. Because of my job, I can't do dat. I am gone many days at
once. It's difficult to date," he says, his eyes looking all melancholic.

"Tell me about it! Everyone in Miami wants the big and
buffed guys with the beautiful model faces. Even with my job, I
find it hard to compete with that."

A sweet smile spreads across his face.

"But you are very nice looking, Ted. Men vould be fighting over you in Germany with your dark skin and eyes. You vould stand out in a good way. You are also a very nice person."

"So wanna take me Berlin sometime, Jergin?" I joke. We both laugh.

"I vill be in Miami in two veeks. If you show me your city, I can return de favor and show you Berlin some day if you ever leave the East Coast for a vacation. The best vay to learn a town is through someone who lives there."

"Deal!" I toast his glass, and he returns the clink.

We talk for the next hour, and before I realize it, the bar is closing. It's 2 a.m. I forgot that Boston still runs on Puritan time. Everything shuts down at two.

We head to the coat check and grab our coats.

"Where are you staying in town?" I ask, as I wrap my neck in my red scarf.

"Oh, at de Colonnade Hotel. Do you knov it?"

This is such a coincidence.

"Yes, that's my hotel. We can share a cab ride there if you want."

"That vould be nice, Ted. I am having fun with you. This is my first time in Boston."

"And this is my first time in Boston with a cute German guy!" I say.

We laugh as we walk outside, and I hail a taxi. We climb into the backseat of a yellow cab, and the whole five-minute ride, my hand rests on his knee and his hand does the same to mine. I wonder if Ray had a similar ride back to the hotel with Ronnie.

20

Brian

"Brian! I'm here! Yoo hoo!" I hear my mom shouting from the front door. I hear the click-clack of her heels echoing against the marble floors. I get up from the patio lounge chair where I was lazily absorbing some sun rays, and I walk over to welcome her back to Miami. She hasn't been here since last year, when Daniel and I bought the property. Sometimes, I forget what a presence she can have in my life. She can deprive the entire room of all the oxygen and carbon dioxide molecules with her hyper energy. Maybe that's where I get my ADD from. It runs in the Anderson gene pool.

She lifts up her sunglasses as soon as she sees me, and I spot the same Anderson blue eyes that stare back at me every morning in the mirror.

"How's my baby boy?" Millie squeezes my cheeks. I hate it when she does that.

"Hey, Millie! Welcome back. As you see, we're still doing construction." She looks around and gives me her uninvited critique.

"Well, Brian . . . you and Daniel have done a lot to this place. The marble tile is so exquisite, nothing like my worn out hardwood floors back at my house. I could use some new floors honey. And the granite counters! Oh, how lovely and you added the baby grand piano. You need to get back to your music instead of focusing on all this real estate stuff and what's-his-name Latin boy. Now how can you even think of breaking up with Daniel for some schlep who gives you good head?" My mom isn't one to hold back. She gets right to the point These are going to be two *long* days.

"Um, thanks, Millie. Let me show you to the guestroom in case you forgot where it is. We have so many rooms here, I forgot what's where," I say, grabbing her two suitcases and walking up the stairs. I glance down, and she's still surveying the living room and the new Romero Britto paintings I bought on Lincoln Road.

"Well, how whimsical," she says, marveling at one of the bigger paintings that looks likes a dancing clown with an explosion of primary colors in the background.

"Millie, settle in and freshen up, we're going to get some lunch on Lincoln Road as soon as you're ready."

"I'll only take a few minutes, Brian. We'll be leaving in no time."

An hour later, I'm still waiting for my mother. She finally descends, taking each slow step down, from the guest room, as if she were a queen about to address her people below. That's my mom. She drives me crazy, but I also love her to death. She changed from her blouse and blue jeans into a loose summer yellow dress. She reminds me of a Bohemian Southern Belle right about now.

"Let's go, Millie! I'm starving. I'm taking to you to this cute place on Lincoln."

"I can't wait!" she says. "It's so good to be back here with my baby boy. *Ah*, Miami," she says, adding last minute touches to her spiked-up wisps of Rod Stewart blonde hair in the hallway mirror.

We finally arrive at the Van Dyke restaurant, my favorite eatery on the Road. We sit outside and lounge under the radiant sun as the waiter brings us our menus and glasses of water filled with crushed ice. Ever since my mother became sober years ago, she won't allow herself to be near alcohol, so out of respect, I order a cool iced tea instead of my usual cranberry with vodka even though I'm going to need a few to get through this weekend.

"So Brian, when I do meet this Eros fellow, your Latino boy toy?"

"I'm going to invite him out for dinner tomorrow night. We'll go out to eat, and you'll meet the Puerto Rican who has captured my heart. You're going to like him." My mother takes a deep breath and rolls her eyes.

"I think you're making a terrible mistake. Daniel loves you. He wants you. So what if he plays on the side? You do too. You just can't let that poison your relationship. You two have such a wonderful connection. You know, Daniel called me the other night before I came down here. He's really worried about you and your future together. He really does love you, Brian."

"I know, Millie. I love him too, but I want passion. I want monogamy. I'm tired of settling for a special love that doesn't do it all for me. Daniel will always be in my life, but what I feel for Eros completely overshadows what I feel for Daniel. I'm tired of being with someone so successful that I feel overshadowed because people are using me to get to him. I'm tired of asking permission to do little things for the house and to buy things. With Eros, I don't feel like I'm being controlled. I want passion, freedom, independence, and incredible sex. It's hard to explain, but I feel I should be with Eros."

"Yeah, you feel that wild dick of yours should be with the Puerto Rican. I'm going to give you some good advice Brian, which I didn't always do when you were growing up. I wasn't the best mom in the world with my bouts of alcoholism, but let me try and be a good mother now. No one has a perfect relationship. We all learn to give and take in life and in love. What you and Daniel have is imperfect but special. When I see you two together, there's a natural chemistry. You make each other smile so much. I can't help but think there's more to this Eros than meets the eye, and you're not seeing it. My intuition tells me you're not getting the whole story, Brian. You need all the facts before you make such a big decision about leaving Daniel."

Did I mention my mother is all about spirituality and intuition too? I remember when I was little, she always knew when something bad would happen. She knew she was going to total her Pontiac Firebird when she rammed it into a tree with me riding shotgun, but she didn't know exactly when it would happen. My face hit the front glass window, and I broke my nose. I had fifteen stitches to sew up the cuts along my eyebrows. Thank God for minor plastic surgery. Daniel paid for that after our first six months together. I remember him telling me in his sexy but rough Israeli accent, "Brian, you have such a beautiful face, one that I adore, but we can make those small scars disappear. I'd be happy to make those painful reminders of your mom's drinking go away. Those memories and the scars should be in the past."

Thinking back, I know Daniel would have been fine if I hadn't done the surgery, but those scars were daily reminders of Millie's addiction to the bottle, and I know how guilty she felt every time she saw them on my face over the years. I still have nightmares every now and then from that accident, the bludgeoning impact of my face against the cold glass.

My mom also knew that I was going to leave her and fly off to New York to make it as a singer. She knew that something recently has been going on in my life besides Daniel. The woman just knows, and I know when she knows something.

"Thanks Millie but remember, I'm just as intuitive as you are. I know I'm not getting the whole story. I'm letting the universe present me the full story when it thinks I'm ready. I can't wait for you to see Eros. He has dark brown curly hair, thick black eyebrows, brown eyes, and a beautiful dark tan." I'm getting excited at the thought of his hard chest and tan nipples.

"Oh, like that guy over there walking with the older man. He seems to fit the description," Millie says, pointing to the other side of Lincoln Road near the Swatch watch shop. I glance over, squint, and do a double-take. I can't believe my eyes. It's Eros and another guy. Huh? The man looks like he's in his mid-forties with a crew cut, glasses, and a matching tan. They're talking as they browse the watches in the display window. They look like . . . a couple? Eros looks so happy and free, without a care in the world. I'm confused, and a stinging burning feeling fills my chest. I feel like someone stomped on my heart and threw it in a pottery kiln. He said he was bisexual and that his roommate doesn't know he's bi or that he messes around with men. What the hell?

"Brian, is that him? And if it is, why is he with that man? They look like a couple," Millie says, covering her forehead with her right hand so she can get a closer look over the sea of outdoor tables marked by bright green umbrellas across the street.

As these emotional rumblings stir inside me, I whip out my cell and dial Eros. The whole time as the phone is tightly pressed against my ear, I watch him and the stranger. The phone rings, and I see Eros pull out his phone. He looks at the incoming call and then puts his phone away. He knows it's me. He's ignoring my call. This isn't adding up. I'll get the story later, the whole story. I leave a message.

"Eros, hey, it's Brian. Call me when you get this. I need to talk to you," I say, flipping my phone closed.

"Yes Millie, that's him. I don't know why he's with that guy, but I'm gonna find out. You can bet on that."

The waiter comes back and takes our order. I tell him I want the grilled chicken sandwich, and Mom orders a Greek salad. But suddenly, I don't feel like eating much right now. I've just been served a plate of betrayal. My appetite has been replaced by anger. My mom can sense that, and she leans closer to me.

"See what I mean? There's something he's not telling you. I bet you pay for everything, right? I bet you haven't been to his place yet, no? And you're risking everything you have, a great partner who does his best to appease you, a beautiful home and financial security for what? *That!*" She points to Eros and his friend. Her gold bracelets jingle with the gesture. "I think I was meant to be here so that you could see what you're getting into. Brian, use your intuition. Trust it. It's screaming at you for a reason, and you're turning a deaf ear, sweetie."

"Millie, not right now! I know what you're saying, and trust me, I'll get to the bottom of this. Let's just eat." I know my mother says she's looking out for me, but she's also looking out for herself as well. She feels threatened by my connection with Eros. She's enjoyed the perks of having Daniel in my life. That little white Cape house in North Carolina? We bought it for her. Her 2005 Jeep Cherokee? We bought it for her. Her trip to Miami? I paid for it, even though it was her idea to come down. She wants me to be in a committed loving relationship but preferably with a successful lawyer or businessman, not a teacher or a waiter. This lunch and this whole weekend? All of this goes on my tab, Daniel's tab. We wouldn't be able to do this on Eros's tips.

A few minutes later, our food arrives, and I begin to chow down, biting hard on every single morsel to keep my mind from racing from one sick thought to another. I can't help but think of all the lies Eros has told me. I know I'm no saint, but I told him from the start that I did have a partner and about our situation. Eros has kept his home life a mystery from me. I need to know more if I'm planning a serious future with him. I've never met any of his friends or seen his apartment. Those are red flags flying right there. Am I just another sugar daddy potential for him? At least I'm cuter than that older guy. Millie tries to change the subject to distract me from my thoughts.

"Maybe after lunch, we can look at some flowers for your front garden. You know how much I like to garden. I think you can use some hibiscus plants, maybe some bamboo for the window sink in the kitchen for good luck," she says, scooping up some of her lettuce and chunks of chicken onto her fork.

"That sounds great, Mom" I deadpan.

"Oh my gosh, you actually called me Mom. Now I know that you're really upset."

Later that night, after a day of shopping at Merrick Place with Millie and a dinner on Miracle Mile at an Italian restaurant, I finally hear from Eros. It's almost 9 p.m., many hours after I left that message. I take the call outside on the deck while Millie watches the Rachael Ray show in the living room. She looks so cute sitting on the sofa and taking notes for new recipes. She leans back into the sofa like she owns this place. A mother's rights, I guess.

"Brian, *mi amor,* how are you doing? How's your mom? I can't wait to meet her."

"Don't *mi amor* me you asshole. I saw you today!"

"Que? What are you talking about? I had to work this afternoon at the restaurant," he says, almost convincingly. He's a great liar. "I got home a little while ago."

"Eros, my mother and I saw you with that older guy on Lincoln Road. I know what you look like. I'm not blind," I say, pacing back and forth on the dock. The cool bay breeze can't calm me down right now. I'm seething with anger, and my face feels red and hot. Does he think I'm an idiot or something?

"Baby, that wasn't me. I swear. I was at the restaurant all day. You can ask Oswaldo, the main waiter there, or even Juan, the other counter waiter. I'll do anything to prove to you that wasn't me. It must have been someone who looked like me. Why would I be on Lincoln Road with a guy who wasn't you?"

Now I'm feeling really confused. I could easily ask his co-workers if he was there today, so why would he offer for me to do that, if he wasn't telling the truth. But the guy looked exactly like him.

"Eros, I swear it was you. I was sitting at the Van Dyke with my mom and we saw you. I was describing what you looked like and she pointed you out, just based on my description alone."

"Well, that's funny, that another *chico* here looks like me. There are so many Cubans and Puerto Ricans and Brazilians here and we all have the same features, *tu sabes.* I guess I should be flattered that you're all worked up that you thought you saw me with another guy. That is sweet, *chico lindo.* I swear, it wasn't me, Brian, you have to believe me. And if you really thought it was me, why didn't you say hi or something. I could have met your mother today."

Maybe it wasn't him. He does make a good point. Now I'm

not sure what to think, and I feel awful for letting Millie think that was him and that he was with another guy today. Not a very good first impression. I'm going to give him the benefit of the doubt. And he's right, I could have easily walked up to him and I didn't. Maybe deep down inside, I knew it wasn't him after all, and I was letting my mother's bad energy toward Eros cloud my judgment.

"So, are we still on for dinner tomorrow night? I really want to see the woman who gave birth to my beautiful *chico*," Eros says.

"Yes Eros, we're still on for tomorrow night. I'll pick you at six with Millie, and we'll get something to eat."

"I can't wait, Brian. See you tomorrow," he says.

"Sweet dreams baby."

"Only if you're in them, Brian," he says.

I know he said that wasn't him today, but something inside me keeps nagging at me. Something doesn't feel right, and I can't seem to put my finger on it. My intuition is redlining. Is he such a great liar or am I a gullible, love-struck idiot? I wonder what Ray and Ted would think of all this. Ray would probably ask me, "Well why didn't you go up to him and confront him there? And besides, why are you upset? You have a partner already." His twin Racso would probably have said the same thing, but I can't imagine him being in this situation with Cindy. For one, they would have been together having lunch with one of their parents, and I can't imagine those two lovebirds having an open relationship. They are completely committed to one another from what Ray has told me. Ted would probably say, "If it looks like a dick, then it's a dick." What does my intuition say? I can't seem to filter out my insecurity about my future and my feelings for Eros. Both are confusing my thoughts; they're all jumbled up in my head and heart. I can't hone in on exactly what is bothering me. I know the guys should be getting back from Boston this weekend, so I'll tell them the details and see if I'm not just imagining things. For now, I'm giving Eros the benefit of the doubt. Like my favorite book *The Four Agreements* states, "Don't assume anything."

I recite those agreements in my head, and I feel better for now. But still, something is bugging me from the inside, and I wish it would go away like the small white sailboat drifting away in the distance in Biscayne Bay.

It's Saturday night, and Eros has surprised me by offering to meet me and my mother at my house. I usually pick him up. It's almost six, and I hear a taxi pulling up to the house. It's Eros, and he looks so handsome. I've never seen him as dapper as he is now. He's wearing khakis and a tight-fitting Polo-type shirt, but it's not Polo. Maybe a Macy's generic brand. He's wearing nice brown shoes. He looks like a Latino Ken Doll, all darkly tanned. He has a bouquet of lilies in his hand. He flashes his smile when he sees me standing in the doorway.

"Hey, *lindo!*" He greets me with a kiss.

"Hey you. Are these flowers for me? You shouldn't have. They're beautiful Eros." I smell his grassy musky cologne which I want to lick off his body.

"*Bueno*, they're for your mom actually." He walks in, and I walk behind him, with my hand on his upper back. I feel his hard back with the slightest touch.

"Millie's all ready. She's in the living room."

We walk in, and I introduce them.

"These are for you, Mrs. Anderson. I thought you might enjoy the beautiful scent of lilies," he says, handing the bouquet to my surprised mother and then kissing her on her cheek.

"Well, nice to meet you too. Thank you for the flowers. They're quiet lovely. Gardening is one of my favorite hobbies in Charlotte, so I recognized the flowers right away. I'll go put in them a vase." She walks into the kitchen and fills a clear glass vase with water and her gift.

I'm surprised that Eros was considerate enough to think of my mom like that. I can tell she liked the flowers. She's a sucker for flowers, which is why her Cape house in Charlotte is filled with them, inside and out. Eros just scored some points with Millie, and

I'm glad. I just want her to forget about the Eros clone from yesterday at lunch.

We get ready to leave and walk over to the Land Rover. Eros gets into the passenger front seat and my mom gets in the back. The whole way, Millie is talking about her flight, her flowers, and the renovations Daniel and I have done to the house. Eros doesn't seem to say much so I try to fill the void and engage him.

"Millie, did you know that Eros worked at a library back in Puerto Rico? He's from San Juan." I look over to Eros and signal with my eyebrows for him to talk.

"Yeah, I loved working there. We had a book club for kids, and they would meet each week and talk about what they liked about their books, which was usually a *Harry Potter* novel. I miss Puerto Rico," he says softly.

"What brought you to Miami, Eros? It seems so far away. Don't you miss your family?" Millie asks, looking out the window while wearing her sunglasses.

"It was my family that brought me to Miami. I'm making decent money at the restaurant, and I send back whatever I can. I talk to my mom and sister pretty often. It's a Latino thing. We speak several times a week."

"Oh I wish Brian would call me more often. I talk to him once a week or so. He's *so* busy. Listen to that Brian, Eros calls his mom almost every day. *Hmmm,*" my mother says, leaning in from the back of the seat.

"Okay Millie, I get your point. You want to talk more often. I got that." I tell her.

We pull up to Larios on Ocean Drive, and I valet the car. Who knows, maybe we'll see the Estefans here, since they own the place. I've heard so many good things about the Cuban food here, and I can smell the black beans and chicken wafting outside.

Once inside, the host walks us to our table near the front window with an amazing view of bustling Ocean Drive and the beach. It's just past 6:30 p.m., and it's still bright outside. I can tell the sun is beginning to dim leaving the sky a darker hue of blue.

Eros pulls out a chair for my mom, and I sit between them. The waiter brings us a basket of freshly baked garlic bread and glasses filled with ice water. We scan the menus, and Eros gently holds the palm of my hand under the table.

"So being Latino, would you recommend anything Eros?" Millie asks him, her eyes and spiked up blonde hair appearing above the rim of the menu.

"I'm more into Puerto Rican food, but Cuban food is pretty good too. If you want a good meal, try the breaded chicken steak with a side of black beans on rice. That's *muy delicioso*. Or there's the *bistec*, the fried steak, with onions on top. You can't go wrong at Larios. That's why Emilio and Gloria bought it from the original owners years ago."

I wink at Eros.

"Thanks Eros. I think I'll get that chicken steak and the beans and rice."

The waiter comes back and takes our order. I settle on the chicken and rice, and Eros gets the shrimp cocktail and a side of fried plantains. To drink, Millie gets a large iced tea, I get a Diet Coke and Eros orders a martini. I interrupt his order.

"Eros, maybe you'll want something without alcohol. How about a virgin piña colada or something else?" I stress to him with my eyes.

"Brian, I really want a martini."

"I think you should get something simple and easy," I say.

"Nah *chico*, I'll get the martini."

My mom excuses herself to go to the ladies' room and once she's gone, I lay it all out for Eros.

"She's a recovering alcoholic. I told you that the other day. It's not nice to order drinks around an alcoholic. It's insensitive."

"Oh shit, sorry Brian. I forgot. I'll tell the waiter to change the drink to a Sprite or something. I didn't mean to be inconsiderate. *Lo siento.*"

Millie comes back, and we munch on bread until our food comes.

"So Eros, how long have you known you're gay? Is your mom okay with it?" Millie blurts out. Eros starts coughing on his piece of bread. I think my mother is just warming up now. Here comes the Millie inquisition.

"I don't think I'm gay. I like men, but I also like women. I'm what you call bisexual. *Mi mama* doesn't know anything."

"Oh that's a cop out. You're either gay or not. Do you prefer men or women?" Millie continues firing away.

"I've never really thought about it that way, Señora Anderson. I really care about your son. I've never felt like this toward a man before," Eros says, squeezing my hand.

"Felt like what exactly?" she says.

"I mean, I have strong feelings for Brian. He's a wonderful guy, and I feel I have learned so much by being with him."

"Millie, he's still figuring out what he wants, even though I think he's a total cocksucker!" I say jokingly. Eros looks at me and smiles, showing off those beautiful white teeth of his. I can't wait to brush the tip of my tongue against them later tonight.

"That's nice to hear Eros, but my son is already in a relationship and him and Daniel have a wonderful if complicated one. Where do you see yourself fitting in here?"

"Millie! *Please* . . . !" I scold my mom.

"Well Brian, I'm just asking. Don't you want to know?"

Eros sips his water and answers.

"I care about your son and enjoy being with him. From what he has told me, this beautiful *chico* is an empty relationship with Daniel. He deserves to feel passion and love again, and I feel that way toward Brian. I know he feels that way about me too. We're taking things day by day and enjoying the moment for what it is."

"Yeah, and you're enjoying the ride Eros. We saw you with that other man yesterday afternoon."

Eros' eyes convey confusion.

"But that wasn't me. I explained that to Brian last night," Eros explains.

"Brian might fall for that but I don't. I saw him with my own pair of eyes and I can clearly say that it was you walking on Lincoln Road with that gentleman."

"Mother! Stop!" I shout at Millie, banging the table with my right hand. Other restaurant patrons suddenly focus their sights on our table.

"Fine Eros. I know what you said, but I know what I saw. I'm just looking out for my boy here. You hurt him, you hurt me. Got it?"

"You have my word Mrs. Anderson. I would never intentionally do anything to hurt Brian. I think I love him," he announces.

"What? You love me, Eros?" I ask him.

"*Si* Brian. I do. The thought of hurting you or betraying you completely makes me sick. I know my heart is with you."

Millie rolls her eyes.

"Me too, Eros. I love you too," I tell him.

We popkiss at the table, and I caress the back of his neck with my hand and feel his small bush of thick curly hair.

"Fine, whatever. You guys love each other. Now where's our food? I want to eat," my mother says.

For the rest of the meal, we stay quiet, eating our delicious dishes. The whole time, Eros and I hold hands at the table, and my heart melts at the intense gazes he throws my way which tear holes into the deepest of my inner core. I know with each glance he's telling me how much he cares for me, and I reciprocate the same message to him. I can't help but feel Eros and I belong to one another. The more time I spend with him, the more I know my destiny is not with Daniel anymore. I've come to a decision. It's time to move on with my life and find my independence and that intense love I've been missing all these years, whether Millie approves or not. Like everyone else, she'll just have to deal with it.

When the waiter brings the check, I immediately grab it and slip my American Express card. The waiter swoops by, picks it up, and smiles.

"Well Brian, this was a lovely place. I can see why the Estefans bought it," Millie says, sipping the rest of her iced tea.

"Yeah, this was a good choice. We have to come here again chico," Eros says, patting my hand gently.

"The Estefans also own Bongo's across Biscayne Bay, next to the American Airlines Arena. We should go there sometime too and maybe dance. It's been so long since I've danced or even seen Millie dance. You have to shake your groove thing sometimes, Mom," I say.

"Oh the only thing that will be shaking is my cellulite, Brian. A dance floor is no place for a woman who's fifty-five, ah, I mean forty-five years old," she winks at me.

I grin at her when I notice the waiter returning with the bill and my card. His eyebrows furrow.

"Do you have another card, Mr. Anderson. This one has been declined," he says, matter-of-factly.

"Declined? Are you sure? Can you try again?"

"We swiped it three times. It's no good."

"That's weird. Our accountant paid that card off two weeks ago," I tell Millie and Eros, who also look confused.

I pull out another credit card, my American Airlines Citicard. "Here, try this one."

A few minutes later, the waiter is back.

"I'm sorry sir but that card has declined as well. We have an ATM near the restrooms if you need some cash."

"Brian, I have some money," my mother says.

"Yeah, me too *chico*," Eros jumps in, pulling out some bills from his wallet.

Then it hits me like the waves crashing against the shoreline in the near distance. Daniel has begun to cut me off, for good.

21

Ray

Two and a half stars. That is what I'm giving this first date, if you can call it that. I am hoping it gets better, if I survive. *(Gulp!)*

"Ray, you have to stay about ten feet away from all the gators and snakes," Ronnie casually informs me as he rides ahead of me on his bicycle. "If you hear high-pitched squeaking sounds, those are the baby alligators. Watch out for the mother!"

Qué cosa! I thought Ronnie was joking when he said we would see gators and snakes up close here in the Everglades Shark Valley. I thought it was one of those overexaggerated Cuban comments. Cubans have a propensity for embellishing stories. Did I mention I hate snakes and reptilian things? The closest I get to them is on-screen, in movies like *Jurassic Park* or *Snakes On A Plane* or the infamous *Anaconda* and its unnecessary and unwatchable sequel. They're creepy crawlies, and just the thought of them fills my skin with pebbly goose bumps. I'm not planning on getting off my bike anytime soon, so I'll keep my distance from the wildlife out here. The only gators I want to see are the friendly ones that smile on people's key chains or the ones that stare back at me from Florida license plates. I can just see the story on Channel 7 now with Ted reporting it. *Deadly First Date. Miami movie critic Ray Martinez was last seen cycling on a narrow concrete bike trail with a friend when he vanished, allegedly into the mouth of alligator. The crew from "Without A Trace" is on the case. More at eleven.*

Yeah, so I'm on a date with Ronnie, and so far, it's been an adventure. We just started pedaling on the bike trail that is flanked by a river of sawgrass on both sides. It's a flat path, and the sun is baking this ribbon of roadway, causing vapors to rise like mirages in the distance. Did I just see something scurry cross the trail up ahead? The heat is playing tricks on me. It's probably a figment of my Cuban imagination. This is a great excuse to see Ronnie's calves and arms. He's wearing a red sleeveless shirt, and his thin arms are nicely toned with a little hair on the forearms. And his calves? He must bike a lot because they are perfectly round and hard. I want to squeeze them like snuggly plush dolls. Even though an army of buzzing dragonflies has decided to piggyback on my shoulders and even though this is beginning to feel like biking hell, seeing Ronnie in shorts and, more importantly, seeing Ronnie again seems all worth it. I smile to myself.

After we got back from the Boston journalism convention, I called him to go out to dinner and to hang, but Ronnie suggested we do something different for our first time hanging out together. His idea of different: cycling fifteen miles on a flat straight line in the soupy heat surrounded by nature and unseen—for now—wildlife. Not romantic in my book but very sweet in his own way. He wanted to show me something fun to do in Miami that people often overlook with all the bars, beaches, and fake boobs. Besides, this is something he enjoys, and he wanted to share with me. In the little time I've known Ronnie, he's surprised me with his outlook and point of view. It's refreshing, and I feel like I'm learning something new about him each time we talk.

"This way, we can enjoy nature and work up an appetite for later. We can chow down at La Carreta on Calle Ocho," was Ronnie's pitch, and I was a sucker for it. I'm a sucker for this super cute guy.

"The trail will take about two hours, depending on how fit

you are, Ray, so in that case, it may take us three hours," he teased on the phone earlier. If Racso could see me now, he'd be laughing his head off. I could use a cigarette right now. My lungs are paying the price for my pack-a-day habit. I'm almost breathless, and we're ten minutes into the ride under the blazing sun. This will definitely take me more than two hours. I got turned on when we got here because Ronnie smeared me in sunscreen to protect my fragile white skin. You'd think I just came off a flight from Alaska with my pale skin even though I grew up under this harsh Miami sun.

"Hey *chico*, wait up! I'm an old man," I gasp out loud to him as he speeds off ahead like a roadrunner on wheels.

"I'll slow down for you Socrates. This way we can talk and ride," he shouts, making a U-turn and coming back my way to ride along my right side. We're cycling side by side now, keeping a lazy pace, and there's not even a breeze to cool me off. Just an intense humidity. We're the only two cyclists on this Saturday afternoon. We're two of South Florida's natives surrounded by—and I don't want to know where they are—the most native of natives. You know, the gators. Ronnie says we can stop along the trail's edge and search the water for signs of wildlife, but there are no guardrails or fences to separate us men from the beasts. I'll keep my feet on the pedals, thank you very much. Damn, I should have brought my Marlboro Lights. I left them in Ronnie's car.

"How often do you come out here Ronnie?"

"At least once a month, when I'm not buried in school work or my stories for the *News*. It's relaxing, isn't it? You can't see Miami here. No signs of the Latin metropolis. This helps me relax and keep my mind off things. It's very spiritual, communing with nature," he says with a big old boyish smile on his face as we maintain a brisk pace. At least he's enjoying the ride, because I'm not. The company is pretty good though.

"I have a cheaper way of relaxing. It's called a cigarette."

He looks down at his handlebars and laughs.

"That's really bad for you, ya know. Remember what happened to Peter Jennings from ABC News? Out of nowhere, he was diagnosed with lung cancer, and his voice became all raspy and hoarse on the air and he died a few months later. All because he couldn't quit the smokes," Ronnie says, scolding me with his big brown eyes.

"Trust me, I know all about the hazards of smoking. I've tried quitting, but it never sticks. It's not as easy as it sounds, Ronnie boy."

"Well, maybe if you knew someone who died of smoking, then you'd have a change of heart," he says in a tone mixed with seriousness and sadness. His eyes drift off to the swampy marsh on his right. I see his profile cast beautifully against the boundless golden wet fields. The scene behind him is something you'd see in the opening montage of *CSI: Miami* where David Caruso is riding on an airboat with his bright orange hair blowing wildly in the wind.

"Did you know someone who died of smoking?" I ask.

"Yeah, my grandfather Mario. I saw the whole thing, from when he was diagnosed to his constant hacking and coughing. He was on a respirator for a while, because his lungs just gave up. My family was devastated. It was five years ago last month," he says, looking at me and then looking away at the marshlands.

"Listen Ray, I don't mean to sound like a drag or anything. I'm telling you this because I care and I don't want to see you get sick or die from something so gross and avoidable as smoking, but the sooner you quit, the better. It's dirty and gross. The damage you've done to your lungs is irreversible. Besides, I want to keep reading your wonderful movie critiques on your blog and in the paper. Without you, I wouldn't know what movies to watch every week. I'd be lost," he says, putting his hand on his heart and letting out a big sarcastic sigh.

"Well, if they find a cure for smoking, trust me Ronnie, I'd take it in a heartbeat. I don't smoke as much as I used to, so I've cut back a little. I used to smoke two packs a day, so I'm weening off, just a teeny tiny bit *chico.*"

"Oooh. One pack a day! That's a great cutback. Before you

know it, you'll be down to—what—half a pack? It doesn't work like that. You have to quit cold turkey. Does your brother smoke?" "Nah, Racso hates cigarettes. It's one of our many differences even though we're identical. People think that twins share a brain and have similar interests, but we don't. Racso likes to play basketball and sports. I prefer to see what movie opened at number one, like my own score card. Racso likes to work out. I prefer to read and cycle around the beach. I like guys. Racso loves women, hence his fiancée Cindy. So to answer your question, he loathes my smoking."

"He's not the only one," Ronnie says mischievously and winks. "Come on, I'll race you!" Ronnie speeds away as if his bike carried some sort of secret built-in jet propulsion.

"I'll meet you at the halfway point, wherever that is!" I shout. Hopefully, it's not too far away. My lungs are working harder than Big Momma running on the beach in that Martin Lawrence movie, *Big Momma's House*, which I gave two stars. Oh no, I think I just saw something rustling in the bushes off the path. I start to pedal faster to catch up to Ronnie Reyes who is a Cuban Speed Racer. I wouldn't mind finding out what's under the hood of his Mach 5.

"Hey . . . wait up! Don't leave me here alone, with these gators!"

I survive the first leg of the trail with all my body parts accounted for. We're at mile eight or the halfway point, and there's this huge observation tower which looks like a wooden alien ship that landed smack in the middle of the Everglades.

We park our bikes on the bike rack, and I see tiny little bunnies dash into the bushes. They remind me of Thumper, from the classic Disney movie *Bambi*. I follow Ronnie who seems invigorated from the ride. I'm exhausted and feel more of my strength drain from me as I remember that I have seven more miles to ride to get back to civilization and my cigarettes. Note to self: Don't ride in the Everglades again. Note to self part two: Don't ever ride again anywhere without a pack of cigarettes on hand.

I follow Ronnie up the winding ramp, about four stories up, to the top of the observation deck, and we lean over the rail and look out. He pulls out two cool lemon-lime Gatorades from his red messenger bag.

"Thirsty? I think you could use some *Gay*-torade. You look like you ran the Boston Marathon or something."

"Yeah, some *Gay*-torade would be quite helpful right about now young Ronnie."

"I forgot, you're an old man, twenty-nine right?" he says, before continuing to drink from his Gatorade bottle, one of the ones with the pacifier-like tops. I down the drink in almost one gulp. It's refreshing. I feel the green liquid slowly cooling my overheated insides and filling up my empty stomach. *Ahhh!* But I'd rather have a cigarette, like, *now!*

As Ronnie looks out at the endless river of grass, which looks like a savanna in Africa, I can't help but gaze at his sweet profile. I focus on those thick eyebrows and his brown eyes as they focus on something below. I follow his gaze, and I see something moving in the murky steamy swamp.

"Ray, look! Do you see it?" Ronnie points downward.

"Oh wow, I see two of them. I think it's *una familia*." It's a dark green alligator with a smaller gator, probably its baby boy or girl gator, splashing and bobbing behind it in the water.

"This is their pond or lagoon. Whenever I come here, they're right there swimming back and forth, their tails propelling them fast and slow. Neat, huh? I call her Gwendolyn and her daughter Ginger. Watch out, Ginger snaps!" I laugh. I can't help it, even though it's a cheesy joke. But coming from Ronnie, it's cute, just like him.

"Would you believe that I've never seen a gator before in my life, besides the college team when they played against UM?"

"Well, there's a first time for everything, Ray, like you cycling with me here," he says, the sun casting a certain glimmer in his eyes.

We stand there for several minutes, but I don't feel the time pass by at all despite the chorus of buzzing mosquitoes, crickets, frogs, the occasional bird, and who knows what else out here. I'm enjoying this wildlife adventure with the cutest and sweetest guy I've met in Miami so far. We lean in closer, and I want to gently kiss those soft red lips of his and taste the small film of Gatorade on his upper lip. I want to gently rub the back of my hand against his flushed red cheeks. I'm thinking, no I'm feeling—that I should kiss him, but then Ronnie suddenly turns and points out some other wildlife I hadn't noticed because my eyes were too fixed on Ronnie.

"See that over there about one hundred feet north of the pond? That's a deer, watching out for the gators."

I look in that direction, and I can barely see a deer's head poking from the dry brush.

"Oh wow, he's pretty close. I hope Gwendolyn isn't hungry. She's a big mama jama," I say.

"Deer are pretty fast out here. They can trot like Bambi on speed. I'm sure he'll be fine. If not, we'll be seeing a live episode of *When Animals Go Wild in The Everglades.*"

Just as Ronnie turns my way, and I'm ready to kiss him again, he takes a big swig of his Gatorade, exhales deeply, and swings his messenger back around his shoulder.

"Are you hungry? We should get going. It's going to take us at least an hour to get back to the park's main entrance," Ronnie says, wiping his sweaty forehead with his arms and beginning to walk back down.

"Yeah, come to think of it. I'm starving. The Gatorade is helping though. Let's go. The sooner we get moving, the faster we get back and the quicker I can smoke a cigarette." I'm feeling pretty miserable craving a smoke right now, but I don't want Ronnie to see that antsy side of me. I want him to remember our first date as something fun and not focus on me bitching about my lack of nicotine.

We trek back down the observation tower and back to the bikes. We start cycling to the Shark Valley hut where we parked Ronnie's old Liberty. It's eight long miles back. Since the trail winds and curves, it's hard to see straight ahead. That makes the ride seem much longer than before.

That whole ride back, we don't talk much. I'm more interested in observing Ronnie and keeping a steady pace. He has this child-like wonder about whatever he sees, like the endless oasis of grass and the sheet of slow-moving water that hugs the bike trail. I find Ronnie intriguing, and I can't wait to just sit alone with him at a restaurant and get to know him better without any of these pesky dragonflies tailgating me. Some other cyclists whiz by us as if they were training for a decathalon. (They're probably rushing back to smoke their Marlboro Lights.) Every now and then, we see a couple or a family walking on the path. I would think that would be hazardous to their health because who knows when a panther or one of the alligators might decide to greet them.

I ride behind Ronnie who is riding without holding the handle bars. He has each hand on one of this knees, pumping his legs up and down like the pistons of a steam engine. From here, I can check out his cute Cuban butt. I'd give that bum of his four stars because of its tautness and roundness. It's not big or small but just right. I can't wait to see his pants off him. With less than two miles to go, I see salvation ahead—the park's entrance—and I pedal with what little steam I have left in my body. Ronnie is as energetic as he was when we got here two hours ago. If anything, he seems more invigorated. We finally reach the end of the trail and cycle back to his Liberty where Ronnie pops the back door and starts to load our bikes. As if he was in a movie, I see him take off his red shirt, like a curtain rising and unveiling a grand show. I see his happy trail funnel up to a scattering of some nice dark black chest hair on his lean, toned frame. He dries off his face with the shirt and looks my way.

"Well, what do you think? Wasn't that fun?"

I am instantly excited, my heart pitter-pattering like a conga beat. Good thing I wore baggy black shorts today or else he'd see another kind of wildlife pop out of my shorts.

"Yeah, that was fun. I feel great. Now if you'll excuse me, I need a cigarette."

I walk toward the hut, smiling the whole way, to smoke my cigarette. Across the parking lot, I watch Ronnie carefully load my bike into the truck. When he's ready to leave, he gives me a thumbs up. I can't help but agree.

When I walk back to the SUV, Ronnie puts on a new shirt. It reads "Will Flex For Food!", and I can't help but laugh.

"Will you flex for a kiss?" I casually ask, staring straight into his eyes.

"I don't know. Let me flex and see," he says with a flex that defines a small but round bicep. He smiles back.

Under the bright blue sun-filled sky, we're standing there, a few inches from another when it finally happens. One moment, I'm staring at him asking him about the shirt and looking at his bicep. The next second, we're kissing. I taste the salt on the top of his upper lips as my tongue softly wiggles its ways inside his mouth, tickling his tongue. A powerful rush of endorphins fills my body, creating a wave of internal tingles. I comb my right hand through the back of his wet wavy short back hair. And as we slowly pull back from the kiss, I look deeply again into those brown eyes. I see my own reflected in them. Something in my heart opens up, like a tulip blossoming in spring. I don't know if it's from the heat or lack of liquids, but the sensation feels good, too good, all over.

"Now I would give that kiss five stars, Ray Martinez," Ronnie says.

"I disagree. That kiss was on a whole other rating scale," I say. Ronnie flashes that friendly smile of his, and we continue to kiss, leaning into each other against the side of the Jeep. Our noses playfully nudge each other's, and we laugh at the sensation. I forget momentarily all about smoking another cigarette. I'm too busy getting my fill of Ronnie.

An hour later, we're sitting across from each other inside La

Carreta restaurant on Calle Ocho, the one with the over-the-top lit giant wheelbarrow out front. (I always think that wheelbarrow is going to come loose one day with our next hurricane and roll down SW Eighth Street causing a big traffic jam.) I tell the waitress that I want a *media noche* sandwich and a mamey shake. Ronnie orders a steak sandwich with fries and a Diet Coke. Whenever I take a sip from my icy water, our eyes meet, and we both grin and look away. Gosh, I feel like one of those girls in Disney's *High School Musical*. I wonder if this is how Papi felt when he met Mami or how Racso was when he met Cindy. I think I understand now. When you meet that special person, you just know without really knowing how. It just strikes you when you least expect it.

"Do you come here a lot, Ronnie?" I ask, breaking some of the fresh hot bread.

"I love La Carreta. I come down whenever I get a chance. It's owned by the same people who run Versailles. It's the same food really, but Versailles is more of the crown jewel with its elegant mirrors and green motif. La Carreta is the underdog with its brown booths and matching wooden interior. Everyone comes here late at night or when they're coming back from the beach. The food is just as good. The décor is just a little on the frumpy side compared to Versailles. They're like fraternal twins, similar but not the same. One is more appreciated than the other," he says.

"Yeah, tell me about it." Maybe I shouldn't have said that. Ronnie may read it another way.

"Is that how you feel about Racso? I thought you and Racso were identical." Ronnie definitely picked up on the double meaning. He pays close attention.

"We're identical but very different. What I meant by that comment was that sometimes I feel like the underappreciated one. He seems to be the apple of my parents' eye. He's straight, the school teacher, and he has a great fiancée. He set the bar pretty high. He seems to be everything they hoped they would have in a son. He doesn't even smoke. All they do is talk about his upcoming wedding. I'm the son they call for trips to Costco or to help my dad fix something in the house. I'm like the on-call Martinez offspring, but mind you, they don't want to know anything about my personal life, not that I have anything going on," I say, winking at Ronnie who is twirling his straw in his glass of ice water.

"But I'm sure you're what your parents hoped for you to be too. You're a movie critic at one of the biggest papers in the state. You're a good person, super cute, too. I would find it hard to believe that they would favor Racso over you. If anything, you have the easier name to pronounce and write," Ronnie says, casually touching my right hand with a tender smile.

"That's one good thing I got out of this deal, an easy name," I joke. The waitress with the poofy red hair comes back with our food, and Ronnie and I chow down immediately. I taste the explosion of pickles, swiss cheese, mustard, and pork from the *media noche* sandwich. Crumbs from the bread rain down the sides of my cheek. Ronnie drowns his fries in a pool of ketchup.

"We may have to call 911 to rescue those fries. They need some saving," I say.

"Well, I'm sure you'll jump in and save the fries for me. Here, have some. You earned it after our two hour ride," he says, grabbing a few fries and plopping them on my plate.

I am truly enjoying this date. Being with Ronnie is easy and fun, and I can't help but stare at him. I hope I'm not being obvious, but whenever I catch myself looking at those beautiful black eyebrows and those brown eyes, I find them staring right back at me. I like this guy, a lot. It's not so much his cute looks. It's his heart. I'm equally drawn to both.

As we continue eating, I suddenly hear the voice of doom. My worst nightmare just walked in with his bride to be, the Cuban-Irish Cinderella.

"Oh . . . my . . . God . . . look Cindy, it's Ray and a *friend*." Of all days for my brother to annoy me, why did it have to be this late afternoon on this date? He's standing by the entrance of the restaurant with Cindy. She waves happily. I nod and then glare at them to go away. It doesn't work. It probably fuels Racso even more to harass me on my date with Ronnie. They gingerly walk over to our table. They don't look like they're going anywhere but here. There should be a movie called *10 Ways To Get Rid of My Brother* and right now, I've got twelve in mind.

"This is such a coincidence," Cindy gushes, looking as pretty as ever wearing her snug blue jeans and a pink blouse. Racso is in a black T-shirt and blue jeans. Pretty typical of him.

"Hey, guys. This is Ronnie Reyes, and Ronnie, this is my brother Racso and his fiancée Cindy. They must be on their way out or something."

They all shake hands, but Cindy, being the affectionate and sweet person she is, reaches down and gives Ronnie a kiss on the cheek.

They exchange pleasantries when I suggest, "Well, you guys probably must be going. We don't want to hold you up from your plans or anything."

Racso's eyes narrow at me and says "Oh, not at all! We'll join you. We're just getting here ourselves. We're starving." The next thing I know, Racso and Cindy slide into our booth, with Racso next to me and Cindy next to Ronnie. I just thought of the perfect sequel for the *"The Texas Chainsaw Massacre."* Call this one, *"The Miami Chainsaw Massacre."*

The waitress comes back and sets down two more placemats and silverware for Racso and Cindy and hands them two menus. They tell her right away what they want: Racso gets the ropa vieja and a Sprite and Cindy orders a croquette sandwich and a Materva soda.

We're all sitting there, and Ronnie, being the nice guy he is, gets the conversation going.

"Ray tells me you're both teachers. I think that's really wonderful. My sister Lisa is going to FIU next year to study education," he says, looking back and forth between Racso and Cindy.

"We like him already, Ray," Racso says, breaking some of the bread and smearing it with mounds of butter.

"We're often underappreciated, and it's sometimes really stressful but every now and then, you have a student who tells you how much they love and appreciate you, and that makes up for all the red tape we deal with from the school board. We're not paid very well, but we get so much in return," Cindy says, tucking her black strands of her hair behind her ears, a habit she does often.

"I get letters from my former students who are now in college, and they sometimes come back and visit me at Gables High. It's good to see that we had an effect on them, that we're not just standing in front of the classroom talking to ourselves. It's about making a difference, even if it's one student at a time," Racso says.

I can't seem to get a word in because Ronnie, Racso, and Cindy are getting into their teaching groove talk which I find endearing. He's connecting with them.

"I often thought about being a teacher, but I love to write. It's my secret pleasure. I find that I'm often writing in my head, writing my ledes, or forming paragraphs and thinking of new ways to say the same thing. I love putting words together the same way an artist mixes colors from paint. It's addictive. It's who I am. I can't help but think I was meant to be a writer but more importantly, do something positive with it. That's why I want to be a journalist. In a way, journalists are teachers, too. We inform and educate," Ronnie says, a look of tenderness written on his face. I sit back and watch Ronnie hold his own with my bro and Cindy. He seems to be making a good impression of them. He fits in effortlessly.

"Good for you, Ronnie. Some people never figure out what they want to do, and you're ahead of the game," Racso says. "You go, boy!"

"Totally. You have to be passionate about what you do. If not, it's just a job and you end up hating it," Cindy says. "The sooner you know what you want to do, the better off you'll be. Just look at Ray. He worked hard, and now he has his dream job." I want to hug Cindy right now. She is such a good person. She's throwing the conversation back to me.

"Thanks, Cindy. But enough talk. Let's eat!" I say.

"I second that motion," Ronnie pipes in and winks at me as the waitress brings Racso and Cindy's meals.

"But first let's make a toast," Cindy says. "To good Cuban food and to good company and new friends," she says, holding up her Materva to all our glasses.

"To great teachers," Ronnie pipes in.

"To never going biking without a pack of cigarettes," I say.

"Bottoms up!" Racso says. "Something Ray would know something about."

Cindy spits out her drink after hearing the comment. Ronnie starts to laugh. The waitress walks by and hears the word "bottoms" and gives us a curious puzzled look. I guess she speaks English and knows gay talk when she hears it.

And I'm speechless for one of the few times in my life.

I stomp on Racso's toe under the table.

"Ronnie, please excuse my brother. Sometimes, teachers can act like their immature students," I say, feeling good about my zinger.

"I'm just playing little brother. It was a joke, okay? Sorry Ronnie if I made you feel, ahem, uncomfortable. I like to tease my little bro."

"Ray, he was kidding around. You know how your brother is," Cindy says, trying to clean up the mess. "Besides, you're a top, no?" she says, with a big wink.

"Please . . . let's just eat!" I declare, shoving a piece of bread into my mouth and Racso's. I notice Ronnie has a smirk on his face from the brotherly bashing. He seems to like my crazy twin and Cindy so far. As everyone starts to eat, Cindy looks up at me and silently mouths, "He's a catch!" with a big wink.

"I know," I mouth back.

22

Ted

I'm having trouble focusing on work for once in my life, but since I've done this for so long and dozens and dozens of times, I can run on autopilot. I'm a TV pro after all. Even on a bad day, from a stuffy nose or the runs, I can get away with it and you'd never know what was going on with me from your side of the tube. Just give me some foundation, put me on camera, and let me roll. Whenever I talk into the camera, I disappear into this mental zone, almost a trancelike state, where I'm completely focused on the words, the footage, my questions, and the story. I stare right into the camera, and the dialogue naturally pours out of me. Time is of no consequence. I just need to tap into that zone right about now and focus. I'm sitting here in the front waiting room of the South Beach Boys and Girls Club at Flamingo Park waiting for Jamie Munoz, this week's *Wednesday's Child* profile. He's nine years old, a fourth grader at nearby South Pointe Elementary. He has black straight hair that could use some trimming at Hannah and Her Scissors or even (gasp!) Supercuts. Jamie also has big, round, downward-turned brown eyes that look sad. I read over his background in the file that his counselor Tina gave me to prepare for my segment. Jamie's mother is in rehab for cocaine abuse, and his father hasn't been in the picture for years. The state took him into custody and has been trying to find a home for him since 2006. He's been bouncing from one foster home to the next. No luck. Poor kid. My heart goes out to all these youngsters who don't have a stable home life. It reminds me of how good I have things no matter how much I wallow sometimes in self-pity about not finding a steady guy. Speaking of guys, the reason I'm finding it difficult to concentrate on Jamie is because of Jergin, the German flight attendant.

I had such a nice time with him last Saturday at Club Café and then back at his hotel room. And for the record, I didn't get to nibble on his German sausage, which was fine by me although I imagined myself doing so. Instead, we went back to his hotel room at the Colonnade and had some drinks from the minibar. He also gave me some sweet rich German chocolate called Milka with colorful purple wrapping. We then cuddled on the bed. No sex. I know, I can't believe it myself. There was something sweet and yet intimate about the whole experience. He told me stories of growing up in Berlin when there was an East and West and how the subway there would pass underground between the two sides. He described how he would see armed soldiers glaring at the train from the station's platform as he went from the free zone to the communist one. Jergin described how English was difficult for him to learn at first in middle school but said he feels more comfortable speaking it now. As Jergin spoke, I felt the warmth and softness of his pale white skin with the tip of my index finger. I was like a cuddlesaurus, my head buried in the nape of his neck. He has the softest peach fuzz on his ears, little blonde hairs, like the back of a small golden puppy. His ears point out just a bit, by the way, but I won't hold that against him. I told him stories about growing up on the Cape and our bad winters. I detailed my adventures with Ray at Score and back at UM. I even told him about Max the chihuahua and how he's the most loyal male in my life these days. What I really liked about Jergin was that he was more interested in me than in my job. He's never seen me on the news in Miami, and to him, I'm just a nice handsome guy, not one of the most famous news reporters in South Florida. With all the hot young Boston boys at Club Café with their ultra lean bodies, Irish blue and green eyes, and straight spiked-up hair, Jergin was drawn to me. I caught his eye. I know I'm an okay looking guy, but I couldn't hold a candle up to Ray, Ronnie, Brian, or even that dick named Rico. Sometimes, people see the fame and celebrity of a person, and because of that, they label them as hot or handsome or extra special. Television does that to a person's perception. It alters it. I know if I wasn't on Channel 7, I wouldn't get as much attention as I do here in Miami. People would probably overlook me at Score. With Jergin, I felt like he really saw me and not the celebrity of me, and that meant a lot. He was genuinely interested in Ted Williams, the guy, not the reporter or host of *Deco Time*.

The night escaped us because before I knew it, it was nine in the morning and he had to get to Logan Airport and on a plane for work.

We exchanged numbers and emails and kissed, long, wet, goodbye kisses. I could taste the chocolate remnants from the Milka bar and the beer from the minibar. I hugged him tightly and kissed him one more time. He told me he would be in Miami in about two weeks for a layover. I grew excited at the thought of seeing him so soon again, but I wasn't going to hold my breath either.

"You can show me favorite places to eat," he said in his broken English which I found endearing although hard to understand at times. "I can not vait to feel de varm Florida sun and to see your handsome face again. I vant to meet this famous Max de dog and maybe your friend Ray."

Thinking back, I should have ripped off his jeans and had my way with him and enjoyed some wild and reckless fellatio. But then again, I didn't want to either. I knew for some reason I would be seeing him again even though he's a flight attendant. You know what they say about flight attendants, they fly from one bed to another with each arrival and departure. It was a nice night in Boston. Nothing gained, nothing lost, but my mind keeps drifting back to Jergin, the blonde swirls of his combed-up hair, those aqua green eyes, the sincerity in his voice. These recent memories are distracting me from my assignment, and my mind should be on Jamie Munoz. I need to completely focus on this kid because he wants to be adopted. Put Jergin out of my mind. Jamie is the priority, for now.

Tina, a small woman with black curly hair wrapped in a bun and Lisa Loeb cat glasses, comes out of her office with a little skinny boy in tow and a big smile.

"Jamie, this is Ted Williams, from Channel 7 News. He's going to spend some time with you this afternoon and ask you questions about what you like to do, your favorite shows, teams. You know, fun stuff," she enthusiastically says into his ear as she bends down and stands behind him and faces my way. I also bend down to introduce myself, even though it will wrinkle my Brooks Brothers gray slacks.

"Hi, Jamie. I'm Ted. We're going to have some fun this afternoon. I hear you're the guy who knows this place inside and out. Maybe you can give me a tour and show me around. How does that sound?"

"Good," he says as a chorus of screeches and squeaks from kids' sneakers thunder in the background of the center. Jamie seems a little shy. I have my work cut out in for me. I need to break him out of his shell. Carlos, our camera man, is outside, and I signal through the front glass windows of the youth center for him to come in. I usually have Carlos wait outside for these *Wednesday's Child* tapings because I don't want the camera to intimidate the kid at first.

I tell Jamie that Carlos will be following us around and for him just to pretend that he's not there.

"Pretend we're big celebrities like Justin Timberlake or Hilary Duff and this right here is one of those TV cameras to capture our every move. You're going to be famous, Jamie."

He just nods. Okay, maybe this approach wasn't a great idea. Most kids would rather have a simple home than be famous.

"Want to show me your favorite thing to do here at the center?" I ask, as we walk through the back doors of the center and outside into the basketball court.

"I love basketball. I want to play for the Miami Heat!" he pipes up, his face lighting up at the word basketball. I found my way in.

"Well, I'm not a very good player, but maybe you can show me how to shoot. I bet you kill on the court! I bet you can teach Alonzo Mourning and Dwyane Wade a thing or two, huh?"

He shyly laughs. I quickly motion to Carlos to start taping as Jamie grabs a basketball from a bin of balls by the door.

We make our way to the middle of the court where a bunch of giggly girls are jumping rope. Just down from them, a group of boys are shooting baskets at the other end of the court. The thump thump thump of bouncing balls mix with the sounds of the whipping swinging ropes and a girl saying "Oh no you didn't. Gurrl, I bet you're prego like Britney with that belly of yours." Um, nice. I'm glad to see our future generation is so impressive. I shouldn't talk. They probably watch me on *Deco Time* talking about the same thing with Trina Tucker.

"Come on, Ted, let's see what you're made of," Jamie says, hurling the ball. I react quickly enough to catch it. Time to roll up my dress shirt sleeves and loosen up my tie.

I dribble the ball and talk to Jamie as we pass it to and from each other.

"So how do you like school? I hear you're a good student, Jamie." I try to shoot the ball into the basket. I miss. Jamie dashes under the hoop, grabs the ball and starts bouncing it in between his legs. He has great control over the ball. He's pretty good.

"I really like math. I think it's easy, like this shot," he says, before successfully making a basket.

"I'm horrible at word problems." I say. "That's why I have an accountant." Jamie laughs. We dribble the ball and pass it back and forth as we make our way up and down to the basket. Each time, Jamie makes it in with the confidence of a seasoned player. I know I'm going to look like a big goof for this segment with Jamie beating me in hoops, but it's for a good cause. My ego can take it. If Jamie finds a home because of this, it would have been worth it. The whole time Carlos is running alongside us, zooming in and filming the action while trying not to get in the way. Jamie forgot he was there, which is great because he's coming off very natural.

"If you could talk to anyone out there, maybe potential adoptive parents, what would you want to them to know about you Jamie?"

He stops for a moment and looks up at me. He catches his breath, licks the sweat off his lips, and begins to talk.

"I'm a really good kid, and I don't know my father, and my mother is sick. I'm nice and easy to be with, and I get good grades, mostly Bs. I just want a regular home and to have my own bedroom like some of my classmates at school so I can put up my Heat posters and Miami Dolphins stickers. My real name is James, but you can call me Jamie. Please give me a home!" he says, keeping his locked eyes on me the whole time. No matter how many of these *Wednesday's Child* segments I've done, these kids always manage to get to me. This is when the viewer sheds a tear. My heart melts, and I feel my eyes about to leak with some tears. I blink hard to keep them at bay.

"You'll make some parents very lucky one day soon," I tell him, patting him on the shoulder. He gives me an impish grin.

I then turn to Carlos and speak directly to the camera.

"If you have a home and have the time and space to share it with this boy who can play some good basketball, please call the number below on the screen. For *Wednesday's Child*, this is Jamie (he waves to the camera) and I'm Ted Williams. See you next time, if Jamie doesn't slaughter me on the court. Back to you in the studio."

And we're done. Carlos cuts away from the camera and takes some pan shots of me and Jamie hanging out on the court. I continue to play with Jamie a little longer, off camera and then treat him to a snow cone that is sold inside the center. Before I leave to go back to the station, I give him a black Channel 7 baseball cap, which has a big "7" in yellow. He high-fives me when I say good-bye.

"Thanks, Ted. Come back, and I won't let you win next time," Jamie says at the front entrance of the center.

"Let me win? I was trying to let you win Big J. You're on!" I say. As Carlos and I begin to drive back to the station in North Bay Village, my cell starts to vibrate. It's Brian. I haven't seen him in about two weeks.

"Hey, Brian. What's up?" I say, sitting in the back of the van, reviewing some of the footage for the *Wednesday's Child* segment.

"Hey, Ted, are you busy?" Brian asks in a serious but concerned tone.

"I have a few minutes. What's going on?"

"I need to talk to you and Ray. I need some feedback on my situation. Are you guys back in town? Could we meet up Friday night at Score. There's a lot to tell you guys."

This sounds juicy.

"Yeah, sure. Is this about Eros or Daniel? Or another boyfriend you're keeping hush hush?" I tease.

"It's about Eros. I need your help and Ray's for an undercover mission. Are you in?"

Now this sounds really good. I'm intrigued.

"I'm in! I'll call Ray. You can bet we'll be there at Score, if Ray doesn't have another hot date with Ronnie."

"Ronnie?" Brian asks.

"Yeah, this cute young journalism student Ray met at the convention. They've been hanging out the last few days. I think Cupid struck Ray's heart."

"Well, we definitely have a lot to catch up on then. See you Friday night."

"Yeah, we'll be there and ready for mission impossible. Count us in." I wonder what Brian is up to. I bet he wants us to check out Eros for him or else why would he need the help of two reporters? I can't wait for this exclusive.

As soon as the van pulls into the station parking lot, I receive a text message. I find myself smiling when I look at the face of the cell phone. It's from Jergin.

I will be there next Friday. I cannot wait to see you again, handsome.

I text message him back.

Same here, Jergin. Same here.

23

Brian

"Why did you cancel my credit cards, Daniel? I can't believe you did that to me," I tell Daniel on my cell as I pace back and forth inside the kitchen. I can see the anger reflected in my image on the stainless steel refrigerator.

"Because you didn't want to make a decision about me and that Puerto Rican guy. So you know what? I made one for you."

He's bitter and sounds somewhat numb over the phone. My intuition tells me there's something else going on here besides Eros. The Daniel I know doesn't back down from a fight. He seems to want to move on pretty quickly, "Now deal with it. Let's see how your new boyfriend takes care of you." Daniel says.

What a dick! He knows I'm indecisive about things and I would have made a decision eventually about my future. For the record, I was leaning more toward being with Eros. That's what my heart wants. But then, my wallet is looking pretty empty without Daniel's help. I couldn't even pay for dinner with Millie and Eros at Larios restaurant. Thankfully, I filled up the Rover with gas earlier in the week. I don't want to sound selfish, but I would have a harder life, financially, without Daniel. I do earn my keep by maintaining our homes, but that doesn't translate well outside our relationship and cozy little world. My last real job was working as a waiter at Food Bar and even there, I would freak out the snotty

New York queens whenever I dropped a plate of food during Sunday brunch. My days were numbered there, and Daniel swept in and took me away from all that hard labor. I'd have a hard time holding down a job nowadays.

I really thought Daniel would fight harder for me. He seems to have cut me off too quickly. His financial bullying is another reason why I would want to move on though. I want to stand on my own and be my own person. I'll never be that if I stay with Daniel. I want to be independent.

"Look, I know you're angry, but I want to be with Eros. I'm sorry Daniel but I'm in love with the guy. I love this feeling, even though it's going to make me poor. I do love you Daniel and I always will, but I can't take this life anymore. We're together but we have sex with other guys, and I want more. Call me a selfish dick, but I want love, one-on-one love." My eyes brim with tears, and I'm having trouble speaking. My throat has constricted, an invisible small ball is lodged in there. Snot runs down my nose. Mom already left for the airport so I'm home alone, now sitting on the marble steps in the living room and looking out through the grand glass front doors. My right hand leans on my head, and I notice, through the slits of the front gate, cars zipping by in a blur as they dash toward the beach on the Venetian Causeway. My life as I know it with Daniel is flashing by me, too.

"Well, maybe I want the same thing, Brian. You're not the only one in this situation. Maybe I want to meet a young cute guy who wants to have sex with me and only me. Did you ever think of that? It's not just you. This is about me, too," Daniel says. Then my inner radar goes off, redlining. Daniel must have met someone recently. Why else would he want to end things so fast?

"Daniel, you met someone haven't you? I can just feel it." My heart does back flips at the thought. I imagine him lavishing some skinny blonde boy with straight hair down to his shoulders with all the bigger-than-life gifts Daniel would surprise me with like a new car, the demo CD of my songs, the house here in Miami Beach.

"Yeah, I have. His name is Bradley. He's twenty and an architecture student in Providence, R.I. He's been coming down to Chelsea the last few weeks, and we have incredible sex. He's a sweet guy, kind of like how you used to be."

"Oh yeah! I bet he's a big old bottom and does whatever you say, right? That's why you're into him. He's young and impressionable. I, at least, fight back with you. You got yourself a little boy to boss around. That's not me anymore."

"I've done nothing wrong, Brian. We're in one big mess that only got more complicated when you wouldn't stop with that Latino. I met someone too, and I'm not going to give him up. Bradley is fun. He makes me feel young. Let's face it Brian, you're not the young guy I fell in love with when we met at Chelsea Piers. You've gained some weight, and you can't even hold a job. Bradley relaxes me, and he knows so much about architecture. I'm actually learning something from him."

"Well, I'm learning something new too, that you're a big prick. Go, have fun with Bradley, but remember I own half of this house and New York is still my home." I get up and walk outside to the front driveway. I stand in front of our majestic house, with the lush coconut palms that ribbon the property and the beautiful brick circular driveway. I am reminded all of the houses and projects we've built together: the expansion in our Chelsea condo, the Newport home, and this, the Miami villa, my favorite of them all.

"You can have the Miami house. It's yours. I always thought of that place as more yours than mine, since you're always there. But New York . . . you can't touch that. That's my condo, and it's in my name. You can do whatever you want with the Miami house. It's yours. Sell it and live off the profits. I don't care. Share it with your new man," he says, before hanging up.

I should have seen this coming. It was bound to happen, Daniel meeting someone he's more compatible with sexually. I know he's angry with me right now, but he's really a pussycat deep inside. He needs some time to vent and simmer down. There's a reason I fell for Daniel in the first place, his big heart, and I know we can work through this, as friends. I take a seat on our front steps, and I feel that familiar South Florida breeze brush up against my skin. It's comforting. I close my eyes, and I see the reddish circles from inside my eyelids as the sun beats down on my face, warming it. I take a few deep breaths and absorb the energy of the sun. I hear the breeze hiss through the coconut palms as it were speaking to me, trying to comfort me.

I know things between Daniel and me will never be the same, but I'm trusting this feeling I have about Eros. I knew where I stood with Daniel. I know where I stand now. I just want to move forward and see what life has to offer me.

I smile thinking about waking up with Eros each morning or feeling his strong arms each night in our bed. It's time for me to move on and embrace this fiery passion and love I feel for Eros. He's my future. I know I'll have to tighten my purse here and there, but the possibilities delight me. I can return to my singing and give private lessons to my neighbors, who have been asking me to for years. I can volunteer at a school or a church and sing with the choir. I know Ray and Ted can get me in touch with the proper contacts for that. I can even downsize. I don't need this grand Miami palace. I can live nicely with a smaller cottage on the mainland. This house and our projects in Chelsea and Newport symbolize my relationship with Daniel. They were beautiful properties to look at, but they needed much work on the inside. Nobody ever noticed. We kept up pretenses, and it's time to drop the façade. I've been boxed-in far too long. It's time to break out of this fancy display case that has been my life.

We just didn't make great lovers, that's all. And I know Daniel will never let me starve. I still believe in him and although he's mad at me, I sense he still believes in me. We've always understood each other so well, and that's why my heart and this home will always have a place for him.

I decide to channel all this emotional energy through my music and put it out there. When I play the piano and sing, the music cleanses me of my thoughts. It purifies me. Just as a writer might write in a journal or a diary, I use the piano as my tool of self-reflection. God knows I've written about so many men in my pop songs which have never seen the light of day. But that's okay. This is for my benefit, my own healing.

I scoot my bench under the piano, and I start to play. When I sing, the music pours out of me. It's a creative journey and one that I do alone. No matter what's going on in my life, music comforts me, the same way the breezes outside soothe my skin. I start to play a somber melody, a slow song that is part rhythm and blues and somewhat pop—like an old Jon Secada song. I start singing the lyrics as they emerge in my mind. I grab my synthesizer and add a heavy bass beat to my piano playing.

> *Lonely . . .*
> *Inside.*
> *Realizing the love has died.*
> *I tried to change . . .*
> *My mind.*
>
> *I painted, a picture.*
> *Of this so-called perfect life.*
> *It wasn't enough*
> *To make things right.*
>
> *No one is to blame.*
> *I've tried before.*
> *Moments were good,*
> *But I need more.*
>
> *Need healing for my heart.*
> *Time has come for us to part.*
> *To find my own way, find my start.*
> *I gave you all I had to give.*
> *And now, it's time,*
> *To give you up.*

I play the song a few times and write down the lyrics. I title the song *Give You Up*. Maybe one day, I'll share it with Daniel. But for now, it reflects this moment.

I take a dip in the pool and swim some laps, feeling the warm water refresh my body and soul. I towel off, lay back on the lounge chair and dial Eros to tell him the news.

"*Hola chico!*" he says in his sexy Latin voice. "Are you okay? You sound sad."

He reads me so well.

"Daniel and I officially broke up this afternoon. It's okay though. It was something that had been over for a while. We had to do this."

"I'm sorry to hear that, Brian, but in a way, now you're free to be with me. We don't have to worry about your ex or anything. The house is yours, right?" he asks.

"Yeah, the house is mine. He gave it to me. I'm not going to be able to stay in New York anymore, at least for a while. I'm going to have to get my things and bring them down here."

"*Bueno*, take it easy. I'll see you tomorrow," he says.

Tomorrow? I want to see him tonight. It's only four o'clock. What does he have planned for tonight that I can't see him? Again, my intuition is flying off the charts.

"What about tonight? I thought we can go and have some dinner in Coconut Grove or something to celebrate my break-up and our freedom."

"I'm on my way to work. I can't really talk. I'm working late tonight, until closing. We will celebrate tomorrow *chico lindo*," he says in an almost trying-too-hard-to-sound-convincing tone.

"Sure," I say, feeling annoyed. "We'll celebrate tomorrow then. Maybe I could use a night alone."

"*Bueno*, we'll talk tomorrow," he says.

"Yeah, have a good night at work." I flip my phone off, and I lay in the chair thinking about Eros and his sudden work shift tonight. He didn't mention before that he was working tonight. Something about this feels off. Actually, I still haven't been inside his place. He always has me drop him off. Before I seriously consider having Eros as a permanent part of my life, I have to get to the bottom of some lingering nagging questions I have about his home. I dial Ted to see if he and Ray are back in town so we can meet up at Score. I have an idea, and I'm going to need their help to pull it off. Operation Undercover Puerto Rican Lover is about to begin.

24

Ray

I can't believe Brian talked me into doing this. I can see the preview now, *Miami movie critic and Channel 7 reporter—Peeping Toms in South Beach. More news and then some at 11.* I don't know what's worse, having Racso announce that I'm a big old bottom in front of Ronnie or actually standing outside of Eros's building with Ted while Brian sits in his Land Rover as the look-out guy. My phone vibrates. It's a text message from Mr. I-Don't-Trust-My-Puerto-Rican-Lover.

Do you see anything? Is he in there with another guy?

Ted and I are looking up Eros's apartment number in the lobby of this beat-up old building in South Beach on Lenox Avenue. It's a dark street full of weathered apartment complexes that have long lost their Deco charm. Tucked away on some of the side streets between Fifth Street and Flamingo Park is subsidized family housing, which is shadowed by some unmanicured trees. This is a slice of South Beach you don't see in those splashy ads for new condos in *The Miami News*—the side of the Beach that city promoters and politicians would rather you didn't know about. This building reminds me of the old South Beach, the one used as a backdrop for

Scarface and the original *Miami Vice* episodes. This is the South Beach that became an afterthought after Christo draped the small islands in Biscayne Bay with floating sheets of pink plastic. I didn't know these buildings still existed. But then again, I live on West Avenue, in between two Starbucks.

"I found his unit. He's on the first floor, unit five, toward the back," Ted says, in his undercover reporting mode. I can tell because he's hyper and charged up, as if he were about to go live on air during a riot or hurricane.

"Let's move," he whispers, gesturing with his hand in a circular motion like a platoon sergeant in the field.

"Ted, cut it out. We're not in *Mission Impossible*. In fact, this should be called *Dumb and Dumber*. I can't believe Brian got us to do this." I start giggling. My Corona buzz swims through my system. It's like I'm a college student once again, doing something silly but fun, like the time Ted and I stole ten traffic signs on the UM campus one Friday night. And, just like tonight, we were drunk then, too. I'll never forget how the barricade blinked persistently in the back of my Toyota Tercel hatchback. We finally had to dump it in the UM pond because we couldn't figure out how to make it stop blinking. Luckily, campus police didn't catch us. And now here we are again, on another infamous adventure, which indirectly began at Score where we had a few drinks before meeting up to embark on *Stalking Eros*.

"You have to admit, this is fun, Ray. We're going to find out who Eros really lives with. We're gonna catch him with his pants off, I tell you," Ted says, his eyes narrowing as he pats his gelled black hair to make sure it's still groomed. For the record, Ted's hair is so tight and thick that even if Hurricane Andrew blew back into town, it would remain intact. The rest of Miami would be in pieces, though.

My nicotine craving kicks in, and I whip out a cigarette. Just as I light it, Ted scolds me. "What you are trying to do, give us away or set the building on fire? Put that thing away."

"I just need a few puffs," I say, sucking on the drag. "Stop it with the bitchitude. You get so bitchy when you drink, Ted."

Ted rolls his eyes. "Fine, Marlboro Man. Just smoke *that* way, toward the street."

Ted then gestures for me to follow him around the side of the building, and like a good drunk nicotine-addicted soldier, I do. We peek into one window. *Ooops.* I didn't need to see that. It's a straight couple having sex on their Pier 1 papasan cushion chair. The woman with black straight hair is riding him like a bull, and her mane of hair whips back and forth with each dip making the giant oval chair look like it will tip over. I start to tiptoe down to the next unit, but I have to grab Ted and peel him from the window.

"Did you see that guy's cock? It's huge" Ted says, mesmerized by the live porno playing out in front of him. "I may have to come back here with a news crew."

"Ted! They're going to catch us. Let's go," I whisper loudly, yanking him by his shirt. Of all things, Ted is wearing his Nordstrom's light-blue dress shirt from tonight's evening newscast. I'm wearing my *Bad Boys* T-shirt and blue jeans. We're as conspicuous as Will Smith wearing a yarmulke for Yom Kippur in a Miami Beach temple.

Ted and I slowly move down the side of the building, and we find the last unit, Eros's apartment.

"Psst. This is it, Ray. There he is, in the kitchen."

I squat a little and peek over the windowsill with Ted at my side. We playfully elbow each other for more space. We're in a tight narrow walkway with our backs barely touching a fence that is shrouded with some waist-high, needled bushes. I think I just saw a cat scurry by. *Meow.* Yep, definitely a cat.

"Do you see anyone else?" I ask.

"Nah, just Eros making some oatmeal. Who eats oatmeal at midnight?" Ted says.

We text message Brian on my cell.

We've got visual confirmation. He's here in the apartment. No sign of his roommate. I punch the words into my phone's keypad.

Brian responds. **That asshole! He said he had to work.** He ends the text with a scowling facial expression.

Ted and I remain at the window sill, and I get a good look at the rest of the place. It looks as if an older person lives here because there's a beaten-up sofa wrapped in never-ending plastic which is typical of most Hispanic households here. Personally, I think it's a cheap Cuban thing (something Papi and Mami do as well) to preserve the fabric of the furniture from human sweat, but that's another story, something for *The News's Sunday Style* section. I see an older Zenith TV set from the early 1990s with a few missing buttons. The coffee table is draped in a light faded green tablecloth. I see black and white photographs of a couple filling the back wall. The place looks dated, from the 1980s, as if someone bought new furniture and furnishings once and left it at that. Something isn't adding up here.

A hidden symphony of crickets harmonizes (probably in heat like the couple next door), and I think I just heard a frog. I'm mistaken. That was Ted who just burped. His vodkas and grapefruit cocktails are talking back, and, apparently, they have a lot to say.

"Excuse you!" I tell Ted.

"Sorry," he says covering his mouth. He's swaying a little. Of course, we only would do something this immature if we were drunk and stupid enough to fall for this when Brian brought up the idea.

"I think I see someone coming out of the room," Ted says, squinting through the window.

We take a closer look, and it's a hot guy. Wow. It's a guy wearing a nurse's top with matching light blue surgical scrubs and super white sneakers. His arms are buffed, and they sport a nice golden tan, which compliments his black crew cut and goatee. He's talking with Eros. We can't hear a thing besides all the wildlife back here including Ted.

"I bet you that's his secret lover," Ted says, scaring my eardrums with another one of his burps.

"Shhh! Your burps are gonna give us away," I say.

The male nurse grabs his black man bag and shakes Eros's hand. The conversation seemed pretty professional. No seductive glances or lingering handshakes.

"Can you hear anything?" Ted asks.

"Yeah, your stomach. Now shut up!" I say.

The man nurse, or murse, leaves, and Eros closes the door. He sits on the sofa and turns the TV on. He grabs a pillow from the closet and some sheets and makes the sofa into his bed. How strange.

"Maybe Eros is sick or something," Ted whispers.

"I'm gonna need that nurse if you don't stop with those smelly burps. What the hell did you eat for dinner Ted, bologna slathered with barbecue sauce? Is this what Trina Tucker puts up with sitting next to you on *Deco Time*? No wonder she's always in a bad mood."

"Sorry Ray-Man, my stomach is little upset," Ted says. "Oh wait, something is happening."

We glance back through the window, and I see an old lady inching her way into the living room with a walker. She has a nest of gray hair, and she looks a little like Eros, with her dark eyes and thick eyebrows, that were once black but are now bushy gray caterpillars. She's wearing a faded red robe. She looks weak and ashen. The side of my mouth curls downward as I scrutinize her more closely. She's in pain.

Eros gets right up and springs from the sofa to help her. Through his hand movements, I can tell he's telling her to go back to bed. Her face is a mix of sadness and resignation as she struggles to move forward with much effort. It looks like she hasn't been out that much. Eros walks her back to another room, her bedroom I suspect.

"That might be his mother," Ted says.

"Nah, Brian said his mother lives in Puerto Rico. This is someone else, another family member. Maybe an aunt?"

Now I feel awful for standing here with Ted spying on this old woman and Eros. This is an utter lack of respect and an invasion of privacy. This isn't right, and I feel disgusting for being drunken enough to participate in this. I can mentally see Racso and Cindy nodding in disapproval with Papi and Mami right behind him, their arms folded. What would Ronnie say, seeing me do this right now? I'm embarrassed just thinking about this. How would I explain this if we were caught by a policeman or a security guard, although by the looks of this building, they might be able to protect us from the real peeping Toms and those giant crickets.

"Ted, let's go. This isn't right. If Brian has trust issues with Eros, he should take it up with him. This isn't our problem, and what we're doing is illegal, in case you haven't noticed. We're two grown men standing outside the back of someone's apartment. How bad is that?"

"Yeah, I suddenly feel like a dick," Ted says.

We crouch our heads under the window sills and scurry back to the sidewalk and down the street to Brian's Land Rover. We tell him what we saw.

"I think you need to have a long talk with Eros. He's not telling you the whole story, and I'm sure there's a good reason why," I tell Brian, as soon as we hop into the Land Rover I can smell the leather of the seats. I feel like I'm sitting inside a giant Florsheim shoe shop. I light up a cigarette and blow the smoke out through the passenger window and let my cigarette ash blow away in the breeze so I don't stink up Brian's beautiful SUV.

"Ditto! Now, can you drop me off back at Score. I think I need to sit down and have another drink."

"Thanks guys. I really appreciate all your leg work here. I knew I could count on you two." Brian says, as he begins to drive us back to Lincoln Road parking lot. By the look on his face, I can tell a mix of emotions alternate inside him, questioning Eros and his honesty. I would probably feel the same way if I suspected Ronnie had been lying to me. As Brian drives, I think about how naturally and beautifully things have been developing between

Ronnie and me. He's pretty easy to read. His face speaks before he does, and so far, there hasn't been anything to lie about.

My mind wanders to our first date, where I survived the bike trip in the Everglades and later chowed down at La Carreta when Racso and Cindy invited themselves to dinner. Afterwards, Ronnie and I headed back to my place where I poured us a couple of glasses of white wine under the soft glow of a few gingerbread-scented candles. (Yes, I'm a regular Pottery Barn animal so sue me.)

As Ronnie sat back on my denim-blue sofa, he looked so relaxed, and it was contagious until Gigli awoke from her doggie nap. Gigli, the attention-needing dog, ran out of my room and began licking Ronnie like he was her favorite doll. Her tail wagged so fast, it looked like a black blur. So, I guess Ronnie passed the Gigli inspection and apparently, everyone else's. If Ronnie is good enough for my dog, who am I to argue?

"Good doggie! You're so pretty, Gigli," Ronnie told her, brushing the side of her face with his hands. I remember looking at his profile cast against the wall. I felt smitten watching him take the time to play with my beloved *perrita*. "Now, who's your daddy? Who's your cute daddy?" Ronnie said in a ga-ga voice. He winked at me as Gigli slobbered all over him, in a good way.

That night, as we drank our wine, we exchanged some sweet kisses. The whole time, Gigli perked up her little black ears and watched us, as our shadows blended into one.

When we touched, it wasn't primal or barbaric. There was something sweet and tender about our physical contact. Making out was an exquisite and delicious pleasure. I eventually led him by the hand to my bedroom (sorry, Gigli wasn't invited to come along) which is filled with framed movie posters from some of my favorite flicks, *The Godfather*, *Lord of the Rings*, and *Reality Bites*. We stood by the lip of my bed, and our hands generously rubbed and massaged each other's chests and shoulders as if we couldn't believe this was happening. I felt his toned body and tickled the black soft hairs that covered his chest and funneled down to his navel.

We fell onto my queen bed and rolled around playfully, giggling and enjoying the moment. It didn't take long for our clothes to fly off (landing on top of my dresser and covering Al Pacino's face on one of the posters.) Before I knew it, we were making love. We explored each other's bodies with a mix of patience and passion. We took it slow and savored each moment, every touch. When we finally came, it was the most intense orgasm I had ever felt, and I think Ronnie could say the same thing. We collapsed side by side, each covered in a film of sweat. I cradled him in my arms for the rest of the night.

Later on, when I got up to get some water, I let Gigli back into the room. She immediately hopped on the bed and snuggled in between us. I remember looking at Ronnie and Gigli and thinking how this was one of the most endearing scenes I had ever witnessed. It couldn't have been more perfect than if it had been in a Hollywood film filled with the kind of magic that engrosses a person into the story. Ronnie slept soundlessly, his chest rising and falling as his head faced toward the window and the small crush of South Beach high-rises in the distance. Gigli slept slumped near his stomach, her paw near his belly button. I sat back and watched them and felt something inside me hatch. With Ronnie there it felt even more like home, and the thought of him sleeping over in the future sent an insatiable tingle through me. It felt right, an unexplainable natural feeling.

Brian's voice abruptly snaps me out of my Ronnie flashback. Oh yeah, I was so caught up in recounting the other night that I zoned out and forgot that I'm here with Brian and Ted and that we just played out a scene from *Spy Kids*.

"Ray, thanks again. I appreciate it," Brian says, leaning his left hand on the side of his head, looking pensive. We're parked outside the Lincoln Road parking garage near Macy's, which will always be Burdine's department store in my nostalgic eyes.

"Trust me, just talk to Eros and ask him point-blank about his living situation," I say, climbing out of the car and closing the door.

"Yeah, find out why that little shit has been holding back," Ted says, hopping out of the back seat. Okay, more like stumbling out of the back seat. He's a bit tipsy.

"I'll see you guys later. Let me know how it all goes down. I'm heading back to Score, girls!' Ted says, as he begins his walk back. I don't think he should drink anymore, but Ted has always been good about not overdoing it with liquor. The walk might do him some good. And besides, I'm done. I just want to be in my bed under my goose down comforter.

"Yeah, let me know what happens, Brian. I'm going to head on home and maybe call Ronnie. He said it would be okay to call him after I met up with you guys. We're planning to go to Vizcaya Gardens tomorrow for a picnic," I say, walking up the flight of urine-soaked, garage stairs to my car.

On my drive back home under the bright glow of the street lights that dot 17th street, my mind is on Ronnie and what he's up to tonight. I smile at the thought when my cell phone buzzes. It's a text message. It better not be Brian again with another one of his wonderful spy ideas. And it better not be Ted drunk dialing, or texting. It's from Ronnie.

Hey McCutie. I'm headed to sleep. Had a long day at the university. Thinking of you. Sweet dreams.

I type a message back.

You too. Looking forward to our picnic tomorrow.

25

Ted

I'm back on Lincoln Road wobbling my way back to Score. Ray went home, and Brian is one his way to his McMansion to deal with Eros and the mysterious old lady in his ghetto apartment. Whatever.

I glance at my watch. It's 1 a.m. Still early enough to have another drink. I'm pretty thirsty after running around and playing James Bond with the guys. I plop myself at one of the café tables and order myself a vodka with grapefruit juice. My buzz is wearing off, I think. I'm not sure. I'm feeling quite happy, full of energy, even a little hyper. The manboy waiter comes my way with my drink already prepared. I love him.

"Here's your drink, Mr. Williams," he says, batting his blond eyelashes. "You're the only one who orders this."

"Thanks," I say to him, slurping the bitter-tart rim of the glass. This tastes good. I feel the coldness of the drink sliding down my throat. I down the drink in one long swallow and motion the waiter for another. A few minutes later, he returns with my encore. The vodka makes me feel warm on the inside, but it doesn't take away the fact that I'm alone and single on a Friday night. Ray has Ronnie to go home and talk to. Brian has Eros, whatever his situation is, to cuddle with. Those fuckers! And me? I've got a cute chihuahua. He's not enough though. I want my own special somebody. I'm getting tired of waiting. I gulp more of my drink. My eyes are getting fuzzy. I pull at the top buttons of my dress shirt to fan myself. My chest is pretty sweaty.

I finally did meet someone, and he just happens to live in another freakin' continent, literally a world away. While our meeting was brief, I've been impressed with Jergin's consistency. He has called me or text messaged me each day since we last saw each other in Boston. Sometimes, it's just a quick hello to say he's thinking about me. Other times, we talk about our days. It feels good that he's putting so much effort into trying to get to know me. He can have any guy in pretty much any city, yet he's not giving up on me. The other night, we were on the phone for an hour. He called me from London. It was in the afternoon there, and I got the call just after my live newscast at 11. I stayed up for another hour listening to his sweet German accent as he described all the different cities he had flown to that day and all the funny stories about his passengers. I don't know about you, but I couldn't handle spending my work day some 35,000 feet in the air. The recycled air is bad for the skin. What I find really endearing about Jergin is that he's determined to find a flight back to visit me here in the next two weeks, all because we seemed to click from our first meeting at Club Café. I find this somewhat romantic, something out of a cheesy gay novel. Maybe Tommy Perez of *Boys of Boston* could write about me and my German boy for his next book. I'd call it *I'm In Love With a Deutsche Boy.*

So then why I am sitting here feeling like shit? Because I know in the end, he's a flight attendant who lives in Germany. No matter how good he sounds, I can't be with him right now or drive over to his place whenever I want. I'm tired of this bullshit. I finish the rest of my drink and start walking. I'm wobbling again. I can't drive, so I decide to walk it off by strolling around South Beach.

I hang a left of Meridian Avenue, passing the art galleries and the once-decorated Deco apartment buildings whose painted facades need refreshing. I amble in between the tightly parked cars that line both sides of the streets not leaving an inch of space to maneuver out of. No wonder car insurance is so expensive here. Your car gets banged up just from sitting overnight. I focus straight ahead, but my vision is quite fuzzy. Maybe I shouldn't have gotten two more drinks. I start laughing. *Ooops.* I almost walk into one of the light posts. Excuse you!

I decide to cut through Flamingo Park to make a full loop back to Score. Hopefully, by then I'll be in better shape to drive home and throw myself on my bed. I could crash at Ray's. He's only a few blocks away, but he has one of the most uncomfortable beds. It's like sleeping on a mattress made of hardwood, and then there's Gigli, who must sleep on the bed with him. At least Max sleeps in his own doggie condo in the living room.

I walk through the enveloping darkness of the park, and I see some other guys in my peripheral vision. I bet they're cruising. I see one guy who quickly disappears in the darkness. Another pair of guys walk together to a parked Subaru down the street. This place is like a nocturnal carnival. I start to walk faster. I don't want to get caught, but how did I get here again? As I approach the edge of the park, near the baseball field, I notice a hot twenty-something guy walk right by. His brown eyes lock on me the whole time. I noticed his toned arms hanging from his sleeveless red shirt. I feel my cock raging in my pants. I turn around, and he's standing, staring at me with a crooked smirk. I smile back. He nods up at me. I don't know what takes over me, but I start to follow him. My cock is the pied piper, and I follow where it leads. He slows down so I can keep pace.

A few minutes later, we're walking side by side under the soft glow of the white street lights.

"Hey, you're hot, man," he says in a voice that makes me believe that's he nineteen or so.

"You too," I respond.

"Follow me," he instructs me with that crooked sexy smile of his, and I follow. My dick tingles and coils in my underwear, trying to bust through. My whole body reflects that lust.

We arrive at a desolate corner of the park behind a clubhouse near the track. He puts his hand on my shoulders, and I notice how the soft light causes his brown eyes to twinkle. He starts to unbutton my shirt quickly and abruptly pulls my it out of my pants.

"Hey, take it easy. That's a three hundred dollar shirt, buddy!" I say, as he opens up the rest of my shirt, leaving my torso exposed.

"I want to suck that cock of yours," he says.

"Yeah? Well what are you waiting for? Come and get it."

He bends down and starts unzipping my pants. I feel his hands dig into my underwear. I imagine Jergin being the one putting his hands all over my cock. I can just see his beautiful face kissing mine. My dick becomes as hard as an unbendable stick at the thought. Then I feel his warm moist mouth on my cock.

The guy slurps and moans as he goes down on me. My eyes are closed and focusing on Jergin. I'm lost in the thought, my cock spurting bits of pre-cum into this guy's mouth. Then I hear another voice and see the redness in the inside of my eyelids, as if a bright light is beaming on my face.

I open my eyes, and I'm blinded by the white flare of a flashlight.

"Well, it looks like we've got a breaking story right here," I hear a rough masculine voice say.

I cover the rim of my eyebrows with my hand. I gaze down and back up again, and I see a dark blue uniform, a gun, and then a badge. The picture focuses into full view. It's a Miami Beach police officer. Ah, shit!

The young guy who was sucking my cock gets up, wipes his mouth and looks down, shame etched all over his face.

I zip up my pants and tuck in my shirt.

"Officer, this isn't what it looks like . . ." I plead.

"Oh yeah, you're gonna tell me that your dick wasn't in that guy's mouth right there," he says, flashing the light on Mr. Young Guy, who covers his face with his hands.

"Well, I mean, ah . . ." I stumble for the right words, but there aren't any. I can't talk my way out of this one. A picture speaks a thousand words, and this one is screaming a million.

"How old are you kid?" the cop asks him.

"Nineteen!" he says, still looking down.

The officer asks to see his license, and he hands it over.

"I'm gonna tell you something, and I'm only gonna tell you this once, so you better listen. Do you know how stupid it is for you to be out here, in this dark park, having sex? Have you heard of AIDS? Herpes? Are you an idiot?"

"I wasn't going to let him ejaculate in my mouth. I was just having fun," the young guy says.

"You call this fun, getting down on your knees in a park where kids come and play during the day?" The cop approaches the young guy—I never did get his name—and talks right into his left ear as if it were a microphone.

"You realize you can get mugged, attacked, even killed? Do yourself a fucking favor and get out of here. Go home and study or something. Do something productive with your life. This is a warning. If I ever catch you hear again, I'm taking you to jail where I'm sure a lot of guys will want you to suck their cock and it won't be by choice, dickwad! Do you understand me?"

"Yeah, I'll never do this again. I promise," he says, scurrying away into the darkness.

Now it's just me and the cop, and I have no idea if he will extend me the same break. I hope so, but I can't talk myself out of this. He caught me red-handed, and he can easily make a name for himself by being the one to arrest Ted Williams. Oh God, please please get me out of this, I pray as I look up at the twinkling South Beach sky. I'll do anything. I'll give up my BMW and my spa treatments every other weekend. What was I thinking? That's just it, I wasn't thinking. I was drinking, and this is the second time I let my loneliness and drunkness get the best of me. I imagine all the possible scenarios. I lose my job and my cottage. I have to give Max away to a foster home for pooches because I don't have a job anymore to support him and his doggie condo. No other station would ever hire me again. I become the story, tainted bad news. Ray would be embarrassed to be seen with me. Jergin wouldn't even want to date me. My life would be over. News at eleven. The thought pumps so much adrenaline that I'm somewhat sober and more lucid.

The cop turns my way and leans into me.

"Now what do you have to say for yourself, Mister TV Reporter?"

I smell his fresh, minty breath. I'm close enough that the black whiskers of his mustache appear to me like giant black naked trees in a forest.

"I'm really sorry, officer. I guess I had too many drinks and decided to walk them off and I found myself here. I swear, I'll never do this again."

He takes a few steps back and paces back and forth.

"You know how lucky you are? You have a nice job. From what I've seen on the news, you seem like a professional, a nice guy. I've even watched your community stories and your weekly *Wednesday's Child* segments. You seem like a good guy, but what you did tonight is fucked up. You should know better. You're a role model to a lot of kids," he says. I stand there paralyzed, listening to everything he has to say. I wonder why he brings up children. Maybe he's a father.

"Then you come out here and let some dude suck your cock? Don't you know better? I know you know better. Take it to a hotel or to your house, but don't do this in public. Do you realize where you are?"

I gulp, trying to swallow my entire cardiovascular system back into my body.

"Flamingo Park?"

"Ten points for Mr. TV Reporter. But where are you exactly?"

I look at the building, and it's the back of the Boys and Girls Club. Now I feel like more of an idiot. I was here with the Channel 7 cameras the other day for my adoption segment.

"I recognize the clubhouse now. I know what you're saying," I say.

"Some of these kids want to be just like you when they get

older. What would they think if they saw you here, especially Jamie. You remember him, don't you?"

An instant flood of memories hit me. He was the nice kid I played basketball with a few weeks ago for one of my adoption segments. Oh shit, what if he had been here tonight and seen me?

"Yeah, I remember him. He was a shy but good kid. I let him beat me a few times." I smile at the memory.

"Well, thanks to you asswipe, Jamie found a home. He's in good hands. He's staying with some old friends of my wife's, and they're happy to be his foster parents while they go through the paperwork to adopt him. Jamie has a good home, and it was because of you dickhead."

My smile widens at the thought, imagining Jamie having his own room and shooting hoops with a father figure while his foster mom watches them from a kitchen window where she is baking him chocolate chip cookies. Maybe he'll have a dog to walk and take care of. I bet he'll be a good son. This is one of the reasons I became a TV reporter, to help people, even though I do the cheesy *Deco Time* segments. Flashes of shame hit me. Why did I come back to this park and put my life, my job, and the future of other kids who need my help to find homes at risk for a quick blowjob?

I tell the officer how happy I am that Jamie has a home. I'm praying that my good community service deed will make him see that I'm not just a horny park pervert.

"He's a good kid. I knew someone would eventually give him a nice home," I say.

"Well because of you, he has a home, and I would hate for Jamie and his foster parents to find out that the guy who helped them in all this went to jail for a blowjob in a park. It would taint the whole adoption thing. So this is what I'm gonna do Mr. Williams," he says, leaning in closer to my face so that we're centimeters apart. I could kiss him right now, but I don't want to end up dead or with a broken arm. His masculine authority is turning me on in a weird way.

"I'm gonna cut you a break this one time, for Jamie's sake. But you listen to me pencil dick . . . you better not ever come back here, got it? Too many kids benefit from your work. Think about them and Jamie the next time you think about going on your late night wild cockhunt in the park. I want you to remember this moment and how close you came to losing everything shithead," he says, pinching his index finger and this thumb to emphasize his point.

I swallow as if I'm trying wash away the whole experience down my throat like the drinks I had a few hours ago. I'm relieved when I hear him say "cut you a break." I could have lost everything over a nameless hot mouth on my dick. Thank you God for watching out for me. I promise you I'll never do this again. Next time, I'll stay at Ray's or catch a taxi home. No more vodka and grapefruits for me.

"Oh my God, thank you so much, officer. I swear, this will never happen again. I swear! I can't thank you enough," I say.

"I never want to see your face again, unless it's helping another kid on your show or on the news talking about what a great department I work for. Now go on, get outta here. Go back home."

I extend my hand to shake his, but he ignores it. He just nods, turns around, and walks away back toward the street and the parked cars.

I pull myself together, patting my head with my fingers to make sure it's still there. I wipe the film of sweat that beads on my forehead. I came so close to ruining my life. I can't afford to be this self-pitying guy who wants a boyfriend so bad, that he loses himself in alcohol and in Flamingo Park. It's just not worth it. As I start to walk back to the parking garage behind Lincoln Road, I think about how lucky I am and how God has given me so much. I have my health despite the zits I have to cover up with make-up before I go on the air. I have Ray, the greatest best friend in the world, a family who loves me, a dog who adores me, and a job that allows me to cover so many different stories that it's never boring. And I get paid obscenely well for all this. And most of all, I get to provide a community service with the adoption segments. If it wasn't for my recent show, Jamie wouldn't have found a home. Who knows how many other kids out there need my help. They don't need me locked in some jail cell for getting off in a park.

A few minutes later on my long walk back to my BMW, I stop at David's Café to grab a bottle of water to cool me off. I keep thinking about the cop's words and the anger behind his words when he spoke. He was really upset that someone who helped a kid like Jamie would stoop so low to be in a park for a blowjob. I know better, and from now on, I'm turning a new leaf. Forget about finding the guy of my dreams. I just want to focus on being happy with my friends, my dog, and my life. I have a blessed life, and it's about time I start acting thankful for it. As I sip my bottle water and let the events of tonight rewind in my head, I feel my cell phone vibrate. I whip it out, and it's blinking red which means a new text message. I open it up, and I laugh to myself. It's a message from Jergin. If he only knew what happened tonight. Well, he doesn't need to know. What happens in Flamingo Park, stays in Flamingo Park.

I am coming in next weekend. I can't wait to see your handsome face. Have a good sleep.

I smile at the thought of seeing him again so soon and I can't help but laugh at the timing of all this.

Life has a funny sense of humor.

26

Brian

I'm still processing all this. Eros lives with an old lady? What is that all about? I remember him telling me that his mom and family lived in Puerto Rico. And he said he had a straight roommate, but from what I sensed, it was a guy who wouldn't understand that Eros likes men. So who is this sick woman Ted and Ray described? Why would he keep that a secret?

I spent the night tossing and turning in my white silk sheets, trying to piece together any clues from our conversations these past weeks. Nothing adds up. Now I'm sitting up in my bed with my legs crossed and eyes closed, concentrating. I'm waiting for the answers to come to me, for the universe to send me what I need. I clear my thoughts and summon all my intuitive power. Nothing. I try again for a few minutes. Nothing. All I see—and feel—is Eros's love, his laugh, his smile, the meals he's cooked for me, the vision of him trying to ride the jet ski. All these beautiful memories. I want more of them to add to our collection. So my answers will have to come from Eros. First thing tomorrow, I'm going to show up at his door and confront him. But for the rest of the night, I can't sleep. Not even the cool breezes seeping in through my open grand bay windows help comfort me tonight. I have to remember that nothing is what it seems, even if the picture looks a little distorted right now. I have to believe in my heart that there's more to this than meets the eye. I need to hold on to that feeling. I've come too far breaking away from Daniel not to.

I'm a paranoid mess, and it stems from being in love. For so long, I had things my way with Daniel. The good life. We dined at the fanciest restaurants in Manhattan and Newport and traveled the world. Yet, whenever I felt the urge, I could go and hook up with a hot guy. I liked that freedom that our relationship gave me, but it was all an illusion, the money, the commitment. We were friends and roommates, not lovers. But now with Eros, I have so much at stake. He has my entire heart, something Daniel only had a piece of. When you love someone so passionately, you get possessive of that person. I want Eros with me and no one else. I don't want to even entertain the idea of him being with someone else even if we considered a threesome one day. I did that with Daniel, but I can't do that with Eros. I'd be too jealous. I want to protect what we have from all outside interference and catty, envious gay men. I want to preserve this beautiful spiritual and physical connection we share, like a secret language that only we know. That is why I'm beating myself up here, trying to dissect what this elderly roommate is all about. Deep down in my heart, without a doubt, I know I want to be with Eros and start a new life but not with all these confusing episodes. For us to have a healthy future, we need to trust each other. I need to get to the bottom of this.

I need to channel this energy somehow though since it's going to keep me up for a while. I get out of bed and walk downstairs to my beloved grand baby piano. I sit at the bench and quickly run my fingers rapidly along the soft ivory keys, making a melody that sounds similar to the opening of ABBA's *Dancing Queen* just before the singers kick in belting *You can dance*. . . . I goof around some more on the piano, feeling out the keys until I hit a series of notes that feel right like an old ballad. A slow song is being born. A song about my feelings for Eros. The words come to me.

Don't hold back
Let me in

I'm here for you
This is happening.
Our love is real.
Just let me in.

Many hours later, it's noon, and I'm feeling centered and focused from the piano playing. I drive to Eros's apartment, walk up the steps to the first floor of the building, and make my way down the hallway to Eros's unit. I notice the beige carpet is worn out and icky and there are smudge marks and fingerprints dotting the walls. I don't blame him for not wanting me to come over. This sort of reminds me of the dingy apartment I had in New York before Daniel whisked me away.

I hear the creaking of the wooden stairs above and people arguing in the unit I just passed. At the end of the hallway, I arrive at Eros's door and knock. He opens it, and he's surprised to see me.

"Brian! What are you doing here?" he says, keeping the door open just enough to fit his head. I can't see beyond his gorgeous Puerto Rican face. As mad as I am, I just want to kiss him right now and jump him, but I need to focus on the issue at hand. Besides, make-up sex is the best.

"We need to talk, and I mean now! I'm not leaving. I'm sick of your stupid lies."

"Shh! I need you to be quiet. I'll explain in a second. Meet outside, okay?" he says, looking back into the apartment momentarily.

"Fine! I'll be by the front of the building." He closes the door, and I walk away, jiggling my keys in my hand. I slam the front door.

A few minutes later under the blazing sun, Eros comes out, and we stand outside the front of the building, which looks even more run down than last night with its cracked and peeling paint and its garden of overgrown weeds.

"*Papo*, why are you here? I told you that I can't have visitors because of my roommate," he says in anger which causes the veins in his neck to protrude. I'm getting horny just looking at him, standing in his tight white tank top which contrasts with his mocha skin even more than usual. He's in black sweat pants, and I see the large bulge from his Puerto Rican cock. I glance back at those beautiful dark eyes.

"Yeah, your so-called straight roommate! You said he was a guy. From what I understand, it's an old woman."

"*Qué cosa?* Who told you that?" Eros says, looking stunned that I know the truth and scratching his head.

"Some friends told me. I'll leave it at that. But that's not the point. Why couldn't you be honest with me? Why have you been hiding that old lady? Who is she?"

Eros starts pacing, his fists are clenched, and he's breathing hard and fast. Those neck veins are getting fatter by the second. I've never seen him this upset before. He better not even think about hitting me. I may sing, but I can definitely fight and hold my own.

"That's none of your business," he says.

"None of my business! Well fuck you! I love you Eros, and that makes it my business. How can we plan a future if you won't be completely honest with me? Just tell me, who is that woman? It won't change the way I feel about you. Talk to me."

"You don't understand Brian," he says, turning his back and sitting on the cement ledge by the front door.

"Help me understand," I say, coming over and rubbing his back. No matter how angry I am with Eros, I feel I should try and comfort him as he tries to explain this. Whatever it is, it's not easy for him to talk about it and I want him to know that I support him, even though I'm upset. That's what lovers do.

He takes a deep breath and turns around.

"I'm embarrassed to say this to you but that's my great aunt. I didn't just move here to help out my family in Puerto Rico but also to help care of Tia Marta who hasn't been doing too well these last few months," he says.

I start to laugh and I can't help myself.

"That's the big secret Eros, you live with your old great aunt?

Oh my gosh, this is so funny," I say, uncontrollably laughing. I feel this heaviness lifting off my shoulders. So much confusion and anxiety over something so simple. Eros takes care of his aunt who sounds like she's on her deathbed.

"That's not funny," Eros says, turning back around on the ledge.

I try to control my laughing.

"Baby, why didn't you just say so? I think that's very sweet of you, taking care of your old aunt." He turns around again with his arms folded like a little kid.

"Because she doesn't know that I'm into guys and besides, I'm in my thirties and still living with my family. It's embarrassing. Only losers do that. When you talk about Daniel, you seem so proud of him, for all his success in business. Look at all the wealth you have together. When you talk about your friends, they're professionals with money and cool jobs. I don't have any of that. I'm just a waiter taking care of his aunt and dealing with being in love with a guy for the first time."

My heart swells so much for this guy. I think I love him even more right now. Eros is such a hard worker and so proud of who he is and most of all, he's loyal to his family. He feels bad because he doesn't think he's good enough for me. I disagree. He's more than I could ever want in a guy.

"Oh baby, you don't have anything to be embarrassed about. I'm very proud to call you my boyfriend," I say, giving him a tight strong hug. I rub his back, feeling every inch of him.

"You are?" he asks.

"Yes. I am. I love you the way you are. Just be you." His eyes water a little, and he holds my hand and kisses the top of it.

"So now that that is settled, who was that guy you were with a few weeks ago on Lincoln Road, the hunky older guy. And don't claim that wasn't you. I can spot you a mile away."

He smiles sheepishly, looks down, and takes another deep breath.

"That was Marta's male nurse Juan. He asked for my help in

picking out a watch for his partner. He's been such a great care-taker to Marta that I thought I'd treat him to coffee and dessert one afternoon when another nurse came to relieve him."

I can't help but laugh some more.

"You really are the worst liar. I knew that was you the whole time," I say. "Why couldn't you just admit it then?"

Eros looks away. "Because then I'd have to tell you about Marta. I wasn't ready *chico*."

"You know I love you, right Eros? You can tell me anything. But you have to promise me that you'll be completely honest with me from now on, got it? You have to work on that. I can't be with someone if I don't trust them or they don't trust me. I want you to be my last boyfriend." I say, sitting next to him on the ledge as my fingers rub the back of his neck.

"I promise, *chico*. The whole truth. *Te amo!*" he says, giving me another hug.

"*Te amo,* too."

27

Ray

I'm here in the newsroom filing my review of *28 Days More,* the third installment of the *28 Days* series. I'm giving the movie four stars. I know, I know. It's a horror flick. But still. Like the first installment, the director aimed to create a scary movie where the horror is rooted in something more cerebral than just a *Texas Chainsaw Massacre*-type scare fest. It's one thing to have a zombie leap out from a dark alley and send you running from the theater. It's another when an everyday man ditches his family as an army of zombies descends on them for dinner. The creepiness is in the social chaos as the townspeople try to maintain a grip on reality. Yes, there is eye-gouging gore here, but it's the psychology behind the public hysteria that fuels this movie. I love this stuff! As I write the review, I get an instant message from Ronnie who is at school.

I hope your day is full of sunshine. You're my movie man, five stars, all the way.

It's been a few weeks since Ronnie and I have been, well, I don't know what you'd call it. I guess we're dating, but we haven't labeled it or anything. I see him at least twice a week, which is not easy with my all my screenings, his crazy course load at FIU and his part-time internship at the *News.* And he does live in Hialeah *en la ciudad que progresa,* as we Miami Cubans like to joke because the city is an example of urban planning done all wrong. Each block has a house, a warehouse, a duplex, a shopping plaza and then another house, warehouse, duplex, etc.—endlessly repeated on a western path to Hialeah Gardens, which seems to have followed the lead of Miami-Dade County's second largest city. So basically, I try not to take up too much of Ronnie's time. The guy needs to focus on school and graduating—not me. I'm not going anywhere anyway. But when we do see each other, we add another layer of memories to our ever-growing collection.

The other day, we had a romantic picnic at Vizcaya. Ronnie brought subs from Subway, and we sat on the lush lawns of the gardens, near the maze of bushes. I thought it was somewhat cheesy to bring subs for such an elegant, majestic garden, but it was the thought that counted. On another date, I brought him to the screening of *Shrek 4,* which was light and cute, but the tale of the lime-green ogre and his princess is wearing thin. It's time for DreamWorks to move on from the franchise and start from scratch with a new story, though I wouldn't be surprised if *Shrek 5* popped out of the land of Far Far Away (which is really Hollywood) next Memorial Day weekend.

The part-time critic from the paper north of the county line couldn't make the screening. So that left Ronnie and me alone in the theater, cuddling and sharing a tub of ultra buttery popcorn and large Diet Cokes. It's the little moments with Ronnie that stay with me. I call them my Ronnie observations. He always opens the door for me when we head out in his Jeep Liberty. It shows what a gentleman he is. He always pulls the chair out for me at the restaurants we've eaten at, such as Versailles and the Big Pink near Fifth Street. He always begins our talks with how my day went and always makes a point to ask about my family and Gigli. When he stays over at my place, he spends time playing with Gigli, as if she were his own. He even walks her when I sleep in Saturday mornings after we have spent the night before engaged in wild and intense sex that leaves me breathless and covered with a sweaty sheen. If there were something about Ronnie I could complain about, it would be his babbling. When Ronnie starts talking, he gives you an earful. He rambles and remains stuck on a particular topic, like a CD on replay. Just the other night we settled in my sofa to watch one of my favorite movies, *The Departed* (2006) and just as I was about to press play, Ronnie spent twenty minutes talking about one of his recent articles. The conversation went something like this:

"So how was your day, Ronnie?" I asked him, putting my feet up on his lap as I began to set up the DVD with the remote.

"Ray, it was great. I interviewed this guy who painted his house in mid-Beach entirely purple. He's been making the neighbors see red because the purple house stands out. It's painted like Barney-the-dinosaur purple. So I interviewed the guy and he gives me an entire tour of the house. Ray, everything was purple, from the sofa, to the carpeting, to the walls, to the chairs. Well, various shades of purple, like lavender. And when I asked him if there was anything else that was purple, he blurted out in his Jamaican accent, 'Yeah, my balls. Wanna see?' And after that interview, I went to Miami Beach City Hall and spoke to the head of code enforcement, who told me that the purple tones are breaking the city's color code and that inspectors have left several written warnings on the man's door. After I left City Hall, I went to the office to start making more phone calls and . . ."

See what I mean? The guy keeps going and going like an Energizer bunny with OCD. He ends up stuck on one thought. So I tried to interrupt.

"So you have a colorful story and you wrote it and it runs this Sunday. Now let's watch the movie," I said, fiddling with the remote for my giant flat screen, high-definition TV set.

"But that was just one story. I'm also working on another story about the town of Surfside and another real estate aesthetic issue there," Ronnie said, his eyes flickering with enthusiasm as he was about to launch into another tall tale.

"Okay, tell me later. Let's just relax and watch the movie,"

I urged and Ronnie finally quieted down and let Matt Damon and Leonardo Di Caprio do all the talking.

Don't get me wrong. I love listening to the guy's stories, but he needs to wrap it up after a few minutes. I can't get a word in sometimes. I have to be patient because he's young and slightly immature and these are things he will eventually grow out of—I hope.

That's another thing, his age. I'm twenty-nine, but I feel so much older next to Ronnie. We're in completely different stages of our life. College was a lifetime ago for me. When I hear Ronnie talk about his journalism classes and the writing labs he has to do once a week, I feel like I'm back with Ted at UM. Then there's our situation. Are we simply seeing each other which is more casual than seriously dating? I haven't shown any interest in anyone else, and I don't think Ronnie is seeing any other guys because whatever spare time he has, he spends it with me and Gigli or over at his parents' house in Hialeah. The other night with Ted and Brian at Score, I was talking about the subject over a round of drinks.

"Oh c'mon, you guys are so dating! You have an understood unspoken commitment," Ted said, drinking some seltzer water. For some reason, he's taken a break from the vodka and grapefruits lately, which I think is a good thing. He had been steadily drinking more these last few months.

"Do you sense that you're dating and that you're in a committed relationship? What does your intuition say, Ray," Brian said, leaning back in his chair and putting up his sneakers by the edge of our table as he got all philosophical and spiritual on me.

"I'm pretty sure we're dating. It just hasn't come up," I said.

"Well shit, if I had Jergin here and I saw him a few times a week, I think we'd be dating, Ray. When it comes up, state your case," Ted said. "But from the looks of it, you're boyfriends."

"Again Ray, let time define what the essence of your situation is with Ronnie. The universe will present the answer to you when you least expect it," Brian said as Ted rolled his eyes.

"Char Margolis is in the room, people. No, my bad. It's the author of *The Four Agreements,* ladies and gentlemen. They are communicating through Brian Anderson," Ted announced to an invisible crowd as he teased Brian who flicked his wet straw back at him and stuck out his tongue.

"Ray, who cares what you guys are? The point is, you're together and getting to know each other," Ted said, checking his cell phone every five minutes to see if Jergin had text messaged him, like he's been doing since they met. It's nice seeing Ted smitten with a guy again. It suits him.

"My intuition tells me you guys are really in tune with each other. Just go with the flow," Brian piped in, his eyes fixated on his phone as he texted Eros. What is with everyone and text messages? It's a virtual form of passing notes.

So I'm going with the flow, as Brian suggested that night. Racso asked me the same question about Ronnie and our status, and I told him we're "just hanging out." He wants to invite Ronnie over to the house to meet Mami and Papi with Cindy there too. He thinks it's time our parents see me with another guy, and he thinks they would like him. I'm not sure how I feel about that. I know Mami would eat up Ronnie like one of the sweet flans she concocts every week in the kitchen. But Papi? I'm not sure how he would handle me bringing a guy, and not just any guy, but a *guy* who has planted his hooks into parts of my heart.

Papi is the sweetest man and one of the hardest working too, but when he doesn't like something, he tells you loudly, no matter where you are or what you're doing or whom you are with. It's his Cuban temperament. He says things loud. Says things with passion.

An hour later, I finally file my review of *28 Days More.* I make some suggestions of DVD rentals on my movie blog, *Rated R* and then head out for the day.

I'm driving on the Venetian Causeway on my way back to the condo. I dial Ronnie as I drive.

"Hey, sweetie, how's it going?" I say, while exchanging my U2 CD for some Maroon 5.

"Doing well, just finishing up here at Miami Beach City Hall. I came here right after classes at FIU's North campus. I had to pick up some copies for my next story," he says.

"So since you're in the neighborhood, want to come over? We can get a bite to eat. Or we can play, cutie," I say.

"Yeah, that sounds like a plan. I'm just walking to my Liberty," he says. I hear traffic in the background.

I'm about to hang a right on West Avenue when out of the corner of my eye, I see something closing fast, coming right toward me like a bullet. It's another car. I can't escape it. I grip my steering wheel as tight as I can. The car barrels right into my driver's side, and the impact sends my Nissan into a tailspin. My car jumps the curb and slams into a pole which rocks it to a stop. My right passenger window shatters and sends shards of glass flying everywhere. Like the shaky image of a video camera, it's all a blur. The collision almost sent me flying out of my seat, but my seatbelt locked me in place. My body jerks inside the car, and my head slams hard against my steering wheel. My airbag deploys in my face, burning it.

Everything is as fuzzy as my eyes try to readjust. My horn sounds like a wailing siren. Someone is knocking on my window. What's going on?

"Are you okay? Someone call 911! He's bleeding!"

I close my eyes, and I pass out.

The next thing I know, I'm at Mount Sinai Medical Center lying in a hospital bed. My head is pounding. I feel groggy. I touch my head, and I feel a bandage. I look around, and I see Ronnie in a chair by the side of the bed.

"Hey sleepyhead! You gave us all a scare," he says, getting up and leaning in. He gives me a kiss on the lips.

"What happened? What are you doing here?" I feel disoriented. Then it comes back to me. The accident.

"We were on the phone, and I heard this awful crash, something out of a *Die Hard* movie. I couldn't hear you so I hauled ass and found you in your car. I told the paramedics who you were. They said you have a concussion. You're lucky, but your car isn't. It's a total loss."

"Wow. It happened so fast. I'm glad you're here Ronnie. That was very sweet of you, coming to my rescue," I say, holding his hand. I remember feeling scared before I passed out. At least now I know I wasn't scared.

I hear a bunch of voices growing louder as they approach. It's music to my ears. My family.

"Hey, little bro. I heard you had a little fender bender," Racso says, slapping the palm of my hand. Cindy is right behind him.

"Hey, Ray, how are you feeling? The doctor said you have a little bump on your head. You'll be writing reviews in no time," she says, giving me a kiss on the cheek.

Right behind them comes Ted, Brian, Mami, and Papi. Ronnie moves out of the way as the cavalry settles in.

"You almost made the five o'clock news Movie Man," Ted says. "That was one hell of a crash. Thank God you're okay. They arrested the other driver. He was drunk, Ray. Drunk as in Paris Hilton drunk."

"No way. This was a drunk driver? Oh my gosh, I could have been killed," I say in disbelief.

"Well, actually, you're making the 11 o'clock newscast. Apparently, your little accident caused a big back-up on Alton Road and West Avenue during rush hour."

"Yeah, tell me about it. I had to ditch my Land Rover and walk to your crash scene," says Brian, who brought with him some sage incense sticks for the hospital room.

"*Ay dios mio* Raysito!" Mami blurts out once she sees me wide awake. She runs over, pushes everyone out of the way and plunges her head into my pillow and smothers me as she hugs me. I can't b-r-e-a-t-h-e.

"*Oye* Mami, calm down. I feel okay. I can feel all my body parts, and my lungs' lack of oxygen. I just have this bad pounding headache." She grabs her rosary and puts it around my neck and kisses the top of my forehead, near my stitches.

"*Oye* Raysito, how are jou doing?" Papi asks. They are standing over me, just like when Racso and I were sick in bed. Whenever one of us got sick, the other did as well, and Papi and Mami took turns checking on us and giving us our pills.

"Papi, I'm okay. I'm just surprised to see everyone here. How did you guys find out about the accident? I didn't realize I was so popular."

One by one, everyone looks to the door where Ronnie is standing watching this whole Cuban spectacle.

"*Tu amigo* Ronnie called us," Papi says.

"Yeah, Ronnie found your phone outside your car, and he dialed everyone and told us what happened. Apparently, he got there before the cops did," Racso says.

I look across the room, and I wink at Ronnie, mentally thanking him for staying with me until help arrived. That was really nice of him to do. He must have figured out where I was on my way home and high-tailed his Jeep Liberty there.

"Yeah, thanks again, Ronnie," Ted says. "If it wasn't for you, I wouldn't have found out that my best friend was in trouble."

"No problem guys. I did what I would have wanted someone to do for me," he says, opening the hospital door. "I'm going to give you guys some privacy. Again, it was nice seeing everyone again. And Mr. and Mrs. Martinez, *fue un placer a conocerlos,*" Ronnie says, telling my parents what a pleasure it was to meet them.

"*Gracias*, Ronnie. Jou have to come to our house for dinner one of these days ass a tank you for being with my baby. Anyone that can help our son like jou did is a friend of the family *por siempre,*" Mami says, covering her mouth with her tissue.

Papi then walks over to Ronnie before he leaves and shakes his hand.

"*Muchas gracias* Ronnie. Jou are welcome to our home anytime," he says.

And just like that, my parents meet my first serious boyfriend. Maybe this accident was a good thing after all. Ah, no. My head is killing me. Sometimes the fear of something is actually much bigger than the reality. All of these mini-movies in my head where Papi might throw out my boyfriend or disown me were just fantasies, paranoia, my rampant imagination running wild, and then some.

As everyone fusses over me, Racso leans over and whispers into my ear, "See, I knew Papi and Mami would like your little boyfriend. Now you can invite him to the wedding. Just hope that bump doesn't leave a scar. We can't have that at our wedding, little bro."

"Well, I'll do my best to not look like a victim of *Crash* for your nuptials, Racso."

Ted jumps in.

"Oh don't worry. A little borrowed make-up from Channel 7 will clean that right up, Ray. You'll look like a star."

"Thanks Ted, Brian, Racso, Cindy, and everyone here."

"That's what friends are for!" Ted and Brain say at the same time.

"And that's what brothers are for," Racso jumps in.

"And future sister-in-laws!" Cindy pipes up.

As everyone surrounds me and asks me a million questions about the accident and what I remember, which isn't much, I can't help but think about Ronnie and what he did for me. Not just any guy would do that. He could have assumed I dropped the phone and gone about his day's errands. But he sensed something was wrong and scrambled to find me. And for that, he will always hold a special place in my heart.

28

Ted

"See that over there? Those are the little islands in Biscayne Bay where families have picnics on the weekends. It's like having your own little island in Miami. You need a boat to get there,"

I point out to Jergin, my cute German flight attendant friend/play buddy/potential boyfriend. He's back in Miami, and can I tell you how happy I am to see him? He's only here for two days on a layover, but it's just enough time to pick up where we left off in Boston. As I drive, Jergin covers his forehead with his hands to block out the sun so he can check out the view of the bushy little islands. We're on the Julia Tuttle Causeway with the top down on the BMW. The hot wind blows his hair in all directions. His face is already turning red from the heat. He's so cute.

"Do you think we can go there some time? It looks quiet and relaxing," Jergin says, peering out at the islands. "Miami is so beautiful. You can go anywhere here on a boat or a car. I love coming here."

"We can do whatever you want, Jergin. I'm your tour guide this weekend. No one knows Miami like I do, well, except for Ray." Jergin looks my way and smiles. He gives me a slightly wet kiss on the cheek.

We're heading south on our way to the Miami Metro Zoo at the *far* end of the county where the most rural farmland sits. Not the most romantic thing, but I bet Jergin has never seen alligators, flamingos, or giant giraffes in Berlin. It's been a while since I've been here myself. My last visit was two years ago for a breaking news story. A giant female giraffe escaped, began galloping along the roadway, zipped across the saw grass behind the zoo and toward suburban homes in Homestead. She was found in someone's backyard, eating bananas from a property owner's trees. It was one of those only-in-South-Florida stories. We had great footage. It was the most read story on our Web site as well.

"How far is this?" Jergin asks, the sun beating down on us as we zoom over one of the steep bridges on the causeway, which links Miami to Miami Beach. The bridges each look like a giant lowercase letter "n" from downtown Miami. We have a brief but incredible view of both cities, with the flat tranquil waters of Biscayne Bay reflecting the sun.

"Oh, about thirty minutes. I'll floor it." I slam the accelerator, and we jut into fast-forward motion, at eighty miles per hour. We whoosh by all the SUVs and splashy sports cars that dot the Interstate.

Jergin grabs the sides of the convertible and holds on for dear life. I hear him shout *Vhoa!* I think he meant to say "Whoa."

Twenty minutes later, we arrive at Metro Zoo, and I pull up next to the rows of minivans and SUVs. After I pay the admission fees, we stroll in, and Jergin and I check out the map which highlights which animals are where. The zoo sits on 740 acres and runs about three miles around. It features eighty-one exhibits, so it's going to be a long afternoon. I don't mind. I'm with Jergin, and that's all that counts. We start with the river hogs exhibit. These giant boars are all muddy and, apparently, horny. One hog humps the other, and we hear them oinking, grunting, and snorting.

Jergin laughs.

"Maybe they met at Score," he says.

"Or in Boston!" Jergin is a little devil. I think he may be foreshadowing what's to come.

We take our time, strolling through the zoo, passing kids running from one exhibit to the other as their parents scurry to catch up to them. If they were my kids, I'd keep them on a tight leash. Max would never do that. He's a well-behaved dog.

As we walk, Jergin marvels at all the trees that line the fences. Each exhibit has a gorge or a moat separating the animal habitat from us human gawkers. When we walk by the white tigers lazily lounging in their shady respites, I can't help but wonder how far they can actually jump.

"I've never seen a tiger," Jergin says, leaning over the fence to get a better view.

"Look, one is scratching the other's back. How sweet," he says. I start to rub Jergin's back mimicking the tiger's. This date is so nice, mellow, and fun.

We continue roaming the zoo, passing the gazelles, apes, and energetic zebras (they were running around, chasing each other. Something must be in the air.) By the murky alligator pond, we sit on one of the long, brown benches under a shady tree and relax. My legs ache from all the walking. I lean back and make myself comfortable. Jergin suddenly rises.

"I vant to use restroom. I vill be right back," he says standing up. His khaki shorts and light green shirt bring out the aquatic green hue in his eyes even more than usual. Jergin looks a little dorky with his pale white skinny legs and loose shirt, but I like him nonetheless. He's growing on me, and I like this feeling. Again, he chose to spend his time off in between flights with me, Ted Williams, and no one else. I can't help but think that means something, that I mean something to him, even in a small way.

"Sure, go ahead. I'll be getting my strength back and keeping Gwendoyln the gator company." As Jergin disappears, I sit back and relax. A gaggle of parrots shriek in the background from their performance area. The soft wind rustles the leaves of the nearby trees. A few minutes later, Jergin returns with a scoop of chocolate ice cream.

"Here, for you. I thought you could use something cold," he says. My heart beams. That was so sweet of him. He also brought back another cold bottle of water. Jergin waits on me as if I was the finest gem in Miami, and it's a good feeling.

"I hope you like chocolate. I wasn't sure, but I vanted to surprise you and thank you for bring me here," he says.

I'm not a big fan of chocolate. I prefer mint chocolate chip with vanilla ice cream, but I couldn't tell this to Jergin. He stood there with the ice cream cup in hand, and I didn't have the nerve to tell him that chocolate doesn't really do it for me. But because I like him and I appreciate his thoughtfulness, I scooped the chocolate as if it were the best ice cream in the world. When I finish eating, he takes a napkin, wets it with the bottled water and wipes the edges of my mouth. I guess I had some chocolate stains. I could get used to this. I'm sure the passengers on Lufthansa are treated very well with Jergin around.

I still don't know too much about Jergin, yet these little moments show me that he is a considerate and kind person. I believe actions speak louder than anything, even though my livelihood depends on the visuals and what I have to say. He looks at me with those green eyes of his, and a real smile plasters my face, not one of my camera-ready fake grins. It's been so long since someone gave me such a sincere and intense stare like that. In his own way, Jergin makes me feel special, desired, and appreciated. He likes me for me and not because I'm on TV. Having the most famous face in the region could never replicate what I'm feeling now. Jergin has nothing to gain by my TV connections. He's happy to be here with me, Ted Williams, the lonely gay man.

"Um, what are you looking at? Do I have more chocolate on my face?"

"No. You are all clean. You just have these beautiful dark eyes. I can look into them forever. I cannot tell vhere the pupil begins or ends," he says, giving me a soft kiss on the lips.

We continue walking through the zoo. We study the colossal elephants and gaze in awe at the baby koalas imported from Australia. Even though I was here before for a news story, I never really felt like I saw the zoo. I didn't take the time to stroll around and admire all of life's diverse creatures. Sometimes I get so caught up with the adrenaline rush of my news stories, the shallowness of the *Deco Time* events, and my pity-parties at Score that I forget that there is so much more to do here. With his simple and kind presence, Jergin is helping me realize that now.

I spend the next two days with Jergin by my side. We rent bicycles and ride them in Coconut Grove. We trek along the main highway which is fringed by old trees on both sides. Jergin points out how the sun filters through the trees and casts shadowy spots, like dark butterflies, on the roadway. We cycle and admire all the grand old Miami estates that line up along the Grove with their old Florida Mediterranean facades and lush lawns. We also bike up scenic Coral Way by Le Jeune and Red Roads where the same shadowy spots dot the roadway, a cooling gift from Mother Nature on such a humid day.

We have a romantic dinner later that night at Morton's, eating the juicy and sizzling sirloin steaks. We walk along the shops and galleries on Miracle Mile and peek into the various bridal stores and men's clothing shops.

"Why is this called Miracle Mile?" Jergin asks, as we walk and hold hands on the dimly lit streets. Other couples and families saunter by, dashing in and out of Starbucks and Barnes and Noble with their mocha lattes and desserts. The breeze carries the smell of coffee from the cafés as if the City Beautiful wore it like its own perfume.

"I think it's called Miracle Mile because it's a miracle if you can find parking around here during the afternoon and evening. There's always traffic," I joke. Jergin quietly laughs back. "I used to go to college nearby at the University of Miami. Ray and I would always hang out here. Sometimes I miss living in the Gables. There's nothing quite like this city in Miami. All the streets have exotic Spanish names like Menores or Segovia. This is like a small town in Spain in the middle of Miami," I say.

"Or Berlin. I would love to show you my home like you have shown me yours, Ted. It would be my honor to show a vell-respected and very handsome man like yourself a piece of my country," he says, rubbing the back of my neck where it reaches my hairline.

"*Danke*. I vould love that," I say, mimicking his German accent.

He laughs at my attempt.

We spend the rest of the night back at my cottage. I show Jergin my growing hibiscus trees out front as they burst with various shades of red and orange. He meets Max who keeps jumping him at the knee, like he does whenever he likes someone I bring home. When Jergin asks to see some video reel of my more recent stories, I try and change the subject. I'm enjoying the fact that Jergin is interested in me, and I don't want him to see what a big celebrity I am in South Florida. I show him photos of my parents and my sister and of me and Ray from our days in college. It feels good being able to share my life and the most important people I know with this guy. He seems genuinely interested in seeing where I came from and who I call family. Jergin laughs at one particular photo where Ray is carrying me in his arms on graduation day.

"Ray isn't that strong. I'm still amazed he was able to carry me. We were so excited to be done with UM."

"That is a sweet photograph. He looks like a good friend," Jergin says, holding my hand as we sit side by side on my sectional brown leather sofa.

"He really is. He's my best friend. You'll meet him one day. I promise. But for now, I want you all to myself."

After leafing through the photos, Jergin closes the album and starts softly kissing me. We unbutton each other's shirts slowly and make our way to my backyard which faces the small canyon of high rises along the Intracoastal. We fall into my hammock and sway back and forth, the beach breeze whispering in our ears. Within a few minutes, we're naked, rocking back and forth like a baby in a cradle. I smell his Calvin Klein cologne every time I nudge my nose behind the nape of his neck. We tickle each other as we swing in the hammock. It feels like a carnival ride at the Dade County Youth Fair.

When it slows down, Jergin climbs on top of me, sending a rush of blood coursing through my cock. For hours, we fuck like some of the animals we saw in the zoo today until we finally release our loads. As we lay together catching our breaths, I notice how my dark skin beautifully contrasts with his hairless, milky white arms. As much as I am enjoying my time with Jergin, I know it won't last. He flies back to Berlin in a day, and I'm already missing him. But I'm used to this romance dance. When you live in Miami, most of the hot potential-boyfriends are tourists or models. They're seasonal imports. I'm just getting tired of meeting someone I think I could have a future with, only to learn that he doesn't live here or will only be here short term. I know I'm setting myself up for heartbreak with Jergin, but I'm not expecting anything too serious with him. By not expecting things, I won't disappoint myself. And for now, I'm having fun with my German boy, even if I know our moments are fleeting. Like the news, it's all about the now, and I'm reveling in it—until tomorrow.

29

Ray

"*What am I doing here?* I'm trapped in a Land Rover with three gay guys. They've abducted me for my bachelor party. This . . . is . . . my . . . worst . . . nightmare!" Racso whines to Cindy on his cell.

"And they're playing the Scissor Sisters," Racso continues. "I want to press a secret eject button and fly back to Coral Gables, pronto!" he says before finishing the call with one of his gooey *I-love-you-Cinderella* goodbyes.

Brian, Ted, and I giggle as we drive down to Key West for Racso's first and, most likely, last gay-straight bachelor party.

"*Oye*, Racso, this will be fun. I had to go through a lot of work to plan this, right guys?" I say. Brian and Ted respond at the same time, "Right!"

Ted jokes, "My news photographer will be there, too, to document the festivities for *Deco Time,* so put on your best face, Racso. Your students will probably be tuning in."

Ted is sporting his yellow-lens Ray-Ban sunglasses. He sits with me in the backseat reading a magazine called *Broadcast News,* about the latest happenings in the industry. Brian sits at the wheel touching the radio dial, his hair, his goatee, and just about anything that seems to distract him. Racso rides shotgun desperately gazing at the cobalt-blue Atlantic Ocean that seems to fold itself over the horizon from U.S. 1 to Cayo Hueso. We pass stretches of Egyptiangreen waters on the Gulf side, hordes of seafood joints, piles of lobster traps, and screaming tourist traps. (Swim with the dolphins! Buy factory outlet sandals! Ride a glass-bottom boat!) This should be putting Racso in a tropical state of mind, but all it seems to be doing is making him uncomfortable. He doesn't like surprises, and he has no idea what's in store ahead. I have a special surprise guest, but I'll save that for later.

Racso turns down the radio for a second.

"Bro, how did I get myself roped into this, again? I don't want a big flashy party. I'm a low-key kinda guy. I drive a Toyota Corolla," he says. "Oh yeah, this was Mami's idea. Cuban Catholic guilt. Mami's secret weapon"

"Yeah, it works every time," I say. "See, you're here with the Muskequeers."

I enlisted Mami in helping me convince Racso to go along with me for this bachelor party. She thought that I should be the person to do something for Racso before he gets hitched because he really doesn't have any close guy friends. Immediately, all these ideas began popping in my head. I wanted to make it a night that he would always remember—a fun night out for the Martinez men, like old times in high school—and give us a chance to bond before he starts his life with Cindy. I probably won't see him as much after they're married since they plan to move to Kendall, the land of endless developments in dreaded, sprawling suburbia.

At the house two weeks ago, Mami explained to me how she pitched the idea to Racso as she prepared him a *media noche* sandwich for lunch.

"*Tu hermano* loves jou and wants to give you a nice party. So let him. Jou only have one *hermanito*. He has been planning this for weeks. Be nice,"

Mami recounted the story to me.

"*Pero* Ma . . ." Racso whined back.

"No!" she interrupted. "Jou will do this for your brother, who is doing this for jou. Okay?"

Racso always caves in when it comes to Mami. That's why he

decided to live at home to save money to buy a place for him and Cindy. Yeah, that was Mami's idea. Deep down, she just wanted him home since I had moved out of the house as soon as I secured a dorm at UM. I know, it may sound strange for a Miami guy to get a dorm when his parents live five miles from the campus, but I like to be different and stand out.

"Hey Racso, can you pass the chips?" I say, extending my hand through the slit between the two front seats. I just finished reading the latest *Entertainment Weekly's* movie section and *Daily Variety* when Racso tosses a bag of Tostitos my way.

"Well, thanks. Cheer up, Racso. You'll have fun. We'll have a gay old time," I say devilishly with a wink.

"That's what I'm worried about, little bro."

Ted jumps in to the conversation, or story, as he usually does. He doesn't wait for an invitation.

"You're with Ray, Brian, and me. How can you not have fun? Trust this trio, this will be the best bachelor par-tay. *Ever!*" Ted says, leaning in, his face just above Racso's shoulder, his teeth as white as the puffy clouds in the distance over the ocean.

"Wait till you see what we've got planned," Brian turns to Racso, his manic dark blue eyes excited like a crazy man's. He's playing with his goatee again. "Drag queens galore!"

Racso opens the window to the vast ocean to his right and yells, "*Help! Save me!* I'm trapped by my gay twin bro and his friends. *Get me out of here!*"

In retaliation, we blast the Scissor Sisters CD up a notch. This is going to be one long ride.

After we check into the La-Ti-Da guesthouse on Duval Street, we all take turns showering. Racso goes first since he's about to be hitched and this is his party and he can shower first if he wants to. Yes, I got one room for the four of us, but it's the biggest room in the guesthouse, on the second floor, overlooking Duval Street. In the distance, the ocean beckons like a gleaming jewel.

Two hours later, after everyone has showered and primped and at least three of us have plucked, I lead the group on a dusk stroll on Duval Street before we eat. Everything in Key West is part eatery, part drinkery. We walk down Duval, past all the T-shirt shops and boutiques and Starbucks. When did that open? I could use *un cafecito* to wake me up. I feel slightly tired from the four-hour drive from the Gables, but I'm getting excited looking at the parade of shirtless young guys and hairy men cruising on the boulevard. One of them reminds me of Ronnie, which makes me smile.

As we walk, Racso checks his cell phone. It's Cindy, sending him a text message.

I hope you're not having too much fun at your bachelor party. You better not! Love you sweetie.

I peek over his shoulder to read the message. He texts her back.

I miss you Cinderella! Can't wait to be your Prince.

He smiles at me, and I return the smile. I know Cindy is going to be a great sister-in-law. She's already part of the family. Soon, she'll be Cindy Martinez.

"So, are you ready for your bachelor party? It's going to be a night you'll never forget. Tom Hanks in *Bachelor Party* has nothing on us," I tell Racso.

"Wasn't that the movie where the donkey keels over after snorting some coke and ends up in the elevator of the hotel?" he asks.

Ted and Brian laugh.

"Donkeys are the least of your worries," Ted says, waving to some fans who recognize him from the other side of Duval.

"You ain't seen nothing yet. I sense a big surprise ahead," Brian says, walking behind me, Racso and Ted.

"Are we going to a gay bar?" Racso says, swallowing big gulps of air. "I'm marrying a woman, not another dude."

"Oh shut up, Racso. Whether it's gay or not, it's a party. We're going to celebrate your waning days of bachelorhood. Deal with it. You're not going to die from partying with the three of us," I scold Racso. We pass all the badly sunburned tourists riding colorful scooters that sound like chainsaws gone wild on Duval Street.

After we chow down a scrumptious dinner at the Blue Heaven restaurant, which looks like someone's two-story house with its blue and pink façade and chickens that waddle freely among the diners, we stroll back to Duval in the soupy evening heat. The destination is a club called Aqua, where I made the party arrangements. Posters of drag queens beautify the front window. It says, "Special event tonight: The fabulous Mia Mi."

"This way, Racso. Don't be scared. They don't bite," I say, gesturing for him to follow.

"Yeah, they only bite if you ask them to," Ted says, snappng his pearly white teeth to make his point.

Brian covers his mouth and laughs.

We make our way into the club, which decorated with balloons and ribbons that stream from one side of this small bar to the other and read "Welcome to Racso's Bachelor Party!" Some guys call out my name as I get closer. I'm happy to see my cousins Tom, Juan and Jose. Papi emerges from the darkness of the back bar. He drove down with the other guys.

"Surprise!" Papi says, giving me a tight hug. "Welcome to jou bachelor fiesta, *hijo*." I can tell that Racso is touched that Papi is here. It now occurs to him that he's in a gay bar along with our most macho cousins.

A pretty red-headed waitress named Patty comes by and welcomes us.

"You must be the poor fella who's gonna get hitched," she tells Racso. But upon closer inspection, I see it's not a Patty. It's a Pat, a guy dressed as a woman with a short red skirt and a tight black top. Well, I thought it was a woman. You can never tell these days. The boobs look pretty real, like Cindy's.

"Sit right down. I'm getting you a nice cool Corona. That's

what a little bird told you that you liked," Patty or Pat says to Racso, standing by my side.

The guys grab Racso and plop him into a chair by the lip of the stage. Everyone is hollering as a drag queen named La Huesa appears on stage. She introduces herself and welcomes Racso and the gang to the party. She points at Racso so that everyone knows he's about to be the next passenger on the marriage train. The people in the bar cheer my brother on, and the guys deliver hearty pats on the back, as if he had won the Teacher of the Year award. (He was a finalist this year, by the way.) I sit next to Racso, both of us holding Coronas in our hands.

The show begins. A real woman comes out in a small thong, with pasties covering her plump breasts. To this, Racso shouts, "Yeah!" and she starts to fondle a stripper's pole in the middle of the stage to the tune of *Mustang Sally*. She struts over to Racso and licks his right cheek. As he blushes, I feel my face warm up from the buzz of my drink and the heat seeping into the bar. Cindy would kill Racso if she saw the stripper kiss him, but she's not here. This is Racso's party. After living with Mami and Papi and struggling to get his students to appreciate both American literature and *The Miami News,* Racso should have this time to let loose and have fun.

As soon as she's done, another drag queen struts out. She has dark curly hair, similar to Gloria Estefan's mane of locks. But this drag queen's name is Mia Mi, a play on Miami. She does Gloria's famous hits, and tonight, she's not using a recording. She's singing live, just like the Cuban Conga Queen. She belts out *Turn The Beat Around,* kneeling down and shaking her boobs in Racso's face. Then she performs *Go Away.* We all bust out laughing and drink more beer. Brian and Ted start twirling each other on the dance floor like John Travolta in *Saturday Night Fever.*

Racso probably won't admit this, but I know he's having fun. He's busy laughing and toasting his beer bottle with the other guys. It's a scene I'll always remember. I like seeing Racso like this.

Another performer, a real woman this time (I think), appears and starts singing sexualized versions of Shakira songs. She looks a lot like the real Shakira when she was more blonde and curly haired. She pulls me on stage, gyrating and shaking her hips. I correct her right away, "No no . . . You've got the wrong twin. It's my brother who's getting married," I say, pointing to Racso below. "Get him up here!"

A few seconds later, both Racso and I are dancing on the stage, being courted by this Shakira drag queen (turns out she's a he) who is singing *Whenever, Wherever.*

After a few more songs by Mia Mi and La Huesa, we all settle at our tables and drink, drink, and drink some more. Four beers later, I'm feeling quite dizzily buzzed, a happy old drunk. I hear laughter as Papi tells some funny stories about how Racso and I would try to confuse people in our family when Papi and Mami forced us to go a party. I would pretend to be Racso and he would pretend to be me, and we would play tricks on them.

Papi then starts babbling about all the different cockroaches he encounters while exterminating the hotel rooms of celebrities in South Beach. As everyone drinks up, I pull Racso aside to talk one on one with my *hermano*.

"Bro, this is quite a night," he says, sitting on his chair backwards and tipping his Corona toward mine. Yeah, we love to drink Corona, one of our few commonalities besides our looks.

"Well, it's the least I could do for my one and only brother. It's a gay-straight bachelor party. Something different, you know," I say.

We take some more gulps, and I can tell Racso is pretty trashed. He sways in his seat like a genie, but he's having a good time. As we talk, I notice Ted and Brian on stage with a karaoke machine. I hear the beginning of *Dancing Queen.* The dudes are slurring the words as they try to read the lyrics off the monitor— or maybe that's just how they sing because I didn't see Ted drinking. Who knows? Papi is laughing at them.

I try to focus on Racso, and when I see two of him, I realize I've had one too many.

"What's wrong?" Racso asks.

I grow serious and start babbling. I don't know where this is coming from, but it pours of out me in a rush, like the Corona in reverse.

"Racso, why do you always pick on me? You're always on my case about something. I don't get it. I don't get on your ass about stuff," I say, slurring my words slightly and surprising myself with the confession. Years of bottled-up feelings are unleashed.

I take another swig and burp.

"What are you talking about, little bro? I tease ya but, you know, I'm just playing."

"Yeah, but sometimes you can be a real dick about it," I snarl.

"What, little bro?"

"Yeah, when you talk about how you hate being confused as the gay movie critic or gay this or gay that, it pisses me off. It's fucking rude, Racso, which happens to rhyme with asshole, if you say it just right," I blurt out in one swoop. I narrow my eyes and squint at him. I look away with my hand clenched tightly on my bottle.

"Ray, I'm just playing. Seriously. I don't care if you're gay or not. You're my bro, and I love you. I just like to tease you because you fall for it all the time ever since we were kids."

"But did you have to do it all the time? I'm so sick of it. It becomes grating after a while," I huff.

"I didn't realize how much my badgering bothered you, Ray. You seem really pissed. That was never my intention. I just like to goof around with you," Racso explains. "If I tease you, it's because I love you, man. You've got so much going for you, and sometimes, you're like your own pity party. You have a great job with great pay, which I don't have even though I love teaching. You have great friends. That's one thing I've always been jealous about, bro. You have good friends, especially microphone man Ted. When we went to our separate colleges, you found Ted as your hang out buddy, and I met Cindy. I don't have any close friends. Didn't you ever wonder about that?" Racso continues, putting his hand behind the back of my head as if to comfort me.

I'm surprised by his confession. Racso, jealous of me? Either that or I'm really wasted.

"What do you mean? You and Cindy are always going out and doing stuff with other people."

"Those are *her* friends, Ray, not mine."

"But I don't understand, Racso. You're jealous of me? You've got the perfect girlfriend. Mami and Papi put you on this pedestal, the perfect all-Cuban-American *hijo* with his bride-to-be and a respectable career as a teacher. If anything, I've always been envious of *you*, of what you have. Your students adore you. Cindy is great."

We sit and look at each other, a near-perfect mirror image except for our haircuts and clothing. Our hands are on our beers, and our eyes remain locked wordlessly. Suddenly, we bust out laughing, hysterically.

"So what we're saying is we're jealous of each other?" I say.

"I guess so. How stupid is that?" Racso scoffs. "We're real idiots!"

We start laughing. Racso starts his dry-heaving, and that only makes me laugh harder.

"Man, my twin ESP thing has been really off all these years. There's nothing to be jealous of, little bro. Besides, that Ronnie guy seems pretty cool. I like him, so does Cindy. And Mami and Papi seem to think he's a good guy," he says.

"Ditto, Racso."

"Seriously, if I bust your balls, little bro, it's because I miss you. You weren't just my twin brother in high school, you were my best friend. I didn't need to make other friends in school because I had you."

My eyes start misting. It must be from me sitting under the vent of the strong air-conditioner in the club, making the bar chilly and eyes watery.

"Get outta here. I don't believe you," I say, mocking him in disbelief. I wipe my eyes.

"Honest to God, Ray. And when I started at FIU, I had trouble making new friends. I just had classmates. Then I had Cindy, and she became my girlfriend and my new best friend but still, I missed us doing all those things we used to do in school, like the movies, road trips, hitting bars. Suddenly, you had someone else to hang out with, and you've been doing that with Ted and now Brian. I'd love to have a clique of guy friends like that. I love hearing your stories about your Friday nights out on the beach."

"Well, you can have that too, Racso. I never invited you because we go to gay bars, not really your thing, but if you don't mind, you're welcome to hang with us. *Mis amigos* are your *amigos*. Right Ted and Brian?" I shout over to them.

They nod and continue singing "Milkshake" which leaves Papi looking very confused. I can just imagine what he's thinking the song means. Brian and Ted can't get through a verse without giggling like two little girls from a Saturday morning McDonald's commercial. I, too, feel spasms of joy. It could be from the party and the booze or maybe from knowing how much Racso loves me.

"Thanks, little bro. I promise I won't tease you too much anymore. I was just playing. I don't mean anything by it," he assures me, putting his hand on my shoulder.

"Thanks, Racso, and you're always welcome to hang out with me and the guys. We have a lot of fun. It's a nice end-of-the-week work release. Come out with us when you're back from your honeymoon."

"I love you, little bro," he says.

"I love you too, *hermano*."

We hug and pat each other hard on the back like bongo drums. I give him a big wet kiss on the cheek, and Racso messes up my hair. I mess up his too.

We look over by the lip of the stage and see Papi dancing with Mia Mi. He's twirling her like he would dance with Mami in the kitchen. I wonder if Papi knows he's dancing with a guy dressed as a woman.

He catches my stare and walks over to where Racso and I are hugging and drinking.

"And what's going on here? *Qué pasa?*" he asks.

"Oh nothing, Papi!" we answer at the same time.

"Now that's what I like to see, *mis hijos* loving each other, like two good Cuban *hermanos,*" he says, eyes shining with Cuban pride. "Now let's all dance with Mia Mi. This is a bachelor party after all. Right, guys?

"Right!" everyone in the bar shouts back.

30

Ray

Five stars. That's what I'm rating this big fat Cuban wedding. Racso is finally marrying Cindy, and I'm proud to be the best man. I feel honored that Racso would ask me because he could have asked one of our straight cousins or one of his co-teachers at his school. I'm so flattered to be up here supporting my other half.

I'm standing along the steps of the altar of St. Patrick's Church in Miami Beach at my twin's nuptials. The flower girl and ring boy have already made their trip down the aisle as did Gigli. (We had to include her in the ceremony somehow, so she walked down the aisle in a little yellow doggie dress.) The bridesmaids in soft yellow dresses slowly glide down the aisle to the soothing sounds of the harpist stationed in the corner. Beautiful bright yellow and pink flowers bedeck each pew, and the sun filters through the stained glass Biblical scenes with Jesus Christ and Mary. As the wedding continues, the light cascading through the arched windows glows brighter, from streaks of yellow to brilliant rays that highlight parts of the church with specks of gold. With my eyes, I motion to Mami to stop crying, and I gesture to Papi to keep her down. She's crying more than Cindy, and it's Cindy's wedding. Papi looks at me perplexed but proud. I can tell he hasn't seen Mami cry like this in a long time. Perhaps Racso's wedding is reminding them of theirs back in Havana.

Mami has been wailing all afternoon, and it's getting embarrassing but it's probably the only wedding she'll see for one of her twins. Unless Ronnie and I get hitched in Massachusetts one day. Yeah, Ronnie and I are a couple, and I'm in love. I like the way that sounds—*in love*. Gee, I must sound like one of the female leads in a romantic comedy. But I have to admit, being in love is such an incredible feeling, something that makes my heart pitter-patter at times in a good way when I least expect it. It's a mix of feeling good, proud, scared, and nervous. Whenever I think about a project, a trip, or doing something to my condo, I can't help but imagine Ronnie in the big movie picture in my head. I guess that's what love does to you. It makes you plan ahead for what's to come, and I enjoy imagining him in some future scene in my life. I imagine that Gigli agrees with me because Ronnie treats her like his own. He's her step-dad, and she loves sleeping next to him more than me. Gigli is an affection slut, so she'll go with anyone who spends more than five minutes feeding or cuddling with her. So much for me. Speaking of Ronnie, I see him in the row behind my parents.

He's sitting with Ted and Jergin, who flew in for the weekend from Berlin to be with him again. I've been impressed with Jergin's commitment to Ted. He always finds a way to visit my best friend, no matter how tired he is from his travels. So far, he's been here every other weekend, and things seem to be working out for them even though it's not Ted's most ideal relationship or anyone else's. Knowing him and the rest of the gay population, he'd rather have a boyfriend in the same zip code, heck in the same continent, but Ted has learned that you can't pick the person you fall in love with. Love finds you, even from as far away as Germany. There I go again, sounding like a gooey romantic comedy.

Like a slow-moving panoramic shot, my view moves from them and pans over to Brian and Eros. I'm happy to report that Brian and Eros are enjoying the happy state of coupledom. A quick summary on Brian: he sold his McMansion on the Venetian Causeway and with the profits, he and Eros bought a smaller house, a bungalow, in Little Havana. (Brian made Eros sign a prenuptial agreement, by the way, to protect his assets. I call him the gay Trump.) This way, Brian gets to hone his Spanish while Eros feels more at home with all the Spanish that is spoken in the Calle Ocho neighborhood. Eros is now a student at Miami-Dade Community College's downtown campus where he's studying education. He wants to be a high school counselor and help fellow Latino kids deal with being gay. Brian has hinted that they plan to travel to Vermont for a little romantic get-away and to have a civil union ceremony there, so I may be driving up to Vermont from Boston sometime next year. Yes, that's right. I said Boston. But I'll get to that in a just a second. Good things come to those who wait and right now, this is the good part of the ceremony.

Racso and Cindy are at the altar holding hands and exchanging their vows. Their eyes are locked as if they're the only ones in the big old church. When he glances my way momentarily, I wink at him as if to say "I'm so proud of you bro." Racso nods back as if to say "Bro, I can't believe I'm doing this." I still don't have the twin ESP thing and if Racso were focusing right on me, he'd know what I was thinking but it's of no consequence. I've learned lately that Racso is my true best friend, someone I can look at and not just see myself physically but see who I really am. He will always be there to support me and I for him, as I am showing him today standing by his side. Today is one of the rare occasions we look like each other's clone. We both had to cut our hair for the wedding so now we look like mirror images with our matching spiked-up black hair. (It was Mami's idea to do this, styling our hair and clothes just as we were little kids.) After the wedding, I may let my hair grow out.

I zoom back to Racso. His eyes lock back on Cindy, who looks absolutely stunning. Her black straight hair is up in a bob and masked by a lace-like veil. When Racso lifts her veil, everyone gasps in awe. Mami wails again. *Qué pena!* I think she's crying for two reasons. One is the wedding. The other involves me and the upcoming new chapter in my life. Before Racso and Cindy say their "I dos," Father Juan interrupts and speaks to the guests in the pews.

"Before they officially become husband and wife before the eyes of God, Racso and Cindy wanted to express how much they loved each other through a special song. They asked a close friend of Ray's to sing it for them. Here now singing *Amarilli, mia bella* by Italian composer Giulio Caccini is Brian Anderson."

Brian steps up to the side of the altar, grabs the microphone, and taps it a few times. He then smiles at everyone sitting in the pews. He takes a deep breath and begins to sing the Italian aria a capella. Hearing Brian sing reminds me of a smoother Josh Groban and pebbles of goose bumps run up my back when he hits a high note that thunders throughout the church. As if by cue, a white dove flies into the church and then disappears through one of the open stained glass windows. But Racso and Cindy didn't notice. They were too busy looking at each other, Cindy's eyes are brimming with tears. Racso dabs them with a handkerchief, one that I gave him with his initials on it.

Brian finally ends the song, and a chorus of applause fills the church. Silence then falls on the church and Racso and Cindy finally exchange their vows.

"And I now pronounce you husband and wife," Father Juan announces.

Each breaks out in a grand smile that would melt the hardest of hearts. They embrace in a deep wet kiss. Mami wails out loud some more, stands up, and waves to them as the new husband and wife step down and walk back up the aisle. A crescendo of organ music reverberates throughout the cathedral's sweeping arched ceilings. The guests stand up and applaud as the couple dashes out the door. We are close behind, peppering them with rice. With our arms around each other, Ted, Brian and I stand by the lip of the church's main entrance and toss as much rice as we can hurl.

"Cindy looks so beautiful. We should probably put this on

Deco Time as a recent fabulous wedding," Ted says holding up his camera to digitally record the rice throwing as Racso and Cindy make a run to the stretch limo.

"How did I do? I was thinking of posting some of your video on my Web site to promote my music," Brian says, all dapper in his black suit with blue tie.

"Yeah, I gotcha. Don't worry Mr. American Idol. I'll email you the footage so you can upload the footage. You did great or as Paula Abdul would say 'We just love you.' " Ted says, with the camera obscuring his face as he records.

"Isn't this great? All of us here, in nice suits, sort of like Score but in the daylight?" I say, lighting up a cigarette to commemorate the nuptials and the end of a long day.

"Yeah, *wonderful,* Ray," Ted says sarcastically, now pointing the camera in my face and then laughing.

"Seriously, remember earlier this year how different things were. I was single. Ted you were Mr. Mingle. And Brian, well, you had a guy."

"But I'm in a better place, now, Ray and Daniel and I are still friends," he says.

"Yeah and I've got a guy who I barely see. We spend more time apart than together but you know what guys, it's worth it. It makes Jergin and I appreciate our time together. I'm not complaining. It's all good," Ted says.

"So when do you and Ronnie take off for Boston?" Brian asks.

Oh, I forgot to tell you about that. Remember that gay and lesbian journalism conference I attended last winter in Boston? I dropped off some of my clips to the Nieman Foundation for Journalism at the Harvard University booth. They provide fellowships for journalists who spend two semesters at Harvard focusing on a specific area or their specialty. As much as I enjoy reviewing films, I wanted to try something different for a few months, to recharge my creative batteries and this seemed like a good opportunity. This is Harvard, after all and the highest level of education I received was a bachelor's degree in journalism. So how could I say no when I was offered a slot? I figured I could take classes there for a year, get to know a city completely different than Miami and be on my own for bit and away from my family. The fellowship offers a stipend and housing so I could live off that and write some freelance reviews for *The Boston Daily* for some extra money. After the fellowship, I can return to *The Miami News*—or move on to something else in my field, perhaps even teach film criticism at UM or FIU. The icing on the cake here is that Ronnie landed a one-year development position at *The Boston Daily* in its Metro section. So we're going to be in Boston at the same time and learning the city together and finding new places to walk Gigli. It's a great way to get to know each other as well, away from our Cuban comfort zones. We won't be too homesick because we'll have each other and of course, Gigli.

Just as Racso and Cindy embark on a new life together, I am also spreading my wings. I know it will be hard being away from my parents, but I feel there is something more out there than South Beach, the *News* and the confines of the movieplex. I don't want to be in Miami to review *Miami Vice III*. I want, as Brian would say, to follow my Cuban spirit, and Boston seems to be calling. I'm nervous about what Boston has to offer and what life would be like there, especially without a car. I'm leaving my dilapidated Nissan with Racso who is excited to finally get his hands on my sports car. I wonder what the winter will be like but what I do know for sure is that I will have plenty of familiar faces visiting. Ted says he'll fly up to visit his old Beantown and take me to Club Café again and to see his family on the Cape. Brian and Eros plan to stop by when they visit Vermont. Racso and Cindy have already reserved a week to spend with me. And of course, I'm looking forward to adapting to a new city with a great guy who happens to be the star in my eyes and my heart.

As we all stand and wave to the newlyweds, my cell phone

starts to vibrate in my pocket. Who the hell can be calling now? Pretty much everyone I know is here at the church. I quickly whip out the phone while keeping my eyes trained on the departing limo.

I open up the flap phone and I start laughing when I see the ID. It's a text message from Racso. He's about to embark on his honeymoon and yet, he finds time to harass me, his little bro. I wonder what he wants.

The message reads, **Thanks again for being my best man. I love you little bro.**

I smile, wave and silently mouth, *"I love you too."*

But somehow, I sense that my brother already knows that.